A BELLBROOK MURDER MYSTERY COLLECTION BOOKS 1-3

REAGAN DAVIS

COPYRIGHT

CONTENTS

A WELL CONSTRUCTED MURDER

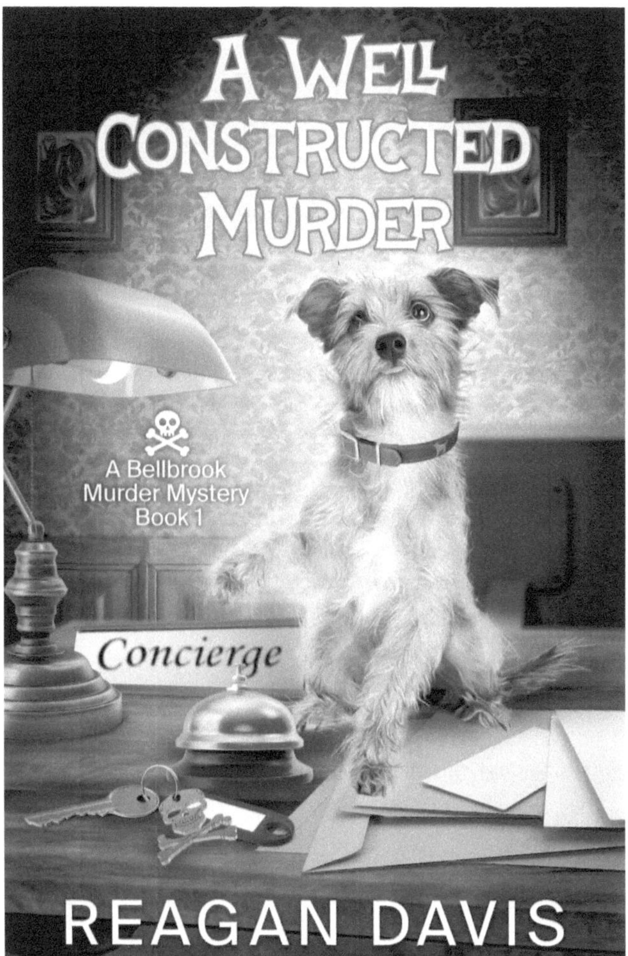

A WELL CONSTRUCTED MURDER
A Bellbrook
Murder Mystery
Book 1
Concierge
REAGAN DAVIS

COPYRIGHT

FOREWORD

Dear Reader,

Despite several layers of editing and proofreading, occasionally a typo or grammar mistake is so stubborn that it manages to thwart my editing efforts and camouflage itself amongst the words in the book.

If you encounter one of these obstinate typos or errors in this book, please let me know by contacting me at Hello@ReaganDavis.com.

Hopefully, together we can exterminate the annoying pests.

Thank you!
Reagan Davis

CHAPTER 1

A LITTLE GUCCI

October 19TH

The shiny red pickup truck turned left at the bottom of the driveway and disappeared into the distance. Karla let out a relieved sigh. Another close call. Why was *he* there? Was *he* looking for her? Karla knew her luck would eventually run out. How long could she avoid someone in a town as small as Bellbrook?

Turning onto the long driveway the pickup truck had just left, she glanced at the dashboard clock. It had been two weeks, two days, two hours, and twenty-two minutes since Karla Bell had first realized she was alone.

Karla liked being by herself. She was a proud, independent woman. But being by oneself wasn't the same as being alone. As long as she had Grandma May, Karla was never alone. Unaccompanied, maybe, but never alone. And never unloved.

If Karla was a balloon, her string would be tied to

Grandma May's wrist. She could float as far away as she wanted because, with Grandma May holding the string, she could always find her way back.

Two weeks, two days, two hours, and twenty-two minutes ago, at Grandma May's funeral, the realization struck her that, for the first time in her life, no one was holding her string. She was scared and alone in a crowded church.

Untethered and terrified, she'd swallowed her fear in the church that day. And she continued to swallow it every time it stirred deep inside her, demanding to be felt.

Karla came to a stop in front of twin cottages. Mirabel, the cottage where Grandma May had lived, and Bellflower, the unoccupied, decrepit cottage also owned by the Bell family.

She shifted the car into park and unbuckled her seatbelt, watching as Dylan Fitzgibbon stomped out of Bellflower. He marched toward his white pickup truck, tore the magnetic FITZ IT RIGHT THE FIRST TIME sign from the driver's side door, and flung it into the bed of the truck. He then jumped into the driver's seat and sped away.

The dust cloud stirred up by Dylan's angry departure settled on his father's matching white pickup truck, which was still parked in front of Bellflower and still displayed its FITZ IT RIGHT THE FIRST TIME sign.

"What do you suppose that was about, Gucci?" Karla asked, unclipping the doggie seatbelt.

The scruffy mixed terrier tilted his charmingly dishevelled head and perked his button ears at the sound of his name. His impossibly long tongue unfurled from the side of his mouth.

Karla patted her knee and jerked her head to the side. Gucci leapt across the centre console with ease and landed in her lap.

She exited the car, and while setting the rambunctious terrier on the driveway, she spied Rosalie Howard behind the side-by-side cottages. Rosalie often cut through the Bell property on her daily walk, marking the midway point of her route by stopping at Mirabel for a cup of tea with Grandma May.

Old habits die hard, Karla thought, comforted by Grandma May's familiar voice in her head.

The thud of the car door grabbed Rosalie's attention, and the young octogenarian caught Karla's eye, smiled, and waved. Karla responded in kind and was about to walk over to her late grandmother's best friend to say hello, but Leon Tyson appeared, seemingly from nowhere.

He approached Rosalie with a booming, "Hello there, Ms. Howard. How are you on this lovely fall day?" and flashed her a megawatt smile.

Karla couldn't hear their words, but their faces and hands moved in the familiar, exaggerated way they did when people were being neighbourly and cheerful.

As they spoke, Leon rested his hands behind his back, clasping his right wrist with his left hand, his right pinky finger twitching sporadically as he spoke.

Mentally and emotionally exhausted at the thought of more small talk—if anyone else looked at her with pity and asked how she was holding up as they lightly touched her arm, she thought she might scream—Karla ducked out of sight before Leon spotted her.

Gucci tugged at his black Chanel leash and matching collar, whining and pulling Karla toward Mirabel.

His urgency gave Karla pause. She picked up the cream and beige dog, stroking his wiry coat.

"Shhh." She hushed his whimpers and, with her free hand, tucked her shoulder-length blonde bob behind her ear, cocking her exposed ear toward the cozy cottage.

Voices. Familiar. Raised. A man and a woman. They were too muffled to be intelligible from outside Mirabel cottage, yet distinct enough to discern the contentious tone of their conversation.

"Brace yourself, Gooch," Karla warned with a sigh, using his nickname, and returning the terrier to the ground. "This sounds like one of their feistier arguments."

She sighed and squared her shoulders, preparing to referee another argument between the two non-siblings.

THEIR VOICES WERE loud enough to drown out Karla and Gucci's entry, despite Karla having closed the cottage door behind her with an intentional and loud *thud*.

From what she could gather, Lynn, her mother, and Harry, the estate caretaker, were having a noisy disagreement about Harry removing furniture from the cottage without Lynn's prior knowledge. They stood on opposite sides of the small Victorian-era writing desk that had functioned as Grandma May's bedroom vanity for as long as Karla could remember.

Karla had spent hours at that vanity when she was a little girl playing dress up with Grandma May's makeup and jewelry. Just thinking about it, Karla swore she picked up a whiff of Grandma May's perfume.

She was distracted from her olfactory memories when Lynn shouted at Harry and yanked the dainty desk toward her. Harry gave a curt response and tugged the desk back toward him.

Karla wondered how many miles—four inches at a time back and forth—the poor desk had travelled since their argument began.

Karla was certain she had told Lynn about Harry relocating the contents of Mirabel today. Hadn't she? Karla wracked her brain, trying to recall *when* she relayed this piece of information to her mother but came up blank. Maybe she didn't. *Shoot!*

Lynn blurted a not-safe-for-work adjective. This was Karla's cue to intervene on Harry's behalf and protect him from the not-safe-for-work noun she knew Lynn was about to call him. Lynn had a fondness for hurling that specific pair of curse words at her verbal sparring opponents.

"*I* asked Harry to move the furniture," Karla interjected. "Fitz is demolishing the inside of Bellflower, then he's coming to demolish Mirabel before he renovates and restores both cottages." She placed a protective hand on Harry's arm. "Harry is helping me move Grandma May's belongings somewhere safe."

"Why is this the first I've heard about it?" Lynn's blue eyes were wide with hurt, fixated on her daughter's green eyes.

Gucci whimpered at the end of his leash, straining to get within petting distance of the squabbling duo. His quill-like tail swished back and forth in the air above his backside.

"I thought I told you," Karla admitted. "I'm sorr—"

"Here we go!" With an eye roll that would make a rebellious teenager proud, Lynn tossed her hands in the air and brought them down hard against her hips. "You never told me," Lynn shouted. "When are you going to grow up, Karla Sheridan Bell, and stop punishing me?!" She slapped her hands against her chest. "I get it. I was a horrible mother."

"I wasn't punishing you, *Mother!*" Karla hissed.

Spitting the word *mother* at Lynn like a verbal grenade was Karla's favourite weapon.

"I thought I'd told you about the furniture. I'm sorry. Since Grandma May died, I've had a lot on my mind.

"Are you saying I haven't?" Lynn challenged. "You might have lost your grandmother, young lady, but I've lost my mum." She slapped her chest again. "You have no idea how that feels."

Being referred to as a young lady took Karla aback for a moment. No one had called her that in the last ten of her thirty-nine years.

"You're right," Karla agreed. "I don't know what

it's like to lose my mother. But I know what it feels like not to have one."

Harry attempted to cover his shocked gasp with an improvised throat clearing. He shifted his weight, clearly uncomfortable with his proximity to the brutal exchange of words between mother and daughter.

"Something you want to say, Harry?" Lynn challenged, crossing her arms in front of her chest, and arching one professionally shaped eyebrow.

Harry shook his head.

"Good," said Lynn. "This is a *family* matter." She shook her head. "None of your concern."

"Harry *is* family." Karla's whisper wasn't to quiet her words, it was to quiet her anger.

Harry Kincaid wasn't family in the biological sense, but he was family in every other way that mattered. Following in his father's footsteps, Harry had worked for the Bell family his entire adult life. His title was Gamekeeper. But he was more than that. Harry was the glue that kept the Bellcroft estate together. Officially, he managed the outdoor part of Bellcroft, the Bell family estate. His official duties included groundskeeping, outdoor maintenance and repair, gardening, and seasonal maintenance. Harry was part of Bellcroft and Bellcroft was part of him. Grandma May used to say that Harry was as much a Bell as any blood-born Bell—maybe even more.

Unofficially, he was the only doting uncle-big-brother-cousin figure Karla had ever known. Harry had been part of her everyday life growing up. She had seen far more of Harry than her mother, that was for sure. Harry had been one of the few constants in

Karla's life. He was family. Karla would never say it out loud, but Harry felt more like family than her mother, Lynn, had ever been.

Though Harry and Lynn were the same age, Harry looked older. His bushy gray beard, mop of silver hair, and weather-beaten, careworn skin aged him. He reminded Karla of an old Irish fisherman; he just needed a pipe and a cable-knit sweater.

"I'll get this out of your way." Harry picked up the small Victorian-era writing desk that had been the centrepiece of their argument and escaped the tense atmosphere inside the cottage.

Gucci tried to follow him but ran out of leash before he reached the door. Defeated, he lay down with a heavy sigh, rested his chin on his front paws, and stared longingly at the door, waiting for Harry to come back for him.

"You should've checked with me, Karla," Lynn said in a softer, less confrontational tone. "Mirabel is my home."

"Actually, it's not," Karla reminded her. "Grandma May left Bellcroft to me, including all the buildings and contents. She left her bank accounts to you. We're standing in my house."

"But I grew up here," Lynn pleaded. "I live here."

"You haven't lived here since you were eighteen," Karla disputed, shaking her head. "Why are you still in Bellbrook, anyway? Shouldn't you hurry back to Roy?"

"You know his name is *Ray*."

Karla shrugged. She didn't care what his name

was. He was temporary. Ray was Lynn's boyfriend du jour. Meal ticket. Sugar daddy. Whatever.

Karla knew the routine; their unhealthy dynamic would run its course, and they would break up. Lynn would run back to Bellbrook to recover until she found her next victim/ boyfriend. Then she would disappear again. Lather, rinse, repeat.

"I'm staying in Bellbrook," Lynn announced, "to help you and support you. Grandma May's death is the biggest loss you've ever had. I want to be here for you. I know I haven't always been the best mother, but I want to do better. It's time for us to mend fences."

Lynn locked eyes with her daughter and held the gaze a little too long, not batting her false eyelashes once. This was how Karla knew Lynn was lying. When Lynn lied, she challenged her victim with intense, prolonged eye contact. It was her Tell. It was the first Tell Karla ever figured out when she was eight-and-a-half years old.

She didn't know which part of Lynn's statement was a lie, but there was a lie in there somewhere. Karla knew it would come to light sooner or later. Lies always did.

"Grandma May was like a mother to me," Karla said, hoping the words stabbed Lynn like a knife. "But her funeral was almost three weeks ago. I'm fine now. I have lots of support. Do what you do best and rush back to Ray."

Lynn's posture slumped, as though her daughter's dismissal was a punch in the gut. That's when Karla noticed Lynn was wearing the same black dress and shoes that she had worn to Grandma May's funeral.

"Why are you dressed like that?" Karla gestured at Lynn's sombre outfit.

"Mr. Hughes's funeral was this morning," Lynn replied, smoothing the front of her black dress and tucking a stray blonde tendril into her French twist. "And it's a good thing I went. You were nowhere to be found, and someone had to represent the Bell family." She pointed at Karla and wagged her maroon-polished index finger. "The Bells put the Bell in Bellbrook. We're pillars of the Bellbrook community. People expect us to represent the town and attend events. Good and bad. What would Grandma May have said if Mr. Hughes had been buried without a Bell in attendance to pay respects and support poor Anna, his heartbroken widow?"

GAWD! Lynn had a flair for the dramatic. It's amazing she didn't have a shelf of Academy awards.

"You're the last person to lecture me about being a Bell," Karla asserted. "You left this town and abandoned your responsibilities when I was a baby. The only time you visited was when you were between men or needed something from Grandma May."

Karla knew exactly what it meant to be a Bell. Most of the time, it was confusing. Living in Bellbrook with the surname Bell made her an aristocrat in the eyes of the locals, and a local in the eyes of the real aristocrats, who kept vacation homes on the outskirts of town. No matter where she went or who she was with, she always felt like an outsider. Except for Grandma May, of course. Karla was never an outsider with Grandma May.

"Where were you this morning that was more

important than Mr. Hughes's funeral?" Lynn demanded as Harry re-entered the cottage and brushed past them toward Grandma May's bedroom.

In truth, Karla knew she lacked the mental and emotional bandwidth for another funeral so soon—and in the same church, no less. The mere thought left her emotionally paralysed. So, instead of putting herself through it, she'd moved boxes of sentimental belongings out of Mirabel to her best friend's garage before Fitz showed up to gut the place.

"I hardly knew Mr. Hughes," Karla explained, keeping the real reason to herself. "And I don't know Mrs. Hughes very well. It felt inappropriate to attend. The funeral home's website said friends and family only. I didn't want to intrude. I sent flowers to Mrs. Hughes and donated to her chosen charity."

Harry breezed through the room again, this time carrying the wooden chair that matched the small writing desk he and Lynn had played tug-of-war with earlier. Watching Harry and the chair disappear through the front door, Lynn clenched her fists at her side and stomped her black kitten heel on the wood floor.

"Where am I supposed to stay while this place gets renovated?"

"Go back to Ray," Karla suggested. "Or dip into your inheritance from Grandma May and rent a room at the Nestled Inn."

"I can't afford to live at a bed-and-breakfast," Lynn lamented. "That money has to last for my retirement."

Retirement? What Lynn would retire from was a mystery to Karla. Apparently, it was a mystery to

Gucci too, judging by how he quirked his head to one side like he'd just heard a strange sound.

Karla acknowledged that, while Grandma May had left Lynn a tidy sum, the inheritance wasn't bottomless. It was enough money to afford Lynn the luxury of doing almost anything she wanted, but not enough to do nothing ever again.

Karla suggested Lynn might get a discount at the Nestled Inn by negotiating a weekly or monthly rate.

"Where will you stay?" Lynn asked.

"With Rob," replied Karla.

Lynn rolled her eyes. "Family should stick together during times like this."

Rob is family, Karla thought but said nothing, refusing to rise to Lynn's attempt to goad her into another argument.

"Anything you want me to move out of Bellflower, Karla?" Harry asked when Lynn and Karla caught him poking his head through the ajar door.

"I'm afraid not," she replied. "I'm told most of it is unsalvageable."

"Are you sure?" Harry asked. "Have you assessed the situation yourself?"

Karla shook her head. How could she assess the situation when she'd never been inside Bellflower? Grandma May had it shuttered and locked up tight when Karla was a little girl. Grandma May always said she would get around to sorting out the cottage next door, but one thing or another always got in the way, and she never did. Now, it was Karla's responsibility to restore both cottages to their former glory and figure out what to do about the large manor house and grounds nearby.

"I haven't," Karla admitted. "But I'm going to. That's why I'm here. Believe it or not, I didn't come here to break up your argument. Fitz called and asked me to stop by Bellflower. He wants to show me something before he starts the demolition."

"Why don't I come with you," Harry offered with that familiar, protective tone in his voice. "We can see if there's anything inside worth salvaging, and I can have a word with Fitz about his demolition plans."

Since Karla told him she'd hired Keith Fitzgibbon to renovate the twin cottages, she'd gotten the sense that Harry didn't agree with her choice of contractor. He hadn't said anything specific, but Karla knew him well enough to know he had reservations.

They asked if Lynn wanted to go with them and see the inside of Bellflower one last time before Fitz gutted it.

"I don't have time for a stroll down memory lane," Lynn replied brusquely. "I have to pack and find somewhere to live before my home is torn down around me." She huffed and shook her head as she turned toward the bedrooms. "I can't believe I'm being evicted by my own daughter," she added just loud enough for Karla to hear as she walked away.

THE AIR inside Bellflower was musty and thick.

A small herd of dust bunnies scattered in the wake of Karla crouching down and gathering Gucci in her arms. As she tucked him under one arm and wiped dust from the pads of his paws, she wished she had one of those masks that construction workers use.

"Fitz?" she called. "It's Karla Bell."

"His truck is outside," whispered Harry. "He must be here somewhere."

"Hello? Fitz?"

Dust particles hovered in the single streak of sunlight that crept through the boarded-up kitchen window.

"Fitz!" Harry's booming voice made Karla flinch.

They stood in silence for a moment, listening for Fitz's reply. Nothing.

"I'll find him." Harry pointed to his ear under his thick mop of silver hair. "He's probably wearing head-phones or something."

Karla nodded and hugged Gucci close.

One careful step at a time, she followed Harry deeper into the dank, stale house. The dusty air tickled her eyes and nose.

Bellflower's floor plan was the mirror image of Mirabel, making the cottage eerily comforting and creepily familiar.

"Fitz!" Harry lunged into the second bedroom. "Keith!" He shook the man's arm. "Keith Fitzgibbon! Can you hear me?"

"He can't hear you." Karla placed her free hand on Harry's shoulder. "I think Fitz is dead."

CHAPTER 2

MAX'N'CHEESE

KEITH FITZGIBBON, a.k.a. Fitz, was slumped against the wall with his legs stretched out in front of him, and his head tilted to one side. His hands rested on the floor on either side of his tall, husky body, palms up.

Harry checked Fitz's left wrist for a pulse and looked up at Karla, shaking his head. Then, his cautious hand moved toward the sheet of paper that rested on Fitz's rotund, overalled belly.

"No. Don't touch it," Karla warned, taking a step toward him. "Don't touch anything."

"Right," Harry agreed, nodding and straightening his long legs until he returned to his full standing height. "I'll call your dad."

Karla nodded and craned her neck to read the sheet of paper on Fitz's belly. The paper was crinkled as though it had been crumpled into a ball then uncrumpled.

It was a note scrawled in pencil.

IT WAS MY FAULT.

The block letters were faint, just dark enough to be legible. The note was signed with Fitz's signature, also in pencil.

Taking in the scene, Karla assumed Fitz must have written the note with the red carpenter pencil on the floor near his right hand, next to the pneumatic nail gun laying at his fingertips. The pneumatic nail gun that he had presumably used to shoot himself in the forehead. A streak of blood smeared down the wall, as if Fitz had been standing when the nail gun fired, then slid down to his final position.

A shudder crawled up Karla's spine, and her nose twitched with dust irritation.

Gucci shook his furry head against her hand, and Karla realized she had been unconsciously covering the dog's eyes to spare him from witnessing the tragic scene.

"The police are on their way," Harry said, gently steering Karla away from Fitz. "Your dad said we should wait outside and not touch anything."

"Harry," Karla said, resisting his attempt to guide her. "Look at the blood smear on the wall." She pointed at the red smudge.

"Looks like Fitz was standing up when it happened," Harry said, arriving at the same conclusion as Karla. "Poor soul." He shook his head and clucked his tongue. "He must've slid down the wall afterward."

"How did the note land so perfectly in the centre of his belly?" Karla wondered aloud.

"That's for the police and the coroner to figure

out," Harry said, once again steering her toward the door. "I'm sure there's a reasonable explanation."

Karla was sure there was an explanation too, and she hoped it wasn't that Fitz had been murdered.

OUTSIDE, the bright and unseasonably warm fall day was a stark contrast to the dark, lifeless atmosphere inside Bellflower.

Within minutes, police cars, uniforms, and first responders had overtaken the small cottage. Organized chaos. It looked like a mass of confusion, but everyone wearing a uniform seemed to have a purpose. They knew what to do and where to go, which was more than Karla could say. Trying to stay out of the way, she silently wondered if the entire Bellbrook police department was there.

"What's going on?" Lynn asked, running out of Mirabel, her outstretched arms reaching for Karla as she closed the gap between them.

"It's Fitz," Karla said.

Lynn wrapped a protective arm around her daughter's shoulder.

"Is he OK? Did he have an accident?" she asked, her eyes searching Karla and Harry for answers.

"Fitz is dead, Lynn," Harry said, his hand positioned to steady her if necessary.

"What?" She looked to Karla for confirmation. "Fitz? Dead?"

Karla nodded. "We don't know the details," she

fibbed to avoid describing the grisly scene. She wasn't ready to talk about it yet. She was still processing.

"Hey, Sis!"

Karla's head spun toward her half-sister's voice.

"Max!" She wrapped her free arm around her sister and squished Gucci between them.

Maxine Sheridan was eleven years younger than Karla. Despite their generation gap, and despite Max spending every summer of her youth in her mother's hometown in Japan, Karla and Max were close. They had a bond. They were sisters, but at the same time, they were both only children. They might have shared a father and grown up in the same small town, but they grew up in different worlds. They both knew the loneliness of feeling like outsiders and shared a silent understanding and appreciation for one another.

The half-sisters couldn't have been more opposite in appearance. Both women took after their mothers. In fact, the lack of resemblance between them and their father was so pronounced that their father would often joke he must have been constructed entirely of recessive genes.

Karla had inherited Lynn's wavy, blonde hair and Max had inherited her mother's straight, black hair. Karla inherited Lynn's facial features but with a slightly different eye colour—Lynn had blue eyes while Karla's were green. Max inherited her mother's brown eyes. The only feature the sisters shared was their mutual height of five feet, five and a half inches. Though Max's police uniform created the illusion that she was the taller and more physically imposing sister.

"I need to ask you a few questions," Max said, rubbing Gucci's head and letting him kiss her chin.

"Let me take the dog," Lynn offered, already reaching for him. "Gucci can help me pack while you deal with"—she gestured to the surrounding chaos—"this."

"Thanks." Karla gave Lynn a tight-lipped smile and relinquished the terrier.

"We can go inside Mirabel," Max suggested.

"No, we can't," Karla retorted. "Unless you want Lynn to take notes about our conversation."

The sisters decided to sit in Max's patrol car. As Karla opened the passenger-side door, she spotted Harry. He was talking to the police chief and mimicking—as best he could while upright and without a nearby wall—Fitz's position when they found him.

"How are you?" Max asked, squeezing Karla's hand. "Are you in shock? Maybe a medic should check you over."

"I'm fine." Karla flicked her wrist dismissively. "Or at least, I will be." She smiled as proof of her resilience. "Let's get this over with."

Max produced a notebook and pen. She opened the notebook to the next blank page and jotted a quick note at the top. "Start at the beginning," she said.

So, Karla told her sister everything, starting with the red pickup truck that drove out of the driveway just before she arrived, Dylan Fitzgibbon's hasty exit from Bellflower, Harry and Lynn's argument, and ending with her and Harry telling Lynn that Fitz was dead.

"Are you sure it was *his* red pickup truck?" Max asked.

"Positive." Karla would know that pickup truck anywhere. She'd been avoiding it since her return to Bellbrook.

"Do you know why *he* was here?"

"No idea," Karla replied, without letting on that she was dying to know the answer herself—pardon the pun.

"Other than the red pickup truck and Dylan, did you see anyone else near Bellflower today?"

Karla thought back. Though it had been barely an hour, it felt like a lifetime since she exited her car and placed Gucci on the driveway.

"Rosalie was on her midday walk," she said, pointing to the spot behind the cottages where she had exchanged a smile and a wave with Grandma May's best friend.

"Did you talk to her?"

"No," Karla replied. "I was about to, but Leon Tyson showed up. They were talking and I didn't want to interrupt. I don't remember seeing his car, though. Either he was parked on the other side of Fitz's truck, or he arrived after me and I didn't notice."

"How long were Rosalie and Leon behind the cottages?"

"I don't know," Karla replied. "Harry and Lynn were arguing in Mirabel. I went inside to referee."

"So, Lynn and Harry were already here when you arrived?"

"Yes." Karla nodded. "Harry had been making trips in and out of Mirabel all morning. He was moving Grandma May's things to the manor house. And Lynn said she'd spent the morning at Mr. Hughes's funeral."

"How long were the three of you inside Mirabel together?"

"Long enough for Lynn and me to have an argument, and for Harry to remove a couple small pieces of furniture." Karla shrugged one shoulder. "I didn't pay much attention to the time."

"Why did you and Harry go next door to Bellflower?"

"Fitz phoned me this morning," Karla explained. "He wanted to show me something before he started dismantling the interior. Harry offered to come with me in case there was anything inside the cottage I wanted to keep. Fitz and I had agreed to meet after lunch."

Instead of living by the clock, like the rest of the world, the people of Bellbrook marked time relative to the milestones of their daily lives. Events were planned around frustratingly vague events like mealtimes or the position of the sun. People made plans for *after breakfast* or *late afternoon*. And the ever dubious *over coffee*. The ambiguity and general disregard for standardized time in Bellbrook was something Karla found particularly difficult to navigate. In her corporate life, she had lived by the clock. Time was the god that she and everyone else worshipped and followed. Her previous home in the suburbs might have lacked the cultural and commercial attractions of the big city, and fell short of the charm and neighbourliness of small-town Bellbrook, but at least suburbanites agreed to live their overscheduled lives abiding by the same clock. Everyone knew, with confidence, where they were supposed to be and when they were supposed to be there.

"Do you know what Fitz wanted to show you?"

Karla shrugged again and shook her head. "I have no idea. He never got the chance to tell me."

"Did you or Harry touch or move anything when you found Fitz?"

"I didn't touch anything," Karla confirmed. "Harry shook Fitz's arm and checked his left wrist for a pulse. He tried to touch the suicide note on Fitz's belly, but I stopped him before he disturbed it."

"How do you know it was a suicide note?" Max asked.

"I saw it. I read it," Karla admitted. "The pencil was so light, I had to squint, but I read it. All four words."

A rap on the windshield startled the sisters and interrupted their conversation.

Max smiled at the officer, who tapped on the glass, and lowered the driver's side window to hear what he had to say.

"Chief wants to talk to you," said the young officer, lifting his chin toward the cluster of uniforms near the porch.

"Both of us?" Max asked him.

The officer shrugged and walked away.

Max closed her notebook. She and Karla exited the car and made their way toward the police chief who was already heading toward them. They met halfway between Max's patrol car and Bellflower's wrap-around porch.

"How are my two favourite daughters?" Chief Dean Sheridan asked, chuckling at his own joke.

Dean Sheridan, chief of the Bellbrook Police Department, often used the phrase, *my two favourite daughters*, when both his daughters were present. He thought it was hilarious. Every time. Everyone else laughed to be polite. At least, he'd stopped explaining the joke each time by following up with, "It's funny because they're the only two daughters I have."

"Hi, Dad," Karla said, letting his large, strong arms envelop her in a brief but tight hug.

"You're the last person I'd expect to find at a crime scene, Kar-la-la."

Dean had called her *Kar-la-la* or *La-la* all her life. She hated it but taught herself to cringe on the inside.

"Crime scene?" Karla asked. "Fitz's death was a crime?"

"We treat every unexpected death like a crime scene until the coroner tells us otherwise, La-la. It's procedure," Dean informed her, readjusting his service cap and briefly exposing a grey flattop that you could carve a roast on. "Maybe you'll get a taste for it and join the family business, hmm?"

"Don't hold your breath," Karla replied. "I'm quite happy running *my* business."

"And good at it too," Dean added with a wink.

It was true. Karla loved her job, and she missed it. She was the founder and CEO of *Just Task Me!*, an exclusive concierge service that catered to ultra-high net worth clients and promised *world-class service with small-town attention to detail.* Her clientele read like a list of Fortune 500 bigwigs and movers and shakers from multiple industries. She had originally moved back to Bellbrook to take care of Grandma May, but Grandma May's health took an unexpected turn for the worse. Karla had found herself planning a funeral instead of dividing her time between tending to her grandmother and establishing the East Coast branch of *Just Task Me!* like she had planned.

"I hope Max'n'cheese is taking good care of you."

Unlike Karla, Max cringed outwardly at her Dean-bestowed nickname.

"Of course, I'm taking care of her." Max gave her father a slight eye roll. "And don't call me *that* at work," she added in a hushed tone.

"Sorry, Officer Sheridan." Dean grinned.

Max updated Dean on her conversation with Karla. She told Dean she'd like to visit Rosalie and Leon to question them and get their statements.

Dean agreed and commended his daughter's investigative skills. He then informed them that he was about to visit Dylan Fitzgibbon and inform him of his father's death.

It hadn't occurred to Karla that somebody would have to notify Dylan that his dad was dead. She hoped Dean wasn't too late, and Dylan would find out through the proper channels instead of the town rumour mill. There was a good chance the news had already become common knowledge, and friends and neighbours were starting to reach out to Dylan, offering condolences and dropping off comfort food while gently prodding him for information about Fitz's sudden death.

Karla had the inexplicable urge to accompany her sister and father to collect statements and question witnesses. Why? Karla wasn't a cop. She had no interest in helping with a murder investigation. Or did she? She had discovered Fitz's body, after all. And he died in a house that she owned. Maybe it made sense that she felt obligated to see the investigation into his death through to the end.

An unmarked, white, windowless van appeared, driving up the long driveway.

"Coroner's here," Dean announced to his officers. "You'll have to notify Dylan, Officer Sheridan." He nodded to his youngest daughter who nodded back, accepting the assignment. "I need to stay here with the coroner, but Dylan can't wait. The news will be all over town in no time."

On second thought, Karla decided to stay at Bellflower a little longer and hear what the coroner had to say about Fitz's death.

CHAPTER 3

A REAL-LIFE REDHEAD

THE CORONER'S van was parked next to Karla's car. Karla paced between the vehicles, stopping occasionally to lean against her car and raise her face toward the warmth of the sun. More than once, she caught Lynn watching her through Mirabel's living room window. They exchanged nods and awkward waves.

One time, Lynn mouthed, "You OK?"

Karla nodded and gave her a thumbs-up.

She checked the time on her phone. Who knew it would take the coroner so long to visit a death scene?

Finally, the front door opened. Dean appeared first, followed by the coroner.

Karla waved her whole arm over her head, bouncing up and down on the balls of her stiletto-heeled, chocolate brown ankle boots.

The coroner waved back with equal enthusiasm, gave the police chief a quick hug, then raced down the porch steps like a child rushing out of school at the end of the day.

"I hoped you'd still be here!" the coroner said as she approached the white van.

Rob's thick ponytail of loose ginger curls bounced as she jogged toward Karla. The sun reflected off her red tresses, creating a copper halo on the top of her head that reminded Karla of the first time she had ever laid eyes on her best friend.

It was their first day of kindergarten. Five-year-old Karla had only ever seen red hair on TV and in picture books. It had never occurred to her that red hair grew on real people in real life. Robyn Mayhew's ginger locks, alabaster skin, and clusters of reddish freckles had mesmerized young Karla. She had convinced herself that the little red-haired girl was a magical creature disguised as a five-year-old kindergartener.

"Are you a fairy?" Karla had whispered, so as not to tip off the other kids that someone magical was in their presence and blow the red-haired fairy's cover.

"No," Rob had replied, her red ponytail swinging in the sun as she shook her head.

"Are you a mermaid?"

"If I was a mermaid, I would be in the ocean. Duh!"

Karla couldn't argue with that logic.

"What are you?"

"Just a kid," Rob had replied with a shrug.

"Me too."

They had been best friends ever since. No matter how much distance separated them, or how much time passed between visits, when they were together, they were five-year-old girls again. Whatever time or distance had separated them was forgotten.

"You were in there forever," Karla teased, hugging

her friend. "I was starting to think you were doing a full autopsy right there inside Bellflower."

"Ha ha," Rob responded. "The autopsy will have to wait until tomorrow." She checked the time on her watch. "I have patients this afternoon."

In addition to being Bellbrook's coroner, Dr. Robyn Mayhew was also the town doctor.

"I was kidding," Karla said, now serious. "I didn't think you'd need to perform an autopsy for a suicide."

"I'm not convinced Fitz died by suicide," Rob admitted, unlocking the coroner's van and opening the barn door-style doors at the back.

"I knew it!" Karla hissed under her breath.

"What do you mean, *you knew it*?" Rob asked.

"There's no way Fitz placed the note on his belly after he died and slid down the wall," Karla theorized. "The scene was laid out too perfectly."

"You're not wrong," Rob admitted. "There are other inconsistencies at the scene that warrant further investigation too."

"Like?"

"Shhh," Rob hushed, nodding behind Karla. "We'll talk at home later."

Karla turned to see her father closing in on them.

"Looks like your renovation will have to wait, La-la," he said. "We won't be able to release the scene for at least a few days."

"Oh?" Karla asked, hoping for more information. "Why not?"

"Well, we need to take photos and gather evidence. Then we have to wait for Dr. Mayhew" —he smiled proudly at his daughter's best friend—"to determine official cause of Fitz's death."

"Fitz didn't take his own life?" Karla looked back and forth from Rob to Dean, waiting for a definite answer.

The police chief and coroner both avoided eye contact and mumbled vague answers under their breath.

Fitz was murdered. Neither Dean nor Rob would admit it out loud, without a formal post-autopsy coroner's report, but their body language and what they didn't say spoke volumes. Fitz's death was a homicide.

Oh my! Karla felt like the world was closing in around her. Suffocating her. She stepped backward, then stepped backward again, digging her stiletto heel into the toe of the uniformed officer who was rolling the gurney out of the back of the coroner's van.

"Sorry," she mumbled to the young constable whom she remembered seeing earlier when he knocked on the window of Max's patrol car.

"No worries," he said, taking one hand off the gurney to steady her. "Steel-toed shoes." He shrugged one shoulder. "I didn't feel a thing."

Karla chuckled uncomfortably and used the side of the van to steady herself.

"It's OK, Karla. Breathe," Rob instructed.

"Deep breaths, La-la."

Karla nodded and tried to ignore how suddenly loud and stifling hot the world had become.

Breathe? How could she breathe when everything was wrong? Murders didn't happen in Bellbrook. Bellbrook was her safe place. When the world bit her, Karla retreated to Bellbrook—to Grandma May—to lick her wounds until she was strong enough to face the world again. Now, Grandma May was gone, the comfort and stability of her career was halfway across the country, and someone had been murdered in Bellbrook. In Bellflower of all places. Inside what was technically Karla's house.

"What's wrong?" Lynn demanded. The screen door slammed shut behind her. "Why is everyone crowding around Karla?" She speed walked toward them from Mirabel. "Karla? Are you all right?" She forced her way into the circle and rubbed big, slow circles on Karla's back.

Karla had no doubt Lynn had been watching them through the window.

"I'm fine," she insisted. "Just a bit lightheaded."

It wasn't a complete lie. Karla hadn't eaten since breakfast—a serving of yogurt with berries and a sprinkle of granola—and it felt like days ago. Her stomach was cavernous and starting to rumble.

"You need food and water. You can't stand outside this long without water." Lynn tapped on the shoulder of the nearest uniformed officer. "We need a bottle of water." She bulged her eyes at him. "Now." He looked at the police chief for approval, then scurried away.

"Nice to see you, Dean," Lynn said curtly with a nod.

"Lynn," Dean said, returning the nod. "You're looking well. Life in The Everglades agrees with you."

Lynn gave him a small smile and ignored his compliment. "I'd offer your officers tea and coffee," she said, changing the subject, "but the kitchen is empty. He even emptied the flaming fridge and unplugged it." Lynn nodded toward Harry, who was talking with another uniformed officer on the Bellflower porch. "He's not much to look at, but he's amazingly efficient. He emptied the entire cottage in a single morning."

"No worries," Dean said. "It's the thought that counts."

"It'll have to be," Lynn scoffed.

Karla's parents had an awkward but cordial relationship.

Dean had always been awkward around women. Especially the ones he had been married to, not married to, or fathered.

Dean and Lynn were never a proper couple. They dated casually and briefly at the start of their senior year of high school, and Karla was the result. Upon learning she was pregnant with Karla, Dean offered to marry Lynn, but she declined his proposal.

Grandma May once told Karla that Dean had offered to marry Lynn because he loved her, not out of obligation because she was pregnant. But Lynn didn't love him, and her plans didn't include settling down in Bellbrook and raising a baby. Lynn Bell had planned to conquer the world. And a few months after giving birth to Karla, that was exactly what she set off to do. She left her baby girl in the capable, loving arms of Grandma May and never looked back. Well, almost never.

Dean was as active and involved a father as an eighteen-year-old could be. He rather stumbled through his young adulthood, training to be a police officer, starting his career, and embarking on several short-term relationships until he met Max's mum. Thrilled that someone finally agreed to marry him, he got her down the aisle within six months of meeting. Then Max came along, and the marriage fizzled. His wife, like the women Dean had dated before her, claimed that Dean was *emotionally unavailable* and said he *wasn't vulnerable enough*. Dean gave up on finding true love. He jokingly told his daughters he must not be cut out for marriage. He might have given up on women, but he never gave up on fatherhood. He was a good provider and did his best to relate to his daughters. He provided for them and showed them he loved them by letting them play with the lights and sirens in his patrol car and buying them ice cream before dinner on school nights, against the wishes of Karla's grandmother and Max's mum. He also fixed things like cars and toys, even if he couldn't fix their broken hearts or hurt feelings.

"Before you leave, Lynn, I'll need you to give a statement to one of my officers," Dean said.

"Of course," Lynn replied. "Anything to help." She shrugged. "I didn't see or hear anything, though. I was at Mr. Hughes's funeral all morning. Fitz's truck was here when I got back, but I never saw Fitz. I assumed he was working inside Bellflower."

She snapped her fingers. "But Leon Tyson was here." She nodded, remembering. "He was standing on the porch at Bellflower, peering in the windows."

Dean pulled out his notebook and pen. "Did you speak to Leon?"

"No," Lynn replied, shaking her head. "I don't think he saw me. He was staring into the window pretty intently. But I was surprised he got here from the funeral before me. I only made a brief appearance at the condolence call. All the fuss had overwhelmed poor Anna Hughes, and she went upstairs to lie down, so I left. I thought I was one of the first people to leave, but he must've left before me if he beat me here."

"You saw Leon Tyson at Mr. Hughes's funeral?" Dean clarified.

"I think so." Lynn stroked her chin thoughtfully. "There were so many people. I saw everybody and nobody, if you know what I mean. Leon was wearing a black suit when I saw him on the porch, so maybe I just assumed he was at the funeral."

"Did you see anyone else around Bellflower today?" Dean asked.

Lynn shook her head. "Just Harry. Then Karla arrived and they found Fitz together."

"Was Dylan Fitzgibbon's truck here when you arrived?" Dean asked.

"I don't think so," Lynn replied, staring into nothingness as she searched her brain for the answer. "I only recall seeing one FITZ IT RIGHT THE FIRST TIME truck."

The young officer whom she had dispatched to find water returned and handed Lynn a bottle of water and a snack-size bag of almonds. Lynn unscrewed the cap and handed the water to Karla. "How'd Dylan take the news about his dad's death?" She directed her question at Dean. "I'd make the poor boy a casserole, but like I said, the kitchen's empty."

Karla swallowed a mouthful of water then inhaled a long, deep breath. *Can she stop complaining about the stupid kitchen?! For goodness' sake, a man was murdered while we were next door arguing about a hundred-year-old writing desk!* Karla had to remind herself that Lynn didn't yet know Fitz was murdered. As far as Lynn was concerned, Fitz had suffered a mysterious, fatal workplace accident.

Lynn opened the bag of almonds and handed it to Karla.

With only one free hand, Karla tipped the bag into her mouth.

"Max is with Dylan now," Dean replied.

"Delivering news like that must be the worst part of the job," Lynn sympathised. "I don't envy Max right now."

Karla didn't envy her sister either, but part of her wished she was with Max, asking questions and finding out what happened between him and Fitz that caused Dylan to stomp away from Bellflower in such a hurry.

CHAPTER 4

TREATS AND BRIBES

OCTOBER 20TH

"This is a nice surprise," Karla said when Rob arrived home unexpectedly in the middle of the day.

If not for Gucci's excited yelping and barking, Karla would have been oblivious to Rob's presence because she was so engrossed in her email inbox.

"I'm working from home this afternoon." Rob patted her laptop bag and set it on the kitchen island. "I need to write up and file the coroner's report for Fitz's autopsy."

"Right." Karla nodded. "What about your patients?"

"The Doctor from Beaver Creek is helping. He offered to see the patients that couldn't reschedule."

"Good," Karla commended her friend. "I'm glad to hear that you and The Doctor From Beaver Creek can get along and work together, despite everything that's happened between you."

Beaver Creek was the town next to Bellbrook. The

doctor from Beaver Creek was Rob's ex-husband. Though his name wasn't banned, per se, Karla could see the pain in her friend's eyes whenever someone mentioned it. Thus, they had an unspoken agreement to refer to him as *The Doctor From Beaver Creek* until Rob's feelings about the pending divorce were a little less raw.

"Well, our professional relationship is good, unlike our personal relationship, which is a hot mess." Rob sighed and shook her head. "And our co-parenting relationship is a work in progress."

"You guys are wonderful parents," Karla assured her. "Josie is the most thoughtful, well-adjusted nine-year-old I've ever met." Karla chuckled. "I might hire her to be my life coach."

"Imagine how much more thoughtful and well-adjusted she'd be if she had a happy, functional, two-parent home," Rob mumbled as she pulled a glass from the cupboard next to the fridge.

"Thanks to her parents, Josie has two happy, functional, cooperative one-parent homes." Karla opened the fridge and pulled out the pitcher of lemon-raspberry-rosemary infused water she knew her friend was about to reach for. "You're a great mum, Rob, and Josie is an awesome kid."

"I miss her so much when she's with her dad every other week." Rob looked longingly in the direction of her daughter's unoccupied bedroom. Then she shook her head and smiled at Karla. "What have you been up to?" Rob asked, sneaking a peek over Karla's shoulder. "Is that a list of suspects? People who you think might have killed Fitz?"

"Sort of." Karla shrugged. "More like a list of people who were around Bellflower when Fitz died."

Rob ran her finger down the page, reading each name under her breath.

"Red pickup truck?" She glared at Karla. "*He* was at Bellflower yesterday?"

His name was another name that they had silently agreed to avoid.

"I saw *him* leave."

"Are you sure it was *him*?" Rob asked.

"Positive."

"What was *he* doing there?" Rob wondered out loud, then gave Karla a head-to-toe appraisal. "Why are you still wearing your jammies? It's almost lunchtime."

Another ambiguous time reference. What did *almost lunchtime* mean? Close to noon, after 1 p.m.? Karla glanced at the time on the microwave: 11:45 a.m.

"I had a video meeting with my business partner and our management team," Karla explained. "I did my hair and makeup because they could only see me from the neck up." She shrugged one shoulder. "Our meeting ran longer than expected, then I made this list, and got focussed on replying to emails. I guess I forgot to get dressed." She glanced down at her navy silk pajamas with white satin piping.

Rob gave Karla a skeptical side-eye glance. "What did you have for breakfast?" she asked, returning the water pitcher to the fridge.

As if on cue, a growl emanated from Karla's empty belly, answering Rob's question.

Karla rubbed her hungry tummy to reassure it that food was imminent.

"Are you taking your meds?" Rob asked, then took a sip of water.

"Yes, doctor." Karla resisted the urge to roll her eyes. "Most of the time," she added under her breath.

"Time blindness, hyperfocus, forgetfulness… they're symptoms of your ADHD."

"I know," Karla said. "The meds help, but they don't fix all my symptoms."

The doorbell and Gucci's subsequent barking interrupted their conversation and saved Karla from the medication compliance lecture she knew she was about to get from her best friend.

"Dad! Max!" Karla said when she opened the door to find her uniformed family members on the doorstep.

"We brought treats!" Max announced over Gucci's excited barking.

Dean held up a tray of takeout cups from Déjà Brew in one hand, and a distinct, pink confectionery box from Upper Crust bakery in the other. Her stomach doubled its rumbling efforts at the thought of Upper Crust bakery's maple crullers.

Karla stood aside so her father and sister could enter the house.

"Treats or bribes?" Rob asked jokingly, relieving Dean of the tray of coffee cups.

"Both," Dean replied. "We were hoping to talk to you about Fitz's autopsy."

Max removed the lid from Gucci's Puppyccino and picked him up so he could enjoy his gourmet treat.

Over coffee and pastries, Rob gave Dean, Max, and Karla a summary of her autopsy findings. Dean asked how the nail from the nail gun had killed Fitz and whether his death was instant.

"Violent fragmentation of part of the brain stem," Rob explained between sips of cinnamon rooibos chai. "The brain stem controls breathing, heart rate, and blood pressure, among other vital functions." She nodded. "He would have died instantly. Probably before he processed the sound of the nail gun being fired."

"Isn't the brain stem in the back of the head?" Karla asked, unconsciously rubbing where the back of her head met the top of her spine. "Wasn't Fitz shot in the forehead?"

"He was shot twice," Rob revealed.

"That means it had to be murder, right?" Karla asked.

"Yes," Rob confirms. "The first shot killed him. A dead man can't fire a nail gun."

"So, the first shot was to the back of his head, and the second shot was to his forehead?"

Rob nodded.

"Why did the killer shoot him twice?" Karla wondered aloud. "Surely they realized he was dead after the first shot."

"Could be a case of overkill," Dean speculated. "The killer was emotional and did more than necessary to kill their victim."

"Overkill can indicate a personal connection between the killer and the victim," Max continued. "It suggests they may have had strong feelings about their victim."

"I suspected Fitz was murdered when I saw the nail gun," Dean added, putting down his almond bear claw. "Fitz was left-handed. The nail gun was found next to his right hand."

"So was the pencil," Karla remembered. "If Fitz's killer staged the scene to look like suicide, they mustn't have known Fitz was a lefty."

"Which means whoever did it probably didn't know him well enough to know he was a southpaw," Max continued, finishing Karla's thought.

"Or they were so flustered, they forgot," Dean countered.

"Did the killer force Fitz to write the note?" Rob asked.

"We don't think Fitz wrote it," Dean disclosed. "The signature doesn't match. And whoever wrote it had a very light touch. Fitz's handwriting samples indicate he would have applied a lot of pressure to the pen or pencil."

"Maybe the killer wrote the note *after* they killed Fitz," Max suggested.

"Fitz was a big man," Karla said. "He would have put up a fight."

"There were no defensive wounds or marks on Fitz's body," Rob advised.

"Is it possible Fitz didn't see his killer coming?" Karla asked.

Max and Dean nodded.

"Any fingerprints?" Rob asked, tearing apart her chocolate croissant.

"None," Dean replied, shaking his head. "The nail gun and pencil were wiped clean. Another indication Fitz was murdered. The only fingerprints on the note belonged to Fitz and his son, Dylan. But we expected to find Dylan's fingerprints on the note since it was written on the back of his resignation letter."

"Resignation letter?" Karla asked. "Dylan resigned from the family business?"

"Apparently," Dean confirmed.

Karla knew there must have been some sort of drama in the Fitzgibbon household for Dylan to resign from the family construction business and do it in such a formal manner that he handed his father a letter of resignation.

The doorbell rang again, causing Gucci to erupt into a barking frenzy as he raced toward the door.

"Hi, Lynn!"

Karla took a bracing breath when Rob said her mother's name.

Lynn exchanged greetings with everyone gathered around the kitchen island.

"What brings you here?" Karla asked.

"I was just passing," Lynn explained. "The Nestled Inn is just up the road." She jerked her thumb in the direction of the nearby bed and breakfast. "Anyway, I saw two patrol cars out front and thought I should stop in to make sure everything is OK." She glanced at the coffee cups and confectionery box. "I see you're fine."

"Dad and Max stopped by to talk to Rob about work stuff," Karla explained.

"Speaking of work stuff, is it true that Fitz was murdered?"

"Where did you hear that?" Dean demanded.

"Around," Lynn replied with a shrug. "Everyone in town is talking about it."

"Stupid rumour mill," he muttered under his breath. "Yes, it's true. Unofficially."

"How did Dylan take the news of Fitz's death?" Lynn asked, directing the question at Max.

"He was shocked," Max replied. "He had a lot of questions, and I didn't have very many answers. We had only just found Fitz, and Rob hadn't conducted the autopsy yet. I'm going to visit him when I leave here to give him a few details and ask him more questions."

"I could go with you," Karla offered. "I don't mind."

Not only did she not mind, but Karla was eager to go with Max. She wanted to hear what Dylan had to say about Fitz's death and ask him why he resigned from the family construction business.

"I'm not sure it's a good idea, La-la," Dean said. "It's not usual procedure for a civilian to observe an investigation."

"But I've known Dylan since he was a little boy," Karla argued. "I have a perspective about him that no local cop could have."

"I agree with Dean," Lynn said as if someone had asked her opinion. "What if Dylan is the killer? You don't need to be tangled up in this case. It could be dangerous. Let the professionals deal with it."

"Fitz was found in my house," Karla argued. "For

all I know, he would still be alive if I hadn't hired him to renovate the cottages. And I found him. I feel obligated to help solve his murder. I could just happen to show up to pay my respects at the same Max shows up. It would be coincidence. Anyway, I could be helpful"—she shot Dean and Max a knowing glance—"I can tell you if Dylan is lying."

"She's right, Dad," Max agreed. "It wouldn't hurt for Karla to listen and observe. And her… special skill might be handy."

"What special skill?" Lynn asked.

"Karla's a human lie detector," Max announced proudly.

"How?" Lynn asked, narrowing her gaze on Karla. "Why is this the first time I'm hearing about it?"

Because it's something I only share with people I spend time with.

"I have a knack for telling when someone is lying." Karla shrugged.

"How?" Lynn demanded again.

"It's hard to explain," Karla replied.

"I have a theory," Rob said, raising her hand like she was in school and wanted the teacher to pick her to answer the question.

"I'm listening."

"It's possible that Karla's neurodivergence makes her consciously aware of details in her environment that most neurotypical people would not be consciously aware of. She also processes sensory inputs much faster than the rest of us, allowing her to find seemingly invisible patterns or deviations from patterns."

"In English please, Dr. Mayhew," responded a wide-eyed Lynn.

"Karla has ADHD and probably SPD—sensory processing disorder—which makes her hypersensitive to very small details that the rest of us ignore with our conscious brain. Not only can she distinguish these small details, but she can process them fast enough to extract patterns and predict behaviour." She pointed at her laptop on a nearby table. "Karla's brain is like a superfast computer with a very small memory."

"Are you saying my daughter is a human polygraph test?" Lynn asked.

"Kind of," Rob replied. "For most of us—unless we're psychopaths—lying causes stress. Even small insignificant lies are stressful. To release the stress, our bodies increase our heart rate, sweat fidget, or create other small quirks and tics to take the pressure off. It's totally normal and its involuntary and subconscious."

"We can't stop doing it?" Max asked.

"You can try," Rob replied, "but probably not, and if you do, your body will substitute a new tic or quirk to replace the one you stopped."

"You don't have AHDD," said Lynn, looking at her daughter. "You were academically gifted. You could read at a grade five level in kindergarten."

"ADHD," Karla corrected her. "And I do have it. I've had it all my life, but I didn't know until Rob diagnosed me. Women are often misdiagnosed well into adulthood."

"You get it from me!" Lynn swatted Karla's shoulder. "Your lie detecting is just like my weather forecasting."

Everyone around the kitchen island rolled their eyes in unison and prepared themselves to hear about Lynn's barometrically sensitive sinuses and left hip.

"I always know when a low front is moving in. My sinuses sense it long before The Weather Network's high-tech forecasting equipment. The worse my sinus pain, the worse the downpour will be. In 1999, I was living in the Bahamas and had sinus pain so bad that I threw up hours before Hurricane Floyd made landfall. But in the winter, it's my hip"—she bent her knee and rotated her hip to demonstrate—"depending on the pain level, I can tell you how much snow is coming to within one centimetre."

"I suppose," Dean announced, returning to the original subject and saving everyone from another weather prediction story, "if La-la happened to be at Dylan's house when Max happened to show up, and if Dylan didn't ask La-la to leave, there's nothing I could do about it."

"Good!" Karla slapped the quartz countertop. "Let me get my purse!"

"And clothes, maybe?" Max called as Karla left the kitchen.

Karla looked down at her blue silk pajamas.

"Give me five minutes," she called, changing course toward her bedroom.

CHAPTER 5

FUR, DROOL, AND KISSES

IT TOOK Karla longer than usual to get dressed. For the first time in her adult life, she couldn't decide what to wear.

Karla's extensive designer wardrobe, shoe collection, and cache of carefully curated accessories were more than a testament to her successful, lucrative career. They were her suit of armour against a scary world.

Her wardrobe, combined with her sleek hair, flawless makeup, impeccably manicured and pedicured hands and feet, and apparent self-confidence, conjured an air of automatic authority usually reserved for men. In addition to affording her the same professional credibility as her male colleagues in the corporate world, the persona Karla had created—Corporate Karla as her alter ego was known—made her more intimidating and less approachable, which was exactly what she had wanted. If people can't get too close, they can't lie to you. Or leave you.

While Corporate Karla had served her well in her previous life, it was over the top for Bellbrook.

The problem was, Karla had worn the disguise and exuded the attitude for so long that she had, over time, *become* the persona she had created. This was becoming increasingly apparent since her return to Bellbrook last month. Corporate Karla did not like being forced into dormancy and, in certain situations, insisted on being allowed out to play.

Most of her wardrobe was in storage until the renovation was complete and she could settle in at Mirabel. She'd brought only the essentials to Rob's house. Despite Karla's essentials being at least five times the size of most people's wardrobes, nothing seemed quite right to wear to a condolence call at Dylan Fitzgibbon's house.

She had wanted something formal enough to reflect the sombreness of the situation, but casual enough to make her relatable. She hoped that making herself as approachable as possible—a big step outside her current comfort zone— would encourage Dylan to trust and confide in her. Like he used to.

After much deliberation, she returned her black Alexander McQueen slim sheath dress with cap sleeves, V-neck, and flattering fitted waist to the closet and settled on her olive green, sleeveless jumpsuit with tapered ankles. She accessorized the outfit with a thick tan belt, chunky, brown, block-heel pumps with ankle straps, and her gold-brown Birken bag—because a Birken bag was appropriate for any occasion and, therefore, essential.

She completed her friendly and accessible look

with a black, leather moto jacket and her natural, wavy hair. Karla couldn't remember the last time she had left the house without scorching her blonde waves into stick-straight submission with the blistering heat of a 440-degree flat iron.

Karla slid the black wicker basket over the same arm as her Birken bag and rapped on Dylan's door. She listened to his dog's deep barks as she picked up the covered casserole dish with an envelope taped to the lid that someone had left on the doorstep.

"Back, Cash!" bellowed a voice from inside the house. "Down! Sit! Good boy."

The inner door cracked open.

Karla craned her neck and aimed her smile at the small opening.

Dylan opened the door just enough to poke his head through.

"Hi."

"Hi, Dylan," Karla replied. "Do you remember me? I used to —"

"Of course, I remember you, Karla."

He raised his index finger to indicate he would be right back. The door closed, then almost immediately opened again with Dylan bent at the waist, gripping the collar of his impossibly huge dog.

"Come in," he said, shuffling backward from the door, dragging the largest most reluctant canine she'd ever seen.

The dog was so big, Karla wasn't sure if she should pet him or strap a saddle to his back and take him for a ride.

She stepped inside.

"This isn't from me. It was on the doorstep when I arrived." She placed the casserole dish on the cluttered hall table, then gestured to the dog. "May I pet him?"

Karla had never met a dog—or cat, or any other animal for that matter—that she didn't love. The feeling was reciprocated. Karla and animals had a natural, easy mutual love for each other. Animals were much easier than people. Animals wore their feelings on the outside. She knew where she stood with an animal. Unlike people whose actions didn't always match their words.

"As long as you're OK with dog fur, drool, and kisses."

"Three of my favourite things," she joked, extending her hand so the dog could sniff it. "Good boy," she said when the dog lowered the top of his head under her hand so she could rub him.

"His name is Cash," Dylan said with a hint of pride. "Most people are terrified of him at first, but he's a gentle giant. He wouldn't hurt a soul."

"Who could be scared of such a good boy?" Karla asked with puckered lips, directing the question at Cash. "Handsome boy!" she said, crouching down, taking the St. Bernard-Great Dane mix's massive head in both hands, and rubbing his ears.

The delighted dog basked in her attention. The breeze from his enormous, wagging tail moved the pile of unopened condolence cards on the hall table.

"Why did you name him Cash?" she asked.

"Because it takes so much money to keep him fed," Dylan replied with a sigh. "And when he was teething, he chewed through hundreds of dollars' worth of shoes and furniture." He gathered the casserole dish and a pile of cards from the hall table. "If I leave food out, Cash will eat it as soon as I turn my back." He nodded toward the kitchen. "Come and sit down."

"I guess there aren't a lot of places that are out of Cash's reach," Karla said.

"We've—*I've*—had to get pretty resourceful to keep stuff away from him."

Karla watched Dylan shuffle around a bunch of mismatched casserole dishes to make room in the fridge for the latest arrival.

"Coffee? Tea? I think someone dropped off a bottle of rum earlier," he offered, pointing toward the cluttered countertop.

"No thank you," Karla replied, holding out the black, wicker, cauldron-shaped basket with black ribbon tied in a bow around the handle. "I thought you might have more than enough casseroles."

Dylan took the basket and indicated that she should follow him to the living room. He sank into an easy chair, and Karla perched on the edge of the sofa across from him. Cash sat on the floor next to her, resting his humungous head on the armrest and gazing lovingly at her. She rubbed the top of his soft, furry head as she and Dylan spoke.

"Fun Dip?" he asked, amused. "I can't believe you remembered."

"Of course, I remembered," she said. "The store only had six packages left, so I cleared them out."

Karla had hoped Dylan's favourite childhood candy would help take his mind off the events of the past twenty-four hours, if only for a minute. It had always done the trick when he was little.

She had worried that departing from the usual condolence offerings of comfort food or flowers might have offended him. After all, she hadn't seen him in twenty years. For all Karla knew, adult-Dylan might have hated Fun Dip or become a stickler for social protocol.

The black, cauldron-shaped basket had been her attempt to make the fun, nostalgic gift more suitable to the tragic reason for her visit. Karla had searched the store for something appropriately sombre to put the candy in, but there weren't any wrapping options for condolence gifts. Even the black gift bags gave off celebratory vibes. When she had seen the display of Halloween baskets, Karla asked the store clerk if there were any black baskets without orange pumpkin ribbon or glow-in-the-dark skeleton ribbon wrapped around the handle.

"What's the occasion?" the clerk had asked.

"Condolence call," Karla had replied.

"Fitz's boy?"

Karla nodded.

"I have some black ribbon under the counter somewhere…"

Rrrrip. The sound brought Karla back to the here and now.

Dylan had already opened a package of Fun Dip and was stabbing the pink edible candy stick into the flavoured, coloured sugar. She could smell it. The sweet stickiness and the pending sugar rush. Watching him focus so intently, Karla caught a glimpse of the little, curly-haired, brown-eyed boy he used to be. Now, Dylan Fitzgibbon was a grown-up, curly-haired, brown-eyed man with a beard and hairy, tattooed forearms.

I feel old, she thought with a sigh.

"You used to bring me a package of Fun Dip every time you babysat me," he recalled, then licked the red sugary powder off the stick. "It was my favourite candy, but my parents never let me have it because they thought the sugar made me too hyper." He chuckled as he stirred the stick through the sweet powder. "I was scared that, if my parents found out, they wouldn't let you babysit me anymore." He licked the stick again. "A couple of times, I suspected my dad knew. He'd say something weird or cryptic about candy, then wink at me."

"Who did you think bought the Fun Dip?"

"No way!" Dylan exclaimed. "My dad knew? He was in on it?"

"He sure was," Karla confirmed. "He bought them in bulk. I kept them at my house and brought one package every time I babysat you, just like Fitz had instructed."

When she was a teenager, Karla had had a standing arrangement with Dylan's parents. She babysat him every Tuesday from 4 p.m. until 7 p.m. Tuesday was their weekly date night, or so they had said. They would come home gushing to Dylan and Karla about the fancy dinner they had in Beaver Creek or the movie they had seen.

After Mrs. Fitzgibbon left her husband, she came clean to everyone in town. For more than a year, the

Fitzgibbons had been seeing a marriage counsellor in Beaver Creek every Tuesday. Apparently, Fitz was a serial adulterer. Mrs. Fitzgibbon found out when one of his mistresses confronted her at the grocery store. She claimed that, after talking to the mistress, she returned home and packed bags for her and Dylan. She had planned to pick him up from school, make the seven-hour drive to her parents' house, and never step foot in Bellbrook again.

But Fitz had come home early and caught her packing. She said he cried and begged her to stay. She claimed marriage counselling was his idea. According to her, they had started with monthly appointments, but soon, Fitz had wanted to go more often, so they attended weekly sessions together. Fitz had begun attending sessions by himself for individual coun-selling. It turned out Fitz was having an affair with the receptionist at the therapists' office.

Mrs. Fitzgibbon was less forgiving that time and unwilling to give her philandering husband another chance. She and Dylan moved out. They stayed in Bellbrook so Dylan could maintain a relationship with Fitz. Dylan spent the rest of his childhood living with his mother on weekdays and his father on weekends. Mrs. Fitzgibbon remarried a few years after the divorce. She and her new husband recently retired and moved to the West Coast. With Fitz dead, Dylan had no more relatives in Bellbrook. Just a quirky, tight-knit community of nosy busybodies who loved him like family and would continue to overwhelm him with homemade food until the town was out of casserole dishes.

"I'm sorry for your loss," Karla said softly. "Fitz was a town fixture. Bellbrook won't be the same without him."

"Thanks," Dylan replied, without looking up from the candy he was swirling with the Fun Dip stick and tapping his heel rhythmically on the floor. "I'm sorry about your renovation."

"Don't worry about the renovation," Karla assured him with a flick of her wrist. "In the grand scheme of things, the renovation isn't important. It's waited this long, so it can wait a while longer." She shrugged. "Besides, my dad said the police will be able to release the cottage in a few days."

"By the time you find a new contractor and they fit the job into their schedule, weeks or months could pass before anything happens."

"I won't search for a new contractor if you want the job," Karla offered, feigning ignorance about the resignation letter on Fitz's belly and Dylan's hasty departure from Bellflower just before she and Harry found Fitz's body.

Still not looking up from his Fun Dip, Dylan's heel tap evolved into an anxious knee-bounce. He clenched and unclenched his jaw as he poked the candy stick into the sugary powder. The sudden air of irritability and tension lingering between them was almost palpable.

"I no longer work in construction," Dylan blurted.

"I hadn't heard," Karla responded. "Which is unusual. News usually travels through Bellbrook faster than the speed of thought."

"It's a recent development." Dylan stopped

bouncing and poking and dropped the stick in the pouch of sugar. He locked eyes with Karla. "No one knows yet. I only told my dad yesterday."

"I guess that explains you resignation letter."

"How do you know about that?"

"I found your father," Karla tells him. "Your resignation letter was nearby."

Karla was careful not to disclose where the note was located relative to Fitz's body, that the note had been written on the back of the resignation letter, or the four penciled words scrawled above Fitz's forged signature. Dean had told her this information was a holdback. So was the location within the house where Fitz was killed. Dean hoped holding back details that only the killer would know, would make it easier to pinpoint Fitz's murderer.

"I'm sorry," Dylan said, his voice thick with emotion. He leaned forward, rested his elbows on his knees, and dropped his head forward. "I'm sorry you had to see that." He looked up at her. "They wouldn't let me see him. I told Max that I wanted to go to Bellflower, even if I couldn't go inside, but she said it wasn't a good idea."

"In my experience, Max is usually right," Karla said with a sigh. "It's one of her most annoying qualities." She winked to let him know she was joking.

Dylan's head slumped again. He sniffled and cleared his throat.

Distressed by his owner's emotional state, Cash lumbered to his side and sat on the floor at Dylan's feet, resting his huge, fluffy head in his owner's lap.

Dylan buried his head in the scruff of Cash's

substantial neck, and the young man's shoulders heaved silent sobs.

"Can I get you anything?" Karla asked, not sure what to do but wanting to do something—anything— to ease his pain. "Water? Tissue? I can find that bottle of rum someone dropped off."

Dylan shook his head and nuzzled deeper into Cash's fur.

Karla stood and scanned the living room and kitchen for something useful. She slid the paper towel from the spool on the kitchen counter and brought the entire roll to him.

"It's my fault," Dylan said, tearing off a sheet and crumpling it in his fist. "I shouldn't have left. I knew he was upset, but I never imagined he would do this." He blew his nose into the crumpled paper towel.

"This isn't your fault, Dylan."

Unless you killed him, Karla thought as she rubbed his back in the same, comforting way Grandma May used to rub hers when she was upset. She bit her lip to stop herself from telling Dylan that their argument wasn't the reason Fitz died. Dylan deserved to know that Fitz didn't take his own life. Someone else took it and staged the scene to hide their brutal actions. But it wasn't Karla's place to tell him. Max should be there any second. Updating Dylan on the status his father's death would be her unpleasant task.

"What did you and—"

The tinny chime of the doorbell, accompanied by Cash's explosive barking, interrupted Karla's question.

"He won't stop barking until I answer it," Dylan said, rising from the sofa.

"I'll go." Karla placed her hand on Dylan's shoulder and gave him a gentle push back into his seat.

"I don't want to see anyone," Dylan said.

She nodded. "I'll get rid of them." *Unless it's Max.*

CHAPTER 6

A HEAD-SCRATCHER

IT TOOK both Max and Karla to wrangle Cash and stop him from charging through the door when Max entered the house. Once Max acknowledged the hyper hound, and gave him some love, he calmed down and proudly led her to Dylan in the living room.

Karla excused herself to the kitchen while Max informed Dylan that the Bellbrook police were investigating Fitz's death as a murder.

"Murder?" Dylan shouted from the living room. "That's not what you said yesterday!"

She listened as Max explained to Dylan how the police had gathered evidence and scrutinized the scene. Then she explained how the coroner's findings had confirmed the police's suspicion that Fitz had been murdered.

"I couldn't tell you this yesterday because I didn't know. It was just speculation until the coroner completed the autopsy, and we finished gathering evidence."

"You said it was self-inflicted!" Dylan retorted. "I've been blaming myself. I thought he did it because of me."

"I didn't say it was self-inflicted," Max corrected him. "I said, *it's too early in the investigation to be certain, but at first glance, there's no apparent evidence of foul play.*"

"Double-speak for suicide," Dylan argued.

"You can stop blaming yourself," Karla said, handing Dylan the glass of water he didn't ask for. "Your argument wasn't a factor in Fitz's death."

Dylan swallowed a large gulp of water. "But I still have to live with the memory of our last conversation. A loud, angry argument that ended with him throwing a crumpled-up piece of paper at my back as I stormed off."

Karla perked up at the words, *crumpled-up piece of paper*, recalling the forged note scrawled on a once-crumpled sheet of paper.

"Tell us what happened," she urged. "From the beginning. It'll be good for you to get it off your chest, and you never know, you might have inadvertently noticed something that will help the police find Fitz's killer."

She lowered herself onto the sofa across from him. Max joined her. Cash maintained his loyal stance by his owner's side.

"I can save the police a lot of trouble," Dylan stated, pulling himself up to his full-seated height. "I know who killed my dad."

Karla and Max leaned forward in their seats.

"Who?" they asked in unison.

"Leon Tyson."

"Leon?" they asked again in stereo.

"Why would Leon kill Fitz?" Max asked.

"Because my dad was blackmailing him."

"Fitz was blackmailing Leon Tyson?" Max asked, her tone of voice hinting at a touch of confusion, skepticism, or both.

Dylan nodded.

"Why?" Karla asked.

"I don't know the details," Dylan explained, "but it had something to do with an affair."

"Whose affair?" Max asked.

"Leon's, I think. But I don't know for sure," Dylan admitted. "I overheard a conversation between them the other day. Dad and I were working at different work sites. I needed to borrow his reciprocating saw. He didn't answer my text, so I drove to his worksite to pick it up. When I arrived, Dad and Leon were arguing. They didn't know I was there. I kept my distance, so they wouldn't catch me eavesdropping. I only heard part of the conversation, but I heard enough to get the gist of it."

"What did you hear?" Max's notebook was open, and she hovered her pen nib over the blank page.

"Leon said it was getting dangerous. He said if they got caught, he would lose everything, his job, and his family. Dad said Leon was overreacting and tried to brush him off. Then he said, 'If you back out, Leon, I'll tell everyone what you've done, and you'll lose everything anyway.'"

It sounded to Karla like Leon would have lost either way. If he didn't continue with their mysterious scheme, Fitz would expose his secret. And if he continued to cooperate, Fitz would have been able to use the information to increase his demands of Leon whenever he wanted.

"What about the affair?" Max asked. "You said this blackmail scheme involved an affair."

"Later that day," Dylan continued, "I confronted my dad with what I had overheard. First, he denied it. He tried to convince me that I'd only heard a small part of the conversation, and I heard it out of context. But I wouldn't let it go. I told him if he didn't tell me the truth, I'd quit my job, leave Bellbrook, and never speak to him again. Finally, he admitted he had discovered Leon was having an affair. In exchange for keeping quiet about it, Leon agreed to overlook the occasional building code violation on my dad's worksites."

"So, your dad would cut corners to save money?" Max deduced.

Dylan nodded. "He said he only cut corners occasionally and swore on *my* life that he would never compromise anything that was a safety risk or could lead to someone getting injured."

Karla silently wondered how many corners Fitz would have cut had he lived to renovate the cottages. She also recalled the apprehension she had perceived from Harry when she told him Fitz would be handling the renovations. She wondered if Harry knew about Fitz's substandard work.

"That's rough, Dylan. I'm sorry you were dealing with that," Max said in her friendly, non-cop voice.

Karla had forgotten that Max and Dylan were

friends. He was only a couple of years older than her, and they'd grown up in the same small town, attending the same schools.

"It sucked," Dylan agreed. "But it was a wake-up call. My father wasn't the person I thought. I mean, if he lied to me about this, what else did he lie about?"

Karla and Max shook their heads, unsure if Dylan's question was rhetorical or if he expected a response.

"I knew I could never trust him again, and if any of his corner-cutting resulted in someone getting hurt, I wouldn't be able to live with myself."

"Is that why you resigned?" Karla asked.

"Mostly." Dylan nodded. "But to be honest, I never wanted to be a contractor anyway." He slowly scratched the top of his curly head and let his hand linger there. "So, I decided this was the push I needed to pursue my dream of becoming a paramedic."

"Really?" Karla asked. "You never mentioned becoming a paramedic when you were little. You always said you wanted to be a builder, just like your dad."

"I did," Dylan admits. "But I really liked science and biology in school. And I want a job where I can help people. I never talked about it before because I didn't want to disappoint my dad." He slowly scratched his head again. "He always wanted me to take over the business."

"How did Fitz react when you resigned?" Max asked.

"Not well," Dylan replied, shaking his head. "I wanted him to know I was serious, to prove I wasn't just blowing smoke because I was mad at him. So, I wrote a formal letter of resignation. I gave it to him yesterday at Bellflower, and after he read it, his face turned red. He called me some ugly names."

Dylan's eyes glistened with moisture as he recalled their final, nasty conversation. "He said I would be back when I realized how tough the real world was. I told him I would never work for him again. He crumpled up my resignation letter. I realized our conversation would get worse if I stayed, so I told him we could talk about it later when he was calmer. He threw the paper ball at me as I walked out."

"Was that the last time you spoke to Fitz?" Max asked.

Dylan nodded.

"Any texts or emails between you since that argument?"

He shook his head.

"Does Leon know you are aware of the arrangement he had with Fitz?"

"I haven't spoken to Leon since before I overheard them arguing." Dylan shrugged. "But I guess my dad could have told him before he died."

"Where did you go when you left Bellflower yesterday?" Max asked.

"Here," Dylan replied. "I picked up Cash and took him to the new dog park. Then, I was online most of the day, researching paramedic programs and filling out applications."

Dylan's cellphone rang, interrupting their conversation. It was his mother. She called to check on her son, advise him of her flight information, and assure him that she would arrive in Bellbrook early the following morning.

Karla was relieved that Dylan wouldn't be alone. She was painfully aware how overwhelming it was to plan a funeral and keep up with the onslaught of administrative demands that need to be dealt with when someone dies. She was confident that Dylan's mother would share the burden with her son.

Dylan placed the call on hold and advised them that he would probably be on the phone for a while.

Karla and Max took this as their cue to leave. Karla pressed her business card into Dylan's hand and mouthed, *Call me anytime*, after she hugged him good-bye. They gave Cash a goodbye rub, then left.

Karla's head swirled with questions. Was Dylan telling the truth about his argument with Fitz? Did it end like Dylan claimed, or did it end with him nailing Fitz to the wall, literally? Did Leon kill Fitz to end the extortion? If Dylan was correct about the blackmail scheme, Fitz's death was the ideal solution for Leon. A dead Fitz could neither make further demands of him nor expose Leon's secret. Also, Leon was near Bell-flower before she and Harry found Fitz's body. Lynn and Rosalie saw him too. Karla decided it was time to visit the town hall and ask Leon some questions about her building permits.

"I forgot you used to babysit Dylan," Max said as they walked together to their cars.

"I forgot you went to school together," Karla rebutted.

"I had a crush on him when I was ten." Max

chuckled and shook her head. "If you tell anyone, I'll never forgive you!"

"You had a crush on Dylan?" Karla stopped in her tracks and looked Max in the eye. "But he's a boy."

"Sometimes I like boys." Max shrugged.

"Boys can be difficult," Karla warned. "I speak from experience."

"So can girls."

They laughed.

"What do you think about Dylan's story?" Karla asked.

"I'll check his online history and see if he told the truth about being online most of the day, but it's a shaky alibi," Max admits. "Hopefully someone saw him at the dog park. A witness would help verify his timeline, and they might have noticed if Dylan was acting strange or anything."

"I hope you find someone."

"Dylan might not have stood out, but Cash would have. It's hard to forget a dog the size of a small horse."

"Do you think Dylan killed Fitz?" Karla asked, hesitant that she might not like Max's answer.

"I hope not," Max replied. "What do you think?"

"He lied," Karla disclosed. "At least I think he lied." She paused. "I'm certain he lied. His Tell is the same as it was when he was ten." Karla slowly scratched the top of her head and let her hand linger for a moment.

"Is that Dylan's tell?" Max asked, mimicking the gesture.

Karla nodded. "He lied about never wanting to be contractor."

"What about his alibi, the argument with Fitz, and the blackmail?" Max asked.

"He seemed truthful," Karla confirmed. "It's possible he has another Tell that I didn't pick up, but I doubt it. I was on high alert the entire time."

"Why would he lie about never wanting to be a contractor?" Max wondered. "It's not like his childhood dreams are relevant to his father's murder investigation."

"When Dylan was a kid, he worshipped his father and wanted to be just like him," Karla recalled. "He would talk about how smart Fitz was and how Fitz was the best builder in the world. He would play with his construction toys and pretend he was working on a job site with his dad."

"It must suck to find out your dad was a blackmailer who charged people full price, then cut corners and kept their money."

"Exactly," Karla agreed. "I understand Dylan's desire to separate himself from Fitz. There are times I'd rather have been hatched from an egg than be Lynn's daughter. Maybe he lied to convince himself, not us, that he didn't idolize his father."

Could Dylan have killed his father in a fit of passionate rage? Was the realization that the man he idolized was a flawed, complicated human too much for Dylan to process? Did the shock push him over the edge of reason?

Karla still thought of Dylan as the fun, sweet, hyper boy she'd babysat. The boy who initiated an impromptu game of hide and seek when it was time to detangle his curly hair. The boy who cried because of the long-distance telephone commercial on TV. The little boy who was bad at math and had told her that when he grew up they would be the same age, and they could get married and eat Fun Dip for dinner every night. She couldn't imagine him as an angry adult capable of patricide.

"Listen, La-la." Max only used Karla's nickname when she was about to say something serious or make fun of her. Her current tone of voice indicated she was about to do the former, not the latter.

"What?" Karla asked, her heart racing. She braced herself.

"Now that Fitz's death is officially a murder investigation, everyone who was near Bellflower yesterday before you found him is a suspect."

"Excuse me?" Karla wondered if she'd misheard or misinterpreted what Max said. "Are you saying *I'm* a suspect?" She pointed to herself.

Max nodded.

"Harry?"

Max nodded again.

"Lynn?"

Another nod.

"Rosalie?"

Max gave a slow, barely discernable nod.

"You must be joking!" Karla scoffed. "Rosalie is eighty years old, for goodness' sake. I'm not sure she even knows what a nail gun is." She half-laughed at the absurdity of the suggestion.

Karla already had a vested interest in solving Fitz's

murder—it happened on Bell property—but her sudden, unfamiliar yet fierce instinct to get answers for Dylan and protect him, Harry, Lynn, and Rosalie from the scrutiny of a murder investigation steeled her determination. She knew she wouldn't stop until she found the truth and the people she cared about were cleared of suspicion.

"We still have to eliminate her as a suspect," Max reminded her. "You forgot someone."

"Leon?" Karla asked rhetorically. "It goes without saying that he's a suspect. He had the most to gain from Fitz's death."

"So far," Max cautions. "We're still digging into Fitz's life and tracing his movements in the days before his murder. Who knows what we'll uncover? Leon is a solid suspect, but I have a feeling Fitz had more enemies than we realize."

"You know something," Karla accused with one arched brow.

Max pressed her lips together.

"You can't tell me."

Max gave her a very thin smile and a very subtle nod.

"I'll find out eventually."

"I know," Max agreed. "I assume you're on your way to the town hall next?"

"In light of Fitz's death, I have a few questions about the building permits he got for Mirabel and Bellflower."

"What questions?" Max asked.

"I don't know yet." Karla grinned. "I'll think of them on the drive over there."

Max checked her watch. "I'll give you the same head start I gave you with Dylan."

"Sounds good, Max'n'cheese." Karla grinned and unlocked the car door.

"*Argh!*" Max stomped her heavy boot. "I hate that nickname," she griped on the way to her patrol car.

CHAPTER 7

SLOWER THAN MOLASSES
IN JANUARY

KARLA STEPPED out of line to pick up Leon's business card from the display rack under the community bulletin board.

Leon Tyson
Building Permits, Bylaw Officer, Building Code
Enforcement

She noted the inherent conflict of interest with the person responsible for issuing the building permits and the person who inspected the building sites being the same person. Small towns were more trusting and didn't always have the same boundaries as the rest of the world.

Karla checked her text messages, email, and social media accounts. Twice. It felt like she had been waiting in line forever behind the same three people.

"It's nice to see you out and about," a familiar, gruff voice said from behind her. "You've been in Bellbrook almost a month, and you've hardly made a public appearance. Everyone keeps asking what you're hiding from."

Not what, who, Karla thought.

"I've been busy," she reminded Harry. "What are you doing here?"

"Parking ticket." He held up the yellow slip of paper and rolled his eyes.

Harry's phone rang. He glanced at it and declined the call.

"Is it always this slow?" Karla asked, gesturing to the people ahead of her.

"Molasses likes to take her time and talk everyone's ear off," Harry whispered, staring at the reception desk, and waggling his silver, caterpillar eyebrows.

"The receptionist's name is Molasses?" Karla asked, dubious.

"Only behind her back," he replied. "Her name is Mary, or Marcia, or something, but everyone calls her Molasses because she moves slower than molasses in January."

His phone rang again, and again, he glanced at the screen before declining the call.

"Somebody's popular," Karla teased, poking the hand with which Harry gripped his phone.

"Somebody certainly is," Harry agreed with a smirk. "But it's not me." He winked.

"Then who is it?" Karla asked.

"It's you," Harry said. "You're the popular one." He chuckled. "My phone's been ringing since yesterday on account of you."

"I don't understand," Karla said, furrowing her eyebrows.

"My phone has been blowing up since word got around about Fitz's death," he explained. "Trades people, contractors, and everyone in the construction trade from Bellbrook and beyond want to know if you're looking to replace Fitz." He took in her blank expression. "They all want a crack at renovating the cottages."

"Why?" Karla asked. "It's hardly a huge job."

"No, but Bellcroft is."

"Ahhh," Karla said as comprehension swept across her face. "They think if they do a good job on the cottages, they might get to renovate the manor house," Karla concluded.

"Exactly," Harry confirmed. "Renovating Bellcroft Manor will be huge bragging rights for whoever you choose. A top-to-bottom renovation of the largest historical building around could make a career."

Karla was struck with simultaneous epiphanies. First, it was possible that a rival contractor killed Fitz so the cottage job would become available. If this was true, the pool of murder suspects just grew exponentially. Second, Harry and everyone else believed she would be renovating the manor house. A massive and expensive undertaking that she wasn't sure would be possible.

As they inched closer to the reception desk, Karla was hesitant to continue their conversation with so many ears lingering around them.

"I need to talk to you about the renovations," she

whispered. "Actually, you and Lynn and I should discuss a few things."

They agreed to meet the following day. Karla created a group text with her, Harry, and Lynn. She sent a quick text with the time and location, then added it to her calendar. She knew if she didn't, she'd forget to show up, even though it was her idea. Lists and alarms were the only way she could remember where she was supposed to be and when she was supposed to be there.

They passed the rest of their time in line discussing the weather and their plans for the rest of the day. According to Harry, Lynn's left hip was predicting snow in the next twenty-four hours, which seemed absurd to Karla considering the unseasonably warm fall they'd had so far.

"I hope you don't mind, but I'd like to refinish the writing desk from May's bedroom," Harry said. "I'll also fix the sticky drawer and shine the hardware. While I'm at it, I'll refinish and reupholster the chair too."

"That would be wonderful," Karla said, touching his arm. "Thank you, Harry. I would love to put that desk in Mirabel when I move in."

The line finally moved again, and Karla was next. When the person ahead of her approached Molasses at the reception desk, she purposely didn't step forward, staying out of earshot.

"Listen, Harry," she whispered.

He leaned in to hear her.

"Have the police spoken to you since Fitz's death was ruled a homicide?"

He nodded. "About being a suspect, you mean?"

She nodded. "We're all suspects." She gestured around her as though all the suspects in Fitz's murder were gathered in the town hall lobby.

"I'm going to clear our names," she hissed. "All of us."

"You are so much like your grandmother," he said with a smile. "If anyone can do it, it'll be you."

Molasses, whose real name was Maria, according to the nameplate on her desk, paged Leon. Karla dodged her myriad of questions and avoided small talk by pretending to receive an urgent business call and stepping aside to answer it.

"Ms. Bell?"

Karla spun around from the trophy case full of citizenship awards she was perusing.

"Please call me Karla." She extended her hand.

"Leon Tyson," said the tall, lean man with horn-rimmed glasses, and short, cropped dark hair. "Pleasure to meet you."

"Likewise." Karla smiled.

"Where's your cute little dog?" Leon asked, closing his office door and gesturing for Karla to have a seat across from his desk. "Prada? Dior? Armani?"

"Gucci," she said. "He's at home. My roommate is working from home today, and Gucci is keeping her company."

Leon smiled. "I thought you might be here to properly license Gucci and finally get his dog tag."

"Right," Karla said with a nod. "I'll be sure to take care of that."

She had been so busy and distracted with

Grandma May's death and emptying Mirabel that Karla hadn't thought to make sure Gucci was properly registered and tagged. She thought it weird that Leon was aware of Gucci's unlicensed status. Did he keep tabs on every dog in town, or was he checking up on her? If he was checking up on her, why?

"Good," Leon said, nudging his glasses up the bridge of his nose. "It would be a shame if Animal Control picked up your little dog and took him to the shelter."

Leon's demeanour was friendly, but his words and voice were vaguely threatening. The same way the words, *Enjoy your next twenty-four hours* sounded threatening compared to *Have a nice day*, even if the person saying them acted friendly. Was he threatening Gucci? What kind of coward would threaten a small dog?

Karla corrected her posture, straightened her spine, and sat at attention. She'd met people like Leon before. They liked to remind everyone that they hold a position of power.

"I'm sure you have more important things to do than pick on small dogs and their bereaved owners." Karla challenged him with a smile and embraced her alter-ego, Corporate Karla. "I'm here to discuss the building permits Fitz took out for my renovations."

"I was sorry to hear about Fitz," Leon said, shuffling the papers on his desk and moving them from one pile to another. "It must be awful to have someone die in your home."

"Even worse to be the person who found them."

"Oh?" Leon's hands froze mid-shuffle. He dropped

the stack of papers and looked at Karla with narrowed brown eyes. "*You* found him?"

"Me and someone else," Karla admitted. "It was a shock."

"Where was he? Could you tell how he died?"

"I'm not supposed to talk about it with anyone other than the police."

"Of course," Leon agreed as his hands resumed shuffling the stack of papers he'd dropped a moment ago. "Regarding your permits, I assume Dylan Fitzgibbon will take over the renovation?"

Karla shook her head. "Dylan has decided to pursue a different career. He had officially resigned before Fitz died."

"Really?" Leon asked, gazing at his pen cup as he considered Karla's words. "I had no idea. Neither of them mentioned it, and I saw them regularly. In fact, I saw Fitz a few days before he died."

Is Leon's surprise about Dylan's resignation genuine? Either he didn't know about the resignation letter, or he lied to make it look like he never saw it and was therefore not present when Fitz was murdered.

"You didn't see Fitz yesterday when you were at Bellflower?" Karla asked.

With the papers out of the way, Leon placed his elbows on the desk and laced his long, thin fingers together.

"Yesterday?" he asked, then cleared his throat. "I was at Bellflower yesterday, but not to see Fitz." His right pinky finger twitched.

"Oh?" Karla asked. "Why else would you be there?

I hope you weren't making a house call to remind me about Gucci's dog licence."

"Of course not." Leon's chuckle was awkward. "I knew Fitz was starting work at Mirabel, and I stopped by to ensure the permits were properly posted and displayed as per the bylaw." His pinky finger continued to twitch, seemingly unbeknownst to him. "That's all, it was a routine visit. I didn't go inside, and I didn't see Fitz. Just his truck."

"Were they?" Karla asked.

"Were they what?" Leon was flustered, and small beads of sweat were visible on his brow and upper lip.

"Were the permits properly posted as per the bylaw?"

"Yes." He cleared his throat again. "Yes, they were. As I expected they would be."

"Even if they weren't posted properly, you wouldn't have given Fitz a fine or anything, right?" Karla pressed. "I'm sure you would have overlooked such a minor compliance issue." She paused for dramatic effect. "Especially for Fitz."

"I don't like what you're suggesting, Ms. Bell."

Karla presumed from his offended tone and formal address that they were no longer on a first name basis.

"Isn't it true, Mr. Tyson, that you would sometimes overlook minor code violations for Fitz?"

"Never!" Leon insisted, his pinky twitching so hard that it was now tapping the desktop. "Code enforcement is my job, and I take my job seriously. I enforce the rules regardless of who breaks them."

"That's not what I heard," Karla challenged. "But I

guess I heard wrong." She shrugged and stood up to leave.

Where are you, Max? You were supposed to be here now.

"Someone said I was overlooking code violations for Fitz? Who? Who said that?"

"The same person who told me he was blackmailing you."

"Fitz was not blackmailing me."

The steadiness of Leon's voice and sudden stillness of his pinky finger caused Karla to sit back down.

"Something was going on between you and Fitz," she said matter-of-factly. "And you were lurking around Bellflower around the time he was killed."

"I wasn't lurking," Leon reminded her through clenched teeth. "I was doing my job. The timing was just unfortunate."

Unfortunate for Fitz.

"If anyone was lurking around Bellflower yesterday, it was Rosalie Howard," Leon suggested. "Maybe you should throw your accusations at her!"

"Rosalie?" Karla scoffed. "Why would Rosalie kill Fitz?"

"That's for the police to figure out, Ms. Bell, not a bored, bossy, big-city businesswoman with too much time on her hands."

Karla bit her tongue and forced herself to remain stoic at his use of the outdated, misogynistic term, *businesswoman*. She detested any label that defined her by biology or minimized her accomplishments because of her gender. She was a CEO, goshdarnit! Regardless of what hormones coursed through her body or what letter filled the gender designation on her birth certificate.

"As I told the police," Leon continued, "I found Rosalie skulking around Bellflower. She was distracted and mopey. I offered to drive her home, but she refused. She was still skulking around when I left."

"Rosalie doesn't skulk," Karla corrected. "She was mopey because she had just attended Mr. Hughes's funeral. Her second funeral in three weeks. Her daily walk past my grandmother's house was a sad reminder that her best friend had recently died." She stood up and hoisted her Birken bag over her arm. "What kind of coward deflects negative attention from himself by implicating a defenceless elderly woman?"

Karla regretted referring to Rosalie as defenceless. She might not be physically imposing, but Rosalie Howard was far from defenseless. Karla had seen her put bigger, scarier bullies than Leon in their place.

Leon rose from behind his desk and moved to the door.

"This has been an enlightening conversation," he said, opening his office door.

"Yes, it certainly has."

At least they could agree on something.

"I have faith that Bellbrook's capable police department will get to the bottom of Mr. Fitzgibbon's untimely demise and bring those responsible to justice."

He made a sweeping gesture toward the open door, and Karla strode through into the noticeably cooler hallway.

"One more thing, Ms. Bell."

Karla turned to him.

"Be sure to get Gucci's dog licence. It would be a shame if Bellbrook's animal-control officer picked him up. Wouldn't it?"

Bully!

Karla got in line again in the town hall lobby and sent a quick text to Rob, asking her not to walk Gucci until she got home with his new tag.

CHAPTER 8

AN ANGRY PORCUPINE

IN THE MUNICIPAL parking lot across from the town hall, Karla discovered the reason Max didn't meet her at Leon's office. She was talking with Dylan and two unfamiliar women. Max's stance between Dylan and the mystery women gave Karla the impression she was refereeing an argument between them.

"Mrs. Hughes," Karla said, approaching them and recognizing one of the petite brunettes with matching large dark sunglasses. "I'm not sure if you remember me"—she extended her hand—"I'm Kar—"

"Of course, I remember you!" Mrs. Hughes gave Karla a limp handshake. "I'm friends with your mother." She smiled weakly. "Lynn's very proud of you. She talks about you all the time."

She does? Karla wondered what Lynn could possibly have to say about her. They rarely spoke, and Karla never bothered to share the details of her day-to-day life with Lynn, never mind provide her with enough information to talk about her to her friends *all the time*. Unless, Karla suspected, Grandma May had kept Lynn apprised of the details of Karla's life, the same way she used to tell Karla the minutiae of Lynn's life.

Mrs. Hughes gestured to the woman next to her. "This is my sister, Trina." Both women's long hair blew behind them in the breeze like brunette superhero capes.

"I was sorry to hear about Mr. Hughes," Karla said.

It sounded like such hollow platitude. But what else could Karla say that would ease Mrs. Hughes's pain? Words were like nets that were slightly too small. We hope they'll cover what we mean, but they can't possibly hold that much grief or sadness.

"Thank you." Mrs. Hughes patted the back of Karla's hand. "It was a shock. So sudden."

From what Karla had heard through the grapevine—the grapevine being Harry, Rosalie, Rob, and Lynn—Mr. Hughes had suffered a tragic household accident. He slipped in the shower and gripped the grab bar to steady himself, but the grab bar detached from the wall. Mr. Hughes went down, smacking the back of his head on the tile floor. The metal grab bar landed on his face. He was home alone when it happened, and when Anna found him, he was dead. Blunt force trauma, Rob had called it.

"We should get going," Trina said, checking her watch.

"I have an appointment at the bank," Mrs. Hughes explained. "It was lovely to run into you, Karla." Mrs. Hughes gave her a quick hug. "Tell Lynn I said hi."

She looked at Max and smiled. "See you around, Max."

And without a word of acknowledgement to Dylan, the women left.

"She seemed nice," Karla heard Trina comment as they walked away. "She doesn't have the personality of a cactus like people say."

"I'm more like an angry porcupine," Karla called, then smiled.

Mrs. Hughes and Trina turned and gave her an awkward wave.

"Angry porcupine?" Maxed laughed. "You don't do much to change the impression people have of you."

"I don't care what people think," Karla said. "The people who matter know what I'm like, and the people who don't know, don't matter." She shrugged.

"Why did Mrs. Hughes ignore Dylan?"

Dylan shot them a shifty glance.

"Mrs. Hughes asked me about my dad's death," Dylan explained with a shrug. "Like everyone else in town, she wanted to know what happened, and who I think did it."

"Did you tell her your theory about Leon?" Karla asked.

"No," Dylan replied. "I told her I don't know any more than her. The police haven't told me anything."

"Your answer upset her?" Karla asked.

"Not that I could tell. I wanted to change the subject, so I told her I was sorry about Mr. Hughes. I said the same thing you said to her, almost word for word." He gestured at Karla. "But she got upset when

I said it. Luckily, Max showed up. She and Trina calmed her down. Then you showed up."

"Mr. Hughes only died a week ago," Max assured him. "Mrs. Hughes is still in shock. She's cycling through the stages of grief. She's probably exhausted and trying to process tons of emotions. Try not to take it personally. I'm sure you didn't say anything that offended her."

Max was right. The whole town was on edge. Karla wasn't sure if Bellbrook had ever had three deaths so close together. First, Grandma May, then Mr. Hughes, then Fitz. And the fact that one of those deaths was a murder made the situation more traumatic. It was a lot of collective grief for a town that was usually so sheltered from the harsh realities of the outside world.

Dylan pressed the button on his keychain and unlocked his white pickup truck. "I need to get this bag of dog food home before Cash's dinnertime. He gets rambunctious if I feed him late."

"How did it go with Leon?" Max asked as they watched Dylan's pickup truck drive off.

Karla held up her right hand, making her right pinky finger twitch.

"Is that Leon's tell?" Max asked.

Karla nodded again, and Max jotted a quick note in her notebook.

"What did he lie about?"

"He admitted to visiting Bellflower yesterday before we found Fitz's body, but said he wasn't there to see Fitz. I'm not sure if he lied about the reason for his visit, seeing Fitz, or both," Karla explained. "Then, he lied again when he told me that he enforces the rules equally, regardless of who breaks them."

"Maybe Dylan is right. Maybe Leon was ignoring code violations for Fitz."

"Maybe," Karla agreed. "Also, I think Leon lied to Rosalie yesterday."

"About what?"

"I'm not sure," Karla admitted. "When they were talking behind Bellflower, Leon turned so his back was toward me. His hands were behind his back, and his pinky finger was twitching like crazy."

"Rosalie has a mind like a steel trap," Max said. "I bet she'd remember every word Leon said during their conversation."

Karla nodded. "She invited me over for lunch tomorrow."

CHAPTER 9

A FAMILY MYSTERY

OCTOBER 21ST

Rosalie's house was comfortably cluttered and smelled like warmth and unconditional love. The same way Mirabel smelled when Grandma May was alive. Karla thought Rosalie's house hit the perfect spot on the comfort continuum, not cluttered enough to suggest a hoarder lived there, but cozy enough to give guests permission to relax.

"Off, Hemy!" Rosalie shooed the small tabby cat, Purrnest Hemingway, off the kitchen counter. "I hear the police are releasing Bellflower today," she said, spraying and wiping the spot the cat grudgingly vacated.

"Yes, they are," replied Lynn, sneaking a piece of bacon to Gucci under the table. He scampered off to the sunroom to eat the prized treat in peace. "I drove by on my way here. An officer was removing the police tape from the porch and front door. Harry said a tow truck took away Fitz's pickup truck yesterday."

Rosalie hadn't warned Karla that Lynn was also coming for lunch.

"Dad said we have to meet later so I can sign some forms acknowledging the items they removed from Bellflower as evidence," Karla commented as she turned the stiff, plasticky page of a photo album from before she was born.

Rosalie had drawers of photo albums. Karla loved to leaf through them when she visited and ask Rosalie about the familiar and unfamiliar faces. Rosalie always remembered who everyone was, how they knew each other, a funny story about them, and what was happening when the photo was taken.

"Did they take much?" Rosalie asked.

"I think they mostly took Fitz's tools." Karla shrugged one shoulder and scanned the grainy, age-faded photos. "I guess I'll find out later." She turned the page again. "Are you sure I can't help you, Rosalie?"

"Do you think I'm too old to make lunch?" Rosalie asked with mock annoyance. "Cooking for the people I love is one of the few pleasures I have left. Let me enjoy it." She smiled and stroked Karla's cheek.

Rosalie was soft on the outside, and when she smiled, her entire face smiled, not just her mouth. She had pronounced dimples and kept her fine, salt and pepper hair in the same short bob she'd had for at least thirty years. Rosalie came from an era when people dressed every day regardless of their plans. Today, she wore practical blue slacks, a white t-shirt, and a loose, blue floral button-down blouse, untucked and unbuttoned. Her matching blue socks and blue flower earrings tied her outfit together.

Hemy wound himself around Karla's ankles.

She discreetly scratched her denim thigh, offering the kitty a place to settle. He accepted the invitation, leapt onto her lap, and tucked his paws underneath him, creating a fluffy ball of purring warmth.

"Who's this lady?" Karla asked, pointing to an unfamiliar woman with a serious expression on her face, standing behind Gigi's easy chair.

Rosalie squinted at the square photo. "That's Viola Spencer," she said. "She was Gigi's caregiver."

Karla had no recollection of Viola Spencer, and only fragmented memories of Gigi.

"I haven't heard that name in years. I forgot all about her." Lynn tugged the album toward her and craned her neck to see Viola's photo. "Did we ever find out what happened to her?"

"Something happened to her?" Karla asked. "What?"

"Put the photo albums aside for now. Your mum and I will tell you about it while we eat."

Rosalie served each of them a bowl of her famous broccoli cheddar soup, toasted focaccia garlic bread, and a fall salad of mixed greens, pear and apple slices, chopped bacon, and feta cheese, topped with an apple cider vinaigrette dressing. It smelled like comfort and tasted like a hug.

Karla had missed homemade food between her visits to Bellbrook. As much as she enjoyed gourmet food prepared by celebrity chefs at fancy, impossible-to-get-a-table restaurants, nothing warmed her belly and her soul like Rosalie's homemade soup or strawberry-rhubarb pie.

"Grandma May hired Viola to help take care of Gigi," Lynn explained.

Gigi was Karla's paternal great-grandmother and the last occupant of Bellflower cottage. She died before Karla was old enough to form any solid memories of her.

"Why did Gigi need someone to take care of her?" Karla asked.

"She didn't need care in a physical sense," Lynn replied.

"Viola's job was to keep an eye on Gigi and keep her safe," Rosalie explained. "Gigi developed dementia. At first May was able to manage the situation with a little help from me and a few other people, but as Gigi's symptoms worsened, taking care of her became a challenge."

"You see, love, one of Gigi's dementia symptoms was paranoia," Lynn continued. "She started accusing people of stealing from her and bugging Bellflower to record her conversations. She made it impossible for Grandma May and Rosalie to look after her. She was so paranoid that she began hiding her belongings so no one would steal them."

"Then when she couldn't find something she'd hidden, she'd accuse May and me of stealing it," Rosalie added.

"It got so bad that she withdrew large amounts of money from the bank, forgot she'd made the withdrawals, and told the bank manager that Grandma May stole her money," Lynn recalled.

"That's awful," Karla said.

"And most of the time, we couldn't find the money she withdrew from the bank," Rosalie said. "May figured Gigi must have found a great hiding spot somewhere but forgot where it was in between stashing stuff there."

"The final straw was the day Gigi visited her safe deposit box at the bank," Lynn said. "She brought the safe deposit box home with her."

"I didn't know clients were allowed to do that," Karla said.

"They aren't," Rosalie confirmed. "Safe deposit boxes are supposed to stay at the bank. Inside the vault. But Gigi managed to leave the bank with this huge, heavy metal box and carry it all the way home from Main Street without anyone noticing."

"Oh my," Karla said, half-laughing. "I can't believe I've never heard this story before."

"The bank manager wasn't amused," Lynn said. "I'll never forget the scowl on his face when he and the head teller showed up at Bellflower to retrieve the box."

"I forgot about that!" Rosalie laughed and slapped the top of the small, round, wood table. "May spent hours searching for the safe deposit box. She looked everywhere. She kept asking Gigi where it was, but Gigi didn't know what she was talking about. She accused May of losing the safe deposit box and lectured her for bringing it home in the first place."

Lynn and Rosalie laughed until they cried and dabbed their eyes at the memory.

"Did anyone find the safe deposit box?" Karla asked.

"Under her bed, hidden between two folded blankets," Lynn replied, nodding. "But we never found the contents."

"We turned that little cottage upside down searching," Rosalie recalled. "Then we retraced the route between the bank and Bellflower but found no trace of the contents." She arched her eyebrows and shook her head. "She could have hidden them anywhere."

"Really?" Karla asked, enthralled by the mystery of the missing safe deposit box contents. "What was in the safe deposit box?"

"Cash, bearer bonds, savings bonds, stock certificates, heirloom jewelry." Lynn listed off the contents on her fingers. "Grandma May found a pair of pearl earrings a few months later, though."

"I remember that!" Rosalie blurted. "I was there when she found them." She looked at Karla. "May had popped next door to Bellflower to borrow some flour from Gigi. She came back with the flour cannister, and when she reached in with the scoop, she pulled out half a cup of flour and a pearl earring." She chuckled and shook her head at the memory. "We put the rest of the flour through a sieve and found the other earring."

"It sounds like Gigi was the hide and seek champion of Bellbrook." Karla tore off a piece of garlic bread. "What happened to her caregiver, Viola?" She dipped the hunk of bread in her soup, then popped it in her mouth.

"May had to let her go after Gigi's stroke," Rosalie explained. "After the stroke, Gigi couldn't return to

Bellflower. It caused significant damage, and Gigi needed round the clock medical care. She was supposed to go to a care home in Loganville."

"It didn't make sense to employ Viola if Gigi wasn't coming home," Lynn added. "Grandma May gave her a month's wages and a letter of reference with a generous bonus. Also, Bellflower was in a state of disrepair, even back then. The plumbing and electrical were outdated and didn't meet current codes. There was some wood rot in the beams holding the place up. Grandma May worried it wasn't fit to live in."

"Viola left and May locked and boarded up Bellflower until she had time to search it again for the items Gigi had hidden and deal with the deferred maintenance. But there was never time." Rosalie nodded at Karla. "You were little, and she was still managing the manor house as an event venue. She was involved in every community event in town. There was always something more important than Bellflower."

"Did Viola leave town?" Karla asked, slipping a piece of feta to Hemy, still purring in her lap.

"No, she got a room at the Nestled Inn," Rosalie said.

"She didn't want to leave Bellbrook because she was dating that guy"—Lynn snapped her fingers, and her eyes darted around as she searched her mental archives—"what was his name?"

"The butcher's son," Rosalie replied. "The chubby butcher's apprentice in Beaver Creek."

"That's right!" Lynn agreed, pointing at Rosalie.

"She hung around for a while, hoping to persuade him to make it official and put a ring on her finger."

"But he didn't," Rosalie continued. "In fact, he broke up with her the day before Gigi's funeral. Viola was devastated."

Sadly, Gigi never made it from the hospital to the care home in Loganville. Instead, she suffered a second, bigger stroke, and died in her sleep. Karla still remembered Grandma May's words, *I'm sure she did it on purpose. She would have rather died than lived anywhere other than Bellbrook.*

"Poor Viola was so upset that she ran out of the church, sobbing, in the middle of the funeral service," Lynn remembered. "Everyone thought she was distraught over Gigi's death, but I think most of her tears were because she was heartbroken about the butcher's boy dumping her."

"No one ever saw her again," Rosalie concluded. "She took her belongings from the Nestled Inn while everyone was at the funeral and left town without saying goodbye."

Lynn's phone rang, and Karla watched Ray's name and photo flash on the screen.

"I'll take this outside," Lynn said as she picked up her garlic bread and excused herself from the table.

Karla rolled her eyes as the screen door slammed shut behind Lynn.

"I'm surprised she's still here," Karla said, stirring the last bit of soup in her bowl. "This must be a record. I don't think Lynn has spent this long in Bellbrook since she was eighteen."

"I could say the same about you," Rosalie said in a tone that sounded like a warning.

"It's not the same," Karla mumbled. "I didn't abandon my baby. I didn't run away from anything. I was running toward something."

"Lynn left you in the best possible hands," Rosalie reminded her. "You had a whole community of people who loved you. She did what she believed was best for you at the time."

"She did what she believed was best for *her* at the time." She shoved a pear slice in her mouth.

"What would you have done if you were an eighteen-year-old single girl with a new baby?"

Karla didn't like thinking about Lynn as anything other than a villain in her life story, so she changed the subject.

"Do you remember running into Leon Tyson behind Bellflower the day Fitz died?"

"Of course, I remember. My knees might be stiffer than they used to be, but my memory is still perfect," Rosalie replied. "He kept trying to give me a ride home. He acted like I couldn't walk by myself. *Mind how you go, Ms. Howard. That unpaved path is uneven. It would be a shame if you fell.*" She lowered her voice several octaves and mimicked Leon's stern expression. "I told him." She nodded. "I said, my best friend May and I created that unpaved, uneven desire path. Decades of rushing back and forth to each other's houses. That path has seen laughter and tears and heard more local gossip than Molasses down at the town hall. I will never stop walking that path."

Karla had patchy memories of toddling on the

narrow footpath, stooping every few steps to pick dandelions in her white patent Mary Janes, frilly white ankle socks, and white Easter dress dotted with small pink and yellow daisies. And racing with Harry. Sometimes he would pick her up from school, and they would take the path as a shortcut home. He would challenge her to a race. She always won. Her prize was a piggyback ride the rest of the way. When Karla was a teenager, *a certain boy* would walk her home from school. They would amble along the path as slowly as they could, making the walk last as long as possible. They held hands, and sometimes, *he* would kiss her under the canopy of maple leaves.

"Mind how you go, Ms. Howard. That unpaved path is uneven. It would be a shame if you fell," Rosalie repeated, then made a slight huff. "He said it so many times. I teased him that it sounded like a threat."

Karla dropped her spoon in the bowl. "A threat?"

"I was teasing." Rosalie laughed. "It wasn't a threat. It was just Leon being annoying."

A shiver ran up Karla's spine. What if it was a threat? What if Leon was worried that Rosalie had seen something she shouldn't, or that she would tell the police he was hanging around Bellflower? What if Rosalie had accepted his offer of a drive home, and no one ever saw her again?

"What were you and Leon talking about when he first approached you?" Karla asked. "I remember I was about to walk over and say hi to you, but Leon beat me to it. So, I went inside Mirabel instead."

"That's right," Rosalie confirmed. "You had a look

on your face like you were relieved he didn't see you. Then you and Gucci disappeared."

"What did you talk about before I disappeared?"

"Why?"

"I think Leon lied to you."

"About what?"

"I don't know. That's why I'm asking what you talked about."

The screen door slammed shut and startled Hemy awake. His head popped up, and his ears perked to attention.

"What'd I miss?" Lynn asked, dropping her phone in her purse hanging on the back of her chair.

"I was just about to recount a conversation I had with Leon the day Fitz died," Rosalie replied.

"Oooh, I've got good timing." Lynn stabbed an apple slice with her fork.

"We said hello," Rosalie began. "I asked about his wife and kids. He asked about Hemy. We talked about the weather. I blamed global warming, and he told me about an investment company that only invests in companies that will benefit from global warming. Heating and cooling companies, electric cars, stuff like that." She flicked her wrist. "Then we talked about Mr. Hughes's funeral. We agreed the service was lovely, and the eulogies were funny yet respectful. Then I commented on not seeing him at the buffet after the service."

"Leon wasn't at the buffet after the service?" Karla asked, then spun toward Lynn, freaking out Hemy and causing him to leap off her lap. "Did you see Leon at the buffet?"

"I don't remember seeing him specifically, but I left early," Lynn reminded her. "But when I saw him at Bellflower, he was wearing a black suit and black tie. I assumed he was at the funeral and the buffet at Anna's house afterward. You know what Leon is like. He attends everything. Always afraid he'll miss something."

"FOMO," Rosalie said with a nod. "That's what the kids call it."

"FOMO?" Lynn repeated.

"Fear Of Missing Out," Rosalie explained. "Leon Tyson has FOMO."

"You're right," Lynn agreed. "He's a nosy fussbudget."

Amused and shocked by Rosalie's correct use of slang, Karla refocussed the conversation.

"Did Leon say why he wasn't at the buffet?"

"On the contrary. He insisted he *was* at the buffet, and we must've missed each other."

"That's the lie," Karla said with a certainty that radiated from her gut.

Karla was willing to bet her life that was the lie. Leon wasn't at the buffet after the funeral service but wanted people to believe he was. She made a mental note to ask Max if the buffet was Leon's alibi.

"I know it is," Rosalie agreed.

"How?" Karla asked, wondering if Rosalie had picked up on Leon's twitchy pinky finger.

"Because he didn't know that Anna Hughes excused herself almost as soon as she got there to go upstairs and lie down."

"Speaking of Anna Hughes," Karla said, losing focus. "I saw her today at the town parking lot."

Karla's phone chimed, interrupting her story.

Harry: Are you busy?

Karla: No. Are you OK?

Harry: I'm fine. I found something. I think you should see it.

Karla: Where are you?

Harry: My place.

Karla: Be there in ten.

CHAPTER 10

A PROPHECY COMES TRUE

RUNNING along the desire path toward Mirabel, Karla felt bad for rushing out of Rosalie's house without helping to clean up the lunch mess and leaving Gucci for her to dog sit. But Rosalie had insisted. *Go,* she had said. *It must be important because Harry hates texting.*

"Did Harry say what he wants to show you?"

"No," Karla called over her shoulder to Lynn who was a few paces behind.

"Wait," Lynn wheezed.

"Are you all right?" Karla nodded her chin at Lynn's hand, which was gripping her hip.

"It's nothing," Lynn insisted. "The first snowfall of the season, that's all." She knocked on her hip. "Just a twinge. The snow won't accumulate."

Karla glanced up at the heavy, grey sky, recalling Harry mentioning something about Lynn's snow prediction yesterday at the town hall. Snow? This was the first seasonally cool, overcast fall day they'd had, but surely it wasn't cold enough to snow.

"Good to know," Karla said, choosing not to challenge Lynn's left hip.

"Did Harry say the mystery item was urgent?"

"No."

"Then why am I running in my Kate Spade leopard-print flats?"

In addition to her physical resemblance, Karla had also inherited her mother's love of designer clothes, except where Lynn's taste leaned toward trendy and hip fashion, Karla preferred a classic, timeless aesthetic.

"I could tell by the tone that it's urgent."

"You could tell by the tone?" Lynn heaved, still catching her breath. "Of a text message?"

"Fine, we'll walk," Karla said. "But we'll walk fast."

"Deal."

Speed walking through the shortcut Rosalie and Grandma May had created through years of daily visits was still faster than driving all the way around from one driveway to the other. A straight line was always the shortest distance between two points. One of the few bits of grade seven math that had stuck with Karla.

They followed the path until it ended next to Mirabel. Then, they strode behind the cottages and cut through the trees to the Gamekeeper's cabin that had been Harry's home for as long as Karla could remember.

On the forest floor, outside Harry's front door, a shabby yet majestic Irish wolfhound lifted his shaggy, grey head to see what the fuss was about.

"Clancy!" Harry said the dog's name like he was warning the motionless canine to back off.

The prostate, uninterested animal yawned and rolled onto his side, refusing to interrupt his nap to greet them.

Harry opened the front door and motioned for them to enter the log cabin ahead of him.

Harry's small dining table and chairs were pushed up against the wall. In the middle of the room, Grandma May's Victorian writing desk sat on a paint-splattered drop sheet that was probably older than Karla. Flakes of dust and chips of mahogany-coloured stain surrounded the partially sanded desk.

"I used to draw pictures at this desk when I was a little girl," Lynn said. "It sat in the corner of Gigi's living room with a small stained-glass lamp in the corner."

"I remember it from Grandma May's bedroom," Karla added. "She used it as a makeup vanity."

"Grandma May loved this little desk," Lynn confirmed. "It was the only piece of furniture she took from Mirabel after Gigi died."

"I found it in here, just like this," Harry interrupted as he fussed with the desk drawer. "See? I put it back just how I found it."

He handed the shallow, wide drawer to Karla.

Unsure what he was showing her, Karla noticed that Harry had removed the handle. The shiny, newly polished handle sat on the fireplace mantle across the room. She wondered if he was looking for praise or feedback or something.

Then she saw it.

The bottom of the drawer was bowed. She had a flashback to sneaking into Grandma May's bedroom to play with her makeup and jiggling the drawer just the right way so it would open without alerting Grandma May in the next room.

This stupid drawer always jams, young Karla had complained when, one day, Grandma May caught her wrestling with the forbidden thing.

Because you aren't meant to open it, Grandma May half-teased with a wink as she jiggled the drawer in that magical way that always unjammed it. *Put everything back exactly as you found it, please.*

Karla memorized the magic jiggle, and from that day on, she snuck in and out of Grandma May's makeup drawer whenever she wanted. Grandma May had been none the wiser. Or so she thought. Karla suddenly realized, if that were the case, Grandma May wouldn't have shown her the magic jiggle.

"This drawer was always wonky," Karla assured Harry. "Don't worry if you can't fix it." She shrugged. "I kind of prefer it like this."

Harry pointed at the bowed drawer and arched his wiry eyebrows.

"I think he wants you to look at why it's bowed," Lynn surmised.

Karla wedged a thumbnail under the thin piece of warped particle board and lifted it.

"A false bottom," she said, wrenching the thin piece of wood out of the drawer. "What's this?"

Sealed envelopes were taped to the underside of the false bottom. The tape was yellow with age and had lost its stickiness over time. The envelopes peeled off easily, held in place more by habit than actual adhesive.

Karla set the hollowed-out drawer on the drop cloth at her feet. The envelope she chose had yellowed corners and smelled like sawdust as she ran her finger under the dried seal. "Oh my," she said, holding up a small stack of old, musty hundred-dollar bills wrapped in a savings bond.

Lynn stepped forward and chose another envelope. It was packed with bearer bonds folded into fourths.

Every envelope taped to the underside of the false drawer bottom had either money, bonds, or both.

"I bet these were inside the safe deposit box Gigi brought home from the bank," Lynn presumed. "There's a list of the contents. Grandma May kept it in her nightstand. During a rare lucid moment, Gigi told her what was inside the box, and Grandma May wrote it down."

"The nightstand is in the manor house," Harry said. "I stored all the furniture from Mirabel in the ballroom."

"What are we waiting for?" Lynn asked, shoving a pile of folded bonds back inside an envelope.

CLANCY LED THE WAY, lumbering ahead of them and occasionally disappearing to follow his nose into the nearby trees or sniff things and pee on them.

The walk from Harry's cottage to the manor house was chillier than the walk from Rosalie's house. The temperature was dropping, and the sky was darker. The air felt heavier, and the breeze was brisker.

Karla wrapped her thick, grey, open-collar cardigan tightly around her and was thankful she had worn her Uggs.

They wondered aloud where else Gigi Bonnie had creatively hidden the rest of the missing loot, and whether they would find it after all these years.

"It's Anna Hughes," Lynn said when her phone rang. "I'll have to take it. She might need something. Keep going." She swept them away with her hand. "I'll catch up."

She stopped to accept the call, then hung back a few steps while she talked with her friend.

"Harry," Karla said, hooking her arm through his, "do you remember when I told you that I'd hired Fitz to renovate the cottages? You seemed kind of hesitant about my choice. Did you have reservations about Fitz doing the work?"

"I hate to speak ill of the dead, but I'm not going to lie, Karla. I'd heard rumours that his work was getting sloppy, and he was padding invoices and cutting corners. There was always something shifty about Fitz. I was worried about the quality of work he'd do at Bellflower and Mirabel."

"Why didn't you say anything?"

"It wasn't my place," Harry confessed. "At the end of the day, I just work here. The Bells tell me what to do, not the other way around." He shrugged. "I figured if you wanted my opinion, you'd ask for it."

"I always want your opinion, whether I ask or not. As far as I'm concerned, you're just as much a Bell as me and Lynn," Karla said. "The only reason I didn't ask was because you're the gamekeeper. You take care of the outside of Bellcroft. I didn't want to take advantage by asking your opinion on the inside."

"Well, that's just silly," Harry said. "I'm always here for whatever you need. Inside or outside, I will always help you and Lynn any way I can."

"In that case," Karla said. "I'd like you to oversee the renovations. I trust your judgement completely. Hire whoever you think will do the best job. I give you full authority to manage the project as you see fit."

"I won't disappoint you, Karla." Harry blinked and dabbed his eyes. "It'll be the best renovation ever."

"I know," Karla agreed. "And you'll be fairly compensated for your work."

"Anna says hello," Lynn said, jogging to catch up to them.

"How is she doing?" Harry asked.

"As well as can be expected," Lynn replied. "She called to tell me that she ran into Karla today at the town parking lot. She said Karla looked wonderful." Lynn reached behind Harry and gently tugged a lock of Karla's hair. "She said wavy hair suits you."

"She was with her sister, Trina." Karla said. "I didn't know Mrs. Hughes had a sister."

"Trina doesn't live around here," Lynn explained. "But she's been staying with Anna off and on since the summer." She cupped her hands around her mouth. "Trina's been having marital problems," she whispered, as if Clancy might repeat what she'd said. "Rumour has it she had an affair."

"Oh?" Harry and Karla said together.

"Anyone we know?" Harry asked.

"I asked Anna if it was true, but she swears she doesn't know." Lynn shrugged one shoulder. "I'm sure she knows. She probably doesn't want to discuss her sister's private business, and I respect that. But I heard Trina and Fitz had a short affair."

"Fitz?!" Karla shouted. "Fitz who died inside Bellflower?"

"He's the only Fitz I know," Lynn replied. "Apparently it started when Mr. Hughes hired Fitz to help with their renovation over the summer."

"I'm not surprised," Harry said. "Everyone in Bellbrook knows Fitz always had a particular weakness for married women."

"Has it occurred to anyone that one of those women could have killed him?" Karla asked. "Or one of their disgruntled husbands?"

"That would be a lot of suspects," Lynn commented with a chuckle.

"Your mum's right." Harry laughed. "Fitz had more flings than Clancy's favourite frisbee."

INSIDE THE MANOR HOUSE, they found the handwritten list exactly where Lynn said it would be: inside Grandma May's nightstand. It was next to the Bell family bible, pressed between the pages of a Danielle Steel novel like a bookmark.

"Wow!" Karla declared as she perused the list. "How big was the safe deposit box?"

"Bigger than you'd think," Lynn replied.

"If we can find the rest of the assets that Gigi hid, it might mean that we can refurbish Bellcroft and open it as an event venue again." Karla stopped short of finishing her thought: *Without Gigi's money, there's no way we can afford it. We'll have to subdivide the land and sell the manor house. For the first time ever, Bellcroft wouldn't belong to the Bell family.*

"We'll find it." Harry winked. "I feel it in my bones."

Karla wished she was half as confident as Harry sounded.

Over the years, Bellcroft Manor had fallen into disrepair. Maintaining a mansion was more expensive and time-consuming than most people realized. Wing by wing, then room by room, Grandma May was forced to close the once-popular local attraction and event venue to the public until there wasn't enough of the manor house left to rent out. But despite the lack of income from events, the fixed costs persisted. Property taxes, insurance, Harry's salary, water, electricity, maintaining the grounds, it all had to be paid, and Grandma May had spent most of the family fortune keeping the lights on. Had she not died, Grandma May would have been forced to either sell the manor house or find an investor for it in the next couple of years. More than once, Karla had tried to discuss the future of Bellcroft with her, but Grandma May had always hated discussing anything unpleasant and would change the subject.

They spent the rest of the afternoon dismantling and probing the nooks and crannies of Grandma May's belongings. Karla felt like a secret agent searching for a tiny microchip. They checked pockets, drawers, shelves, the backs of furniture, and the bottoms of furniture. They opened jars and bottles, leafed through books, checked behind and inside picture frames, and even inside shoes and boots.

"Nothing," Lynn declared, sweeping long blonde bangs off her face.

They resolved to search every inch of the estate, starting with Bellflower cottage, and agreed to regroup tomorrow.

They reasoned it made sense to begin at Bellflower since that's where Gigi had lived when she hid the family fortune. The two items that had been recovered already—the pearl earrings in the flour cannister and the financial assets in the writing desk—were found inside items that were in Bellflower when Gigi had lived there.

Stepping into the chilly, late afternoon air, Karla gathered her thick sweater around her and turned up the shawl collar against the snowflakes blowing in the chilly wind. She looked at Lynn.

"This hip hasn't been wrong yet," Lynn said, winking and smacking her left butt cheek.

CHAPTER 11

PEPPERLONELY AND MUTTZERELLA

"I don't often get the chance to have dinner with both of my favourite daughters," Dean commented with a laugh.

Karla took the stack of pizza boxes from him, and he scooped Gucci into his bearish arms, cradled him like a baby, and rubbed the terrier's belly.

"How's my grand-dog doing?" Dean inspected Gucci's Louis Vuitton collar. "Why does he need so many different collars and leashes?"

"He doesn't need them, Dad," Karla said. "He wants them." She smiled at the small dog basking in belly rubs. "Don't you Goochie Poochie?" she asked with puckered lips as she scratched the top of his head. "Who's my handsome boy?"

"I hope you don't spoil my future grandchildren as much as you spoil this dog."

Karla and Max rolled their eyes in shared exasperation, and Max let out a heavy sigh.

"Grandchildren are Max's department, Dad," Karla said, grinning at her sister and handing her a plate.

"Thanks for dumping me in it, Sis," Max hissed under hear breath.

"Do I smell pizza?" Rob asked, closing the door behind her.

Gucci squirmed and whined until Dean released him to greet the latest arrival.

"You sure do," Max replied, loading slices onto her plate.

Karla could tell Max was grateful for Rob's timing to change the subject.

"Wine?" Karla held out a glass of pinot grigio to her best friend.

"Yes, please." Rob's shoulders dropped, and her eyes closed blissfully as she took the first sip. "I'll be right back." She placed the glass on the table. "I have to change," she said gesturing to her bright blue scrubs and rainbow rubber clogs. "Save me a slice of Here Comes Treble."

Here Comes Treble is one of Dough-Re-Mi's signature pizzas with jalapeno peppers, bacon, and sausage.

Karla motioned to open the smallest pizza box but hesitated when she saw the crude hand-drawn sketch of a dog on the lid.

"It's for Gucci," Dean explained. "It's called a muttz-erella. They assured me it's made especially for dogs with only high-quality, dog-friendly ingredients."

As if he understood every word the humans said, Gucci appeared at Karla's feet. Sitting at attention, his eyes followed her hands' every move.

"And you think *I* spoil the dog?" Karla challenged, opening the box to reveal a bone-shaped dog biscuit. "C'mon Gooch!" she crooned.

Gucci followed his doting owner into the kitchen without taking his eyes off the treat.

"Sit."

He sat and licked his chops.

"Wait."

He waited, sweeping his quill-like tail across the tile floor like a feather duster.

Karla dropped the muttz-erella treat into his red Le Creuset dog dish.

"Go get it!"

He lunged at the bowl.

Dean wasn't much of an oenophile, so Karla instinctively opened the fridge and grabbed a beer for him.

"Oh." She realized Dean was still wearing his uniform at the same moment she opened the beer bottle. "Are you working tonight? Should I exchange this for water?"

"No," he said taking the bottle. "I'm finished for today. I'm starving and didn't want to take the time to go home and change."

"He spent all afternoon questioning Dylan," Max added.

"Dylan Fitzgibbon?" Rob asked, returning from her bedroom wearing the mint-green loungewear set Karla gave her two Christmases ago. Her red tresses were gathered into a messy top knot.

Dean and Max nodded.

"Did he tell you his blackmail theory?" Karla

asked, handing her father a plate. "He thinks Fitz was blackmailing Leon over an affair."

"He told us," Dean confirmed. "Rumours about Fitz's escapades with various married women have been swirling around town for years."

"Fitz?" Karla asked, dropping a slice of Bach, Bach, Bach—pizza with chicken, barbecue sauce, mozzarella and Colby-jack cheese, and sauteed onions and mush-rooms—onto her plate. "Dylan said Leon was the cheater, and Fitz was the blackmailer."

"Dylan could've been confused," Max said.

"Max'n'cheese is right, La-la," Dean agreed. "Dylan only overheard a small snippet of the conver-sation, and he only heard Fitz's side of the story."

"And he admitted he eavesdropped from a distance," Max continued. "It's possible he misinter-preted what he thought he overheard." She shook her head. "Fitz could have lied to him or let Dylan believe that what he overheard was correct."

As much as she wanted to believe Dylan and was swayed by his confidence about the conversation he'd overheard between Fitz and Leon, Karla couldn't disagree that Max might be right.

"Why would Fitz lie to Dylan about having an affair? Why would he rather let Dylan believe he was a blackmailer instead of Bellbrook's own Casanova?" Karla asked.

"If we could figure that out, we might be able to figure out who killed him," Dean replied.

"I can't imagine Leon having an affair," Rob piped in, pouring herself a second glass of wine. "He's such a stickler for rules. I've seen him walk two blocks to a crosswalk so he wouldn't break the town's jaywalking law. There's no way someone that conscientious would break their wedding vows, much less commit murder."

"Some people are only conscientious when they think someone might be watching," Max pointed out.

"Fitz had a long history of carrying on with women who were already in relationships," Dean reasoned. "Rumour has it his most recent paramour was Trina, you know, Anna Hughes's sister."

"Paramour?" Max snorted a laugh. "The 1800s called, Dad. They want their word back."

"It's a good word. Inoffensive and gets the point across," Dean defended, then turned his attention back to Karla. "Leon has no known history of cheating on his wife, and like Rob said, he's a stickler for rules. His reputation as an upstanding citizen is important to him."

Is his reputation important enough to him that he would kill to protect it? Karla wondered.

"We're considering a theory where Fitz had an affair, Leon found out, and blackmailed him. Fitz began cutting corners on people's renovation projects to pay the blackmail, and Leon looked the other way because he was benefitting from the building code violations," Max divulged.

"That's a big theory," Karla said. "And it contradicts everyone's opinion that Leon Tyson is Bellbrook's law-abiding, moral compass."

"Everyone has secrets, La-la," Dean counselled. "Some people just hide them better than others."

"Speaking of secrets," Karla said. "Harry, Lynn,

and I found some old-timey money and stuff that my great-grandmother hid before she died."

"The money from the safe deposit box?" Dean asked.

"You know about that?"

"Everyone knows about that," Max said. "It's a local legend."

"I didn't know about it until this afternoon," Karla said, somewhat hurt that she was the last person to find out something about her family.

"I didn't know about it either," Rob sulked. "And I've lived in Bellbrook my entire life."

"I was one of the volunteers who helped Grandma May and the bank manager search for it," Dean said. "We did a grid search of the route Gigi would have taken home from the bank." He nodded, his gaze distant. "It took days. I got poison ivy searching in the wooded areas next to the road."

"I always wondered if one of the searchers found the loot and kept it," Max added.

"We think the rest might be hidden inside Bell-flower," Karla said.

"Your grandmother searched that cottage top to bottom," Dean said. "If it was there, she would have found it."

"The loot that was recovered so far came from items that were inside Bellflower. Her hiding places were clever. Grandma May might have underesti-mated Gigi's ability to hide stuff. From what I gather, Gigi was a resourceful woman."

"All the Bell women are resourceful." Dean winked.

"If the loot is hidden in Bellflower, then it's a good thing Fitz died."

Everyone looked at Rob and gasped.

"I don't mean it's good that he's dead," she clarified so quickly that it sounded like the words were in a race to escape from her mouth. "I mean if the murderer hadn't killed him, Fitz would have trashed the old furniture and demolished the inside of the cottage. He either would have unknowingly taken the loot to the dump, destroyed it, or found it and, I hate to say it, possibly kept it."

"Rob's right," Max agreed, then she elbowed Dean. "We should consider that Fitz's killer could be someone who knows where the loot is and killed Fitz to stop him from destroying it or trashing it."

"Or finding it," Dean agreed.

"Harry said contractors from all over have contacted him since Fitz died," Karla revealed. "They want to renovate the cottages in hopes it will lead to the manor job. Maybe one of Fitz's competitors wanted the job badly enough to kill him."

"If the suspect pool includes rival builders, women Fitz had affairs with, and their husbands, the list of suspects would be so long, you might as well use the town phone book," Rob said, piercing the air with the pointy end of her pizza slice.

"Dylan and Leon are still our prime suspects," Dean declared. "And we still haven't ruled out you"—he pointed his thick finger at Karla—"Lynn, Harry, or Rosalie. But we're working on it. I can't imagine a rival builder would kill Fitz just for a *chance* of getting the job," he reasoned. "Besides, you said refurbishing the manor house wasn't in the budget."

"It's not," Karla confirmed. "But it *could be* if we find the financial assets Gigi hid. That money, combined with my money and whatever else I can scrape together, might be enough to make the Bellcroft Manor project possible. I could run the East Coast branch of *Just Task Me!* from the manor and use it as a destination venue for my clients." She waved away the idea. "We'll see. We'd have to find Gigi's money first."

"*Your* money," Dean corrected her as he reached for another slice of Pepperlonely pizza with only cheese and pepperoni. "Grandma May left the property, buildings, and contents to you, La-la. Whatever assets you find hidden in the walls, furniture, or whatever, will belong to you."

Karla wasn't sure Lynn would see it the same way.

CHAPTER 12

COFFEE ON THE ROCKS

OCTOBER 22ND

Karla knew today's scavenger hunt would be a messy, dusty job and dressed accordingly. Since her morning didn't include face-to-face or video meetings, she didn't bother with makeup. She pulled her blonde waves into a low ponytail and paired her oldest, rattiest sweatpants with a faded, oversized sweatshirt bearing her alumni's logo that she stole from a brief college boyfriend. The last time she ventured outside with so little preparation, she had the flu and was on her way to the pharmacy.

After a morning spent replying to emails, touching base with VIP clients, and syncing calendars with her virtual assistant, Karla took Gucci for a walk, then left him at home while she headed to Bellflower to embark on a treasure hunt with Harry and Lynn.

But first, coffee.

The lady ahead of her at Déjà Brew ordered a *coffee on the rocks*, which was the best description of iced coffee that Karla had ever heard. There was something familiar about the woman's voice. When the mystery woman reached back and pulled out her long, dark hair from inside the collar of her black trench coat, Karla made the connection between the voice and the hair.

"Anna? Mrs. Hughes?" Karla gently touched the woman's shoulder.

Anna's posture was slouchy, making the petite woman seem even smaller than usual and easy to overlook. She had managed to make herself so unnoticeable that she was nearly invisible. Her thick, dark hair cascaded around her face like a hood, and oversize, dark sunglasses concealed most of her face. Her long black trench coat added to her camouflage.

"Karla!" Mrs. Hughes raised her large sunglasses with a cringe that suggested she was trying natural light for the first time today. "It's lovely to see you again. We haven't seen each other for years, and here we are running into other twice in one week." She smiled weakly.

"I'm sorry for not attending Mr. Hughes's funeral," Karla said. "But you've been in my thoughts." *Mostly because I want to ask you if your sister, Trina, had an affair with the man who was murdered inside my cottage,* she added in her head.

"I understand, dear." Mrs. Hughes lowered her sunglasses, once again shielding herself from the overwhelming brightness of her new reality. "Funerals are awful." She let out a sigh. "I would've skipped it, too, if I could." She looked up at Karla. "Hardest day of my life, so far." She patted the back of Karla's hand and pressed her lips into a thin line. "You know what I'm talking about."

Karla nodded. She knew exactly what Anna Hughes was talking about.

An almost-forty-year-old-woman losing her octogenarian grandmother to a prolonged, progressive illness was sad but expected. Losing a husband who wasn't yet sixty years old and, according to Rosalie, healthier than a butcher's dog, was tragic. Especially losing him to a sudden, freak household accident.

Karla recognized the exhausted agony in Anna's heavy, red eyes. She recognized it because she had seen it before. In the mirror.

Just over two years ago, Karla's best friend from college was murdered. Aside from Rob and Max, Meghean had been one of the few people who broke through Corporate Karla's protective barrier of frostiness and sarcasm. Meghean and Karla weren't married like Mr. and Mrs. Hughes, but they were friends, business partners, and spiritual sisters. They were soulmates. And when a soulmate dies, part of your soul dies with them.

Some wounds never heal, Grandma May said when Karla had come home to Bellbrook to lick her emotional wounds after Meaghan's funeral. *Some wounds are too big to heal properly so we heal around them.*

Karla watched Anna collect her iced coffee from the barista. Then in the corner, Anna discreetly slipped a flask from her pocket and spiked her drink. A group of yoga-attired women who were huddled around a nearby table murmured in hushed tones while pointing and nodding in Anna's direction.

As Karla placed her order for an Iced Blonde French Vanilla Coconut Latte, Anna left, and the women's murmurs grew loud enough to overhear.

Karla glared at them. If her eyes could shoot flames, every woman at that table would have needed to draw their eyebrows on their faces for the next six weeks.

She caught the eye of a blonde yogi with an inverted bob and bit her tongue. *Shame on you for judging her!*

"So sad," said the inverted bob, shaking her head and clucking her tongue.

Sad that she can't grieve in peace? she wondered, *or sad that you have nothing better to talk about?*

Karla turned away and exhaled loudly, drumming her fingers on the counter, silently pleading, *Please hurry before I give these yoga bitches a piece of my mind.*

"Here you go," said the chipper barista, eyeing Karla's drumming fingers and tense face. She was clearly bracing herself to deal with an irate customer. "Sorry for the wait."

Karla smiled and thanked the barista, slipping a generous tip into the tip jar to ward off the pang of guilt she felt for making the barista think she was upset about the wait instead of the spandex busybodies at the nearby table.

"Karla? Karla Bell?" The yogi with her hair in a scrunchie—obviously their leader—narrowed her gaze on Karla.

"Ladies, this is Karla *Bell*," the queen yogi addressed her followers. "May Bell's mysterious, reclusive granddaughter and the new owner of Bellcroft."

"Nice to meet you, ladies," Karla said to the group in the sweetest tone of voice she could muster. "For the record, I'm neither mysterious nor reclusive." She shrugged. "Just picky about who I spend time with." She flashed them a wide grin and relished their brief but confused expressions as they tried to figure out if she had just insulted them.

"Lynn's daughter, right?" asked another yogi. "I'm a good friend of your mother's."

How did Lynn maintain so many *good friends* in Bellbrook when she didn't even live here? Why do so many people seem to like her so much? Karla didn't understand Lynn's mass appeal.

"You have that big, fancy business that caters to the rich and famous, right?" asked another spandex-clad inverted bob.

"Something like that," Karla replied.

"I bet you have *lots* of good stories to tell," said the brunette pixie cut.

"Are you married?" asked the auburn bob with blonde highlights.

"No, I don't believe in monotony," Karla purred, enjoying letting Corporate Karla out of her cage for a while.

"You mean m-o-n-o-g-a-m-y," the queen yogi corrected her, dramatically stretching each syllable.

"I know what I said." Karla winked.

"Is it true you and Harry Kincaid found Fitz's dead body?" asked the first inverted bob.

This was Karla's cue to make a graceful exit. Max

and Dean had been very specific that she shouldn't feed the rumour mill.

"Well, ladies, it's been a blast, but I must run." She pretended to check the time on her watch-free wrist and flashed them another dazzling smile. Karla knew the best way to deal with fake people was with fake platitudes. When in Rome and all that. "Places to be. People to see. Toodles," she sang, giving them a wiggly wave as she strode away.

On the sidewalk, Karla took a deep cleansing breath, re-caged Corporate Karla, and indulged in a long satisfying sip of coffee.

"They're talking about you," said a voice behind her.

Karla turned to see Trina and Anna standing side-by-side in near-identical black trench coats.

"The Posers," Trina said, pointing at the table of chatting women through the café window.

"The Posers?" Karla asked with a chuckle. "As in yoga pose? That's very clever."

"It's also inaccurate," Trina advised. "They've never actually attended a yoga class."

"But they have yoga mats sticking out of their bags." Karla pointed out.

Trina shrugged. "All I know is no one's ever seen them stretch farther than across the counter to pick up their lattes, and they aren't members of Om Sweet Om."

Om Sweet Om was Bellbrook's local yoga and Pilates studio. Karla was relieved to hear The Posers weren't members because she was considering joining but had second thoughts since her encounter with them.

"They're talking about you," Trina continued. "I can tell because they got all animated when you left"—she did an unenthusiastic version of jazz hands—"and keep looking toward the door where they last saw you."

"You're used to the big city where people mind their own business," Anna added. "It made you forget it's not like that around here."

"I'm not bothered," Karla said. "Let them talk." She had another gulp of coffee.

"It doesn't bother me, either," Anna said, crinkling her nose.

Karla was telling the truth. She wasn't bothered. She had developed an emotional callous where rumours were concerned. Growing up in Bellbrook was like exposure therapy for gossip. It cured her of fearing what other people thought. In fact, the reason Karla looked and acted the way she did was to *encourage* people to talk about her. She reasoned that if people were going to talk anyway, she may as well control the narrative and keep them focussed on things that didn't matter and couldn't hurt her.

"Listen, Karla," Trina said, looking at the sidewalk and shuffling her feet. "I'm sorry about what I said yesterday at the town parking lot." She looked up and met Karla's gaze. "I know you don't have the personality of a cactus." She crinkled her nose. "It was just something I overheard."

"Honestly Trina, it's fine," Karla said, admiring Trina's willingness to take responsibility. "I know I can be a little prickly sometimes." She smiled. "Actually, I overheard something about you, too." Karla hoped she wasn't about to offend Trina so hard that the woman would stomp off without giving her the answers she was probing for. She sipped her coffee while Trina formed a response.

"Oh yeah?" Trina asked. "What'd you hear?"

"I heard you had an affair with Fitz."

"Fitz?"

"Yes. Keith Fitzgibbon. The contractor who was murdered at Bellflower."

"Ha!" Trina elbowed Anna, who followed her sister's lead and let out a guffaw laced with shock. "I'm not having an affair," she clarified, with her nose crinkled. "Fitz was a nice man, but I'm married." She held up her left hand and wiggled her ring finger.

"I heard that too," Karla informed. "I'm told Fitz had a preference for married women."

"Trust me, Karla," Anna added, crinkling her nose and shaking her head. "There was no affair. I would know if there was." She locked arms with Trina. "We're together all the time. My sister and I don't have secrets."

"I'm sure you hear this all the time, but you bear a strong physical resemblance to each other. You could be twins."

"We take after our father," they said in unison, making it obvious they'd heard this before.

"Did you also inherit his mannerisms? Not only do you look alike, but you move the same and make similar facial expressions."

Anna and Trina looked at each other and shrugged one shoulder at the same time.

"We're very close," Trina said.

"I can see that," Karla agreed.

"Speaking of sisters," Anna said. "Trina and I had a nice visit with Max today."

"Not on official business, I hope."

"Actually, yes," Anna said. "She asked us some questions about Fitz."

"Really?" Karla feigned shock. "Why would she ask you two about Fitz?"

"Like you, she heard I'd had an affair with him," Trina said.

"That's the small-town rumour mill for you," Karla declared, tilting her head and raising her coffee cup like she was making a toast. "What kind of relationship did you have with Fitz?"

Trina took in a deep breath and blew it out. "Fitz was a nice man," she said again. "Earlier this year, my husband and I were having issues. Nothing huge, but our marriage hit a rough patch. I stayed with Anna for a while so we could have some space from each other and clear our heads. Fitz was helping with their renovation, so he was around. He was a good listener and easy to talk to. We became friends. That's it. I hadn't seen him for at least a month before he died."

"I was under the impression Mr. Hughes renovated the house by himself." Karla directed her comment at Anna. "I didn't realize you'd hired Fitz."

"My husband did most of the renovation work himself," Anna said proudly. "But he hired Fitz for a few tasks that were outside his comfort zone."

"Anna means, she *made* him hire Fitz for the jobs she didn't trust her husband to do himself."

Anna rolled her eyes. "That's not true," she said with her nose crinkled. "We agreed it was best to hire a professional for some of the plumbing and electrical work." Anna sighed, and a tear rolled down her cheek from behind her large sunglasses. "My dear husband worked so hard to turn our house into the retirement home of our dreams. It's too bad he didn't live long enough to enjoy it."

"He would want you to enjoy it," Karla said, patting Anna's arm.

"That's what I keep telling her," Trina agreed.

"You really are much kinder than people give you credit for, Karla" Anna said, in a way that made Karla believe she meant it as a compliment. "I can see why Lynn is so proud of you."

For an instant, a flush of angry heat rose inside Karla. She drained her coffee cup, swallowing hard and forcing the anger back down. What right did Lynn have to be proud of Karla? Her success wasn't Lynn's achievement. On the contrary, Karla's accomplishments, despite Lynn's lack of maternal nurturing or attention, were an act of rebellion against her mother. She had devoted her life to proving to the world—especially Lynn—that she didn't need anyone else. She might have wanted approval, but she didn't *need* it.

"Speaking of my mother," Karla said as an alarm chimed on her phone, "If I don't leave now, I'll be late meeting her and Harry."

CHAPTER 13

A HOLE IN THE WALL

KARLA EXPECTED to find Lynn's car parked at the top of the long, shared driveway. She wasn't expecting the shiny red pickup truck with tinted windows. What was *he* doing here? It was hard to avoid somebody when their truck kept coming and going from your driveway.

Where were Lynn and Harry? Lynn's car wasn't there, and there was no sign of Harry. If he were already inside Bellflower, he would've left the door open, and Clancy would be lounging somewhere nearby.

She shifted the car into park and scanned her surroundings. The red pickup truck's owner was nowhere in sight. Nevertheless, Karla closed the car door as gently as possible and didn't lock it for fear the chirping sound that confirmed the car was locked would herald her arrival and lure the red pickup truck's owner out from wherever he was.

No evidence remained from yesterday's brief snow squall. The midday sun was bright, the sky was cloudless, and the air was seasonally fresh. Birds sang in nearby trees, and the last of the frost-hearty campanulas clung to the white picket fence, fighting against the brisk breeze.

Karla was typing a text to Harry, letting him know she was there, when from the corner of her eye, she spotted movement between the cottages.

Most of him was hidden behind Bellflower. He wasn't facing her, but she'd recognize his strong back and broad shoulders anywhere. He wore a grey and white plaid flannel shirt—untucked—black jeans, and work boots. Karla swallowed hard. Her heart somersaulted inside her chest.

Schwuuup! The sound of a retracting tape measure snapped her out of her thoughts.

He turned toward her, tape measure in hand, adjusting his backwards baseball cap until the brim was in front. His hair was still short and messy on top. Like it used to be.

He stopped.

Though his eyes were shielded by the brim of his hat, she felt him looking at her. His gaze had its own weight and temperature. Karla felt like she was in a fog. This was it. The moment she had been looking forward to and dreading since she drove past the *Welcome to Bellbrook* sign almost a month ago. She sucked in a shaky breath and held it. Her heart pounded against her ribs like it was trying to escape.

His smile pulled at her insides like a magnet. She

resisted the urge to walk toward him. He was harder to resist than gravity.

Twenty years ago, Karla had only wanted two things. She wanted him, and she wanted them.

He wanted Bellbrook.

She returned the smile and swore she could smell him. But that would be impossible, right? He was fifty feet away. And who still smells the same after twenty years?

He walked toward her, rolling up his sleeves. He had the most amazing forearms… and his hands. OMG, his hands! *Don't think about his hands, Karla. Don't even look at them.*

"Hey, stranger!" His voice sent a familiar rumble through her body and made her heart race.

"Hey!"

His grey, downturned eyes were exactly how Karla remembered. Except now, there were creases in the corners that made him look more mature and distinguished than the lanky, still somewhat awkward, nineteen-year-old she had waved goodbye to in this very driveway twenty years ago.

His wiry body had filled out since then. He was solid now. Muscular. He stroked his dark, stubbly chin, and Karla swooned internally at his big, strong hands. *Don't look at his hands, Karla. Look away!*

"H—"

"Y—"

They started to speak at the same time, laughed at the coincidence, and said, "You first," at the same time again, and laughed again.

With the proverbial ice broken, they asked about each other's lives, families, and jobs. Karla listened as Griff gushed about his three kids. She thought about how different her life could have been if she hadn't left.

"Bellbrook hasn't been the same without you. Welcome home." He chuckled. "I never thought I'd say that to you. I can't believe I'm standing here talking to Karla Bell."

"In the flesh." She smiled. "I can't believe Griff Dixon made a special trip to Bellcroft to welcome me home."

"I didn't make a special trip," Griff explained. "Harry asked me to come by and talk to him about renovating the cottages."

"I see." Karla nodded. "Where is Harry?"

She wondered if Harry had intentionally arranged for Griff to come over today, when he knew she would be there, then made himself scarce so she would have to face her past whether she wanted to or not. She also wondered if Lynn and Harry had concocted the scheme together, and that's why, conveniently, they were both missing.

"He said he'd be right back," Griff replied. "We already looked around Mirabel, but he forgot the key for Bellflower and went back to his cottage to get it." He jerked his thumb behind him toward the gap between the cottages. "I was just getting some outside measurements until he gets back." He shook his head and grinned. "You look the same." He reached toward her then stopped himself, shoving his hand in his pocket instead. "You're as gorgeous as the day you left."

"You're just as charming," she said with an awkward laugh.

Woof! Woowoo!

Clancy announced his arrival with a low bark and deep howl as he emerged from the trees.

Karla bent to greet the large grey hound, and Griff gave the dog's side a friendly pat.

"Found it!" Harry called, holding up a keychain between his thumb and forefinger as he stepped out of the thicket. "Finally."

Griff and Clancy jogged and trotted over, meeting Harry halfway.

They spoke briefly, then Harry dropped the key in Griff's hand, and Griff jogged up the steps to Bellflower, then disappeared inside.

"What the heck, Harry?" Karla hissed, tapping the toe of her white sneaker with her hands on her hips.

"Hi, Karla," he said, approaching her with Clancy in tow. "Before you get your trousers in a twist, this isn't what it looks like." He shook his head vigorously, ruffling his silver mop of hair. "I thought Griff and I agreed to meet before lunch, not after. We had a miscommunication about the time."

Karla rolled her eyes. Of course, this could have been avoided if the people in this town would use an actual clock instead of vague time-related benchmarks.

"I wish you'd warned me." She gestured to her oversized sweats and makeup-free face. "I might have made an effort."

"You look great," he assured her. "You always look

your best. Anyway, If I'd warned you, you wouldn't have come."

"You're not wrong."

"This is a good thing," Harry insisted. "Griff was Fitz's nephew," he reminded her. "He might know something about Fitz's murder." He whispered *murder* like it was an impolite word. "And this will give you a chance to ask him why he was here the day Fitz died."

Harry made good points. Karla had completely forgotten that Griff's mother and Fitz were siblings. And he was right that Karla needed to ask Griff why he was near the crime scene before she and Harry found Fitz's body.

"C'mon, Karla," Harry implored. "You were bound to run into each other sooner or later. You live in the same tiny town for goodness' sake. Isn't it better to do it here, in private, instead of somewhere public with the local gossips watching and listening?"

"You're right," Karla admitted, nodding. "We had to see each other eventually, and I should talk to Griff about Fitz's death."

"Do you know where Lynn is?" Harry asked. "She should've been here by now."

As Karla shook her head, her and Harry's phones chimed in unison.

"I bet that's her," he said.

"It is," Karla said as she read the text Lynn had sent to her and Harry. "She lost her keys. She just found them and will be here soon."

"I figured it must be something simple like that," Harry said, as if he was relieved that Lynn wasn't delayed by something more worrisome.

"The sooner we find Fitz's killer the better," Karla said. "It feels like the entire town is tense, and everyone is suspicious of each other."

"The entire town is on edge," Harry agreed. "I've never seen Bellbrook this uptight. Everyone walks around like they're waiting for someone to jump out and startle them."

"Harry! Karla!" Griff shouted as he jogged through the front door and down the porch steps. "You need to see this." He jerked his head toward the cottage.

Karla and Harry looked at each other, wordlessly conveying the dread they both felt at the urgency in Griff's voice.

"Maybe he found more of Gigi's money," Karla suggested hopefully.

"Let's hope," Harry responded as they slow-jogged toward the cottage.

INSIDE THE DARK, musty cottage, Griff led them toward the basement stairs, lighting the way with a flashlight. He descended the creaky wooden stairs first, then used the flashlight to light the way for Karla and Harry.

"Over here," Griff said, pointing with the flashlight.

He and Harry hunched their shoulders and lowered their chins because the ceiling in the old basement was too low for them to stand up straight. The top of Karla's head was only inches from the cobwebbed ceiling beams.

They followed Griff to the wall.

Karla coughed. The stirred-up dust tickled her eyes and throat.

Griff came to a halt in front of a hole in the wall. Karla deduced that the hole was made recently. The dust around the hole was fresh, relative to the rest of the dust. She wondered if Fitz had made the hole in the wall, since Griff wasn't in here long enough, and didn't appear to be covered in dust or debris.

"Look," Griff said, aiming the flashlight beam toward the hole. "I haven't phoned anyone yet. I thought I should show you first."

Karla stepped forward and squinted into the hole.

Griff handed her the flashlight.

Harry peered over her shoulder. She heard him breathing in her ear.

They leaned forward together.

A pile of dusty rags. Clothes, maybe? And a dusty leather gym bag in a style that was popular about thirty years ago.

"What's that?" Harry whispered.

"What?" Karla asked, panning the flashlight along the dirt floor behind the wall.

"The grey thing," Harry said, placing his hand on top of hers and commandeering the flashlight. "There!"

"It's"—she squinted, unwilling to believe her eyes —"a skull?"

"That looks like an arm or leg bone," Harry said, pointing at the bone sticking out from beneath the pile of dusty clothes.

"A dead body?" Karla asked, looking at Griff.

Karla heard Grandma May's voice in her head. *I had to board-up Bellflower. That place is falling apart. It's a deathtrap.* At the time, Karla thought it was just a turn of phrase. Had Grandma May been serious?

He nodded. "I think we should phone your dad."

A SECRET SNOGGING
SESSION

KARLA GASPED, sucking in a lungful of dusty air, then started coughing and hacking.

Harry smacked her back as if she were choking.

Griff grabbed her by the waist and whisked her toward the stairs. She felt like she was floating, but she wasn't sure if it was because she was half-walking as he half-carried her up the stairs, or because his hand was gripping her waist and touching her soul at the same time.

He swept her through the front door and down the porch stairs.

She took a deep breath of fresh, outdoor air, then sneezed.

"You OK?" he asked.

She nodded, still clearing her throat. "Dust," she rasped.

"I'll call your dad," Harry said, stepping away from them and already holding his phone up to his ear.

"There are human remains inside Bellflower," Karla gasped as her respiratory symptoms abated.

"I've never seen a dead body before," Griff said.

"Are you OK?" Karla asked. "You might be in shock. Do you want some water? Maybe you should sit down."

"I'm fine," Griff insisted. "How about you? This is the second dead body you've seen in a week."

"I'm starting to think I'm the common denominator," Karla admitted sarcastically.

"Shouldn't the police have found the remains when they were here for Uncle Fitz's death?"

"I'm surprised they didn't find it too," Karla agreed. "They kept the house as a crime scene for two days."

"I guess this is new for all of us," Griff said. "The Bellbrook police department has never processed a murder scene before. Uncle Fitz was Bellbrook's first murder. Ever."

"Was it, though?" Karla asked. "How do we know the remains you found in the wall weren't the result of murder? Whose remains are they, and how did they get there?"

"I don't know." Griff shrugged. "I was showing myself around the house from top to bottom, like I always do when I'm scoping out a potential job," he explained. "I poked my head into the attic and noticed a hole in the attic floor. The floor around the hole didn't look stable enough to bear my weight, so I checked the main floor, then the basement to see where the hole might have led."

"It led to the body," Karla concluded.

Griff nodded. "I assumed it would lead to some-thing like an old leak or rotted wood."

"Did you make the hole in the basement wall?" Karla asked.

Griff shook his head. "The hole was already there. Someone found the body before me." He stroked his chin thoughtfully, then adjusted his baseball cap. "Whoever it was, they found it recently. That hole looked new to me."

"It looked new to me too," Karla confirmed. "I suspect Fitz found it. He called me shortly before his death and asked me to meet him at Bellflower. He said he wanted to show me something."

Griff looked down and kicked the dirt with the toe of his work boot at the mention of his late uncle's recent death.

"I'm sorry about your Uncle Fitz," Karla said softly. "Harry and I shouldn't have let you go inside Bell-flower alone. Not after what happened to your uncle in there."

"It's fine," Griff insisted. "Harry asked me a dozen times today if I was sure I wanted to go inside Bell-flower. He suggested I only give him a quote for the Mirabel renovation, then we could revisit the Bell-flower renovation later." He nodded toward Harry, who was on the phone several metres away. "In fact, I suspect he *"forgot"* the key to Bellflower on purpose to give me another chance to change my mind about going inside." He used air quotes around *forgot*.

"That sounds like something Harry would do," she concurred with a half-laugh.

"I went inside because I wanted to. I'd never been

inside Bellflower before. I wanted to see the cottage and see for myself where Uncle Fitz was murdered."

"You didn't go inside Bellflower when you were here the other day?" Karla asked. "The day Fitz…" She let her sentence fizzle out before she could finish it.

"Who said I was here the day Uncle Fitz died?"

"Nobody," Karla replied. "I saw you." She pointed toward the driveway. "You were leaving as I was arriving. We just missed each other."

"Right," Griff said, nodding. "I wasn't here long. I didn't go inside, and I didn't see Uncle Fitz. But I heard him."

"Heard him?" Karla asked.

"I heard him and Dylan arguing," Griff explained. "Uncle Fitz phoned me the night before he died. I was at my daughter's soccer game and didn't answer his call. He left me a voicemail message asking me to either call him back or come by Bellflower the next day. Said he wanted to talk to me about something."

Griff pulled out his phone and played the voicemail for Karla. An eerie chill ran through her body at the sound of the dead man's voice. It was like hearing a ghost.

"Do you always keep voicemails?" She asked.

Griff nodded. "Bad habit. I just hang up after listening to them. I always forget to delete them first. Used to drive my wife nuts because my voicemail box was always full when she'd try to leave a message."

"What did Fitz want to talk to you about?" Karla asked, ignoring the comment about Griff's wife. Karla had never met Griff Dixon's wife but was sure she was gorgeous, intelligent, witty, and perfect in every way possible.

"Dunno," Griff shrugged. "When I got here, Uncle Fitz and Dylan were parked side by side." He pointed to where Karla had seen the matching FITZ IT RIGHT THE FIRST TIME pickup trucks when she arrived with Gucci the day Fitz died. "I pulled up behind them. I could hear them shouting from the porch. I decided not to knock or go inside. I'm allergic to drama, remember?"

"I remember," Karla confirmed. "Could you hear what Fitz and Dylan were arguing about?"

"Not really." Griff shook his head. "Dylan was near the front door. I heard him stomping, and his voice was louder. Fitz was farther away. Dylan called Uncle Fitz a liar, and Uncle Fitz shouted a string of profanity at him. I decided it was best to leave and pretend I didn't hear anything. I meant to phone Uncle Fitz later and tell him I was too busy to stop by, but I forgot. Next thing, I heard he had died in some horrible workplace accident."

"Except it wasn't an accident," Karla whispered.

"I know that now," Griff admitted. "Dylan told me. He said Max told him the police initially thought it was suicide, then determined it was murder."

"Do you know if Fitz was dating anyone special before he died?"

"Uncle Fitz didn't talk about his love life much. Like ever." Griff shrugged. "He never brought anyone to family functions either. He said he didn't like feeding the rumour mill."

"Did Dylan ever mention switching careers?" Karla

asked. "Apparently, he's applying to paramedic programs."

"He told me that's what he was doing when Uncle Fitz was killed," Griff confirmed, rubbing the back of his neck. "But that's the first time I've ever heard Dylan talk about wanting to be a paramedic. As far as I knew, he always wanted to work with Uncle Fitz." He poked her arm, and she resisted the urge to lean into his touch. "You used to babysit him. Remember how much he loved playing with his construction toys?"

"He idolized Fitz," Karla agreed. "Why didn't you work with Fitz? You didn't want to join the FITZ IT RIGHT THE FIRST TIME team?"

"You know how I am, K," he said, using the nickname she hadn't heard since high school. "I don't always respond well to authority." He chuckled. "I'm better off as my own boss. Uncle Fitz had a strong personality. We would have butted heads. He was fine with it. He even helped me out when I was getting started by referring me for jobs he had to turn down."

"Have you heard any rumours about the quality of Fitz's work?" she asked, choosing her words carefully so she wouldn't come across as speaking ill of the dead. "Someone mentioned he might have been cutting corners and overcharging."

"I haven't heard about any specific examples," Griff replied. "But I've heard the rumours. To be honest, I could see Uncle Fitz cutting a few corners to help his bottom line. He was always highly motivated by money. He was tempted by more than one get-rich-quick scheme that my mum had to talk him out of."

"Have you talked to Max or my dad?" Karla asked. "You're one of the last people who heard Fitz. You can help them with the timeline of his death."

"They questioned me," Griff revealed. "I didn't see anything," he said defensively. "If I had seen or heard anything suspicious, I would have told the police. It's not like I have anything to hide. I'm an open book."

"You might not think you saw or heard anything suspicious, but that's for the police to decide. It's possible something you think is insignificant is a clue that will help find Fitz's killer."

A line of patrol cars pealed up the driveway, their flashing lights barely visible in the bright daylight.

Here we go again, Karla thought with a sigh.

"K," Griff said, reaching into his front pocket. "Here's my number. Call me if you need anything." He slipped a business card into her hand and smiled.

She smiled back.

Dean's car lurched when he slammed it into park.

"Are you OK, La-la?" he shouted as he ran toward them. "What's this about another body?" He pulled her into him, then pushed her away so he could scan her from head to toe, then pulled her into him again.

After asking her four more times if she was sure she was OK, Dean excused himself to visit the crime scene. He told Karla to yell if she needed him.

In the middle of the parade of police patrol cars was Lynn's late-model hatchback. The car she'd inherited from Grandma May.

"What on earth is going on?" Lynn demanded.

"Found another body," Harry informed her. "But we don't know who it is."

"What do you mean, you don't know who it is?" Lynn looked from Harry to Karla. "Why do you keep finding dead people?" She wrapped her arms around Karla's shoulders and squeezed the breath out of her. "Thank heaven you're OK," she whispered.

"Actually, I found this one," Griff interjected, raising his hand. "I found the remains alone, then showed Harry and Karla because I couldn't believe my eyes."

"I should have been here," Lynn squeezed Karla again, but Karla stiffened and wiggled out of the embrace. "That's twice in a week you've had a traumatic experience, and I wasn't here for you."

Story of my life.

"Are you sure you're all right?" Lynn asked, tucking a stray clump of hair behind Karla's ear.

"I'm fine," Karla assured her, swatting Lynn's hand away from her face. "Harry and Griff were here. We had each other's backs."

Max and another officer approached them. The unfamiliar officer invited Harry to have a seat in his patrol car and give his statement. Max invited Griff to wait by her patrol car, telling him she'd join him in a moment.

"Dad's going to take your statement," Max said. "As soon as he's finished checking out the scene."

"Will I be able to stay with her?" Lynn asked. "I wasn't here for any of it. I arrived at the same time as you, so I don't have to give a statement."

"I'm sure it'll be fine if you're there," Max replied. "But Dad has the final say."

Lynn nodded.

"I'm glad you came home to Bellbrook, La-la. You're good for business," Max teased with a grin. "Seriously, are you OK? Do you need anything?"

"I'm fine, honestly," Karla told her sister. "I'm not sure about Harry and Griff, though."

"We'll keep an eye on them," Max assured her. "So will everyone else in Bellbrook when word gets out." She gave Karla a wink and left to join Griff at her patrol car.

"He's aged well, hasn't he?" Lynn asked, nodding her chin toward Griff, who was leaning against the patrol car with his long legs crossed at the ankles while he scrolled on his phone.

"I guess." Karla shrugged. "Yeah. Whatever."

"Don't tell me, *whatever*," Lynn scoffed. "It doesn't take a scientist to sense the chemistry between you and Griff Dixon." She shimmied her shoulders. "It's electric."

"I think electricity is physics, not chemistry, Mother."

"You know what I mean." She nudged Karla's shoulder with her shoulder. "He's getting divorced, you know."

"I know. Rob told me. I don't live under a rock."

"They've been separated for months," Lynn continued. "Apparently it's very amicable, you know for the kids' sake, but there's no chance they'll get back together."

"I'm not interested."

"Liar."

"He has kids. I have to focus on getting the East Coast branch of *Just Task Me!* up and running and renovating Mirabel so I'll have a home." Karla shook her head. "It's too complicated."

"You'd be a great stepmum."

"We aren't even dating. Will you stop trying to marry me off to a man who isn't even divorced yet?! Gawd!" Karla crossed her arms in front of her chest and rolled her eyes.

"I would've gotten here sooner, but it took forever to track down my keys," Lynn said, changing the subject.

"Where were they?" Karla asked, relieved to talk about anything other than Griff Dixon's marital status.

"I left them at Anna Hughes's house this morning," Lynn explained. "We went for an early morning walk, like we often do when it's not too hot, too cold, or too wet. Afterward, I went inside for a glass of water and left my keys on her kitchen counter. I didn't realize they were missing until I was getting ready to meet you and Harry. I called Anna but she wasn't home. She and Trina had gone to Déjà Brew—she mentioned that they ran into you and The Posers. Anyway, she was at the hairdresser getting her roots done, so she couldn't tell me if I'd left my keys on her counter. But she said Trina would be there, and I was more than welcome to walk over and look for my keys."

"You found them at Anna's?" Karla guessed, gesturing to the keys in Lynn's hand.

"My keys weren't the only thing I found at Anna Hughes's house."

"Oh?" Karla's interest was piqued.

"I found Trina canoodling on the couch with a certain uptight, pompous Bellbrook Bylaw officer."

"Leon Tyson?" Karla hissed, so no one else would hear.

Lynn nodded.

"Are you sure?"

"Positive," Lynn replied. "I saw them through the window before I rang the bell." She looked over both shoulders, then leaned into Karla and whispered, "His car wasn't there. I ended up finding it on the next street over. Leon and Trina were having a secret tryst."

"You're absolutely positive?"

"See for yourself."

Lynn unlocked her phone and opened her photos. The photos were grainy and taken from a distance, through a window, so the quality wasn't great. It could have been any two people smooching on a sofa. But what were the odds that someone else would have a secret snogging session on Anna Hughes's sofa? The man's profile certainly resembled Leon Tyson, but Karla wondered if she only saw the resemblance because of the power of suggestion. And the woman could be any petite woman with long dark hair. In fact, if Lynn hadn't mentioned that Anna was at the salon having her roots tended to, she would have assumed it was Anna.

"What did they say when you interrupted them?" Karla asked, handing Lynn's phone to her.

"I didn't interrupt them," Lynn clarified. "I was very careful to make sure they didn't realize I had caught them in the act."

"How did you get your keys back?"

"I hid beside the house and sent Trina a text," Lynn explained. "I told her I was on my way there to find my keys and warned her I would ring the bell when I arrived." She grinned smugly. "Seconds after I sent that text, Leon Tyson scrambled out the back door and over the fence. I waited a minute or two, then walked up to the front door, and rang the bell. Trina answered, acting all casual and aloof. I found my keys, apologized for the intrusion, and left. I walked down the sidewalk, for appearance's sake, in case Trina was watching me, then doubled back and hid beside the house again. Sure enough, Leon hopped over the fence again and walked into Anna's house through the back door. He's very nimble for someone in a three-piece suit."

"Wow," Karla said, her head spinning with thoughts about what this meant and how it might relate to Fitz's murder.

"I took the long way home," Lynn continued. "I walked down the street behind Anna's house and, sure enough, found Leon's car parked on the side of the road. Legally, of course. Leon would never park illegally."

"Of course not," Karla agreed. "He might cheat on his wife with someone else's wife, but he'd never break a parking law. Perish the thought."

CHAPTER 15

RESERVE-A-TROLL

WHILE KARLA and Lynn were talking and waiting for Dean to question Karla, Rob showed up in the white, windowless coroner van and exchanged waves with them as a police officer escorted her inside to the crime scene.

Soon after, Dean emerged from the house. He, Lynn, and Karla sat on the porch steps at Mirabel so Karla could answer questions and give her statement.

"Could the bones belong to Viola Spencer?" Lynn speculated after Dean was finished asking Karla questions. "No one ever heard from her again after she left Bellbrook."

"I think it's a definite possibility," Dean agreed. "Hopefully, Rob can confirm it. She said the remains had been there for decades. She said she might have to consult with an anthropologist to help her with the autopsy."

"That sounds like a long process," Karla said.

"She said the teeth looked pretty good, so she

might be able to make an initial identity with dental records, then confirm it later with DNA and such."

"Does Rob think the person in the basement was murdered?" Karla asked.

Dean shrugged. "She believes the remains belonged to an adult female, but she was hesitant to narrow down the age or speculate on a cause of death."

"Whoever the mystery woman is, someone somewhere must be looking for her," Lynn observed. "Surely somebody loves and misses her."

"The good news, if there's anything good about finding a dead body, is that the house was locked and boarded up, so the body wasn't disturbed by animals or weather. Rob says that will make the autopsy a bit easier."

"Do you think someone killed her and hid her body in Bellflower because they knew it was sealed off from the outside world?" Karla asked. "What if Fitz was killed because he found the remains?" She stood up and paced in front of her parents while rapid-fire thoughts coursed through her head. "Maybe whoever killed the mystery woman killed Fitz too. Maybe they heard about the renovation and tried to move the remains, but Fitz caught them." She was speaking fast now. Almost too fast for Lynn and Dean to follow along. Her mind was like a jungle, and each thought was a vine. She swung from vine to vine faster than she could process the vine she was currently hanging on to. "Was this what Fitz wanted to show me? What if he told someone else about the remains? He could have inadvertently told the killer." She bit the inside of her cheek. "That would mean the killer was someone he knew."

"Sit down, love. You're making us dizzy," Lynn said.

"Your mother's right, La-la. You'll wear a hole in the porch."

Karla ignored their pleas. "I thought Trina or Leon might have killed Fitz," she thought out loud. "But this new—I mean old—body changes things. Now I'm not sure."

"Why, Trina?" Dean asked, trying to make eye contact with his fast-pacing daughter.

"Because she's having an affair with Leon Tyson," Lynn replied on behalf of their daughter. "I saw them with my own eyes and have photos to prove it." She looked at Karla. "But Trina was with Anna when Fitz was killed. Anna excused herself to lie down, and Trina went with her to help her settle, then Trina came back downstairs to the wake. After she returned, I left. Trina couldn't have done it."

"But Leon could," Dean uttered under his breath. "Maybe they were working together."

"Maybe what Dylan overheard between Fitz and Leon was correct after all," Karla suggested. "Maybe Fitz discovered that Leon and Trina were having an affair and blackmailed Leon. Trina said Fitz was a good friend and good listener. Maybe she confided in him about the affair, or maybe he caught them in the act."

"I caught them in the act," Lynn reminded them.

"As long as Fitz was alive, there would always be a possibility that he could expose the affair. If that happened, Leon and Trina would both lose their reputations and probably their marriages. They both had a huge motive to kill Fitz."

"And Fitz just let everyone believe he was having an affair with Trina when it was really Leon?" Dean asked.

"Why not?" Karla shrugged. "Fitz never seemed to care what people said about his personal life. Trina told me that she and Fitz were friends. Maybe he didn't mind covering for her."

"But neither Leon, nor Trina lived in Bellbrook thirty years ago," Lynn argued. "Trina moved away when she got married, and Leon's family moved here fifteen years ago. They couldn't have killed the mystery woman in the basement."

"Maybe the mystery woman's death was unrelated to Fitz's murder," Dean hypothesized.

"I hope so," Lynn said. "I don't think poor Anna could cope with her sister being a prime murder suspect. She's been through so much lately." Lynn stood up and brushed nothing off the thighs of her leggings. She looked at Dean. "Is it OK if I take Karla home? She's dealt with enough today. She needs a break."

"I'm fine. I don't need to leave," Karla pleaded, hoping to hang around long enough to talk to Rob about the remains in the basement.

"Well, there's no point in staying here, love. I don't think you, me, and Harry will get a chance to search for Gigi's treasure today."

"You might not have to search for it at all," Dean added.

"Why not?" Lynn asked hesitantly.

"Because the old leather duffle bag we found next to the remains is full of cash, jewelry, bearer bonds, and other valuables that match the inventory list from the missing safe deposit box."

Karla's and Lynn's jaws dropped.

"No one buries a headline like you, Dean," Lynn said, shaking her head.

"THANK YOU, but I ordered fizzy water." Karla nudged the glass of cabernet sauvignon toward her mother.

"Red wine contains resveratrol," Lynn explained, sliding the glass back toward her daughter, "a compound found in grapes that diffuses stress by impeding the functioning of an enzyme which controls stress in the brain." She smiled with pride. "Your best friend Rob taught me that. It's doctor-talk meaning, red wine will settle your nerves."

"My nerves are good. I don't need any reverse-it-all, or reserve-a-troll, or whatever you called it."

"Listen to your mother, young lady!"

"Rosalie! You're a sight for sore eyes," Karla said, sliding over to make room in the booth.

"I can't stay long," Rosalie warned. "I'm meeting the Petal Pushers for a drink soon."

"We'll take you for however long we can have you," Lynn added with a smile.

"Hello, ladies," Harry said, sliding into the booth next to Lynn at The Pavlovian Pub. "Is this for me?" he asked, eyeing the wine glass in front of him.

"It'll settle your nerves," Karla advised him.

"Then, I might need the whole bottle," he chuckled before taking a long sip.

"Where's Griff?" Lynn asked, peering around Harry as though Griff might be hiding there.

"He said thank you for the invitation, but he had to pick up his son from school and chauffeur him to swim practice."

A twinge of regret stirred within Karla. Was it regret that Griff wouldn't be joining them for a post-trauma-sharing libation, or regret that, had she made a few different choices, she could be watching her son's swim practice right now in a humid public pool, on uncomfortable metal bleachers beside her husband? Either possibility terrified her.

"Dean and I think the remains might belong to Viola Spencer," Lynn informed Harry and Rosalie. "What do you think?"

"I think you're right," Harry agreed, nodding. "No one else has ever gone missing from Bellbrook and never turned up again."

"Exactly!" Lynn and Harry clinked glasses, pleased with their deductive reasoning.

"What was the woman wearing?" Rosalie asked, slowly spinning her wineglass on the circular Pavlovian Pub beer mat.

Harry looked at Karla, unsure how to reply.

"She wasn't really wearing anything," Karla explained, without giving away details that the police wouldn't want her to divulge. "It was more like her clothes had collapsed around her remains."

"What did they look like?" Rosalie urged. "Did

you see the colour? Was there a coat? Jeans? High heels or running shoes?"

Karla opened her mouth to respond.

"Wait," Lynn raised her index finger toward Karla while looking at Rosalie. "Do you remember what Viola Spencer wore to Gigi's funeral?"

"I can picture her clear as day, like it was yesterday," Rosalie replied.

Before she left to join her gardening club, The Petal Pushers, at a reserved table elsewhere in the pub, Rosalie told them what Viola wore to Gigi's funeral—the last known sighting of the mysterious Viola Spencer.

Karla sent a text to Rob, asking if Rosalie's recollection matched the clothes found with the mystery remains. She knew Rob was busy moving the remains from Bellflower to the morgue, so she didn't expect an immediate response.

"If Viola died right after she went missing, she could have died wearing that outfit," Harry observed.

"Why would Viola run out of Gigi's funeral and go straight to Bellflower?" Lynn challenged. "There was nothing there for her, and the place was locked up."

"She could've had a key," Harry countered. "What if she knew where Gigi had hidden the contents of the safe deposit box and went back to Bellflower to steal it?"

"It makes sense," Lynn agreed. "Viola lived at Bellflower while she took care of Gigi. She had access to the entire house. She could have found the loot, or maybe in a lucid moment, Gigi told her where it was."

"Gigi's funeral would have been the perfect opportunity for Viola to sneak back to Bellflower, collect the loot, then slip out of town without being seen," Karla reasoned. "Grandma May, Harry, everyone was away from Bellflower at the funeral. Remember how you said everyone in town assumed Viola was upset about Gigi's death and getting dumped by the butcher's son? She probably hoped everyone would assume she left town because she was grieving and heartbroken, and that's exactly what happened. Except she didn't get out of town. Instead, she found herself behind a basement wall in an abandoned house where no one would find her for thirty years."

"I like your theory better than the rumours I've heard," Harry muttered into his wine glass.

"You've already heard rumours?" Karla asked, shocked that she was shocked by the efficiency of the Bellbrook rumour mill.

Karla had wondered what people were saying about the second body. She hadn't dared mention it out loud for fear of giving the rumour mongers ideas. If the thought that perhaps Grandma May knew about the body in the wall had crossed her mind, it must have occurred to other people too. In a town as small as Bellbrook, locals wouldn't be satisfied with simply having such thoughts, they would verbalize them. Karla knew it was a matter of time before speculation around her grandmother's potential knowledge about the body in the wall would become fodder for the local rumour mill. Karla needed to find out who was at rest in the wall, how they got there, and how she could prove that Grandma May had nothing to do with it.

"There's some speculation that May knew about the body behind the basement wall at Bellflower and locked up the house to keep it hidden," Harry confirmed. "They say that's why she never got around to fixing up the cottage."

"What?!" Karla and Lynn shouted in unison.

"Shhhh," Harry urged, making a calm-down gesture with his hands. "You know what people are like. If they don't know the answers, they make up far-fetched stories to fill in the blanks."

"Grandma May would never have covered up a death," Karla insisted.

"Of course, she wouldn't," Lynn assured Karla, then turned her attention to Harry. "My mother was as honest as a saint." She narrowed her eyes. "Who said it?"

"Never mind."

"Tell me!"

"No." Harry took a swig of wine. So much for settling his nerves. "You'll confront them and make a scene. Then, people will assume the rumour hit a nerve, so it must be true."

"I want to know who's spreading lies about my family." Lynn's palm landed hard on the wooden table. "Tell me right now, Harold Baxter Kincaid."

"No way, Lynn Maybelline Bell."

"Enough!" Karla interjected, placing her hand between their faces like a barrier. "You're acting like children. People are staring."

"He started it," Lynn said with her nose in the air.

"*He started it*," Harry mimicked in a whiny voice, crossing his arms in front of his chest.

"It doesn't matter who started it," Karla snapped, wondering when she became the adultiest adult at the table. "The best way to deal with rumours is to ignore them or prove them wrong."

"Which one are we doing?" Lynn asked.

"Both," Karla replied. "We'll ignore the gossip and solve both mysteries. The Bell name will be cleared, and the killer, or killers, will be behind bars." She looked from Lynn to Harry with wide eyes. "Got it?"

They nodded.

Harry excused himself to go to the bar and order appetizers for the table.

Karla suspected Harry's real motivation wasn't hunger, but a desire to put some space between him and Lynn while they both calmed down.

"That man is infuriating," Lynn hissed when Harry was out of earshot.

"That man cares about us. Especially you," Karla chided.

"He cares about you, and he cared about Grandma May. He tolerates me."

"Not true," Karla countered. "He was worried about you when you lost your keys and were late meeting us at Bellflower. I could tell. He worried that whoever killed Fitz had gotten to you."

"Really?" Lynn's tone softened, and she sighed. "I guess he means well. He can't help it if he's infuriating."

"He's family. If you can't be civil to him, be quiet."

Lynn hushed her with a look that told her Harry was on his way back to the booth.

"Karma," Lynn announced, topping up her glass

and changing the subject. "If Viola Spencer was trying to steal Gigi's money and jewelry, karma broke those floorboards to teach her a lesson. That's how the universe delivers justice." She took a long sip of red wine.

"Griff suspects the wood in the attic floor was rotten," Harry said, sliding into the booth next to Lynn. "Probably from an old leak in the roof. He didn't say anything about karma."

"Karma might have stopped Viola Spencer from stealing the family fortune, but that doesn't help us access it," Karla said. "The duffle bag and its contents are evidence in a police investigation. It could take years to get it back."

"We've waited this long, love. We can wait a little longer. I'm sure Dean will do whatever he can to speed up the process."

"What will you do with the money after the police return it?" Harry asked no one, leaning back while the server placed napkin pouches of cutlery in front of them.

Karla waited, expecting Lynn to reply. After all, Grandma May left her financial assets to Lynn, and the land, buildings, and contents to Karla. A duffle bag stuffed with cash, gold, jewelry, and investment certificates behind a basement wall kind of straddled the line between both inheritances. She expected Lynn to stake a claim for it.

"That's up to Karla," Lynn replied.

"It is?" Karla asked out loud instead of in her head.

Lynn paused mid-sip and looked at her.

"I thought we could split it," Karla suggested. "I've

already got a mansion, two cottages, and a nice piece of seaside real estate."

"Listen, love," Lynn began in a soft, sympathetic voice and placed her wine glass on the beer mat in front of her. "I know on the surface it seems like Grandma May favoured you in her will. But she had a reason. She was a very strategic woman. Nothing she did was accidental. Ever. Just like you."

They paused while the server delivered a platter of three-layer nachos and an order of hot artichoke spinach dip with toasted baguette slices for dipping.

"Grandma May didn't just leave you a mansion by the sea, she left you a huge responsibility. The property has been neglected. When the estate became too much for Grandma May to maintain, she gave up. She knew you'd have what it takes to restore Bellcroft to its former glory and that you would figure out how to best preserve our family legacy. She knew what she was doing when she made her will. She wanted to be certain, that if Gigi's safe deposit box contents were anywhere on that property, you would find it. This money belongs to you. I'm not bitter or jealous. If anything, love, I'm glad she left the biggest and hardest part of the inheritance to you. Because you can handle it. You're the only living Bell who can restore our family home."

And with that speech, the responsibility of preserving the Bell family legacy settled heavily on Karla's shoulders.

"I'm not sure if the money in the duffle bag, combined with my savings, will be enough to restore both cottages and the manor house." Karla hated being the bearer of disappointing news. "Then there are the ongoing costs. The property would have to earn enough income to cover its fixed expenses."

"You don't have to do it alone, love." Lynn reached around the pile of steaming nachos and took her daughter's hand. "I'll help however I can. You can use my inheritance to help pay for whatever you need to do."

Karla felt a sense of certainty in her gut that this was the reason Lynn was still in Bellbrook. She knew the magnitude of Grandma May's legacy would hit Karla like a ton of bricks. This was what Lynn meant when she said she needed to stay and support Karla.

"What about your retirement?" Karla asked, recalling Lynn's comment that her share of the inheritance was her post-retirement financial plan.

"It'll work itself out." Lynn smiled. "The universe hasn't let me down yet."

"I don't want to brag," Harry interjected, "but I've got a tidy sum squared away. It's amazing how much you can sock away when you live for free on your employer's land. I'd love to invest it all in Bellcroft."

Their support left Karla feeling relieved and pressured at the same time.

"Thanks," she said before she was interrupted by the chime of her cell phone.

"I hope that text isn't about another dead body at Bellflower," Lynn teased.

"Don't even joke about it," Harry jested in return.

"It's Rob," Karla said. "She sent a photo of the clothes that were found with the remains." She held out her phone so Lynn and Harry could see the photo of an outfit spread across a metal medical table with a measuring stick next to the shoes and skirt for scale. "Dark burgundy skirt, black satin blouse, dark burgundy blazer, black pantyhose, and black, low pumps."

"Exactly how Rosalie described Viola's funeral outfit."

How did you get behind the basement wall, Viola Spencer?

BULLIES & LIARS

OCTOBER 23RD

Karla wasn't a paranoid person, but she was always aware of her surroundings. So, she couldn't help but notice the animal-control officer following her and Gucci on their morning walk. The man in the Bellbrook town van wasn't even trying to be discreet; they'd even exchanged waves and smiles at one point. Was this a veiled threat from Leon Tyson? Did he want to make it clear to Karla that he could get to her through Gucci whenever he wanted? The only thing Karla hated more than liars were bullies. Leon Tyson was both. She knew the only way to deal with liars and bullies was to call them out and take away their power.

"Dad? Max?" Coming inside after their walk, Karla was surprised to find her father and sister sitting on the sofa, sipping blueberry-basil infused water. "Why are you here? Did we have plans that I forgot about?"

"Hi, La-la," Dean said.

Like she was making a toast, Max raised her water glass toward Karla and nodded in greeting.

Karla detached Gucci's black studded Versace leash from the matching collar, so the eager pup could run into the living room and launch himself onto the sofa to greet Dean and Max with as much enthusiasm as ten non-terrier dogs.

"Rob let us in," Dean said, tipping his head toward Rob who was in the kitchen making a new pitcher of infused water. "We came by to give you an update on the remains in the basement at Bellflower."

"Give *me* an update?" For an instant, this confused Karla, and she wondered why Dean and Max would include her in case updates.

"You're the homeowner," Max explained. "You're an interested party, if not a co-victim of a possible crime."

Co-victim? If her death was murder, Viola was the only victim as far as Karla was concerned.

"We're still waiting to confirm a couple of things, but we've concluded that the remains likely belonged to the woman Bellbrook knew as Viola Spencer," Dean confirmed. "Unfortunately, we can't notify Viola's next of kin because we can't find them."

"As far as we can tell, Viola Spencer never existed," Max added. "We can't find any official records for someone with that name and birthdate, and the tax information she provided when May hired her was fake."

"People don't abandon their old life and reinvent themselves for no reason," Rob pointed out, joining them in the living room. "Viola must have been running from something when she came to Bellbrook."

"Maybe whoever she was running from caught up with her," Karla suggested.

"We don't think so," Dean said. Then, he and Max looked at Rob.

Karla looked at her too.

"This is off the record," Rob said as a verbal disclaimer. "Until we've done more tests, and I've consulted a few experts, these are *unofficial* findings. Understood?"

"Totally," Karla agreed, repositioning herself and nestling into the club chair so she was facing Rob. "Spill."

"I don't think Viola Spencer, or whoever she was, was murdered," Rob disclosed. "There's no evidence of foul play. The cause of death was cervical fracture. Her remains displayed injuries consistent with a fall."

"She fell and broke her neck?" Karla asked, attempting to translate Rob's doctor-speak.

"Yes," Rob confirmed. "Her injuries are consistent with falling through the attic floor, crashing through the main floor, and landing behind the wall in the basement. Her death was instant."

"Griff walked us through the crime scene and showed us how he found her," Dean continued. "There was a lot of wood rot from an old leak in the roof. The leak was patched, but the damage was never dealt with, and the wood was unstable. Viola stepped on it and fell through. The momentum she picked up on her way down, combined with more structurally unsound wood, helped her breakthrough the floor behind the wall on the main floor and land in the basement."

"Griff suspected Fitz probably found the remains the same way," Max added. "Fitz probably looked in the attic, saw the hole in the floor and followed it to the basement. The basement wall around Viola's remains would have been misshapen"—Max made a curve with her hand to indicate how the wall would have bowed outward—"and discoloured because of the bacteria and gasses that would have been trapped behind the wall during the decomp process..."

"Got it." Karla waved her hand in a stop motion, not needing anymore graphic details. "Upon seeing the misshapen, discoloured wall, curiosity got the better of him, and Fitz made a hole to see what was going on behind it."

"Precisely," Dean said.

"But *why* was Viola Spencer in the attic at Bellflower?" Karla asked.

"We believe she was stealing the valuables we found in her duffle bag," Dean confirmed what everyone had already suspected. "She probably hid the valuables in the attic beforehand, so no one would find them before she was ready to make her move."

"She saw the perfect opportunity during Gigi's funeral because everyone in town was otherwise occupied," Max continued. "When she snuck into the attic to retrieve the stashed loot, she fell."

"And she never let go of the duffle bag," Rob added. "I believe she died gripping it."

A shiver ran up Karla's spine.

"This version of events supports Lynn's karma

theory," Karla said, grateful that one of the mysterious Bellflower deaths had a non-murderous explanation that didn't implicate anyone she loved.

"If Lynn's got a direct line to karma, can you get her to ask karma for some help with Fitz's murder case, please?" Max asked and Karla sensed from the undertone of frustration in her voice that she was only half joking.

"Did you hear about Leon and Trina's shenanigans?" Karla asked.

"Dad told me." Max nodded with a sigh. "Trina and Leon have a good motive, but we have witnesses who place both of them at Mr. Hughes's wake when Fitz was murdered."

"But Lynn, Rosalie, and I saw Leon loitering around Bellflower just before Fitz turned up dead," Karla refuted. "How could he be in two places at once?"

"This is the problem with eyewitness testimony." Dean shrugged and sighed as if everyone in the room understood and shared the shortfalls of eyewitness testimony.

"Isn't eyewitness testimony a good thing?" Karla probed.

"Depends on the situation," Dean replied. "In this case, it's not as reliable as I'd like. You see, our memories are highly susceptible to suggestion. Especially when dealing with multiple witnesses." He leaned forward and rested his elbows on his knees. "Let's say you witness a hit and run. While you're waiting for the police to arrive, you talk to the other bystanders and exchange stories about what you saw. You remember seeing a person in a green coat. You don't remember much else about, but you remember the green coat. A fellow bystander asks you if you saw the woman in the brown coat. Now that you've heard the suggestion that the coat was brown and worn by a woman, there's a good chance you'll adjust your memory so that you believe the coat was brown or green-brown, or something, and a woman was wearing it."

"So, if one or two people claim to have seen Leon and Trina at the wake, other people will work him into their memories too," Rob concluded.

"Exactly," Dean said. "Especially when people expect to see a certain thing. Like, everyone would expect to see Trina and Leon at Mr. Hughes's funeral."

"Then there's Dylan," Max added. "I couldn't find any witnesses to confirm he took Cash to the dog park, and his online alibi is shaky at best. We can place him inside the cottage, arguing with Fitz before you and Harry found his body, which is pretty compelling."

"Griff was at Bellflower too," Karla disclosed. "He left just as I arrived."

"We know, La-la," Dean said. "As of right now, Griff isn't a suspect."

"And his statement corroborates part of Dylan's statement," Max added. "It corroborates the argument Fitz and Dylan had, and Dylan's insistence that he stayed close to the door so he could leave before their argument got more heated. It gives Dylan's story credibility."

A wave of relief rose within Karla and left her body in a long exhale.

"My money's on Leon," Karla announced.

"Why?" they asked in unison.

"Because he's rattled. He doesn't act like someone with nothing to hide," Karla replied. "When I asked him if he overlooked building code violations for Fitz, he lied. At least I think he lied. He has a Tell."

Max twitched her pinky finger the way Karla did when she showed her Leon's Tell, and everyone nodded.

"He got offended and made vague threats about Animal Control picking up Gucci. Then today, Gucci and I ran into the same animal-control officer every time we turned a corner on our walk."

The adorable terrier perked up when he heard his name and jumped on Karla's lap. She stroked him as she spoke.

"You never told me this!" A bright shade of red heat washed across Dean's face.

"He also said some weird stuff to Rosalie when she ran into him at Bellflower the morning Fitz died. Something about her falling on the path between her house and Mirabel. She didn't take it as a threat, but given the context of his other odd behaviour, I think he could have been trying to intimidate her."

"He'll be disappointed then," Max said. "Rosalie Howard doesn't get intimidated easily."

"Leon can be kind of socially awkward, but I can't imagine him threatening anyone," Rob said.

"Is there a town bylaw against threats?" Max asked jokingly. "If there's a bylaw, he definitely wouldn't do it."

"I plan to visit him today," Karla said, having just decided. "I'll let you know if I find out anything new."

"Why?" Dean demanded. "Maybe you should stay away from him until this is over, La-la."

"The discovery of Gigi's money changed my financial situation. I'm making plans to restore the manor house and use it as the new *Just Task Me!* headquarters. I'm going to visit Leon to ask him about building permits and licences and stuff," Karla said, making it up as the words left her mouth.

"I'll go with you," Dean offered.

"I'm a big girl, Dad. I can handle myself. Besides, it's not like Leon will kill me in the busiest building in town in his glass-walled office."

"If Leon is guilty, he'll be more cautious about what he says in front of the chief of police," Max added. "I think there's a better chance that he'll let his guard down and say something useful if Karla goes alone and pushes his buttons."

Karla smiled at Max's show of support.

"Fine." Dean gave up. "But I'll be right outside if you need me, La-la."

CHAPTER 17
A MISOGYNIST SAYS WHAT

LEON WAS IN A MEETING. Molasses recommended that Karla make an appointment and come back, but she didn't want an appointment. She wanted to use the element of surprise to her advantage. She figured that, without time to prepare beforehand, Leon would be easier to catch off guard and more likely to say something self-incriminating.

"You might have a long wait," Molasses warned.

"That's fine." Karla smiled. "I'll be over there"—she pointed to the stone bench next to the indoor water feature—"checking my email and catching up on some work until Leon is available." She smiled and walked away before Molasses could argue with her.

While Molasses focussed on helping the next person in line, Karla craned her neck and stretched her body, trying inconspicuously to look down the hall. She wanted to know who Leon was meeting with. It was no use. Years of yoga and Pilates had helped keep Karla agile and flexible, but not enough to peer around corners. She drummed her fingers on the back of her phone and brainstormed a way to sneak a peek into Leon's glass office. Then she saw it. The sign for the restrooms had an arrow that pointed down the hall that led to Leon's transparent, fragile fortress.

Karla stood and smoothed her forest-green cigarette pants, buttoned the matching forest-green single-breasted blazer, and perfected her posture. She was prepared to unleash Corporate Karla if necessary. Corporate Karla knew how to match wits with liars and bullies.

She strode down the hall with her head held high, as if she belonged there, but walked on the balls of her feet to minimize the clicking of her stilettos on the marble floor. She didn't want Leon to hear her approaching.

At the end of the hall, she came face-to-face with another RESTROOMS sign. The arrow pointed left. Leon's office was right. She turned right.

Leon was pacing in his glass fortress. His hands were behind his back with his left thumb and middle finger encircling his right wrist like a handcuff. How apropos. He paced the same four or five steps, blocking her view of whoever was sitting in the chair he was pacing in front of.

After a few minutes of her eyes trailing left and right like she was watching a tennis match, Leon stopped pacing. When he lunged for the phone on the corner of his desk, it gave Karla a clear view of the person in front of whom he had been pacing.

She gasped! What was *he* doing there?

"We have to stop meeting like this."

Karla nearly jumped out of her skin at the nearness of the soft, unexpected voice in the otherwise silent hallway.

"Mrs. Hughes!" She flinched and brought her hand to her neck.

"That's an evolutionary defence mechanism, you know," Anna Hughes nodded at Karla's hand which was still clenched just below her neck. "My husband was an avid fan of the nature channel. He watched more wildlife documentaries than I can count," she recalled with a nostalgic gaze. "I used to watch with him sometimes. That's how I learned that wild animals instinctively protect their throats when they perceive a threat. Predators like to go for the throat. Throats are vulnerable."

"I don't think you're a threat, Mrs. Hughes," Karla said, smiling and lowering her hand. "You just startled me."

"Call me Anna," the petite brunette insisted. "Mrs. Hughes was my mother-in-law." She giggled at her own joke, and Karla giggled with her. "I didn't mean to scare you. I'm surprised you didn't hear me coming. Footsteps echo off these marble floors like we're in a cave or something."

"I was distracted," Karla admitted.

"Yes. You look a little confused. Can I help?"

"I was on my way to the ladies' room and took a wrong turn," Karla fibbed. "It's like finding my way through a glass maze."

Anna gave Karla directions—a straight line in the opposite direction—and even offered to accompany her to the door.

Karla declined.

"I know how you feel," Anna sympathized. "Since my husband died, it feels like the whole world has shifted slightly. Everything is exactly the same as it always was, yet nothing is quite the same as it used to be. You know what I mean, dear?"

"Yes," Karla replied. "Unfortunately, I do."

"I'm afraid it's not the world that's changed, it's us."

Karla nodded.

"You'll find your new normal," Anna assured her. "You uprooted your entire life to move back to Bellbrook. Then your grandmother died ahead of schedule, and you found two dead bodies in the cottage next door. A month like that is bound to ruffle anyone's reality." She smiled sweetly.

Grandma May died *ahead of schedule*? Karla was struck by the casualness of Anna's observations. She had a way of making a series of traumatic events sound almost mundane.

"I'm sure you're right," Karla agreed. "What brings you to the town hall today?"

"I need to speak with Leon Tyson," Anna said, then pressed her lips into a tight, thin line.

"Me too," Karla admitted. "Nothing serious, I hope." *Are you here to confront him about his affair with your sister?*

"Not serious," Anna said, smiling with her nose crinkled. "But necessary nonetheless."

Karla was certain that if Anna didn't know about Leon and Trina's affair yesterday, she knew today. There was no way Lynn would find out something so scandalous about her friend's sister and not share it with her. Especially since Lynn had photographic proof.

"Molas—Maria said he's in a meeting, and she doesn't know when he'll be free."

"Whatever." Anna flicked her wrist and made a sweeping motion. "I told her I'm interrupting him. She said she'd call and warn him. I've been trying to talk to him for days. It's easier to nail jelly to a wall than to corner Leon Tyson for five minutes."

Your sister, Trina, doesn't seem to have that problem.

Anna shifted her weight to peer around Karla into Leon's office. "Is that Griff Dixon?"

Karla turned her head and pretended to notice, for the first time, Griff sitting across from Leon.

"Oh, I guess it is," she said. "Wonder what he's doing here."

"Lynn told me that you and Griff spent some time together yesterday." Anna grinned and wiggled her head like it was about to explode. "She said the electricity between you was so intense that the sparks you two gave off practically singed her."

She made it sound like Griff and Karla were on a hot date, not discussing a renovation and stumbling across thirty-year-old human remains.

"My mother has a knack for exaggeration."

"Does she?" Anna winked. "If you say so."

"Well, I really need to use the ladies' room," Karla announced by way of ending this discussion. "Good luck with your interruption."

Karla didn't look back. When she reached the ladies

room she went inside, figuring if she at least washed her hands, it meant she didn't lie to Anna about needing to use the facilities. Leaving the washroom, she stopped at the fork in the hall. Should she go back to the stone bench and wait her turn to see Leon? Or should she sneak down the hall, peer into his office, and pretend she got lost again if someone caught her? She opted for the latter and snuck down the hall on the balls of her feet.

Griff had left. Leon and Anna both stood. The desk was between them like a partition.

Anna's mouth opened wide when she spoke, and she gesticulated wildly with both hands.

Leon stood still. His mouth was pursed into a tight pucker, like he was forcing himself not to speak.

Whatever *not serious, but necessary nonetheless* subject they were discussing must have been heated.

Could Anna have put together the same clues as Karla and come to the same conclusion? Maybe Lynn told Anna about Leon and Trina's affair and the blackmail scheme between Leon and Fitz, and Anna realized that Leon and Trina had a strong motive to kill Fitz. But Anna would never accept that her sister killed Fitz because no one wants to believe their sister is a murderer, and because Trina was at Mr. Hughes's wake when Fitz was killed. Maybe Anna stormed into Leon's office to tell him that she wouldn't stand by while the police investigate Trina for a murder Leon committed. She could threaten to expose Leon and Trina's affair, and the blackmail scheme, and put Leon in the frame for Fitz's murder. If any of Karla's assumptions were true, Anna could be in danger. Leon might go after her next to protect his tower of twisted secrets.

Karla returned to the stone bench next to the indoor water feature and unlocked her phone. She was about to type a text to Dean and Max, asking them to keep a protective eye on Anna Hughes, when she heard the rapid clicking of footsteps coming down the hall.

Anna appeared at the threshold of the hallway. She was panting. Her eyes were large and panicky.

Leon followed her, but, with his slow jog, was too far behind to catch her. He reached the lobby seconds after Anna broke into a run. With tears in her eyes, she picked up speed and charged through the double doors at the town hall entrance, disappearing into downtown Bellbrook.

Leon stopped and scanned the lobby. Anna was nowhere in sight. Karla watched as he caught his breath and straightened his tie. He glanced around, assessing who was present and what they might have observed. His eyes met Karla's, and he froze.

She smiled and gave him a small wave. "You just missed her," Karla purred.

Leon rushed toward her. "Shhh!" he urged, his shifty eyes glancing furtively around him.

"She couldn't get away from you fast enough." Karla twisted her face into an expression of mock confusion. "It was almost like she was trying to escape."

"Why don't we discuss this in my office." Leon smiled and gestured for Karla to go ahead of him.

"DID you put her up to that, Ms. Bell?" Leon demanded as he closed the glass door behind them.

"Did I put whom up to what, Mr. Tyson?" Karla asked, annunciating each word with intention. "You'll have to be more specific. You have so many secrets that it's hard to keep track of which one we're talking about."

Leon shook his head. "I have no secrets, Ms. Bell." He smacked his chest with both hands. "What you see is what you get." He grinned.

"Hmm…" Karla tapped her index finger against her chin for dramatic effect. "I see a liar, an adulterer, an extortionist, a small-dog bully, and possibly… a murderer."

Leon took a deep breath, trying to contain his emotions and retain his composure.

Thank you, Anna for rattling him for me, she thought with satisfaction.

Under the guise of impatiently shifting her weight, Karla positioned herself within arm's reach of the door. Just in case.

"None of it is true, Ms. Bell. Your suggestions are absurd," he began in a soft, even voice. "Are you delusional? It would be understandable if you were. You've lost your grandmother and found two dead bodies. That would be enough to push the strongest men over the edge, never mind you women with your delicate constitutions."

Delicate constitutions? Is this 1850?

"Misogynist says what?" she mumbled as she coughed into her fist and pretended to clear her throat.

"What?" Leon said. He placed his hands on his hips and tilted his ear toward Karla. "You said something?"

"Nope," she replied, wide-eyed and innocent as she could. "I didn't say anything. Just cleared my throat."

"You said something, Ms. Bell. I heard you. What did you say?"

"Nothing." She shrugged one shoulder. "Maybe you're having an auditory delusion. It would be understandable. You've been blackmailed for an illicit affair and became the prime suspect in a murder investigation. And that's just this week. It would be enough to push even the strongest women over the edge, never mind you men and your fragile masculinity."

"I'm not any of those things you called me," Leon said, ignoring the twist on his own insult that Karla just served him.

Karla raised her hand and spread her fingers. "You're a liar. You lied about being at Mr. Hughes's wake when Fitz was killed." She bent her thumb toward her palm. "You're an adulterer. I've seen the photos." She bent her index finger.

"Photos?" Leon hunched forward, made fists, and rested his knuckles on the desk.

"You're an extortionist because you participated in your own blackmail by overlooking Fitz's building code violations so he could cut corners and use the money he saved as the blackmail payments you owed him." She lowered her middle finger.

"You're a small-dog bully because you indirectly threatened to arrest Gucci if I didn't register him, then had your dog catcher follow us in his van."

"Now I know you're delusional, Ms. Bell." He laughed, and some spittle flew out of his mouth and landed on the desk.

She ignored his remark.

"And, since you were at the crime scene, lied about your alibi, and had a motive to kill the man who was blackmailing you, you are possibly a murderer." She lowered her pinky, then lowered her hand to her side.

"Did Anna Hughes put you up to this?"

"Why would she?"

"She did, didn't she?" he demanded. "I can't give her what she wants. I can't give her what doesn't exist."

"What did Anna want from you?"

"Don't play coy with me, Ms. Bell." He wagged his long index finger at her. "I'm not falling for it. I know Anna sent you."

"Anna Hughes is as much the reason I'm here as you are the reason that the pet police are following Gucci and me."

"There's no such thing as the pet police, and I didn't ask anyone to follow you, Ms. Bell."

"Whatever." She sighed. "What did you say that made Anna cry?"

"Nothing." Leon shook his head. "This an emotionally fragile time for her…"

"Don't explain grief to me," she interjected. "Did she confront you about your affair with Trina?"

Leon inhaled a deep breath, and as he exhaled, his demeanour relaxed. Relief. Why would Leon be relieved at the mention of his extra-marital affair with Trina? Was he relieved it was out in the open?

He removed his glasses and swept his forearm across his face, like he was wiping away sweat. Then he held his glasses toward the light and inspected the lenses.

"Yes," Leon replied, his right pinky twitching as he cleaned his left lens with his tie. "She called me all kinds of rude names and yelled at me for taking advantage of her sister."

"Oh," Karla said, shocked by the frankness and ease of his confession.

"Anna said if I ever contact Trina again, she'll give the photos to my wife, tell the police about the arrangement Fitz and I shared, and lobby the town council to fire me."

"Oh." Karla wasn't expecting Leon to provide more information than she asked for. She was unprepared for him to be forthcoming.

"That doesn't explain why Anna was crying," Karla observed. "It would explain if you were crying, but not her. What else happened between you?"

"Nothing," Leon said, his right pinky twitching as he returned his glasses to his face. "She said something about how she wouldn't have to deal with this if her husband were still here, burst into tears, and ran out of my office."

"Maybe I should check on her," Karla said, moving toward the door and calling Leon's bluff.

"Yes, perhaps you should," Leon agreed. "She was very upset." He sat down at his desk and laced his fingers together in front of him. "Was there anything else today, Ms. Bell?"

"I was going to talk to you about permits for renovating Bellcroft, the manor house, but I think that can wait." She let go of the door handle and let the door close. "One more thing. You were at Bellflower for a long time the day of Fitz's murder. You were already there when Lynn showed up, and you were still there when I arrived and saw you talking to Rosalie. It doesn't take that long to confirm a few building permits were properly posted in the window." She crossed her arms in front of her chest. "What were you really up to?"

Leon reached under the nose pads of his glasses with his thumb and index finger. He pinched the bridge of his nose like he was already fed up with today, and it was barely noon.

"I wanted to talk with Fitz," he admitted.

"About what?"

"Work stuff."

"Did you speak to him?"

"No," Leon claimed. "I knocked on the door, but no one answered. The door was unlocked so I let myself in. Fitz was in the basement. It sounded like he was taking down a wall or something. The dust stirred up by his hammering aggravated my dust allergy, so I had to get out of there. I sat in my car for a while, hoping he'd come outside, and I'd be able to catch him on a break."

"Did Fitz come outside?"

"No," Leon replied. "Dylan showed up. I heard them arguing from outside, so I left. I sat in my car and texted with Trina for a while. Griff Dixon came and went without going inside, either. When Dylan left, I got out of my car and saw Rosalie Howard." He waved her off with his hand. "You know the rest."

"You need to tell this to the police," Karla said.

"I only tell the police what my lawyer advises me to tell them."

Well, then I'll tell the police for you.

"Was there anything else, Ms. Bell? I feel a headache coming on."

Karla shook her head.

"Very good." Leon nodded and turned his attention to the computer monitor on the other side of his L-shaped desk. "Have a nice day."

CHAPTER 18

A PROFESSIONAL
SWINDLER

STEPPING into the brisk fall air, Karla replayed her baffling exchange with Leon. Something big was going on. Bigger than Leon and Trina's not-so-secret affair, and bigger than Leon and Fitz's scheme.

Karla knew from Anna's telltale nose crinkle that she had lied about the *not important* reason for her visit to Leon today. What did she want from him? Leon said he couldn't give Anna what she wanted because it didn't exist. What a strange riddle! Whatever they discussed was important enough for Anna to run away in tears.

Leon lied too. His pinky twitched the entire time he told Karla how Anna confronted him about his affair with Trina. Whatever Leon and Anna discussed must have been serious if Leon was willing to fess up to the affair so easily and risk damaging his reputation, tearing apart his marriage, and losing his job.

"La-la!"

Karla searched for the familiar voice.

"Over here!"

She found Dean hailing her with one arm while his other arm rested on the open window of a Town of Bellbrook utility van. The dog catcher! Did Dean track down the man who followed her and Gucci this morning?

Karla looked both ways and jogged across the street to join them.

"Hi, Dad!"

"La-la, this is Javed." Dean stood aside so Javed could poke his head through the driver's side window.

They exchanged smiles and nods.

"You're the animal-control officer who followed me and my dog this morning," she declared. "Who sent you?"

"I'm sorry," Javed said shaking his head. "Chief Sheridan was just telling me that I spooked you and your little dog. That wasn't my intention. No one sent me. I followed you under my own free will."

As far as apologies go, this one wasn't very comforting. Regardless of who sent him, Javed just admitted he intentionally stalked her and Gucci.

"Javed runs a renovation and repair business part time," Dean explained. "He was working up the nerve to approach you about giving you a quote to renovate the cottages."

"But you seemed engrossed in your thoughts, and I had trouble working up the nerve to introduce myself," Javed continued. "I'm sorry if I scared you."

"You creeped me out, Javed," Karla chided, realizing how crazy she must have sounded to Leon when she accused him—twice, but who's counting—of trying to intimidate her with the pet police.

Why didn't I say animal control? Or dog catcher? No wonder Leon thought I was delusional.

"Do you know Harry Kincaid?" Karla asked.

Javed nodded. "Everyone knows Harry."

"He's in charge of the renovation. You should speak to him."

"But I think he already gave the job to Griff's company, Fixin' by Dixon," Dean said, looking at Karla for confirmation.

"I think so too," Karla said. "But anything related to the reno goes through Harry."

"Got it," Javed said with a nod. "Again, I'm sorry for freaking you out."

"Well, that's another mystery solved," Dean said as Javed pulled away from the curb and drove off.

"Since yesterday, you've solved the mystery of whose remains were at Bellflower and the mystery of the creepy animal control officer. You're on a roll," Karla teased. "Just one more mystery to solve."

"It's a big one, La-la," Dean said as they crossed Main Street.

As they walked toward the parking lot where Karla had parked her car, she told Dean about her conversation with Leon, her interaction with Anna beforehand, and Anna's hasty, tearful departure from the town hall.

"It sounds like Leon admitted to his affair with Trina, so you'd stop asking questions," Dean surmised.

"That's what I thought!" Karla agreed.

"What could he and Anna want to hide that would be worse than his affair with Trina?" Dean pondered aloud. "Could Trina be pregnant?"

"No!" Karla replied, stifling a chuckle. "Trina is sixty-two years old, Dad. How many pregnant sexagenarians have you known?"

"I dunno, La-la," Dean replied. "Women are a mystery to me." He guided her around the corner toward the parking lot entrance. "If Leon and Trina didn't get themselves in trouble, the only thing that would be worse than the entire town finding out you're a fraudster and an adulterer would be the entire town finding out you're a—"

"Murderer!" they concluded in unison.

Dean's phone dinged, and they stopped while he checked it.

"Urgent?" Karla asked.

"Depends on your priorities, I guess," Dean said as he typed into his phone. "It's Max. She thinks she figured out Viola Spencer's real identity."

"That qualifies as urgent." Karla nodded.

"I told her to meet us in the parking lot." He locked his phone screen, pocketed his phone, then placed a hand on Karla's back and urged her along.

"HER REAL NAME WAS VALERIE SIMPSON," Max explained as Karla and Dean leafed through printouts of Valerie Simpson's mugshot collection. "She was originally from Winnipeg, Manitoba."

"She died a long way from home," Dean commented.

"She had other aliases too," Max continued. "She was a grifter who left a trail of outstanding arrest warrants between Winnipeg and Bellbrook. Her other names were Veronica Styles, Victoria Simon, and Vanessa Stone. She moved from town to town, befriending people and conning her elderly or vulnerable victims out of their life's savings."

"Were you able to contact her family?" Karla asked.

"Yes," Max replied. "They filed a missing person report one week after Gigi's funeral. Her sister said Viola—I mean, Valerie—had a long history of bad decisions, but she always called them at least once a week. The last time they heard from her was the day before Gigi's funeral. She told them she hoped to see them in a few weeks. They never heard from her again. They've provided photos and have offered to provide DNA so we can confirm the remains Griff found belonged to Viola—I mean Valerie Simpson."

"Sad," Karla muttered. "Her family has been worried about her for over thirty years. That's too long to wonder if someone you love is dead or alive."

"There's no doubt in my mind that she died during the commission of a crime," Dean said. "If she hadn't fallen through those rotted floorboards, she and Gigi's money would be long gone. That's one case we can officially close." He wrapped his large arm and hand around Max's shoulder and squeezed until her face scrunched up. "Good investigative work, Max'n'cheese."

"Dad! We're on duty," Max hissed with clenched

teeth, looking around to make sure no one saw the chief of police's display of paternal pride.

"Sorry, Officer," Dean said, releasing his youngest daughter.

"WHAT ARE YOU DOING HERE?" Karla asked.

Gucci bounced on his hind legs, excited to see his owner and desperate for her to acknowledge him.

"Catching up on paperwork," Rob said, gesturing to the files scattered around her open laptop. "It's easier to get stuff done here than at my office. Fewer interruptions."

"Until I moved in with you, I never realized how much paperwork you do," Karla commented, squatting down to give Gucci rubs and kisses. "I always thought your job was examining people, ordering tests, and writing prescriptions."

"It's because of the autopsies," Rob explained. "I've done three autopsies this year so far." She held up three fingers for emphasis.

"So far?" Karla asked with a grin. "Are you expecting more autopsies? Should I warn Dad and Max to brace themselves for an even bigger workload?"

"I hope not," Rob replied with a giggle. "I've never done three autopsies within weeks of each other." She pulled her red hair into a ponytail and secured it with the hair elastic she always wore on her right wrist. "I'm just reviewing my findings. You know, crossing the T's and dotting the I's. Making sure I didn't miss anything."

"I'm sure you didn't," Karla said. "You're the most thorough, detail-oriented person I've ever met."

"Looking at the findings with fresh eyes and reviewing them together has given me a new perspective."

"How?" Karla stood up, with Gucci in her arms and stroked him while she and Rob spoke.

"For starters, all three people died because of trauma from the neck up."

"Is that uncommon?" Karla asked, placing Gucci on the sofa and joining Rob at the dining room table.

"One third of all trauma deaths are related to neck and brain injuries," Rob advised. "So, yeah, having three out of three trauma-related deaths be from trauma above the neck is statistically unique."

Rob shuffled through the papers in front of her and pulled out two sheets of paper with human outlines on them. Both sheets were annotated with hand-written notes, arrows, and circles around the head and neck area.

"Look at these Autopsy Summary Reports," she continued. "Mr. Hughes and Fitz had the same cause of death. The circumstances of their deaths and the instruments of their demise were completely different, but their injuries were remarkably similar. The odds of this happening would be very small."

"Unless it was intentional," Karla observed, comparing the side-by-side reports over Rob's shoulder. "I guess it's even more unique because they happened so close together and in the same small town."

Rob started to say something, but Karla couldn't hear her over the sudden ringing of the doorbell and Gucci's frenzied explosion of yelps.

"I'll get it," Karla shouted over the small but loud dog.

"Hello, girls! Hello, Gucci!" Lynn swept into the house and strode past Karla into the kitchen without stopping. "These weigh a ton," she groaned, placing two reusable shopping bags on the island, then shaking out her hands. "I carried them all the way from Paradise Aisles."

"Why didn't you take your car?" Karla asked, unpacking the first bag while Lynn greeted Gucci and snuck him a dog treat from her jacket pocket.

"I'm trying to walk more and drive less," Lynn explained. "Better for me and better for the environment."

"What's this?" Rob asked, walking into the kitchen and assessing the groceries spread across the marble island.

"I'm teaching Karla how to make Grandma May's famous pasta casserole tonight," Lynn said, rubbing her hands together in anticipation. "You'll be home for dinner, won't you, Rob?"

"I'll be here," Rob said, nodding and grinning. "I wouldn't miss it for anything. Karla cooking is about as rare as a solar eclipse. I want to experience the miracle for myself."

"I cook!" Karla defended. "Sometimes." She shifted

uncomfortably. "When I can't get a table at a decent restaurant."

"Good!" Lynn interjected. "I've invited Max too. But she hasn't gotten back to me yet."

"I wouldn't count on Max," Karla said. "She and Dad are crazy busy at work. They just figured out Viola Spencer's true identity, and they're still trying to solve Fitz's murder."

"They know who Viola Spencer was?" Rob asked.

Karla told Lynn and Rob about Viola's long list of aliases, her travelling con game, and her family's thirty-year search for answers.

"Imagine!" Lynn said with a gasp. "A professional swindler right here in Bellbrook! She fooled the entire town. When she showed up in Bellbrook, everyone felt sorry for her because she was all alone and had fallen on hard times. People around here couldn't do enough to help her. And the whole time she was planning to take what she could get and disappear."

"Those rotted floorboards could have saved countless future victims from losing everything," Rob pointed out.

"Well, I hate to drop off groceries and run, but Anna's having a horrible day. I promised Trina I would stop by and visit."

"Her emotional state wasn't very good when she left the town hall earlier," Karla commiserated.

"How do you know?" Lynn asked.

"I was there," Karla admitted, then she told Lynn and Rob about her interaction with Anna, and her brief observation of Anna and Leon's interaction.

"I'll try to persuade Anna to tell me what went on

between her and Leon," Lynn offered. "She might open up to me if I can get Trina to give us some space. I know Trina means well and wants to take care of her sister, but she's smothering poor Anna with her constant fussing. I think Anna is getting fed up."

"Are things tense between Anna and Trina because of Trina's affair with Leon?" Rob asked.

"Things are tense since the affair has become the subject of local gossip," Lynn replied. "I suspect Anna already knew about the affair but didn't say anything. But now that most of Bellbrook knows, I'm afraid Anna might feel like Trina stole the spotlight. Everyone is so focussed on Fitz's murder and Trina and Leon's affair that they've stopped talking about Mr. Hughes. I'm afraid poor Anna feels like we've forgotten about him."

"Leave the groceries," Karla offered. "I'll put them away. You tend to Anna."

"I'll be back at 5 p.m.," Lynn said, walking toward the door. "Don't start cooking anything until I get back."

No worries, Karla thought.

"I'M VERY PROUD OF YOU," Rob said, washing the vegetables Lynn dropped off and placing them in a colander in the sink to dry.

"Thanks," Karla replied, putting the shredded asiago and meat in the fridge. "It's only a casserole. This doesn't mean I like cooking. I still hate it, but I want to learn to make some of the dishes Grandma May used to make."

"That's not what I meant," Rob clarified. "Though I'm proud of you for learning to feed yourself too."

"Making a reservation and ordering takeout are legitimate methods of feeding myself."

"I'm proud of you for giving Lynn a break and not punishing her anymore," Rob explained, ignoring Karla's defense for not cooking.

"I'm trying," Karla admitted. "Lynn is making a real effort to get along. Especially since I found Fitz's body. And she wants to help with restoring the manor house. Somehow, we've ended up on the same team."

"May would be very happy to see you and Lynn getting along."

"I hope so," Karla said.

"This week has been full of strange occurrences," Rob observed, putting the pasta in the cupboard. "First, two almost identical, yet statistically unlikely causes of death, and now Karla Bell cooking a meal and willingly enjoying it with her mother."

That was too many coincidences for Karla's liking.

CHAPTER 19

THE BARKING LOT

KARLA AND GUCCI had never been to The Barking Lot. Since his midday walk was later than usual, and he had so much pent-up energy to burn off, Karla thought today would be the perfect day to check out Bellbrook's new leash-free dog park. And if there was a small chance she might run into someone who remembered seeing Dylan and Cash at the park the day of Fitz's murder, that would be a happy coincidence.

Max had already canvassed the park and talked to local dog owners, but Max was too busy to canvas The Barking Lot every day. As Karla had to walk Gucci anyway, she figured she may as well fill two needs with one deed, as it were.

The Barking Lot was a large fenced-in greenspace next to Lakeview Park. The leash-free zone featured a double-gate entry system that only allowed one gate to open at a time, preventing dogs from escaping. Karla thought it was quite high tech and clever. There was also a bag dispenser for owners who forgot doggie bags. Random water spigots throughout the park meant fresh water was always available for thirsty pups. Part of the park was shaded with trees, and part was uncovered. There was a hill in the middle and benches scattered around the perimeter for dog owners to watch their pets while resting and socializing with each other.

Karla entered Barking Lot after only getting stuck between the high-tech gates once, then bent over and unleashed Gucci.

He took off like a bullet toward a group of dogs at the base of the hill.

She followed him slowly. The fallen autumn leaves rustled and crunched beneath her sneakers.

"I've never seen you here before, stranger."

"I've never been here before," Karla replied. "Gucci and I are Barking Lot newbies." Cash charged toward her and almost knocked her over with enthusiasm. "Hi, Cash."

"Cash loves it here," Dylan said. "We visit almost every day."

"I can see why," she said. "I've been meaning to bring Gucci but never got around to it until today."

Cash trotted ahead of them, making a straight line toward the pack of dogs at the base of the hill. Most of the dogs were medium or large size, and Karla lost sight of Gucci briefly when he was absorbed by the crowd of long-legs and fur.

Karla and Dylan walked and talked.

Dylan updated Karla on Fitz's funeral arrangements.

"How are you holding up?" Karla asked.

"I'm fine," Dylan replied, scratching the top of his curly head.

"It's OK if you're not fine," Karla reminded him.

"I know," he said, giving his head another scratch.

Clearly, Dylan wasn't as fine as he claimed.

"Have you found a paramedic program?" she asked.

"I'm too late to start this semester," Dylan replied. "But I've applied for January." He crossed his fingers as a sign of good luck.

"You're smart and eager," Karla assured him. "They'd be silly not to accept you."

"I hope they agree with you." He smiled.

Karla's phone dinged, and she paused to read the message.

Lynn: I might be late for dinner. I'll get there as soon as I can. Don't start without me.

Karla checked the time. Lynn wasn't due at Rob's house for another hour.

Karla: Everything OK?

Lynn: Anna's missing. Trina's worried. I promised I'd help search for her.

Karla: Can I help?

Lynn: No thank you. I'm sure she just needed time alone. She would be mortified if we made it a big deal. If I'm late, don't start cooking without me.

Karla replied with a thumbs-up, and she and Dylan resumed walking toward the pack of dogs.

"That's a serious face." Dylan wore a concerned expression.

"It was Lynn," Karla explained. "Anna Hughes is missing."

"Do they need help looking for her?" Dylan asked. "I can put Cash in the truck and drive around…"

"Lynn and Trina are looking," Karla interrupted. "They want to keep it quiet. They think too much fuss will upset Anna."

"I can't imagine her more upset than she was earlier."

Karla stopped in her tracks.

"You saw Anna earlier?"

Dylan nodded.

"Earlier today?"

He nodded again.

"She was upset?"

"Hysterical," he replied.

"Why?"

"I'm not sure," Dylan admitted. "I'm still confused by it."

"Tell me what happened," Karla said, changing direction and veering toward a nearby bench.

"Anna was already upset when she found me," Dylan began as they sat down.

"Found you?" Karla asked. "Had she been looking for you?"

"That was the impression I got."

They watched as a group of dogs, including Gucci, broke into an impromptu game of tag, chasing each other up and down the hill.

"She said no one would tell her the truth, and she needed me to be honest with her."

"About what?" Karla asked.

"That was the part that confused me," Dylan replied. "She wanted me to tell her about a job FITZ IT RIGHT THE FIRST TIME did in July in Loganville."

"You did a job in July in Loganville?"

Dylan nodded. "Dad tendered a bid to build the new amphitheatre in Loganville Park. We got the job and spent July completing it."

"You and Fitz built the Loganville Amphitheatre?" Karla asked.

"We had some help, but Dad and I did most of the work."

"I've driven past the amphitheatre. It's beautiful."

"Thanks," Dylan said, blushing. "It's really just a bigger, more complicated gazebo."

"Don't minimize your accomplishments." She poked him in the arm.

"I'm pretty proud of it," Dylan admitted.

"Why was Anna interested in the Loganville Amphitheatre?"

"I'm not sure," Dylan replied. "But she wanted proof."

"Proof that it exists?"

"No." Dylan shook his head. "Proof of when we built it and proof of who worked on it."

"What did you tell her?"

"The truth," Dylan replied with a half shrug. "We built it in July. Loganville was in a hurry. They wanted it finished in time for their town fair in August. We worked all day and sometimes all night. The town council even paid for us to stay at a local hotel for the last two weeks so we could use our commute time to work on it."

"Was Anna satisfied with your explanation?"

"No," Dylan replied. "It upset her even more. Then, she demanded to know who worked on it. She was particularly interested in the third week of July. I told her that me and my dad were there every day, all day. We had a crew of labourers, and Griff helped part of the week, between his own jobs."

"This upset her?" Karla asked.

"Yes," Dylan replied. "She demanded proof. I showed her photos on my phone that I took at the job site, and I showed her the booking in my online calendar."

"May I see the photos?"

"Sure." Dylan unlocked his phone and tapped the screen a few times. "Swipe left," he said, handing her the device.

Karla scrolled through about two dozen progress photos of the Loganville Amphitheatre. She tapped each photo to see the date and time the photo was taken. Most of the photos were of the structure, but a few had workers in the background or group shots of the proud crew posing in front of it. She looked extra hard at the photos Dylan took in the third week of July. The amphitheatre was nearly finished. There were multiple photos of Dylan and Fitz smiling in front of it, and one of Griff and Fitz pretending to crush the amphitheatre between their thumbs and forefingers.

"Did the photos calm her down?"

"Not at all," Dylan insisted. "She accused me of lying and being part of a conspiracy to protect him."

"Protect who?" Karla asked. "And why was she fixated on the third week of July?"

"Your guess is as good as mine," Dylan said. "She stormed off before I could ask her anything."

"What time did Anna visit you?" Karla asked, trying to figure out if the discussion with Dylan happened before or after Anna's discussion with Leon.

"About an hour ago," Dylan said as Karla's phone rang.

"It's Lynn," she said. "Excuse me."

"I've got to get Cash home for dinner, anyway," Dylan said, standing up. "Call me if you need help searching for Anna." He waved as he walked away.

Karla waved and thanked him for his offer as she answered Lynn's call.

"Hello?"

"Hi, love! We haven't found Anna yet. I wasn't worried before because I thought she just needed time alone. Trina's been making sure Anna is never alone, and I thought she just chose today to rebel."

"You don't sound certain," Karla commented. "Did something happen that changed your mind?"

"Trina called Anna's phone from the landline. The phone rang from the coat rack by the front door. We found Anna's phone in the pocket of her black trench coat."

"She left without taking her phone," Karla deduced.

"Yes," Lynn confirmed. "That's not like Anna. She always takes her cell phone everywhere she goes. Then, Trina realized that her own black trench coat was missing."

"Anna took the wrong coat," Karla concluded. "It's an honest mistake, Mother. The coats are identical."

"But Trina's cell phone was in her trench coat pocket."

"Was Trina's cell phone supposed to be in her coat pocket?"

"Yes!" Lynn said. "Trina swears that was where she left it." We searched the house and called Trina's phone. It's nowhere. We think when Anna took the coat, she accidentally took Trina's cell phone."

"Did Anna answer when you called Trina's number?"

"No."

This was worrisome. If Anna left her cell phone at home on purpose, it implied she didn't want to be found. If she had Trina's phone but didn't answer, it meant she either couldn't or wouldn't talk to anyone. Something horrible could have happened to her.

"Maybe it's time to expand the search," Karla suggested. "Maybe you should call Max or Dad."

She and Dylan exchanged another wave as his pickup truck drove out of the parking lot and past the dog park.

"That's what I think," Lynn agreed. "But Trina thinks Anna will get angry and accuse us of blowing the whole thing out of proportion. Especially if it turns out she just went for a walk or something."

"Can you unlock Anna's phone and use her Friends app to find Trina's phone?" Karla asked. "If you find Trina's phone, you'll find Anna, right?"

"We tried," Lynn said with a sigh that Karla could feel through the phone. "Apparently, Trina doesn't resemble Anna enough to trick the facial recognition on Anna's phone, and Trina doesn't know Anna's password." She sighed again. "Stupid technology," she muttered.

"Gucci and I are just leaving The Barking Lot. I'll drop him off at home and help you search. In the meantime, maybe you should call the police. Even if Trina doesn't agree."

"I'll talk to her again and see if I can convince her."

Karla shouted for Gucci and told him it was time to leave.

He didn't agree and made her chase him around the hill twice. She was grateful she had worn sneakers.

She finally corralled him and attached his leash. She explained the urgency of the situation to him on the way to the double-gate exit.

After managing to navigate the high-tech gate system without getting stranded again, she headed straight for the parking lot.

CHAPTER 20

A TWO-TIME MVP

As Karla and Gucci passed the soccer field, a rogue soccer ball crossed their path. Karla stopped it with her foot, did some fancy footwork, and sent it sailing back to centerfield with an impressive cross kick.

"Nice form." She turned toward the applause. "You're a natural." He smiled.

"I don't want to brag, but two games in a row, I was MVP of the Bellbrook Bruins Soccer Team." She grinned. "I was seven."

"I remember," Griff said, bending down to say hi to Gucci. "I was there. You played midfield, and I played defense."

"You seem to have passed along your love of the sport," Karla said, nodding to the children practicing on the field.

"All three of them play," he admitted with pride. "The twins play on the same team, so we only have to juggle two team schedules instead of three. But it's still chaotic some days."

"I can only imagine." Karla smiled. "I saw you at the town hall today. I would've said hello, but you were in Leon's office."

"Yeah, our daughters are on the same softball team," Griff elaborated. "Leon is the league commissioner next season and asked me to be his deputy commissioner."

Karla wanted to warn Griff that, if her suspicions were correct, he could end up being the commissioner, instead of the deputy, because it's unlikely Leon could commission a children's softball league from behind bars.

"Soccer *and* baseball. Busy family," she said instead.

"Don't forget swimming, karate, and music lessons," Griff added. "Kids are different than in our day, K. Everything is more structured and planned now."

"Did you accept Leon's offer?" Karla asked. "Am I conversing with the new deputy commissioner of the Bellbrook Junior Softball League?"

Griff cleared his throat and stood up straight. "Thank you for offering me the position, Leon. I'm flattered to be considered. However, between work, kids, and other demands, I'm unable to devote the time and energy that the position of deputy commissioner would require. I am, however, happy to help when I can in a lesser capacity."

"Very tactful." It was Karla's turn to applaud and smile. "Now, what was the real reason you turned it down."

Griff's posture relaxed, and his face softened. He leaned into her.

"I wouldn't work with Leon Tyson for all the money in the world," he whispered.

"You've heard the rumour, I take it."

"Which one?" Griff asked. "The Bellbrook gossip network is overworked and exhausted this week because of him."

"You heard the affair rumour?"

"Trina?"

Karla nodded. "And the rumour about Leon's involvement in a blackmail scheme?"

"With Uncle Fitz."

"I'm sorry," Karla said. "It must hurt to hear horrible accusations. Especially so soon after his death."

"It's sad," Griff concurred. "Sad that I'm not surprised by any of it."

"You're not?"

"Uncle Fitz was always looking for an easy way to make a fast buck or sneaking around with someone's wife," Griff says. "Sometimes I wonder what other shady stuff he did that we don't know about."

"Were you surprised to hear about Leon and Trina's affair?"

"Not really," Griff said. "Leon always gave me weird vibes. He was too perfect, you know? Never said or did the wrong thing. Never made a mistake but always looked down on those who did." He shook his head. "Those judging, holier-than-thou types always have the most to hide. I avoid Leon Tyson as much as I can."

"Then you must have been grateful when Anna Hughes burst into his office and interrupted your meeting."

"How'd you hear about that?"

"I ran into her beforehand," Karla replied. "She was on her way to interrupt Leon and force him to speak to her. Do you know what she wanted to talk to him about?"

"Something about an old building permit," Griff said. "I grabbed my coat and got out of there as fast as I could. As I was leaving, she demanded that he produce a building permit from July. As I closed the door, I heard Leon say, *For the last time, Anna. There is no permit. I can't help you.*"

"July?" Karla bit the inside of her cheek. "Anna was looking for information about a job Fitz and Dylan did in July. The Loganville Amphitheatre. Dylan said you helped."

"That's right," Griff said.

"Could Anna have wanted Leon to show her the building permit for the amphitheatre?"

"That would be impossible," Griff replied. "The amphitheatre is in Loganville, not Bellbrook. Loganville would have issued the permits."

"Well, Anna has mentioned the month of July twice today. For some reason, the third week of July is significant to her."

"I can't imagine why," Griff said. "Anna was out of town for most of July."

"She was?" This was news to Karla. "How do you know?"

"Because in the spring, when I gave her and Mr. Hughes a quote to renovate their washroom, she told me she wanted the work done in July when she would be visiting her brother in Alberta. Said she didn't want to live in a construction zone."

"I thought Mr. Hughes renovated the entire house by himself," Karla said. "Trina said Fitz helped him sometimes, and that's how she and Fitz became friends."

"Mr. Hughes renovated the washroom by himself. Uncle Fitz and I gave him quotes, but I'm sure the quotes were just to appease Anna. Mr. Hughes was too cheap to pay for professionals. He was determined to renovate their house on an impossibly small budget. Anna insisted that he hire professionals for the electrical and plumbing work. He promised her he would. He even got Uncle Fitz and I to give him quotes, but then he'd do the work himself when Anna wasn't around. I suspect he renovated the washroom while she was in Alberta and let her believe a professional did it. He even bragged to me about how much money he saved doing it himself."

"Mr. Hughes died in that washroom," Karla reminded him. "He died because the grab bar in the shower came off the wall." Karla started speed walking toward her car.

"Wait," Griff called, jogging to catch up to her. "Where are you going?"

"Do you have to get a building permit to renovate a washroom?" Karla asked, ignoring his question.

"If you move any of the existing plumbing and

electrical, then yes," Griff replied, huffing to talk and keep up with her at the same time. "If you're just doing a facelift and everything stays where it is, then no."

"Would the contractor's name appear on a building permit?" Karla asked as she and Gucci picked up speed when she caught sight of her car.

"It would be on the building permit application," Griff said. "Stop walking for a sec."

She turned and watched comprehension sweep across his handsome face.

"You think Anna blames whoever installed the grab bar for her husband's death." It was a statement, not a question. "And she wants to see the building permit application, so she knows who to blame."

Karla nodded and resumed walking.

Griff grabbed her elbow and stopped her. Her heart also stopped for a beat or two when he touched her.

"If Mr. Hughes did the work himself, there's a chance that he didn't bother getting a permit. He was too cheap to pay the permit and inspection fees," he said, then let go of her elbow.

Karla nodded, hyperaware of the warm spot on her elbow where he'd touched it. She started walking again, rapidly and repeatedly pressing the button that unlocked her car, listening for the familiar chirp.

Griff jogged ahead of her and Gucci and met them at the driver's door.

"Where are you rushing off to?"

"Anna's missing," she said, catching her breath. "I told Lynn I'd help search for her."

"Do you think Leon has her?"

"After our discussion, it crossed my mind," she admitted, picking up Gucci and opening the passenger door. "Let's pretend there was a permit. Assume Mr. Hughes hired Fitz—"

"He couldn't have hired Uncle Fitz," Griff interrupted. "Uncle Fitz worked on the amphitheatre job day and night for the entire month of July."

"Fine," Karla said, buckling Gucci's doggie seatbelt. "Assume he hired someone or did the work himself but followed the rules and got a permit." She closed the door and walked to the driver's side. "What if Leon *overlooked* a few code violations and approved the washroom." She used air quotes for *overlooked*. "Maybe Fitz wasn't the only person Leon was in cahoots with. He could have had arrangements with other trades people to overlook small code violations in exchange for a share of the savings."

"He never tried to set up that kind of arrangement with me," Griff said, sounding somewhere between relieved and offended.

"Doesn't mean he didn't do it with anyone else," Karla said. "If he thinks Anna is onto him, or close to proving his negligence contributed to her husband's death, she's in danger. If he killed Fitz to keep his secrets hidden, why not kill Anna too?"

"I'll come with you," he said, bolting to the passenger door.

"The twins," she said, gesturing toward the soccer field.

He looked back and forth between Karla and the soccer field.

"Promise me you'll call the police, K," he said. "And you'll stay away from Leon if you see him."

"I'll be fine, Griff. Get back to your kids."

TOO LITTLE, TOO LATE?

"Sorry I took so long," Karla said when Lynn and Rosalie stepped out of Anna's house and onto the front porch to greet her.

"That's OK, love," Lynn assured her. "Running late is a common symptom of your ADHD. So is hyperfocus, fidgeting, and forgetfulness." She smiled. "I've been learning about your condition."

"I ran into Griff, then I had to drop off Gucci," Karla explained, ignoring Lynn's newfound knowledge about her condition. "Have you heard from Anna?"

"Nothing yet," Lynn replied, gesturing for Rosalie to sit in the wicker rocking chair next to the front door. "Trina's out searching for her. We decided one of us should stay here in case Anna calls or shows up."

"I'm here to replace Lynn while you two join the search," Rosalie added.

"How will you contact Trina if Anna comes

home?" Karla asked. "Anna took Trina's phone by accident, and Trina's face can't fool Anna's phone."

"That's what I asked," Rosalie said, rocking slowly.

"We tried to unlock Anna's phone," Lynn reveals. "We thought if we could check her messages and her internet history, we might find a clue that would help us find her. We couldn't unlock it, but we discovered that anyone could answer the phone if it rings. Answering a call doesn't require facial recognition."

"So, if Lynn calls Trina on Anna's phone, Trina can answer even though she's not Anna," Rosalie summarized.

This discussion was starting to make Karla feel like someone was drawing a spirograph in her brain.

Lynn explained that Anna told Trina that she was just popping outside to the garage to find something. When Anna didn't come back, Trina went out to the garage to check on her. The garage door was open, but Anna was gone.

"Do you think Anna would mind if I looked in the garage?" Karla asked.

"There's no point, love. Anna's not there."

"I know," Karla acknowledged. "Maybe she left a clue that will help us find her."

They opened the double garage door and took in the scene.

To Karla, it looked like a typical garage. There were shelves for storage lining one wall, a workbench-tool storage unit against the second wall, and trash and recycling pails lined the third wall.

The storage wall and trash wall were tidy and organized. The workbench-tool storage wall was disorganized. Drawers were open and tools were strewn atop the workbench and the garage floor in front of it.

"Are the tools always so disorganized?" Karla asked.

"I don't know," Lynn replied. "I don't think I've been inside Anna's garage before."

They closed the garage door.

"Where should we start?" Karla asked. "It'll be dark soon. We should get going."

Lynn suggested they start by walking the route she and Anna took on their semi-regular morning walks.

They walked in anxious silence, focussing their senses on searching for any sign of Anna. Nothing. No sign of the missing woman. Karla could tell Lynn was growing more worried the closer they got to the end of the route without finding her.

As they walked through the schoolyard on their way back to Anna's house, Karla watched a mum with two toddlers decant water from a large bottle into two small sippy cups. This reminded her of watching Anna spike her coffee on the rocks with something from a flask.

"I think I know where we should check next," Karla said.

"Is THERE a time of day when this place *isn't* busy?" Karla asked, craning her neck to check the tables and booths at Déjà Brew. "It's almost dinnertime for crying out loud. Is coffee just before dinner a new trend I don't know about?"

"You're starting to sound like a true Bellbrookian again," Lynn chuffed. "It's nice to hear."

"What do you mean?" As the question left her mouth, it dawned on Karla that she had used the vague time benchmarks she hated. *Almost dinnertime,* and *just before dinner.* "Never mind," she mumbled, hoping Lynn didn't even hear the question.

"I don't see her, do you?" Lynn asked.

"No." Karla shook her head. "But let's take a stroll past the tables anyway. Just in case."

"Good idea."

"Hi, Bells!" cooed a blonde chin-length bob with lowlights at The Posers table.

"Hi, ladies," Lynn said, heading toward them. "This is my daug—"

"We know Karla," said The Posers ponytailed leader. The Head Poser, Karla decided to call her. "We met her the other day."

"That's right," Karla said with the brightest, fakest smile she could muster. "So nice to see you all again." *Do you ever go home?* "We met the other day. I ran into Anna Hughes while I was waiting in line." She made intense eye contact with the head poser. "You remember, right? Anna"—Karla made a pouring motion with one hand into a pretend cup she was holding in the other—"spiked her coffee."

"I sure do." The head poser nodded enthusiastically. "Anna's been"—the head poser made the same pretend pouring motion as Karla—"spiking her coffee a lot since Mr. Hughes died. She never did it before."

"Did you happen to notice if Anna spiked her coffee today?" Karla asked.

The head poser nodded, and her chestnut brown ponytail bounced. "She sure did." She pointed to the condiment station near the door. "Right over there."

"Both times," piped in the pixie cut.

"Anna was here twice today?" Lynn asked.

"She sure was," the head poser replied. "In fact, you just missed her. She ran out of here and chased Leon Tyson down Main Street about a half an hour ago."

"What?" Lynn asked.

"*She* chased *him*?" Karla asked, confused. She was certain that if anything bad had happened to Anna, it would be because *he* hunted her down, not because *she* chased him.

"She sure did," said the head poser.

"Leon took one step inside Déjà Brew, made eye contact with Anna, and left. He looked like he saw a ghost. She saw him and took off after him," explained the blonde chin-length bob with lowlights.

"Which way did they go?" Lynn asked, already tugging Karla's sleeve.

"Toward the town hall," replied the pixie cut.

"Thank you, ladies," Karla called as Lynn yanked her toward the door.

"But the town hall closed at four-thirty," Lynn said as they hustled down Main Street. "Even if we could get in, I doubt Leon will still be there."

"Just because the office closed to the public doesn't mean no one is there," Karla said, trying to keep their hope alive. "We'll find a way in."

"I'll phone Trina and tell her what The Posers said." Lynn already had the phone up to her ear. "Hopefully this will convince her that we should call the police."

They continued in silence while Lynn waited for Trina to answer the phone.

"Voicemail," Lynn said with a pout. "Why on earth would Anna chase Leon down the street?" she asked. "And why did he turn and leave when he saw her?"

"I suspect Anna believes Leon was involved in Mr. Hughes's death," Karla said.

"That's ridiculous," Lynn scoffed. "Mr. Hughes slipped getting out of the shower. Unless Leon was with him, how could he possibly be involved?"

As they walked, Karla told Lynn about her conversations with Dylan and Griff, and her theory that Anna believed Leon overlooked code violations that caused the grab bar to detach from the wall.

"If she's right about Leon and has proof, he might kill her," Lynn said, picking up speed. "He could be torturing her inside the town hall as we speak."

From the corner of her eye, Karla spotted Molasses getting into her car. She'd recognize that red perm anywhere. She nudged Lynn and pointed.

"Maria!" Lynn waved her hand over her head. "Woohoo! Maria!"

"Hi, Lynn," Molasses said with a smile. "How's your left hip? Any snow or rain you want to warn me about?"

"My right sinus is a bit throbby, now that you mention it," Lynn said, rubbing her forehead just above her eye. "We might get some light rain showers tonight or tomorrow morning." She shook her head and refocussed. "Listen, Maria, Karla and I really need to get inside the town hall. It's urgent."

"Urgent?" Molasses closed her car door, without getting inside. "What happened? Tell me everything."

Karla noticed Leon's car in the parking lot. A sign he was still there. She had to get in there.

"I left something in the ladies' room," Karla blurted the lie, before Lynn could say things that might make Molasses think they were unstable or shared the same altered version of reality. "I really need to get it back."

"I checked the washrooms before I locked up for the day," Molasses said. "I didn't see anything. Maybe you left it someplace else."

"It's very small," Lynn continued the lie. "And very valuable. Sentimental value." Lynn lowered her gaze and dabbed the corner of her eye. "It belonged to my mum."

Award-worthy performance.

"It was one of Grandma May's pearl earrings," Karla added, compounding their lie. "The earring might have camouflaged with the marble floor," she suggested with urgency. "I've already searched every-where else." *May as well keep lying. In for a penny, in for a pound, and all that.* "It's either in the ladies' room or on the floor in Leon's office."

"I can't let you into Leon's office. I don't have a key for his door," Molasses said, taking steps away from her car and toward town hall. "But I can let you into the washroom and help you search."

"Oh," Lynn said. "There's no need for you to crawl

around on the washroom floor, Maria." Lynn shook her head. "It'll aggravate your bad knee."

Molasses had a bad knee? How did Lynn know that?

"Oh, my knee is great now, Lynn." Molasses spoke directly to Lynn and unlocked both locks on the town hall doors without looking. "I had that non-invasive TKA surgery. My knee feels twenty years younger."

"Awww, that's good," Lynn said as she and Karla stepped inside, and Molasses closed the door behind them. "Karla would have had to line up to see you before she saw Leon. Maybe you could check around your desk while Karla and I check the ladies' room."

"Good thinking," Karla added. "Before I saw Leon, I sat on the bench by the waterfall. The earring could be there too."

"I'll check around my desk and the bench. You girls search the ladies' room," Molasses agreed. "If we don't find it, Leon might still be in his office. He's here most nights until at least 6 p.m."

That was exactly what Karla was hoping.

KARLA AND LYNN slipped off their shoes so their sneakers squeaking on the marble floor wouldn't alert Leon.

"We can use them as weapons if we have to take down Leon to save Anna," Lynn suggested, holding up her white sneakers.

As they navigated the glass maze that led to Leon's

office, Lynn held her phone to hear ear twice. Both times she lowered it with a disappointed huff.

"What's wrong?" Karla asked.

"I'm trying to call Trina but she's not answering. I want to tell her what The Posers said."

"Maybe the phone died," Karla suggested. "When you and Trina tried to unlock Anna's phone, did you notice the battery level?"

"No," Lynn said. "It didn't occur to me to look at the battery level."

They slowed down and braced themselves to confront Leon. If he was there. They peered around the corner.

Leon was sitting at his desk, organizing a stack of file folders. His tie was loosened, and the knot rested on the desktop. His top two buttons were undone, and his sleeves were rolled up to his elbows. He was the embodiment of fatigue and defeat.

"If she's not here, then where—" Lynn huffed and stomped toward Leon's office door.

No! Karla thought. *We haven't discussed this. What's our plan?*

"Where is she?!" Lynn demanded, storming through the door. "What did you do to her?" Lynn's eyes scanned the small office like she was expecting Anna to jump out and yell, "Surprise!"

"Who are you talki—" He stopped mid-word when Karla entered the office and stood next to Lynn. "What are you doing here?" He glared at their socked feet. "Why aren't you wearing shoes?" He checked his watch. "How did you get in?"

"You first," Lynn commanded. "Where's Anna? What did you do to her?"

"I don't know what you're talking about."

Karla had to admit, Leon's confusion appeared genuine. His right pinky hadn't twitched once since Lynn confronted him.

"Anna Hughes is missing," Karla explained in her calmest, most even voice. "She was last seen chasing you down Main Street from Déjà Brew toward here."

"I was faster than her," Leon admitted. "I got here and locked the door before she caught up to me."

"Where did she go?" Karla asked.

"How would I know?" Leon said. "I didn't hang around and watch her. I avoid that woman like the plague. She's unhinged." He removed his glasses and wiped his whole face with his hand. "I know Anna is missing. Trina has been texting me updates and telling me how worried she is. So, of course I sent Trina a text and told her about Anna chasing me out of Déjà Brew. If I harmed Anna, like you seem to think, why would I text her sister and tell her that I saw her?"

"To cover your tracks," Lynn accused.

"Delusions must run in the Bell family," Leon said with a chuckle.

"Hey!!" Lynn shouted, but Karla touched her arm and gave her a headshake-facial expression combo that said, *Don't bother.*

"Are you texting Trina on her cell phone?" Karla asked.

"Where else would I text her, Ms. Bell?"

"Trina doesn't have her cell phone," Lynn informed him, then explained to Leon how Anna took

Trina's coat by accident, and Trina's cell phone was in the pocket.

"Impossible!" Leon scoffed and a mist of spittle sprayed his mouth and chin. "Trina and I have been texting each other all day."

"Since lunch, you've been texting with Anna on Trina's phone," Lynn said.

"Preposterous!" Leon sounded confident, but the sideways glance he gave his phone betrayed his doubts. "Trina did seem a little off," Leon said, glowering at his phone with his eyebrows squeezed together. "I thought she wasn't her normal self because she was worried about Anna."

"Trina's not her normal self because she's not Trina!" Lynn said again.

"Call her," Karla suggested. "If Trina answers and we hear her voice, we'll believe that you've been texting with Trina all day. If we hear Anna's voice, you'll know we're right about her having Trina's phone."

"Fine," Leon agreed, picking up his phone.

He placed the call on speaker and placed the phone in the middle of the desk. Trina's phone number flashed on the screen as her phone rang in the otherwise silent office. After four rings, voicemail.

Leon ended the call before the beep and left the phone on the desk. They stared at it and waited.

The phone vibrated and spun.

"It's a text," Leon said, picking up the phone. "Can't talk. Still searching for Anna," he read aloud, then uttered a curse word under his breath and tossed the phone onto his pile of file folders.

"We rest our case," Lynn said.

"What did Anna want when she interrupted you and Griff today?" Karla asked. "You said you couldn't give it to her because it didn't exist. What was it?"

"Copies of the building permit and permit application for the Hughes's washroom renovation in July."

I knew it!

"Was it really non-existent, or did you destroy it?" Lynn asked.

Karla held her breath and kept a careful watch over Leon's right pinky finger as she waited for his response.

"I would never destroy an official document, Ms. Bell," Leon replied, his fingers as still as stones. "It doesn't exist. A building permit was never granted for the Hughes's washroom renovation because nobody applied for one."

"Now, do us another favour. Phone Anna. Trina has Anna's phone, and she's not answering my calls. Maybe she'll answer if she sees your number."

Leon nodded and did as Lynn asked.

They watched as the phone rang. After four rings, voicemail. Leon ended the call before the beep.

"Where are they?" Karla asked, searching Leon and Lynn's eyes for answers. "Are they together?"

"Trina's on my Friends app," Leon told them. "I can tell you where her phone is. That should lead you to Anna, and maybe she can lead you to Trina."

"I hope it's not too little, too late," Lynn said, putting on her shoes.

"Story of my life," Leon said, unlocking his phone.

CHAPTER 22
GESUNDHEIT!

"Do you think Molasses believed we found the earring in Leon's office?" Karla asked as they cruised along Main Street. "I almost fainted when she asked if she could see it."

"I held up a Tic Tac I found in my coat pocket and walked fast," Lynn said. "She saw a small white blur. I'm sure she fell for it." She slammed her phone into her lap in frustration. "Where is Trina? Why isn't she answering Anna's phone?!"

"Has Rosalie heard from them?"

"No," Lynn replied. "She dispatched Harry to track down Trina."

"So now we have a searcher searching for the missing searcher?" Karla mused.

Lynn nodded. "I told Rosalie where we're going. She said if she doesn't hear from us in fifteen minutes, she'll call the police."

Karla nodded in acknowledgement. "Maybe when we find one sister, we'll find the other."

"That's what I'm afraid of," Lynn admitted. "What if Trina harmed Anna?"

"Why would Trina harm Anna?" Karla asked.

"Hear me out," Lynn began. "Fitz used his knowledge about Trina and Leon's affair to coerce Leon into their blackmail scheme."

"Right," Karla agreed.

"What if Fitz blackmailed Trina too?" Lynn suggested. "Why extort money from one person when you can extort money from two?"

"You think Trina killed Fitz to escape his blackmail demands and stop him from exposing her affair with Leon?"

"Yes," Lynn replied. "Then, she tried to frame Leon for Fitz's murder. But somehow, Anna discovered the truth. I'm not sure how, maybe while she was searching for someone to blame for Mr. Hughes's death."

"Trina loves Anna," Karla argued. "I've seen how close they are. Trina would never hurt her. She's been so attentive and supportive since Mr. Hughes died."

"And overbearing," Lynn added. "Is she doting on Anna out of love or fear? Have you heard the saying, keep your friends close and your enemies closer?"

Karla nodded in acknowledgement. "Trina's concern might be less about Anna's wellbeing than about preventing Anna from discovering a tragic truth."

"Exactly!" Lynn declared. "Or maybe Anna is right about Leon overlooking the shoddy work that led to Mr. Hughes's death and found evidence that Trina knew about it."

"She does have access to Trina's phone, and all the information in it," Karla reasoned out loud. "But Trina was at Mr. Hughes's wake when Fitz was killed."

"Half the people at the wake swear they saw Leon too. But we know for a fact he wasn't there."

"Good point."

Karla turned onto the long twisty driveway.

"Turn off your headlights," Lynn instructed. "We don't want to scare her off."

Karla switched the automatic headlights to manual, and they turned off. She pulled over and rolled to a stop. "Maybe we should park here and walk the rest of the way."

They crept up the driveway, arm in arm. The sun had set, and they navigated the twists and turns by memory.

"Where should we look first?" Lynn whispered.

"Leon's Friends app placed Trina's phone between Bellflower and Mirabel," Karla replied. "She could be in either cottage."

Before the cottages came into view, a quick burst of light flashed from the direction of Bellflower. A flashlight? A shooting star?

"I guess we'll start with Bellflower," Karla whispered.

They approached the dilapidated cottage and stood in silence, listening for signs of life. Nothing.

The crime scene tape blocking the door was still intact, but a sheet of weathered plywood laid on the porch below the window it once covered

"Let's go in," Lynn whispered, pulling her keys from her pocket as quietly as possible.

They climbed the creaky steps, and Karla tested the door in case it was already unlocked. It wasn't. Yellow police tape still covered the hole where the key would go into the lock. She nodded at Lynn and stood aside.

Lynn punctured the crime scene tape with the key and unlocked the door. Then, she fisted her keys and placed them silently in her pocket.

The hinges creaked and groaned in protest as Karla cautiously opened the door. She'd only walked through this door twice in her life, and both times there had been a dead body waiting for her on the other side.

Please don't be dead. Please don't be dead.

"Anna?" she called quietly. "Are you here, Anna?"

They crept farther into the dark cottage. The dust was already starting to tickle Karla's eyes and nose. She cleared her throat.

"It's just us, Anna," Lynn used a comforting sing-song voice. "Just me and Karla. We just want to make sure you're all right."

They stopped and used the flashlights on their phones to illuminate the room. Then they cleared the kitchen and washroom. Nothing but dust bunnies, and possibly one mouse that Karla hoped was actually a super-fast dust bunny she and Lynn had disturbed with their movement.

"Shall we check the basement?" Lynn asked.

"Uh-uh," Karla replied, shaking her head. "They say bad things happen in threes. With my luck, I'll find another body down there."

"That's not funny!" Lynn stifled a laugh and

swatted her daughter's arm, chiding her ill-timed, dark humour.

"Let's check the bedrooms first," Karla suggested. "We'll check the basement as a last resort.

They stood in the doorway and checked the larger bedroom with the flashlights on their phones. Nothing.

Karla braced herself to check the smaller bedroom. The bedroom where Fitz took his last breath.

They stood in the threshold and flashed their beams of light into the small room. Karla's beam landed on Fitz's blood smear on the wall. She whisked the light away from the bloodstain, shuddered, and declared the room empty. Her nose twitched, tickled by the dust. She thought she might sneeze, but the sensation subsided.

"Basement?" Lynn asked. "I'll go. You wait up here with your flashlight. It'll give me a beacon to find my way back."

"I'll go with you," Karla said.

She felt a tickle in her nose again, and it began to twitch.

Ah-ah-ah-choo! She sneezed into the crook of her arm.

"Gesundheit!"

How did Lynn do that? How did she make her voice sound like somebody else in another room?

CHAPTER 23

BLINK TWICE

KARLA MADE eye contact with Lynn. "Thank you?" she whispered, hoping her mother would take credit for the ventriloquism-gesundheit trick.

Lynn shook her head, then reached into her coat pocket, and handed Karla a wadded, yet unused tissue.

"Thanks," Karla mouthed, then wiped her nose.

The tissue smelled like stale breath mints, dog treats, and lint.

Lynn raised her index finger to her lips.

Karla nodded in acknowledgment.

"Anna?" Lynn said in a tone of voice most adults reserve for comforting a distraught child. "Anna, dear, where are you?" She tippy toed two steps toward the living room. "We just want to make sure you're OK." She motioned for Karla to tiptoe after her. "Trina's worried about you." Two more sneaky steps forward. "I'm worried too. Why aren't you answering Trina's phone? Did you realize you took the wrong coat and phone by accident?"

"It wasn't an accident."

Like they'd choreographed it beforehand, Karla and Lynn trained their flashlights in tandem toward the disembodied voice.

Anna Hughes squinted into the sudden, harsh brightness and blocked her eyes with the back of her left hand. Her right hand was behind her back.

"I needed her phone to trick Leon into giving me the building permit."

"Did it work?" Karla asked.

Anna shook her head vigorously, and Karla could see suspended dust particles scatter in the illuminated air around her. "There is no permit."

"Anna, why did you hide from us?"

"I hoped you'd leave."

"We are leaving, and you're coming with us," Lynn informed her. "We're taking you home to—"

"No," Anna said resolutely.

Karla was fixated on Anna's missing right hand. Why was it still behind her back? What was she hiding?

"Anna, what's in your right hand?" Karla asked, flashing her beam of light where Anna's hand disappeared behind her back.

"Nothing," Anna said, crinkling her nose.

"That's a lie," Karla said. "You have a Tell. I know when you're lying."

"Lynn mentioned your weird superpower for spotting lies," Anna said, smirking. "Just like her superpower for predicting precipitation. What's my Tell?"

"Show us what's in your right hand, and Karla will tell you," Lynn negotiated.

Karla held her breath as Anna's right hand slowly came into view and revealed the pneumatic nail gun she was gripping.

This explained why the tools were strewn about Anna's garage.

Her hand didn't stop. She brought the nail gun out from behind her back, then raised it to her right temple.

Karla and Lynn gasped.

Lynn lowered her hand from her mouth. "What are you doing, Anna?"

"Returning to the scene of the crime," Anna said. "Well, as close as I can. I should be in the small bedroom, but you're blocking my path so, until you move, this is the closest I can get to returning to the scene of the crime."

She knows the small bedroom is a holdback!

Anna appraised their shocked expressions. "That's what criminals do, right? They return to the scene of the crime?"

Lynn looked from Anna to Karla, clearly confused.

"Fitz died in the smaller bedroom," Karla disclosed to Lynn. "Aside from the police, Harry, and me, only the killer would know that. It's a holdback."

Mouth agape, Lynn spun her head toward Anna. "*You* murdered Fitz?"

Anna nodded.

"That's impossible," Lynn argued. "You were at your husband's funeral. You became overwhelmed on the drive from the service to the wake. When you got there, you went upstairs to lie down. I saw you. I offered to sit with you, but you said you wanted to be alone. I watched Trina take you upstairs, and I saw her come back down. She told me you were tired and fell asleep as soon as your head hit the pillow."

"I snuck out," Anna admitted. "It was easy. I learned from the best. I've been watching Trina sneak around with Leon for months. She had no idea I was onto them."

"How did you get past everyone?" Lynn asked. "There were at least a hundred people inside, outside, everywhere. No one noticed you?"

"I made myself invisible." Anna replied. "I changed into a dress that was very similar to Trina's. Then I let my hair down, because she wore her hair down that day, put on her black trench coat and her sunglasses, and walked out the front door." She shrugged her left shoulder. "A couple of people nodded and said, *Hi, Trina* or *Sorry for your loss*. I just nodded and kept going."

"Put down the gun, Anna," Lynn pleaded. "Your arm must be tired."

Anna shook her head. "An eye for an eye." She sniffled as tears welled up in her eyes. "I thought Fitz killed my husband with his slipshod workmanship." Her voice cracked. "I was wrong." She sobbed. "I killed an innocent man!" she wailed.

"Lower the gun, Anna." Lynn raised her hands in a conciliatory, we-come-in-peace gesture. "Karla and I will stay over here. We won't come any closer. I promise."

Anna's eyes shifted back and forth from Lynn to

Karla several times before she tentatively lowered the nail gun to her side.

"Why did you believe Fitz installed the grab bar?" Karla asked.

"Because my husband TOLD ME Fitz renovated the entire washroom," she shouted. "*Hmph!* Fitz's murder is my husband's fault. If he hadn't lied to me, Fitz would still be here, spreading his low-quality, substandard repairs all over Bellbrook."

"Fitz must have denied it when you accused him," Lynn observed.

"He denied it all right," Anna confirmed. "He insisted that he didn't lift a finger in our washroom. But why would I believe Fitz over my dearly departed husband? Everyone knew Fitz was a liar who thought the rules of human decency didn't apply to him." She gesticulated with both hands, waving the nail gun in front of her. "My husband was a good man." She chuckled and tapped the toe of her foot. "But he was a CHEAP man. If he wasn't so miserly and had paid professionals, LIKE HE PROMISED ME HE WOULD, Fitz would still be alive." She shook her head, indignant. "You know, ladies, the more I process this out loud, the more I realize none of this was my fault. It was my husband's."

Karla had enough sense to know better than to argue with someone who was armed and in the middle of a psychotic break. She hoped Lynn knew better too.

"Fitz was so much bigger than you," Karla pointed out. "How were you able to overpower him?"

"He underestimated me," Anna said. "Also, I've

learned I'm much stronger when someone doesn't take me seriously."

"Fitz didn't take you seriously?" Lynn asked.

"I didn't come here planning to kill him," Anna said. "I just wanted him to admit what he'd done. I recorded our conversation on my phone hidden in my pocket. If I could have gotten him to admit it, I would have had enough evidence to take to the police." She sighed. "I walked over here. I trespassed across your land, so no one would see me. When I got here, Leon was lurking outside. I stayed hidden in the trees behind the cottages so he wouldn't see me. Harry was making trips between Mirabel and the manor house, then Lynn showed up." She nodded at Lynn. "You went inside Mirabel, and I didn't see you again. Then Dylan showed up. He didn't stay very long and left in a huff. Rosalie went for a tour around the grounds and had a conversation with Leon. It was like Grand Central Station here. When Leon and Rosalie left, I let myself inside Bellflower."

Anna paused speaking and stared blankly into the distance as she relived her terrible deed.

"Fitz didn't hear me come in. He was in the smaller bedroom doing something with his tools. Organizing them, maybe? I don't know. Tools aren't my thing. Fitz's murder was the first time I'd ever held a nail gun." She chuckled. "I didn't even know how to use it."

Anna raised the gun to her temple again.

Lynn and Karla gasped.

"What happened next?" Lynn asked with urgency, trying to distract Anna from harming herself.

"We argued," Anna replied. "Fitz insisted he had nothing to do with our washroom renovation or my husband's death. He called me a few unflattering names that only angry, hateful people call women. I won't repeat them. Then, Fitz laughed."

Something in Anna's eyes changed. Her soft, nostalgic expression twisted into rage and contempt.

"He laughed and called me a *silly, simple woman.* How dare he trivialize my pain!" she hit her chest with her left fist. "How dare he minimize his contribution to my husband's death!" Her eyes narrowed. "I knew in that moment that Keith Fitzgibbon had to die. If he wouldn't confess, I would have to take justice into my own hands."

"An eye for an eye," Lynn whispered, repeating Anna's earlier statement.

"A tooth for a tooth," Anna agreed, nodding. "I searched for the nearest thing I could use as a weapon." She held the nail gun in front of her and shook her head. "When I picked this up, I thought it was a drill," she admitted. "I was going to drill him to death."

"Oh," Lynn said. "Well, if it makes you feel better, I wouldn't have known what it was either. I thought it was a giant glue gun at first glance."

They shared a hollow laugh.

"Seriously, though," Anna continued. "I figured if I couldn't make the thing work, it would be heavy enough to beat him with."

"How did you figure out how to use it?" Karla asked. "Since Fitz died from being shot with a nail gun and not from being beaten to death, I assume you figured it out."

"Fitz showed me," Anna said.

"What?" Karla and Lynn said in stereo.

"Fitz gave you a tutorial on how to kill him?" Lynn asked, dubious.

"I pointed the gun at him." She held the nail gun with both hands and aimed it at the wall. "And pulled the trigger."

She pulled the trigger.

Karla and Lynn let out startled yelps, looked at each other, then looked at Anna.

"It didn't go off," Lynn observed.

"I know, right?!" Anna said. "I was shocked too. It's a safety feature. When I fired at Fitz and it didn't go off, he laughed. Then he said, *Stupid woman! The gun only works if it's pressed against a firm surface.*" She walked over to the wall. "I said, *Like this?*" She pressed the gun against the wall and fired. A loud pop echoed through the empty room as the gun discharged a two-and-a-half-inch spiral nail into the wall. "I shot him in the back of his head."

"Did that kill him?" Lynn asked. "Was that how Fitz died?"

"I assumed it killed him," Anna admitted. "He went limp and slid down the wall. He wasn't breathing, and his pulse stopped. But I wasn't worried. If Fitz wasn't dead yet, he would be after I shot him in the forehead." She aimed the gun at the floor and pretended to fire.

"Why did you shoot him in the forehead?" Karla asked.

"Because Fitz needed to die the same way my husband died," Anna replied.

"An eye for an eye, remember?" Lynn reminded her.

"I thought Mr. Hughes injured the back of his head," Karla said.

"After he fell, the grab bar landed on his forehead and damaged his face," Anna explained. "We couldn't have an open casket because of it."

Karla nodded, remembering that Rob's explanation included something about Mr. Hughes forehead. She also recalled Rob's observation about the statistical unlikelihood of Fitz's and Mr. Hughes's identical-yet-unrelated injuries.

"After the second shot, I panicked," Anna recalled. "What if someone walked in and found me here? I found a rag in Fitz's toolbox, used it to wipe the gun clean, then placed the gun near his fingertips. When I pulled the rag out of his toolbox, his red carpenter's pencil fell on the floor and gave me an idea. I looked around for something to write on. I found ball of crumpled paper near the door. When I uncrumpled it, I couldn't believe my luck that it was his son's resignation letter. If the police didn't believe Fitz's wounds were self-inflicted, that letter would have pointed them straight toward Dylan and away from me."

In her peripheral vision, Karla could see Lynn shaking her head in disbelief.

"I did my best to forge Fitz's signature. If it didn't match, I hoped the police would assume Fitz wrote it when he was highly emotional, and it affected his penmanship. Next, I placed the note on Fitz's body so the police would be sure to find it, wiped down the pencil, and placed it near the body."

"You would have let Dylan take the blame for a murder you committed, Anna?" Lynn asked with a tone of disgust.

"In a heartbeat," she said unironically. "At the time. I still believed Fitz killed my husband, and Dylan probably helped him."

"She's telling the truth," Karla said gently.

Lynn's face drooped with disappointment.

Anna lowered the nail gun from her temple.

"I lowered the gun," Anna said, gazing at the nail gun by her hip. "You said if I lowered the gun, you would tell me my Tell."

"You blink twice in a row, fast," Karla lied, blinking twice in quick succession to demonstrate.

Karla would tell Max and Dean what Anna's real Tell was. If they wanted her to know the truth, that would be up to them.

"How did you find me, anyway?" Anna asked, tilting her head.

"The Posers," Lynn replied.

"Ugh," Anna rolled her eyes. "The Posers! Those wannabes wouldn't recognize a Sun

Salutation if it walked up to them and introduced itself. How did they know where I was?"

"They didn't," Lynn replied. "They led us to Leon, who led us to you. He has Trina's phone on his Friends app."

"*Argh*! Why didn't I think of that? I should have known they would stalk each other and turned off the location on Trina's phone."

"Did Trina give you her password?" Karla asked.

"I guessed it on the second try," Anna admitted proudly. "You'll never guess what it was."

They waited in silence.

"C'mon! Guess!"

"Her birthday?"

"Their anniversary!"

Karla and Lynn blurted responses at the same time.

"Leon's birthday." Anna pretended to put her finger down her throat and throw up.

Red and blue flashing lights strobed through the window that Anna used to break into Bellflower.

"You called the cops?" Anna's face was full of genuine hurt and betrayal.

Lynn shook her head. "Not us. Rosalie."

"Does the whole town know I'm here?" She raised the nail gun to her temple.

"Of course not, Anna. Put down the gun." Lynn lunged half a step forward, but Karla tugged her, and she stepped back. "Just me, Karla, Rosalie... and the police."

"And Leon," Karla added.

"I'm not leaving here in a cop car," Anna said, her eyes wide with fear. "I'm not leaving here alive." She pressed the nail gun against her temple, squeezed her eyes shut, and swallowed hard.

"Yes, you are!" Lynn launched herself out of the doorway and tackled Anna around the waist.

The women screamed, growled, and tousled. Karla kept her eye on the nail gun, searching for an opportunity to take it away from Anna safely. But Anna managed to overtake Lynn and held her like a human shield, her forearm around Lynn's throat and the nail gun to Lynn's temple.

The women stood still. Their bodies heaved as they caught their breath.

Discreetly, Lynn slid her hand into her jacket pocket. She gave Karla a barely discernable nod and wiggly eyebrows.

Karla nodded in return.

What are you doing, Mother? What are you trying to tell me?

"I'm doing this whether you and Karla are here or not," Anna hissed, breathless. "It's over, Lynn."

"No, it's not," Lynn grunted.

She pulled her hand from her pocket. She was fisting her keychain with keys sticking out like barbs from between her fingers. She threw the back of her fist in Anna's face, jabbing her in the eye with a key.

Anna doubled over and dropped the nail gun. As she brought both hands to her injured face, Karla swooped in and swiped the gun while Lynn knocked Anna to the floor and smothered her with her body.

"Anytime, Dean!" Lynn grunted and blew her long bangs out of her face as she used the weight of her body to keep Anna from getting up. "Where's your father?!" she demanded at Karla through gritted teeth.

Karla flung open the front door, and police officers swarmed inside, single file, guns drawn.

"Max! Dad!" Karla yelled, excitedly. "Anna killed Fitz—"

"We know, La-la," Dean said, placing his hands on her shoulders. "We've been on the porch for fifteen minutes." He poked his thumb behind him. "We heard everything through the broken window."

"Why didn't you come in?"

"You were doing great," Max said. "You didn't need us. Anyway, we didn't have eyes on Anna, and you guys kept talking about a gun. We couldn't storm into a situation with an armed suspect."

"We flashed our lights, so you'd know we were here," Dean continued. "We were about to kick in the door when we heard a fight break out. We held back. Then, Lynn called me, and you opened the door for us."

CHAPTER 24

A FAMILY DINNER

NOVEMBER 1ST

The cheese was bubbling, and the edges had just the right hint of golden-brown hue.

"It's perfect," Karla whispered to herself as she shoved her hands inside the oven mitts, then slid the heavier-than-it-looked casserole dish out of the oven. She inhaled deeply. "Mm." She carried the steaming casserole dish to the dining room, her head held high with pride. "I think this is the best one yet," she beamed, placing the casserole dish on a cast-iron trivet.

"It should be," Harry said, watching the casserole like a hunter stalking its prey. "It's the third one you've made this week!"

"That's just the three she made by herself," Lynn piped in. "Before she made those, she made two with me."

"What did you do with all those casseroles?" Rob asked.

"She brought one to the station and put it in the break room," Max said, laying her napkin across her lap. "Everyone loved it, and they said to tell you thank you."

"She brought two," Dean corrected. "She dropped off a second one on your day off."

"I took one to The Petal Pushers fall harvest potluck dinner," Rosalie added. "Everyone commented that it tasted just like May's."

Karla felt her face warm as she blushed with pride.

"I dropped off a casserole for Molasses to thank her for helping with your lost earring," Lynn said, winking at Karla.

"Auntie Karla packed me some for lunch yesterday," Josie said, looking the spitting image of her mum, Rob, at that age. "It was good." She shrugged.

Harry served everyone a helping of Grandma May's famous pasta casserole, while the bowl of Caesar salad and dish of Rosalie's homemade sourdough bread sticks were passed around the table.

"Did you give Dylan a casserole?" Max asked.

"No." Karla shook her head. "I visited him the morning after Fitz's funeral, and Dylan's kitchen had more casserole dishes than a crockery shop."

"I heard he got accepted to the paramedic program he wanted," Max said.

Karla wondered if Max's interest in Dylan's future was more than mere neighbourly interest.

"That's right," Karla confirmed. "He's excited to start the next chapter of his life. This new program and career give him something to look forward to. He told me Griff offered him a part-time job while he's in school."

"Did Dylan accept Griff's offer?" Dean asked.

"Yes," Karla replied. "He'll be helping Griff with the renos at the cottages."

"Fitz's service was lovely," Rosalie said.

"I wasn't expecting Leon and Trina to show up," Harry said.

"Can you believe they were together?" Lynn asked. "Arm in arm!"

"I heard they're a couple now," Dean said.

"Trina told me she loved Leon," Harry revealed.

"When did she tell you that?" Rob asked.

"The night Anna was arrested," Harry replied. "Rosalie sent me to find Trina when she wasn't answering calls or texts. I figured either her battery died, or she was in a dead zone. We all know Bellbrook has quite a few dead zones where cell phones just don't work. So, I went from one dead zone to another until I found her."

"Where was she again?" Rosalie asked.

"Down by the water," Harry reminded her. "Near the marina. I told her about Leon helping Lynn and Karla locate Anna, and Trina went all gooey and told me Leon Tyson was the love of her life."

"Apparently Leon's wife threw his belongings onto the front lawn and changed the locks, and Trina left her husband," Dean said, then shoved a forkful of casserole in his mouth.

"Molasses said Leon resigned," Max added. "The mayor told him not to bother working his final two weeks."

"I heard Trina is moving into Anna's house," Harry revealed.

"Where did you hear that?" Karla asked.

"Griff told me," Harry replied. "Trina approached him about giving her a quote to redo the washroom."

"You are kidding." Lynn laughed and swatted him with her napkin, assuming he was joking.

"I'm telling the truth." Harry chuckled. "I swear."

He lobbed a piece of breadstick at her, but Lynn dodged it. It landed on the floor behind her.

Gucci scurried from beneath Josie's chair to claim the doughy prize.

Lynn and Harry's flirty antics reminded Karla of her and Griff when they were Josie's age—nine.

"Did Griff give her a quote?" Rob asked.

"Nah," Harry said, stabbing a piece of romaine lettuce with his fork. "He said he wouldn't go near that job with a ten-foot pole."

"I don't blame him," Rosalie said.

"It'll be strange seeing Trina around town without Anna," Lynn said, pushing a bit of pasta around her plate with her fork.

Anna Hughes was in an undisclosed hospital undergoing an intense psychiatric evaluation. According to Dean, after the hospital released her, she would be transferred to the women's prison to await her trial and sentencing. Dean suspected Anna's lawyer would advise her to plead guilty. Apparently, between Karla and Lynn's accounts of Anna's confession and the police officers having heard most of it through the broken window, there wasn't anything to support Anna's defense. Also, the conversation she secretly recorded between her and Fitz the day she killed him was still on her phone. She literally made an audio recording of the murder. "Slam dunk," Dean had called it.

Karla surveyed the chaotic table, watching the people and dog she loved—her family—eat, laugh, talk, and share inside jokes while they enjoyed Grandma May's famous pasta casserole that *she* made. A warm, comforting heat radiated through her. She no longer felt untethered and terrified. She no longer feared that, without Grandma May to ground her, she would float away. She felt like she belonged. Karla Bell was home.

In her will, Grandma May bequeathed Karla the family land, buildings, and contents, but Grandma May's real legacy was her generous, inclusive notion of family, and a quirky, amazing, supportive family of choice.

"How is the renovation going?" Lynn leaned over and asked.

"They've only been at it a few days, but Harry says we could be moved in by February, weather depending."

"We?" Lynn asked. "Are you and Harry going to be roommates?"

"No," Karla replied, bemused. "I thought I would live at Mirabel, and you would live at Bellflower."

"I thought you wanted to rent out Bellflower to help cover the costs of the manor house?" Lynn asked. "I'm afraid market rent for Bellflower would be outside my budget."

"You wouldn't pay rent," Karla said. "You can live

in Bellflower rent-free as long as you want. It's the least I can do since you're donating your inheritance to renovate and upgrade the manor house."

"We'll be neighbours," Lynn said, grinning and nudging Karla's ribs. "We can visit each other. All. The. Time."

"Let's not get carried away," Karla teased. "But it will be nice to have a neighbour I can rely on."

"You can rely on me, love. For anything. I'll be right next door to help you plan your big event." Lynn glanced around the table, then leaned toward Karla's ear. "Have you told anyone yet?"

Karla shook her head. "No one. The only reason you know is because you were teaching me how to make the casserole when I took the phone call."

"You should tell everyone your exciting news!" Lynn picked up her fork and used it to tap her water glass.

"No!" Karla hissed, trying to take the fork from Lynn.

"Attention!" Lynn tapped the glass again. "Karla has good news to share."

Everyone froze and looked at Karla expectantly.

"I don't really have news."

"Yes, you do," Lynn insisted. "Stop being so modest, love."

"It's not news." Karla shrugged. "It's just my job."

"I don't know where our daughter gets her humility from," Lynn said, looking at Dean, "but it's not me."

"You should toot your own horn more, La-la," Dean agreed.

"Yeah, La-la. Brag once in a while." Max stuck her tongue out at Karla, and they both giggled.

"Fine," Lynn declared, glaring at Karla. "I'll tell them." She turned to the table. "One of Karla's super-duper V-V-V-V-V-V-VIP clients is coming to Bellbrook."

The table erupted with chatter and questions.

"I'm still working out the details," Karla announced, then narrowed her eyes on Lynn. "Which is why I haven't mentioned it yet. There's nothing to mention."

"The client wants Karla to plan a huge VIP event," Lynn announced.

"I wouldn't call it huge," Karla countered.

"I hope they don't want one of those murder mystery weekends," Rosalie teased, already laughing at her own joke. "Goodness knows Bellbrook doesn't need another murder. Even a fake one."

KEEP READING for a sneak peek of Rage Before Beauty: A Bellbrook Murder Mystery book 2.

Click here to read a bonus scene from A Well Constructed Murder

RAGE BEFORE BEAUTY
A Bellbrook Murder Mystery
Book 2
REAGAN DAVIS

COPYRIGHT

Copyright © 2022 by Reagan Davis/Carpe Filum Press - All rights reserved.

Sign up for Reagan Davis' email list to be notified of new releases.

No part of this book may be reproduced in any form or by any electronic or mechanical means, including information storage and retrieval systems, without written permission from the author, except for the use of brief quotations in a book review.

This is a work of fiction. Names, characters, places, and incidents either are the products of the author's imagination or are used fictitiously. Any resemblance to actual persons, living or dead, businesses, companies, events, or locales is entirely coincidental.

ISBN: 978-1-990228-44-5 (ebook)

ISBN: 978-1-990228-46-9 (paperback)

ISBN: 978-1-990228-45-2 (hardcover)

ISBN: 978-1-990228-47-6 (large print)

FOREWORD

Dear Reader,

Despite several layers of editing and proofreading, occasionally a typo or grammar mistake is so stubborn that it manages to thwart my editing efforts and camouflage itself amongst the words in the book.

If you encounter one of these obstinate typos or errors in this book, please let me know by contacting me at Hello@ReaganDavis.com.

Hopefully, together we can exterminate the annoying pests.

Thank you!

Reagan Davis

CHAPTER 1
AN UNCHOSEN ASSISTANT

THE DAY of the murder

Karla stomped her foot in the puddle in the drive-way. Water splashed all the way to the top of her tall, black rain boot, almost soaking her leg.

"I'm coming!" Lynn shouted from the front porch of the cottage next door. "Don't leave without me."

"Like you'll let that happen," Karla mumbled. She plastered a smile on her face and waved to her mother before opening the car door and sliding into the driver's seat.

Lynn locked the front door and bounded across their shared lawn with long, high strides.

"Ooh, it's nice and cool in here," Lynn declared as she positioned herself in the passenger seat of her daughter's car. "The rain hasn't helped the humidity, has it? My right sinus is clear for the first time in days." She tapped her forehead, just above her right eyebrow, as if that would prove her sinus wasn't congested. "I predict the rain will end soon."

Lynn believed her sinuses and hips had meteorological superpowers. She hadn't been wrong yet, that Karla knew of, but Karla was still skeptical about her mother's barometric clairvoyance.

Lynn fussed with the air vents until the cool air flowed exactly where she wanted, at just the right speed. "Air conditioning is much better than in my day. We had to put up with hot air blowing on us until the air conditioner finally cooled down. It felt like forever." She buckled her seatbelt and nodded that she was ready to roll. "I'm not complaining," she clarified. "I don't miss winter!" She shook her head. "I'll take the heat over the snow any day."

Mother Nature was giving Bellbrook a preview of the summer heat waves that were yet to come. This was the first heatwave of the year. And the earliest heatwave Bellbrook had experienced in thirty years.

"This winter was the first Bellbrook winter you've braved since you were eighteen," Karla reminded her mother, shifting the car into drive. "When I was ten, I asked why you never came home for Christmas. You said you only visited Bellbrook in months without an R because you hated snow."

"I've visited you in the winter," Lynn defended. "Just not often or for very long," she added under her breath. "Besides, I spent a winter in Finland once and let me tell you"—she arched her professionally shaped eyebrows and nodded at Karla—"an average snowfall in Helsinki makes a Bellbrook blizzard look like a lovely spring day."

"I'll have to take your word for it since you left me

here with Grandma May," Karla muttered the jab without taking her eyes off the road.

"I've got a notebook, pen, tablet, and the charging cord for my tablet," Lynn said, tapping her orange designer laptop bag with long, French-manicured nails and changing the subject.

Lynn avoided talking about the past. About how she was an overwhelmed, scared eighteen-year-old girl when Karla was born. About how she left her baby daughter in the loving care of her mother, Karla's Grandma May, while she travelled the world and lived a child-free, responsibility-free life, leaving someone else to raise her daughter.

"You didn't need to bring anything," Karla said. "You didn't even need to come. My assistant is only a phone call away."

"She's also in a different time zone," Lynn retorted. "She's too far away and too busy helping the other concierges. You're the CEO of the company, for goodness' sake. You should have a dedicated assistant."

"My assistant has been with me since the beginning," Karla argued. "She's fully trained, competent, and she's my eyes and ears at Just Task Me's head office."

Just Task Me! was the concierge company Karla founded after college. They provided twenty-four-hour-a-day, seven-day-a-week personal, discreet service to an exclusive pool of affluent, influential VIP clients. Just Task Me! employed several concierges and concierge assistants, but Karla personally tended to the company's most elite clientele.

"I know you're fond of your assistant, love, but

she's halfway across the country. You don't live there anymore. You live here now, and you need a support system. She's great for helping you with emails and phone calls and such, but you need an assistant who's right here, right now." She grinned and straightened her spine. "Like me! I'm right here in the flesh. Ready, willing, and able to do whatever you need."

Karla sighed.

Lynn had been lobbying for Karla to hire her since she'd found out Karla would be hosting a murder mystery weekend in Bellbrook for a VIP client. It was Lynn's latest attempt to insert herself into her daughter's life almost forty years after she'd left it.

Everyone kept telling Karla that Lynn was trying to make up for lost time. Trying to build a relationship with her estranged daughter. Karla was trying to be open to Lynn's bonding attempts, but trust didn't come easily for her. Her and Lynn's lives were like two circles in a Venn diagram. The only small overlap their circles shared was Grandma May. But she died months ago, and now Lynn was grasping for common ground to keep their circles connected. The distance between them was no longer measured in miles, time zones, or the number of connecting flights, but there was still a barrier between them. A transparent, solid yet intangible barrier. *Grandma May would have wanted us to be close*, she reminded herself. *Do it for Grandma May.*

"I appreciate your enthusiasm," Karla said. "But I don't need an assistant often enough to justify hiring someone local. Anyway, we already live next door to each other in the same small town. We see each other every day." *No matter how hard I try to avoid it some days,* she added in her head. "You know what they say, 'Too much of a good thing is bad'." She smiled, proud of her burgeoning ability to deflect Lynn's attempts at infiltrating her life. "And you already help by looking after Gucci while I work," Karla added. "If we work together, who will take care of him?"

Gucci was Karla's adorable, dishevelled, spoiled terrier. He had a small and scruffy body and a large, endearing personality. Karla loved Gucci. She loved all animals. Animals didn't lie. Animals were loyal. She didn't have to study them and catalogue their behavioural patterns, searching for small hints of untruth or insincerity.

"You know I love Gucci," Lynn said. "I adore my granddog more than any other pet in the world. I can help look after Gucci *and* help you with Just Task Me! I'm an excellent multi-tasker."

Funny, you couldn't multi-task motherhood. Karla bit down hard on her bottom lip.

"Let's see how this weekend goes and take it from there," Karla suggested as a way of shutting down the conversation.

"To prove that I'd be an indispensable personal assistant, I've created a dossier on your client, Mr. Samir Khan," Lynn announced, pulling her tablet from her laptop bag. "I've researched him and his family on the internet." She unlocked the tablet screen and scrolled through an already-open document. "Their names are popular on gossip sites. Who knew billionaire tech moguls had such sordid personal lives?"

"Most of the stories on those gossip sites are fake," Karla informed her mother. "Manufactured headlines to lure people into clicking, so they'll click on the ads embedded in the fake article. It's called click bait, Mother."

"It sounded real enough to me," Lynn said. "Did you know Samir's wife, Millie, was widowed less than six months before he married her? Or that his brother and best friend hate each other?"

"OK, there might be some truth," Karla conceded, "but it's reported out of context." She checked the surroundings at a four-way stop before proceeding through the intersection. "For example, it's true that Samir and Millie got married soon after her first husband died, but they'd known each other for years. Since their time at Oxford."

"Now that you mention it, the article said nothing about how long they'd known each other." Lynn gave her tablet screen a skeptical glance. "Or that Millie had attended Oxford."

"My bag is on the back seat." Karla jerked her head toward the back of the car. "Inside, you'll find Samir's client file. It's full of actual information about him and his family." She stopped at a red light and turned to Lynn. "When you meet them, under no circumstances are you to mention *any* of the tabloid articles." She narrowed her green eyes. "Got it?"

"Got it," Lynn agreed, nodding, then turned her attention to browsing through the real client file.

Karla savoured the blissful silence as they drove, and Lynn riffled through Samir's file.

"It says here that Samir Khan owns homes all over the world. He has homes on both US coasts, India, the UK, and he prefers to summer in his smaller homes scattered across Europe." Lynn closed the file and returned it to Karla's bag. "Why would someone with homes in the world's most glamorous cities spend a weekend in Bellbrook?" She turned to her daughter. "It doesn't make sense. Why would he stay in a local bed and breakfast when he can stay in the most luxurious accommodation on the planet?"

"The Nestled Inn is a lovely bed and breakfast," Karla championed for the small, family-owned business. "Samir needed accommodation large enough to house his guests but secluded enough to ensure their privacy. He said his wife was eager to experience small-town, East Coast life, and he wanted her experience to be as authentic as possible."

"How authentic can her small-town experience be when she's surrounded by servants and security people?" Lynn asked. "According to your file, Samir's entourage of cooks, maids, butlers, and security personnel is the size of a small army."

"The family and Samir's guest of honour will stay at the Nestled Inn, and his staff will stay at the Seascape Hotel. I've arranged to have them shuttled to and from the Nestled Inn," Karla explained. "His staff arrived last night to get the bed and breakfast ready ahead of Samir's arrival today."

"I still don't understand why they chose Bellbrook, of all places."

"Bellbrook is beautiful." Karla gestured toward the surrounding landscape. The contrast of the bright green foliage against the grey sky and ocean was breathtaking. "It's secluded enough to afford them more privacy than most destinations, and Samir's guest of honour lives nearby," she explained. "This weekend is a celebration. Samir recently added a new app to his tech empire. The app's creator lives somewhere near Bellbrook. Samir said the app's creator refused to meet him anywhere else in the world, so Samir came here. The deal is done, but he likes to celebrate his acquisitions."

Lynn's blue eyes were wide with fascination and curiosity. "I wonder if it's someone we know? Do we have any app developers in Bellbrook?"

"I wish I knew," Karla said. "I've asked Samir for the developer's name and personal information, but he's been too busy to get back to me, and his assistant won't divulge anything without Samir's permission. If he'd at least given me a name, I could've researched the app developer myself and found enough information to make them comfortable this weekend and throw in a few personalized touches. Now, I'll have to figure it out as we go along."

"I read something about this on the internet." Lynn snapped her manicured fingers and once again retrieved her tablet from her bag. "Here it is." She cleared her throat. "TechSavvy, the technology conglomerate founded by majority shareholder Samir Khan, has acquired a new app for its impressive technology arsenal. In a multi-million-dollar deal, TechSavvy has purchased Screw It!, an app that allows users to summon local handy people and trades specialists for small repairs, large repairs, or renovation projects. Screw It! makes finding a plumber, carpenter, or other building specialist as easy as ordering a pizza."

"I've researched the Screw It! app but couldn't find any information on the developer behind it," Karla lamented. "As part of Samir's deal to purchase the app, he agreed to allow the developer to remain anonymous."

"Well, whoever this new multi-millionaire app developer is, we'll figure out together how to cater to them and make them happy this weekend." Lynn winked. "We'll make sure they're so impressed that they put Just Task Me! on retainer, landing you a new, high-profile client," Lynn assured her daughter. "You've always been the type of person who rises to a challenge." She tapped the V-neck of her white pullover blouse. "You get your spunk and resourcefulness from me."

Karla's phone rang through the speakers of her car. *Saved by the bell!*

HARRY KINCAID, flashed across the dashboard display. She pressed a button on the steering wheel to accept the call.

"Hi, Harry," she said. "What's up?"

"Hi, Karla! It's about your client, Samir Khan," Harry said. "We have a problem."

"What kind of problem?" Karla tightened her grip on the steering wheel.

"For starters, it took longer than we expected to get the Nestled Inn ready for your guests."

"Why?"

"First, we had to rearrange the furniture," Harry explained. "Mrs. Khan is a believer in feng shui. They even travel with their own professional feng shui consultant, who makes sure the accommodations are feng shui compliant before Mr. and Mrs. Khan step foot in the place."

"This feng shui phase must be new," Karla said. "I would have warned you if I had known."

"I'll add it to your client's file," Lynn whispered beside her, already clicking open a pen.

Karla nodded in thanks.

"I took pictures with my cell phone before we moved the furniture," Harry added. "That way, I can put everything back before the owners come home."

"I'm sure the owners of the Nestled Inn will be so chill after their all-expenses-paid spa weekend, courtesy of Samir and Millie Khan, that they won't mind a few rearranged knick-knacks."

"I still wouldn't want them to come home to find their stuff's been moved around or missing."

"Missing?" Karla asked. "Why would anything be missing?"

"Well, your clients brought some home comforts with them," Harry explained. "We had to relocate some items from the Nestled Inn to make space. The items we had to move are being stored at the manor house."

The manor house to which Harry referred was Bellcroft, Karla and Lynn's family estate. A large, currently uninhabitable seaside mansion, two cottages—where Lynn and Karla had lived since they returned to Bellbrook—and the gamekeeper's cabin, Harry's home.

"They brought their own linens, their own toilet seats, two large scratch posts for their cats, and two easy chairs—which is a kind of misnomer because nothing about those chairs was easy. They were a hassle to move," Harry continued. "Thank goodness Griff was there to help me."

"Griff Dixon?" Lynn asked. "Why was Griff helping you?"

Karla forced herself not to show any reaction to his name, despite her insides swooning more dramatically than a Victorian-era woman in need of smelling salts.

"He offered," Harry defended. "I tried to tell him I'd be fine on my own, but he insisted."

"Bless him," Lynn piped in from the passenger seat. "Griff is a good boy."

"He's not a boy, Mother, he's almost forty."

"Whatever. My point is, he enjoys helping others."

"How would you know?" Karla challenged.

"I might have been away from Bellbrook until recently, but I know people. I hear things."

"Is the house ready?" Karla asked, refocusing the conversation on her client and away from Griff Dixon.

"Yes," Harry replied. "Just in the nick of time. Your client's motorcade was pulling up as I was leaving."

"On behalf of Just Task Me!, thank you for getting the bed and breakfast ready, Harry. I appreciate it. You'll be generously compensated for your time."

"You'll do no such thing—"

"We're almost at the Nestled Inn, Harry," Karla interrupted, not wanting to argue with Harry about his inexplicable resistance to getting paid. "We'll talk about this later."

"One more thing," Harry said. "I think there's something up with Samir Khan's staff."

"What do you mean?"

"Well, from what I can tell, there's a chef, a lady's

maid, a butler, two other servants, and a bunch of security personnel."

"That sounds right," Karla agreed. "I have their names and contact information in Samir's client file."

"Well, most of them were at the Nestled Inn last night and this morning, unpacking and preparing for the Khan's arrival today. The butler told me they would all be present when the Khans showed up. But I saw the servants rushing out. It was like an urgent mass exit."

"Do you know why?"

"No, but the head of security stayed behind to meet with the police chief to discuss the Khan's security arrangements and whatnot. He and the police chief were in the library when, all of a sudden, the head of security ran out with one hand covering his mouth and the other holding his stomach."

"I see," Karla said. "Thank you for letting me know, Harry."

They ended the call and Karla pulled into the Nestled Inn's driveway, parking behind two very conspicuous large, black SUVs.

"Nice armoured vehicles." Lynn stopped to check her hair in the reflection of one of the SUV's dark tinted windows. "Odd choice for people trying to blend in and have a typical small-town weekend."

CHAPTER 2

MUMSY AND THE NOT-SO-EASY CHAIR

KARLA RANG THE DOORBELL. No answer. Strange. She had expected the butler to open the door. Maybe Harry was right. Maybe the servants had made a mass exodus before their employers arrived. But why? She knocked. They waited. No answer.

"Check if it's unlocked," Lynn suggested.

Karla nodded and cautiously turned the knob, like she was breaking a rule and afraid of getting caught. She inched the door open.

"Hello?" Her voice echoed through the empty foyer.

"Voices in the sunroom," Lynn whispered.

The ladies removed their rain boots, hung their trench coats on the coat rack, and padded toward the indistinct murmur of voices and laughter.

"Ah, Karla Bell." Samir Khan smiled and rose from the light-blue overstuffed sofa. He hesitated ever so briefly, winced, then re-affixed his smile. With outstretched arms, he started toward her. "So nice to see you again!"

She met him halfway. They shared a polite hug and a double-cheek air kiss. He turned his attention to Lynn and placed one hand on his lower stomach, with the tips of his fingers disappearing under the waist of his khaki slacks.

"You must be Karla Bell's younger sister." Samir's tone was flirty and gregarious. His accent was a combination of Indian and posh British.

"Don't be silly." Lynn giggled, blushing and smoothing her long, blonde hair. "I'm Karla's mother, Lynn." She offered her hand.

Samir engulfed Lynn's hand in a handshake that morphed into another polite hug and air kiss.

"So lovely to meet you, Lynn Bell." His smile was wide and genuine.

"You can just call me Lynn," she offered.

But he won't.

Lynn must have missed the notation in Samir's file where Karla noted that he always called her KarlaBell as if her first and last names were one word. She'd stopped correcting him after their third meeting.

"The resemblance is remarkable." He pointed at Karla and wagged his finger. "Now I see where you get your beauty, inside and out."

He wasn't wrong about the strong resemblance. Karla had inherited most of Lynn's features. They had the same wavy blonde hair—though Karla's was shoulder length and Lynn's was longer, similar facial features—except Karla's eyes were green and Lynn's were blue, and similar body shapes—average height, average weight, and well-toned arms and legs from years of yoga and Pilates. Sometimes, when Karla looked at her mother, she felt she was looking in an age-progressed mirror. A sneak peek at what she would look like in eighteen years.

Samir extended his arm and gestured for his wife to join him. He winced again. Karla scanned the other faces in the room to see if they had noticed. If they did, they didn't react.

Samir's wife closed her paperback book, placed it on the coffee table, rose from the sofa, and glided over to him. She was thin with angular features and a small, close-mouthed smile. Her limbs were long and willowy, like a gazelle or a ballerina. She had light-brown hair styled in a trendy mixie cut, large, brown eyes, and alabaster skin. Her demeanor was effortless and gentle, almost fragile. She reminded Karla of a young Audrey Hepburn.

"You remember my wonderful wife, Millie?" He wrapped a proud arm around her thin shoulder and squeezed her into him, bunching her shoulders like an accordion.

Samir Khan was not a tall man. Standing side by side, his shoulder was almost level with his wife's. They could look into each other's eyes without either of them having to raise their chins.

"Of course," Karla said, stepping forward and offering her hand. "It's nice to see you again, Millie."

"And you as well," Millie replied in a voice so quiet, and a British accent so posh, that it made her husband's vivaciousness seem even more animated by comparison.

"Lovely to meet you, Mrs. Khan," Lynn said, stepping forward to greet the soft-spoken woman.

"Please, you must call me Millie," she insisted softly.

"Lovely to see you again, Karla," Raj Khan leapt to his feet and gave Karla a side hug and a pat on the back. "And lovely to make your acquaintance, Lynn."

Lynn nodded and offered Raj a similarly polite greeting.

Raj was a taller, less boisterous version of his younger brother. His face was less expressive, and he gave off a calmer, more mature energy than his perpetually bemused and enterprising younger sibling.

"Colin, so nice to see you again," Karla greeted Samir's best friend and business partner as he waited patiently, standing in front of the light-blue overstuffed chair in the corner of the bright room.

Colin Coventry was ostensibly British. If his upperclass British accent didn't give him away, his mannerisms, tweed jacket, and stiff-upper-lip attitude would.

Karla exchanged pleasantries with Colin and, from the corner of her eye, spied Samir, who pressed the thumb-side of his fist into his gut and released a discreet belch from the side of his mouth. His wife, Millie, appeared, handed him a bottle of water, and rubbed his back. Was Samir unwell?

Lynn asked the group about their travels—too much turbulence on the long flight from LAX. Karla wondered if there could be a link between the turbulent flight and Samir's apparent discomfort.

Karla asked about the accommodation and ensured

everyone had what they needed to feel comfortable and at home.

"Where is your guest of honour?" Karla asked. "I can't wait to meet them."

"He will join us for dinner," Samir declared. "He's a very busy man. Too busy to join us in California," he laughed.

The mystery guest is a man. It's a start.

Karla opened her mouth to ask the guest of honour's name, but Samir spoke first.

"But we don't mind coming to Bellbrook"—Samir glanced at his wife—"do we, Millie?"

"Not at all," Millie concurred. "I can't remember the last time we visited the East Coast in the spring-time," she said with a half-laugh. "I must admit, I've been looking forward to weekending in a small, average town." She smiled. "We prefer to winter in the South after autumning on the East Coast. Then we spend Spring on the West Coast before travelling to Europe for the summer months. We follow the mild weather around the globe because the cold wreaks havoc with Mumsy's arthritis."

"Mumsy?" Karla asked. *Is Mumsy a first name or surname?* "Is Mumsy your guest of honour? The creator of the Screw It! app?"

All four visitors burst into laughter. Samir laughed so hard that he grabbed his side with one hand and his wife with the other to hold himself up.

Karla and Lynn joined in the laughter, too, though they weren't in on the joke.

"You think Mumsy is an app developer?" Millie's voice was hard to hear over the men's laughter.

"Karla Bell, you are hilarious." Samir slapped her shoulder like they were old school chums.

"What's so funny?" asked a serious, British accented voice from the doorway. "I heard your laughter from the second floor. Which doesn't say much about the sound proofing." Her walking stick crossed the threshold first, and Raj immediately offered his hand to assist her. "You sound like a pack of wild hyenas." She sniffed. "Very undignified, I must say."

"Oh, Mumsy, you would have laughed too," Millie said. "Karla asked if you were the developer behind Samir's latest app acquisition."

"Did she now?" The elderly lady scanned Karla from head to toe. "I thought you said she was clever, Samir." She lowered herself into the large, reclining easy chair—that didn't fit the aesthetic of the room—and released Raj's hand with a small nod of thanks.

It must be one of the not-so-easy chairs Harry mentioned.

"You must be Millie's mum," Lynn said with a smile.

"I most certainly am not," the elderly lady protested, leaning her walking stick against the side of her chair.

A Siamese cat slinked into the sunroom after her and wrapped itself around her ankles before leaping onto the elderly woman's lap and kneading the fabric of her practical, grey skirt.

"Mu—Lady Olivia is my mother-in-law," Millie explained.

"I'm sorry," Lynn apologized to Lady Olivia. "I

was under the impression that Samir's parents had passed. I shouldn't have assumed."

"No, you shouldn't," the aristocrat scoffed.

"Your information is correct, Lynn," Raj interjected. "Our parents died when we were children."

"Lady Olivia is my mother-in-law from my first marriage," Millie clarified.

"It's lovely to meet you, Lady Olivia." Karla smiled. "Apologies if my confusion offended you." She pointed to herself with one hand. "I'm Karla Bell, and this is my mother, Lynn." She touched Lynn's arm with her other hand.

Lady Olivia nodded and almost smiled. "Pleasure."

"Likewise," Lynn said, flustered and giving the titled woman a small, confused curtsy.

"Where is everyone?" Karla asked no one in particular, gesturing vaguely.

"We don't know," Colin replied.

"That's what we were discussing when you arrived," Raj added.

"It's a mystery!" Samir said with a mischievous glint in his eye. "Our first mystery of the weekend." He rubbed his hands together. "This is our warm-up before the big murder mystery game tonight." He waved his hand as though he were reading an invisible marquee. "The Case of the Missing Servants."

Everyone chuckled.

"Why don't I phone the butler and find out where they are," Lynn offered, lifting the bag—containing Samir's file and contact information for his entourage—off Karla's shoulder.

"Thank you, Mother," Karla said with a smile.

Lynn nodded and disappeared into the next room with the bag.

"I'm sure they're jet lagged after the journey from the West Coast," Millie suggested. "Preparing for our arrival must be a lot of work. They're probably exhausted and resting at the hotel."

"I'm sure you're right," Karla agreed with Millie. "Harry, my friend and colleague, was helping them prepare for your arrival. Your staff were here late into the night and most of the morning."

"But it's not like the butler not to be waiting when we arrived," Colin reminded them.

"Nor my maid," added Lady Olivia.

The Siamese cat was now curled into a ball of purring fluff on Lady Olivia's lap, and she rhythmically stroked the feline's fur while a second cat slinked into the room and jumped onto the windowsill, fixated on something outside.

"They work hard. I'm sure they'll be along shortly. It's not like we need anything right now. Taking care of ourselves will be a fun adventure!"

"Speak for yourself, Samir," Lady Olivia argued. "I was hoping for a bath and a nap before dinner."

"I would be happy to draw you a bath, Lady Olivia," Karla offered.

"Thank you, but I'll wait for my maid." Her smile was tight and more irritated than kind. "Oh good! You're back." Lady Olivia's stare was trained on the doorway where Lynn stood.

"Any luck?" Karla asked her mother.

"I called the butler, the head of security, and the chef." She shook her head. "No one answered."

"I'll go to the Seascape Hotel and find out what's keeping them." Karla joined Lynn in the doorway and reclaimed her shoulder bag.

"Let them rest, Karla Bell," Samir said. "I'm sure they'll be here soon." He grinned.

I hope so, thought Karla, *because I don't know where I'll find half a dozen servants in Bellbrook with no notice.*

CHAPTER 3

BIG HAT, NO CATTLE

"Billionaires aren't like the rest of us," Lynn announced on the way to the car.

"What do you mean?" Karla asked.

"They travel with their own furniture, use *winter* and *summer* as verbs, and think an adventure is being alone in the house with no servants."

"Samir isn't like that," Karla defended, unlocking the car. "He came from a modest background. Their parents died when he and Raj were young. Raj worked three jobs to support Samir through school. The Khan brothers know what it's like to have nothing. Samir gives vast sums of money to good causes. Particularly causes that further education in underdeveloped countries."

"Yeah, I read about that on the internet," Lynn said, opening the passenger side door. "He might not be an out-of-touch elitist, but her ladyship was pretty snooty."

"Today was the first time I've ever met Lady

Olivia, so I don't know her well enough to draw conclusions."

As Karla backed out of the long driveway, Lynn swiped and tapped the screen of her tablet.

"Don't you think it's weird that Millie's ex-mother-in-law is part of their inner circle?" asked Lynn.

"Lady Olivia isn't Millie's *ex*-mother-in-law," Karla replied. "She's Millie's late husband's mother." She wasn't sure what the distinction was, but she was certain there was one. "And I don't think it's odd at all." She shrugged. "It's nice that Millie and Lady Olivia are close. And it speaks to Samir's character that he supports their relationship. I'm sure Millie's late husband, Lady Olivia's late son, would have wanted them to remain close."

Thanks to her grandmother's influence, Karla had a wide and generous definition of family. She knew family was more than DNA and biology. Family was about love, shared experiences, and choice. Having common ancestors doesn't guarantee unconditional love or mutual understanding. Sometimes, family isn't what we're born into, but the relationships we create along the way as we journey through life.

"According to the internet, Millie's late husband died in a tragic car accident," Lynn said.

"That's right," Karla confirmed. "He was driving alone when his car veered off the road and over an embankment. It was dark, and the roads were wet. The police speculated he lost control of the car when he swerved to avoid hitting an animal."

"It says here they'd only been married a few years when he died." Lynn shook her head and clucked her tongue. "Such a tragic end to a short love story." She sighed.

"He was at Oxford with Samir, Millie, and Colin," Karla added. "Samir and Millie reconnected at the funeral. They stayed in touch, and a few months later, they began dating and got married."

"Samir was on the brink of making his first billion when they got married," Lynn read. She swiped the screen and opened a new search window. "I'm looking up Lady Olivia next," she said. "I wonder if she's royalty?"

"I still don't know the name of Samir's guest of honour," Karla grumbled.

"Lady Olivia isn't royalty, per se," Lynn said, answering her own question and ignoring Karla's frustration about the mystery guest of honour. "It says that she's the daughter of a peer, whatever that means. Her title is a courtesy title." She scrolled down the page. "According to this, Lady Olivia has no money. Her father disinherited her when she married a commoner he didn't approve of. Lady Olivia's late husband was a milk man." She stopped scrolling and turned off the screen. "Lady Olivia is *big hat, no cattle*."

"What does that mean?" Karla asked.

"In my late twenties, I dated a Texan cattle rancher," Lynn began.

Karla sighed, sorry she had asked. *Here we go. Another story from Lynn's exciting, child-free life.*

"*Big hat, no cattle* was the phrase he'd used to describe ranchers who wanted to look rich and successful but weren't," Lynn continued. "He used to say that *real* rich people didn't have to show off their wealth. Their wealth was understated because they didn't have to prove anything to anyone. He said the less successful ranchers tried to make themselves look more successful by wearing expensive clothes and driving luxurious cars. But it was all fake, and they were the poorest of the rich."

"I didn't know you dated a cattle rancher," Karla said.

"He was a real cowboy." Lynn's gaze was distant, and the corners of her lipsticked mouth twitched upward. "Sexy Texan drawl, leather chaps, huge—"

"Here we are!" Karla announced, approaching their long, mutual driveway and interrupting Lynn's trip down memory lane before she learned more about her mother's escapades than she cared to know.

"Hat," Lynn continued. "You interrupted me before I could tell you about his huge, ten-gallon hat." She smirked. "You know what they say about men with large hats..."

"They have large heads?" Karla shifted the car into park at the top of the driveway.

THE RAIN HAD STOPPED, the clouds had passed, and the sun was shining. The ground was dry except for the occasional puddle. Of course, Gucci was drawn to the puddles, sniffing and licking every single one he encountered.

"Yucky, Gooch!" Karla tugged the rose-gold Hermes leash to stop the small terrier from lapping up the dirty water. "You have clean water at home. The workers have been driving their trucks through these puddles all day."

Gucci shook his small head, spraying a mist of puddle water on Karla's beige, wide-legged pants, then continued trotting along the path.

As they reached the end of the path through the wooded thicket, the chirping of birds and chattering of squirrels was replaced by the rumble of construction machines. Shouting workers moved around the work-site with hardhats and determination.

"Hey, K."

The butterflies in Karla's belly fluttered at the familiar voice. Only one person in the world had ever called her, K. She had been so distracted by watching the workers that she didn't hear the shiny, red pickup truck's loud engine sidle up next to her.

"Hi, Griff." She forced her smile to be more casual than it wanted. "How's it going?" She nodded to the bustle of activity in the distance.

"Mostly good," he replied with a smile that encouraged her fluttering belly. "Some projects are ahead, some are behind, but the renovation is on schedule for the most part."

"That's great," she agreed with a nod.

"I'm just on my way out," Griff continued, his truck rolling along next to Karla as she and Gucci ambled. "But I can turn around if you're ready to decide on the crown moulding."

Shoot! I forgot all about the crown moulding! She'd promised Griff she would stop by the manor house this week to look at samples. He'd texted her twice to remind her. He must have thought she was avoiding him. She was, but not intentionally, like usual. Karla stopped walking. Griff shifted the truck into park. Gucci whimpered and pulled, straining against his leash to move them closer to Griff's truck. Karla empathised with the little dog, but she held firm and restrained them both.

"I completely forgot about the crown moulding." She shook her head and threw her hands in frustrated defeat. "I'm sorry, Griff. This week has been crazy at work."

"I get it," Griff sympathized and combed his fingers through his short, brown hair, making it stick up in a roguish, sexy way. "Since you aren't on your way to look at the samples, I'll head out. I have to pick up my youngest at school." He shifted the truck into drive. "The moulding can wait until Monday."

"OK," Karla said, knowing she wouldn't have time to focus on Bellcroft until Samir and his entourage had left Bellbrook. "Monday it is. I promise I won't forget this time."

"I won't let you." He chuckled and winked. "See ya later, K."

Griff drove off, and Karla contemplated walking to the manor house to check on the progress herself.

The manor house was part of Bellcroft, the Bell family estate that Karla inherited from her grandmother. The Bells were Bellbrook's founding family. Bellbrook was more than Karla's hometown; it was her legacy. Her roots were here. Bellbrook ran through her veins. "Remember where you came from," Lynn was fond of reminding her. "The Bell family put the Bell in Bellbrook. This town is in your blood."

Bellcroft was comprised of many acres of premium waterfront property with two small cottages, Mirabel and Bellflower, inhabited by Karla and Lynn respectively, and the gamekeeper's cabin, occupied by the estate gamekeeper, Harry. The manor house, a large, dilapidated mansion, had been free falling into disrepair for almost forty years. Upon inheriting the crumbling estate, Karla knew something had to be done about the derelict mansion. Either the land had to be divided and the mansion sold, or the huge, historical home had to be restored to its former glory and made to earn its keep as an exclusive, oceanside event venue. She chose the latter. Bellcroft would be Just Task Me's East Coast headquarters, the bejewelled centrepiece of her empire.

Griff Dixon was in charge of the massive renovation project. It made sense. He was the most respected contractor around. But his constant presence made it difficult for Karla to pretend he didn't exist. It's hard to ignore someone who constantly picked your brain about marble vs. quartz countertops, harassed you to look at crown moulding samples, and pestered you to choose a finish for the hardwood floors in the library.

Karla checked the time and decided against visiting the manor house today. She still had to feed Gucci, get herself ready to appear at her client's formal dinner tonight, and set up for the murder mystery game afterward. She had a murder to organize!

CHAPTER 4

A PILLOW FIGHT

FOUR FAST KNOCKS. Pause. Two fast knocks. Morse code for the letter *R*.

"It's unlocked!" Karla called.

"Hiya!" her best friend, Rob, called as she entered the cottage.

"In here," Karla shouted from inside her bedroom closet.

"I brought the earrings you wanted to borrow," Rob said, scooping Gucci off the bed and stretching her neck to make it as hard as possible for the excited pup to lick her face.

Gucci squirmed and thrashed in Rob's arms, trying to give her kisses and show her how happy he was to see her.

Rob placed Gucci back on the bed and pulled the small velvet jewelry box from her pocket.

"Thank you!" Karla said, taking the box. "You're a lifesaver." She plucked the earrings from the box and disappeared toward the mirror in her walk-in closet. "They're perfect!" she said, emerging moments later.

She was in full makeup, her blue fluffy robe, and matching blue fluffy slippers. She had pinned one side of her straightened blonde bob to showcase Rob's beautiful diamond drop earrings.

"You look gorgeous as usual." Rob turned to Gucci and puckered her lips. "Doesn't Mummy look gorgeous Gucci-poochie?"

"Thank you for lending me your lucky earrings," Karla gushed. "I promise to return them first thing tomorrow."

"I'm afraid they aren't very lucky," Rob corrected. "They were a gift from my parents on my wedding day. Look how that turned out."

"It turned out great," Karla argued, rummaging through the dresses in her closet. "Thanks to your marriage, I have a clever, adorable, red-haired, brown-eyed, freckle-faced, goddaughter who is your spitting image. She is walking, talking proof that these earrings are lucky."

"It's true," Rob said, grinning with a nostalgic twinkle in her brown eyes. "She's my biggest accomplishment."

"Being a doctor is a pretty big accomplishment too," Karla reminded her. "Don't undervalue your ability to cure people and save lives."

The blush started in Rob's cheeks and spread to her ears. "I hope those temporarily lucky earrings don't run out of luck while you're wearing them."

"Hello? La-la? You home?"

Only two people called Karla, La-la—her father and her sister, Max.

"In here!" Karla and Rob shouted in unison.

"There you are," Max said, appearing in the doorway to Karla's bedroom.

Gucci leapt off the bed and scrambled to greet the new arrival.

"You love your Auntie Max, don't you?!" she cooed at Gucci as she squatted down to greet him, and he bounced toward her face. "Yes, you do!" She slipped him a dog treat from her pocket. While he chomped the small cookie, Max scratched between the terrier's button ears. "Auntie Max loves you too. Yes, she does!"

"Why aren't you wearing your police uniform?" Rob asked.

"My weekend started an hour ago." Max let out a relieved sigh and flopped on Karla's bed with Gucci in her arms. "Thank goodness, I'm not working this weekend," she added. "I'm exhausted from training the new Cybercop all week."

"How's he doing?" Rob asked.

The Bellbrook Police Department had hired a new police officer who specialized in cyber crimes. No one could remember his exact title, so the townsfolk started calling him Cybercop. The name had stuck, and now this poor officer, regardless what his actual title was, would forever be known as Cybercop.

"He's fine." Max shrugged. "Nice guy. Kind of anxious." She looked at Karla. "Your client's security team has been driving us crazy. None of the cops want to deal with them."

"Why?" Karla asked, popping her head out of the closet.

"They act like we have no clue what we're doing," Max complained. "They don't trust us to keep your client safe. The guy in charge told us to stay out of their way unless they call us. They treat us like a bunch of local yokels who only hand out parking tickets and lecture jaywalkers."

"You *do* hand out a lot of parking tickets, Max," Rob teased with a grin. "And I've seen you lecture more than a few jaywalkers." She raised her eyebrows as though she were challenging Max to a duel.

Max scrunched up her face, narrowed her eyes, and slammed Rob's head with a decorative pillow from Karla's bed.

Half of Rob's long red hair came loose from its ponytail. "You did *not* just assault me with a pillow!" she demanded with fake offense and an impish grin. She picked up one of the many decorative pillows that were artfully arranged on the king-sized bed. "Game on!" She cocked her arm and heaved the pillow, hitting Max on the side of the face.

Max recovered from the blow and shook her chin-length, dark hair out of her eyes. "Bring it, old lady!"

Max grabbed a second pillow.

So did Rob.

"Old lady?" Rob scoffed at the mock insult. "I'm not old, you immature little squirt."

Rob was far from old, but from Max's twenty-eight-year-old perspective, thirty-nine wasn't young.

The women pummelled each other with decorative

cushions and laughed so hard that their eyes filled with tears.

Gucci barked and spun in circles on the bed, cheering for both sides.

Karla watched, amused and shaking her head. There was no way she was getting involved, not after the time she'd just spent on her hair and makeup.

"What the heck is going on here?"

Fisted pillows paused in mid-air.

Gucci froze, panting. His impossibly long tongue lolled out of the side of his mouth.

Rob and Max's chests heaved as they caught their breath. "Hi, Lynn," they wheezed out of sync.

"We didn't hear you come in," Rob said.

They lowered the pillows and tried to tame their ruffled tresses while returning order to Karla's messed-up bed.

"I thought you were meeting Harry this afternoon," Karla said to Lynn.

"I was," Lynn confirmed. "Harry wants to repaint his kitchen this weekend, and I was helping him choose a paint colour when my phone rang." She held out her phone as proof. "It was the butler."

"Samir's butler?" Karla asked, hanging a dress on the closet door. "Why would he call you?"

"He was returning my call," Lynn explained. "Remember? I phoned him from the Nestled Inn, but he didn't answer?"

"I remember." Karla nodded.

"Well, the reason he couldn't answer my call is because he's been driving the porcelain bus for the past six hours. He came up for air long enough to return my call. He had to hang up in a hurry because he was going to be sick again. I told him I'd relay his message."

"The butler is sick?" Karla's brain connected the dots, revealing the extent of what this could mean for her client's murder mystery weekend. "Is anyone else sick?" She hoped the answer was no but knew deep down it would be yes.

Lynn nodded. "All of them. The entire entourage." She pocketed her phone and sighed. "The butler figures they either have food poisoning from the lunch the chef made for everyone, or they've all contracted some sort of tummy bug." She shrugged one shoulder. "He suspects something was off with the salmon and hoisin-ginger sauce the chef made for lunch. But apparently, the chef is sensitive and easily offended, so no one said anything, and everyone just ate it."

"Oh my." Karla sat on the edge of the bed, worrying at the inside of her left cheek and formulating a plan. "First, we need to remove the food from the kitchen at the Nestled Inn. If the staff have food poisoning, we can't risk anyone else eating whatever made them sick."

"I'll take care of it." Lynn nodded.

Karla checked the time on her bedside clock. "Dinner is in a few hours. I need to source a gourmet, multi-course meal for Samir and his guests."

"Where are you going to find fancy food in Bellbrook?" Rob asked. "I mean, we have a few decent restaurants but nothing on the same scale as Samir Khan's personal Michelin-star chef."

Max snapped her fingers. "I'll use my patrol car."

She nodded enthusiastically. "We can order from a gourmet restaurant in Loganville or Beaver Creek, and I'll drive fast, with lights and sirens, to pick it up." Max's phone chimed. She knitted her eyebrows together as she read the screen. "Scratch that," she said, shaking her head. "I have to go to work."

"You said you weren't working this weekend," Rob protested.

"I wasn't," Max confirmed, "but with Samir's entire security team sick, the Bellbrook police are taking over his security detail." She shrugged.

"How am I going to replace a butler, a lady's maid, two servants, and a chef?" Karla wondered out loud.

"I can cater to her ladyship all weekend," Lynn offered. "I didn't have plans anyway, other than helping Harry paint his kitchen."

"Mother, I can't ask you to do that," Karla argued.

"You didn't ask," Lynn insisted. "I offered." She gave Karla a small smile. "It's the least I can do. I know I haven't always been there when you needed me, love, but I'm trying to change that. Let me help."

It's not like I can afford to say no.

"Thank you, Mother." Karla smiled at Lynn. "Hopefully, the servants will recover quickly, and you'll only have to help Lady Olivia tonight."

"They could probably use a doctor," Rob interjected. "I'll drive over to the Seascape Hotel and check on the sick people. Make sure everyone is hydrated and assess if anyone needs immediate medical attention."

"That would be awesome, Rob, thank you." Karla smiled and squeezed her best friend's hand.

"Then, I'll meet you at the Nestled Inn and fill in for one of the servants."

"Don't you have to go home and make dinner?"

Rob flicked her wrist dismissively. "Josie's with her dad this weekend. You and Max are working." She shrugged one shoulder. "I've never been in the same room as a billionaire. At least, not that I know of." She grinned. "I'd rather play Downton Abbey with you and Lynn than sit at home alone, binge-watching another medical drama surrounded by bowls of popcorn and ice cream."

"I have an idea." Max held up her index finger and pulled out her phone. "I'll be right back." She disappeared from the crowded bedroom.

"I'll recruit Harry to stand in as butler," Lynn suggested, already typing a text to him.

"Harry's done enough," Karla protested. "I bet he's exhausted."

"Nonsense," Lynn said without looking up from her phone. "He's in. Says he would've been offended if we didn't include him." She locked her phone screen and gave the room a triumphant grin. "I have another idea," she teased. "Remember earlier when you said Samir wanted to give his wife a realistic small-town experience?"

Karla nodded.

"Well, a gourmet meal prepared by a celebrity chef is hardly a typical Bellbrook dinner."

"Right." Karla rolled her hand, urging Lynn to continue.

"So, let's give them a homemade, local specialty they'll never forget."

A wave of comprehension crossed Rob's face. "Rosalie!" She nodded at Lynn. "Brilliant!"

So brilliant that Karla had a brief pang of jealousy, wishing she had thought of it.

"I can't ask an eighty-year-old woman to whip up a meal for six in less than three hours," Karla said.

"You won't need to, love," Lynn assured her. "We'll go through her freezer."

"Which one?" Rob asked with a half-chuckle. "The freezer in Rosalie's kitchen? The freezer in her basement? Or the freezer in her garage?"

Rosalie was a retired widow who loved to cook but had no one to cook for. Karla and Lynn made a point of letting Rosalie feed each of them at least twice a week, but it still wasn't enough to stop Rosalie's freezers from overflowing with home-cooked goodness. Aside from gardening, cooking was Rosalie's only hobby. The winters were long in Bellbrook, giving Rosalie months at a time to indulge her culinary passion. Rosalie often cooked for local community events and hosted holiday meals for friends and neighbours who would otherwise spend the holidays alone. She had been known to single-handedly cater entire potluck gatherings without comprehending the irony of calling it potluck when only one person brought the food.

"Frozen food?" Karla asked. "It feels like we're tricking them."

"They'll never know it's frozen, love," Lynn declared. "Everything Rosalie makes tastes just as good reheated as it does the first time."

"Sometimes better," Rob added. "She might not be

a trained chef, but Rosalie Howard is the best cook in Bellbrook. Heck, she might be the best cook in the country."

"Good news!" Max bounced back into the room, grinning. "I can help. I can fill in for one of the servants."

"How?" Karla asked. "Weren't you called into work?"

"I can do both," Max advised them smugly. "I convinced the-powers-that-be to let me act as a servant, so we would have an armed officer inside the house." She clapped her hands in front of her chest. "They thought it was a fabulous idea."

"That's amazing," Karla commended. Her chest surged with the confidence she'd lost five minutes before when Lynn arrived with the bad news. "OK." She inhaled sharply. "Let's do this! Let's make this the best dinner and murder mystery game ever!"

CHAPTER 5

A WELL-TAILORED SUIT

AT THE NESTLED INN, Karla parked on the road instead of risking her car getting trapped on the driveway if someone were to park behind her. A good concierge always has an exit plan in case they need to make a hasty exit to fetch something for a client. She ended up practicing her parallel parking skills and squeezed her car snugly between Lynn's sedan and Griff's shiny, red pickup truck.

Why is Griff here? She looked around as though he might be lurking close by, eavesdropping on her thoughts. "He must be visiting another house," she reasoned under her breath. She lowered her visor and flipped open the mirror to check her makeup before going inside. She took a deep breath and mentally hyped herself to be the world's best concierge for the next few hours.

Karla stepped out of the car, smoothed her dress, and made sure the pin holding up her hair on the same side as her exposed shoulder was secure. The car chirped when she locked it. She dropped her keys into her sparkly clutch purse and gripped it tight at her hip.

Two steps into the journey from her car to the Nestled Inn's front door, Karla stopped. Who was whistling? She tilted her chin and cocked her ear into the darkness. It was the chorus from the song, "Lady In Red." The whistling grew closer, and Karla spun around, clutching her purse to her chest.

"Sorry, K!" He smiled. "Didn't mean to startle you." He stopped. "Wow. You're beautiful."

"Thank you," she responded, opening her arms to showcase her long, red, one-shoulder sheath dress. "It's by Victoria Beckham."

"The dress is nice too." Griff smirked.

"Why are you here?" she asked, her brows furrowed together.

"Samir and Millie invited me for dinner and a night of murder mystery."

"Wait," Karla said, narrowing her eyes and squeezing her brows together in confusion. "You're Samir's mystery guest of honour? You created Screw It!?" Confusion turned to frustration. "Why didn't you tell me?"

"I thought you knew. Since Samir is your client, I assumed he told you." Griff ran his finger between his neck and the collar of his tuxedo shirt, smiling.

Karla guessed that, working in the construction trade, Griff wasn't used to wearing such structured attire. *Shame, he looks incredible in a well-tailored suit. Gawd, he's gorgeous.*

Karla inhaled and swallowed, hoping it would

push her thumping heart from her throat back to her chest where it belonged.

Griff Dixon wasn't handsome in a musclebound, Hollywood-leading-man way, he was gorgeous in a real-life, hardworking way. When Karla left Bellbrook almost twenty years ago, Griff was the tall, skinny, awkward eighteen-year-old who she watched in her rear-view mirror as he waved her off. Now he was a tall, rugged, confident man. Years of building and renovation work had given him a powerful physique and an outdoorsy glow. Age and experience had given him an air of confidence and maturity. His brown hair was still short and mussed—Karla used to tease him for having a bird's nest on his head—but tousled hair was trendy now, and the silver streaks suited him more than she was prepared to admit. His eyes hadn't changed. They were still grey, mesmerizing, and down-turned. The few burgeoning lines etched in the corners only added to his appeal, making him seem more distinguished.

"When did you become an app developer?" Karla asked.

Griff gave her a half-shrug. "I was always interested in computers and stuff, K, you know that."

"I remember you building PCs and playing computer games, but I don't remember you programming anything." She shook her head. "How many apps have you created?"

"A few for fun, but Screw It! was the only app I released," he replied.

Karla's brain exploded with so many questions. She needed answers. She needed to make sense of this.

"Samir paid millions for that app," she said. "Why are you renovating the manor house? You're a multi-millionaire now. You could do anything you want, anywhere you want."

"I love my job, K, and I employ a lot of people who rely on Fixin' By Dixon to support their families. I intend to keep working as long as I'm able."

"No one knows you built Screw It!" she continued. "My assistant, my mother, and I have searched everywhere for information about the developer. Your name didn't come up once. It's like a ghost developed Screw It!"

"I asked Samir to keep my name under wraps," Griff explained, "and he has been really great about it. He even made it part of the terms and conditions in our contract."

"But your truck is right outside the house where Samir is staying." Karla gestured toward Griff's pickup truck. "Everyone in town will know you were here."

"I'm not worried," Griff said with a chuckle. "Everyone knows I was here last night and this morning, helping Harry get ready for Samir's arrival." He gave her another half-shrug. *When did his shoulders get so broad?* "They'll just assume I came to help out again."

Karla nodded.

"Shall we?" He jutted out his elbow, offering her his arm.

Heat rippled through her body as she wove her hand under the crook of his elbow and rested it on his forearm. They took a few steps, and Griff fiddled with his cufflink, causing Karla's mind to flash back to their high school prom—the only other time she'd seen Griff wear a tux. He was eighteen, handsome, and nervous. His palms were sweaty, and he swallowed after almost every breath.

She had helped him plan his suit so it would match her dress. She was thrilled when he showed up on prom night with a matching corsage for her. His hands trembled when he slid it on her wrist.

"You OK, K?"

Griff's voice jolted Karla back to the here and now.

He nodded at her wrist, and she caught herself absentmindedly rubbing the wrist that Griff had slid the corsage onto twenty years prior.

"Fine," she blurted with an awkward half-laugh. "It's just wrist strain," she lied, rotating her wrist for effect. "Too much typing and mousing." She smiled.

"Did Rosalie Howard just wave to me from the kitchen window?" Griff asked.

Karla stopped walking and tugged his arm, encouraging him to do the same. They locked eyes, and Karla hoped Griff couldn't hear her heart pounding throughout her entire body.

"I should warn you," she said. "When you walk into that house, everyone in town will find out you developed Screw It!"

She felt the weight of his gaze when he tilted his head and narrowed his eyes on her. His stare penetrated her like a laser. "What's going on, K? Why is Rosalie Howard here?"

Karla told him about the sudden, mass food poisoning that had immobilized Samir's staff, her desperation to manifest a five-star meal for six in less than three hours, and everyone's offers to help. "I know this changes things for you, so if you want to leave, I'll cover for you. Samir will understand."

"No, he won't," Griff said with a sigh. "He harassed me for weeks until I agreed to a time and date for this dinner. Samir has a weird superstition about celebrating every acquisition with the seller. He believes if he doesn't, the deal will go bad."

"If you wanted to remain anonymous, why did you agree to meet him in Bellbrook?" Karla asked. "Samir would've flown you anywhere in the world for dinner and mystery night."

"My kids," Griff said quietly. "The twins are in soccer and baseball. My youngest is a competitive swimmer and swims almost every day. They have tutoring appointments, orthodontist appointments, and constantly need to be dropped off or picked up for play dates and birthday parties." He shrugged. "They only live with me fifty percent of the time, but I'm still a full-time dad. When I go away, it affects four other people—my kids and my ex."

"I respect that you want to remain anonymous," Karla said, appreciating the impact that the local awareness of his sudden wealth could have on Griff's children, "so if you want to leave, I'll make sure Rosalie doesn't tell anyone she saw you. I completely understand, and I'll make sure Samir understands too."

Griff blew out a long breath, then turned toward the large Victorian-era house. "It would've come out, eventually. It's impossible to keep a secret in this town," he reasoned. "My kids and ex already know, so it won't matter if they find out." He jutted out his elbow, and Karla snaked her hand through the crook until her hand settled into place on his forearm. "Did you say we're having Rosalie's Roast and Duff?"

Karla nodded. "With roasted root vegetables and pease pudding."

"I do love Rosalie's Roast and Duff with pease pudding." He grinned. "It'll be worth losing my anonymity not to miss this meal."

They resumed walking toward the house.

ROSEMARY AND THYME

HARRY ANSWERED THE DOOR, wearing a crisp, black dress shirt, black suit pants, and a pair of black wingtips. Karla had only ever seen him ditch his faded concert t-shirts, baggy jeans, and worn-in work boots for weddings and funerals. His head of thick silver waves and matching beard were a stark contrast to his makeshift butler's uniform.

Samir's staff's illness had tasked Karla with outfitting a butler, a lady's maid, two servants, and a chef in less than an hour. She had called the only costume store in town, but their maid outfits were more naughty than professional.

After much debate and brainstorming in a group text chat, Karla and her volunteers concluded that the only wardrobe components everyone had in common were black dress pants, black dress shoes, and black, button-down dress shirts. *It'll have to do,* Karla had thought. Max had a slight wardrobe exception; her ensemble would include a black blazer to conceal her holster, badge, and the other police accessories she needed for her job.

Harry moved aside and stood at attention while they stepped into the foyer. Griff guided Karla through the door ahead of him. His touch was light and warm on the small of her back. Goosebumps prickled to life where his hand met her dress and radiated to the tips of her fingers and toes.

Harry ushered them into the lounge where Samir, Millie, Lady Olivia, Raj, and Colin sipped cocktails and chuckled politely at each other's jokes. It was like a scene from Downton Abbey except for the cats. Lady Olivia's twin Siamese cats, Rosemary and Thyme, were curled up on their special blanket in front of the fire, grooming each other and basking in the warmth.

As Griff and Karla entered the room, Harry announced, "Mr. Griffin Dixon and Ms. Karla Bell." Then, he bowed his head and backed himself into the doorway. Clearly, he had seen a few episodes of Downton Abbey too.

"Karla Bell." Samir rose from a wing chair to greet the new arrivals.

He walked toward them, keeping one hand on the button of his tuxedo jacket. A barely discernible wince flashed across his face for an instant. Karla wondered if he was having a wardrobe malfunction or if his earlier tummy troubles were still an issue.

"Griff." Samir and Griff extended their hands. "So wonderful to get together with you, finally," Samir said, shaking Griff's hand with vigor and slapping his shoulder. He turned his attention to Karla. "Are you surprised?" he asked, waggling his eyebrows as he looked back and forth between her and Griff.

Karla opened her mouth to reply, but Samir continued speaking.

"Of course you are surprised! I can tell!" He rubbed his hands together. "When I learned Griff was from Bellbrook, and you were also from Bellbrook, I wanted to surprise you." He chuckled. "I figured in a town this small that you must know each other."

Griff and Karla exchanged awkward glances, then stared blankly at Samir.

"I see I was right." He wagged his index finger at them. "You were very persistent, Karla Bell, constantly asking me and my assistant for the app developer's name and details." He shook his head, amused with the outcome of his plan. "But I told her not to tell you." He clapped his hands in front of his chest, steepled his fingers, grinned from ear to ear, and said, "Oh, how I love surprises!"

"Whiskey sour, isn't it, old chap?" Colin's familiarity gave Karla the impression that he and Griff had met before.

"Sounds amazing," Griff said, following Colin toward the drinks cart.

After exchanging greetings with the rest of the guests, Karla excused herself to check on dinner and set up the murder mystery game in the library.

"Very professional," Karla whispered as she passed Harry, who stood in the lounge entry in stiff silence, waiting to be needed.

"Thanks!" he whispered in reply. "I've been watching YouTube videos about butlering." He gave her a sneaky wink and grin that made her feel like she was nine years old again.

Don't tell your grandmother, or she'll have my guts for garters, he used to whisper when he slipped her a five-dollar bill, so she and Rob could buy candy after school.

Harry Kincaid wasn't family in the DNA sense of the word, but he was family in every way that mattered. Harry had been Bellcroft's gamekeeper his entire adult life, taking over for his father who had been the gamekeeper before him. Karla couldn't imagine Bellcroft without Harry or imagine Harry anywhere other than Bellcroft. He was one of the constants in her life. He was the only fun uncle, protective older brother figure she had ever known. Grandma May used to say, "When Harry Kincaid cuts himself, he bleeds sap from the Bellcroft forest." Karla accepted this as truth until she was eight years old, and Harry hammered a nail through his thumb. His blood was red, just like everyone else's. She was relieved and disappointed at the same time.

On her way to the kitchen, Karla spied Millie from the corner of her eye as she slipped out of the bustling lounge and into the adjoining dining room. She decanted water into a crystal glass, then produced a small tablet from the cuff of her long-sleeved formal dress. Millie dropped the tablet into the glass, and Karla watched the water—at least she assumed it was water—fizz and hiss until the tablet dissolved.

"Must be one of those effervescent tablets," Harry whispered, sneaking up behind her. "You know, for indigestion and whatnot." He patted his tummy. "I noticed Samir rubbing his belly and letting out the occasional, discreet belch. Maybe he's catching whatever his servants have."

"Is that decanter filled with water?" Karla asked.

"I assume so," Harry replied. "I didn't fill it myself, but it looks like water to me."

Karla nodded. "If Millie's potion doesn't help, I'll have a quiet word with Samir and ask if he'd like Rob to examine him."

They watched as Millie wordlessly handed the glass to her husband.

Samir smiled and downed the whole thing in one swig.

CHAPTER 7

IN WHICH LYNN GETS UPSTAGED

THE KITCHEN WAS a flurry of controlled chaos. Rosalie was in charge—of course—making sure everyone either helped or stayed out of her way.

As planned, Lynn, Rob, and Max wore black slacks with black button-down dress shirts and black flats. Lynn and Rob wore their hair in matching buns. Max's dark hair was too short for a bun, so she pulled it into a low, stubby ponytail. Rosalie didn't wear the chefs' whites that Samir's personal chef would have worn. Instead, she wore her favourite *I look as good as I cook* apron, matching fuchsia head tie, and hot pink, rubber gardening clogs that made her appear taller than her four-foot-eleven-inches.

Karla hadn't bothered to source a chef's outfit. The plan was to bring Rosalie's food to The Nestled Inn and leave Rosalie at home. But Rosalie vetoed the plan. She didn't trust anyone to reheat her lovingly prepared feast. Also, she had seen Samir Khan on TV and wanted to see him in real life. Karla agreed because she found it difficult to say no to her elders, particularly when the elder in question was her late grandmother's lifelong best friend.

"We heard you and Griff arrived together." Lynn wiped her hands on a dish towel and rushed over to Karla. "Harry announced your names like you were a couple." Lynn's voice was full of hope.

"It was a coincidence," Karla clarified. The collective sigh of disappointment rivalled a deflating balloon. "We arrived at the same time but not together." She shook her head. "I didn't know he was coming."

"In a thousand years, I never would have guessed that Griff Dixon was a multi-millionaire app developer," Rosalie said. "Good for him! I hope he enjoys every cent of his newfound wealth."

"Who filled the decanters in the dining room?" Karla asked. "Does the large, square decanter have water in it?"

Everyone paused what they were doing, looked at each other, then at Karla, and shrugged.

"The staff must've filled them before they got ill," Max hypothesized.

"Or the guests filled them by themselves," Rob suggested.

Lynn snorted. "I can tell you who *didn't* fill the decanters." She crossed her arms in front of her chest and arched her perfectly shaped eyebrows. "Her ladyship."

"How do you know?" Karla asked.

"Because her ladyship does *nothing* herself," Lynn

griped. "I even had to help her get dressed and put on her jewelry."

"That's what a lady's maid does, Lynn," Max reminded her.

"I sent you video links," Rob said. "Didn't you watch those videos about how to be a lady's maid?"

"I haven't had time." Lynn huffed, tossing her hands in frustration. "I had to remove all the food from the kitchen so no one else got sick. Then Rosalie sent me to the grocery store with a list of food to replace the food I'd tossed. I'd barely finished putting the new food away when Lady Olivia woke up from her nap and started making demands. She constantly needs something. I'm always running around after her. Cleaning up, finding things, and delivering them to her. She made me scoop the kitty litter." She glared at Karla. "You know, she doesn't even say thank you."

"Reminds me of motherhood," Rosalie joked under her breath.

Like Lynn would know what motherhood was like. Karla squeezed her lips together to stop the words from escaping from her brain to her mouth and into the room.

"It's only for a few days," Lynn reminded herself, bucking up. "Maybe less. With any luck, Lady Olivia's maid has a resilient constitution." She plastered a fake smile on her face and added under her breath, "It wouldn't surprise me if she gave herself food poisoning to get a break from her demanding employer."

"Speaking of the servants' mystery illness," Karla said to Rob. "How are they?"

"A few exhibited symptoms consistent with dehydration," Rob started. "I suspect they have food poisoning. I've prescribed IV fluids for a couple of them and lots of rest and clear fluids for the others. I took samples and sent them to the lab." She smiled. "I told them I'd be back to check on them tomorrow." She patted her front pocket. "In the meantime, they have my number if anything changes."

While Rosalie refocussed Lynn and Max on their tasks at hand, Karla had a quiet word with Rob about Samir's apparent stomach discomfort.

"Do you think he could have the same food poisoning as everyone else?" Karla asked her best friend.

"It's possible," Rob replied. "It can take up to six hours for symptoms to start. If he ate the source of the food poisoning before Lynn cleared the kitchen, he could have contracted it." She shrugged.

"I noticed it before that," Karla said. "He was rubbing his tummy when I came over earlier to welcome them to Bellbrook."

"Some people suffer gastrointestinal symptoms when they travel," Rob explained. "Not to mention switching time zones. Jet lag is real for a lot of us."

"You're probably right," Karla agreed. "I've just never been aware of Samir having a history of travel-related illness. But now that you mention it, they were complaining about the turbulence on their flight."

"Turbulence is always worse on smaller aircraft, love. Like on Samir's private jet," Lynn added as she lined the breadbaskets with linen napkins. "Trust me, I've flown in everything from huge jumbo jets to tiny puddle jumpers on every continent except Antarctica."

"Right," Karla said, then told Rob about the effervescent tablet she and Harry had seen Millie dissolve in Samir's glass.

"It sounds like a sodium bicarbonate tablet," Rob said. "You know, those antacid pills that dissolve in water?"

"That's what I assumed too," Karla agreed, relieved.

"I'd be happy to examine him if he'd like." Rob smiled.

"Thanks," Karla replied. "I'll mention it when I get a moment alone with him."

Harry appeared in the doorway. "Lady Olivia sent me," he said to Lynn. "She'd like you to feed Rosemary and Thyme right away."

"Of course she would," Lynn said with an eye roll.

"She said to use the porcelain cat dishes, not the metal ones as those are only for breakfast. And they like to eat up high—like on a table."

"Got it," Lynn said.

"Near a window," Harry added. "Apparently, they enjoy a good view while they eat."

"Of course they do," Lynn said, reaching for the porcelain cat food dishes. "Even though it's dark outside."

"Lady Olivia said to ring their bell when it's ready, and they'll come running."

"When I die, I want to come back as an aristocrat's cat," she mumbled.

Rosalie assembled the first course: clam chowder.

Rob and Max carried the trays to the dining room. She dispatched Karla to tell Harry to announce dinner so the guests could make their way to the dining room.

Across the hall in the library, Karla prepared for the murder mystery game and eavesdropped on everyone in the dining room raving about Rosalie's cooking and how this was one of the best meals they've ever had.

Lynn joined her to practice her part. Having never met a spotlight she didn't like, Lynn insisted Karla let her play the victim in tonight's murder mystery game.

While Lynn rehearsed her single line, "Oh my! I don't feel very well!" over and over again, emphasizing a different word with each iteration and perfecting her overly dramatic demise, Karla slipped into the kitchen to snatch a few forkfuls of Rosalie's culinary creations.

"This is so good, Rosalie," Karla garbled, her mouth full and her eyes rolling back in her head. "I swear, you make the best gravy ever!"

"They can't get enough," Max gushed, breezing into the kitchen. "We need more pease pudding, please." She set the serving dish on the counter. "Millie asked if you would mind sharing your recipes for everything with their personal chef."

"Tell her it would be an honour," Rosalie said, scooping more pease pudding into the china serving dish.

"I'll give you the chef's email address," Karla mumbled through a mouthful of roasted vegetables.

"You missed your calling, Rosalie. You could have been one of those celebrity chefs on the Food Channel."

Max smiled. "Everyone is having second helpings. Well, everyone except Griff and Samir. Griff is on his third helping, and Samir has hardly touched his first serving."

This piqued Karla's interest. "Samir isn't eating?" she asked. "I hope he likes it."

"He insists it's wonderful," Max assured Karla and Rosalie. "He said he's feeling out of sorts and wishes he could eat more."

"Out of sorts how?" Karla inquired.

"He keeps shifting in his chair like he's uncomfortable," Max explained, giving her hips a little wiggle to demonstrate. "And rubbing his stomach." She rubbed circles on her own stomach. "His wife used her napkin to dab sweat off his brow twice. Rob asked him if he was all right when she refilled his water glass. He told her he was fine." She shrugged. "I think he looks clammy, but what do I know?"

AFTER DESSERT—A local delicacy of steamed molasses raisin pudding with butterscotch sauce—the party moved to the library for the murder mystery portion of the evening.

Max was right. Samir looked clammy and uncomfortable.

"Maybe you should retire for the evening," she overheard Raj say to his brother.

"Smashing idea!" Colin agreed. "We can reschedule the mystery game for tomorrow night."

"No one will mind," Millie added.

"I'd love to come back tomorrow night," Griff volunteered, "especially if Rosalie is cooking again."

"No." Samir shook his head. "We've been looking forward to this for weeks. We will do the murder tonight!"

Karla was certain he was referring to the game and not an actual murder.

Much to her relief, Raj and Colin laughed at Samir's slip of the tongue.

"Fine, we'll do the murder tonight," Raj joked in response.

"Let's do this murder," Colin chuffed.

Lynn was ready to play her part. Her lips twitched as she paced in the corner, rehearsing her single line under her breath.

Karla read the murder mystery's fake backstory about a group of people gathered for the reading of the will of their deceased employer when one heir turns up dead: face down, one shoe missing, clutching a mysterious key in her dead fist.

On cue, Lynn appeared in the centre of the room, wheezing with dramatic flair.

What are you doing mother? The victim was poisoned, she didn't die from an asthma attack!

Lynn clutched her chest with one hand and grabbed the back of a wing chair with the other. She looked toward the sky, "Oh my!" She swept the back of her hand across her forehead and gasped. "I don't"—she swooned and swayed, clutching Colin Coventry's arm for dramatic effect—"feel..." She stumbled forward and clutched her chest, then her throat. "Very well."

She crumpled to the floor in a dramatic heap with her fist stretched out in front of her. With one final exaggerated exhale, she unclenched her fist to reveal the key.

"Brava, Lynn Bell," Samir praised, laughing. He placed his thumb and index finger in his mouth and let out an encouraging whistle. "Everyone, a round of applause for Lynn Bell."

The room applauded Lynn's dramatic faux demise. They laughed and took turns recalling their favourite part of her dramatic fake death. Lynn was a committed actor; she hadn't moved a muscle since she hit the floor. Karla was about to give her mother a gentle poke to make sure she was still breathing when a cat—Karla couldn't distinguish between Rosemary and Thyme—slinked into the library, flopped on the floor next to her, and tickled Lynn's nose with its flicking tail. Lynn broke character just long enough to twitch away the itch.

Raj was inspired to recreate Lynn's impassioned forehead swipe and glance toward the heavens. Then, Samir stepped forward, clutching his stomach and groaning. His chest heaved.

Everyone cheered while he recreated Lynn's iconic scene. That was what he was doing, wasn't he?

Samir grabbed the bookshelf and opened his mouth, forcing out a strangled moan. He fell to the floor, taking half a dozen hardcover books with him.

"Well done, darling," Millie said, clapping.

"You deserve an Academy Award," Raj shouted.

"Encore," Lady Olivia cheered.

"Samir?" Worry was etched all over Griff's face as

he looked from Samir's too-still body, to Karla, then to Colin. Colin shrugged, shaking his head.

Something was wrong. Samir wasn't moving. A thick string of saliva trailed from his open mouth to the kilim rug. His eyes were wide, glassy, vacant. Lifeless.

"Rob!" Karla shouted.

Rob and Max were cleaning the dining room and kitchen.

Max ran into the room first. She lunged and slid over to Samir like she was sliding into home base for a grand slam.

Lynn came out of character, took to her feet, and got out of Max's way.

"What happened?" Rob asked, rushing into the room.

With her fingers pressing into the flesh under his jaw, Max looked up at Rob and said, "Samir Khan is dead."

CHAPTER 8

ONE DAD, TWO DAUGHTERS

MILLIE LET OUT a horrified gasp and covered her mouth with both hands. Her eyes opened so wide that her eyebrows almost disappeared into her hairline.

"Millie!" Colin shoved past Lady Olivia and Raj to get to her. "Don't look." He wrapped his arm around her shoulder and pressed her face into the lapel of his black dinner jacket. "Samir wouldn't want you to see him like this."

Rob was performing CPR with Max's assistance.

"Someone call an ambulance," Lady Olivia demanded. "We need a proper doctor, not catering assistants."

"Rob is a proper doctor," Griff explained. "Dr. Robyn Mayhew is Bellbrook's town doctor."

"And the town coroner," Lynn added.

"Oh my," Lady Olivia said. "And she works as a catering assistant on the side?" she asked. "People in small towns really do wear multiple hats."

Karla wanted to explain that Rob was not a catering assistant but an amazing friend who offered to help in a time of need. But given the circumstances, she swallowed her comment.

Rob and Max uttered something to each other that Karla couldn't hear because her heart was pounding in her ears, and adrenaline was whooshing through her veins. Still on her knees, Max backed away from Samir's body and pulled her cell phone from her blazer pocket. Her thumbs flew across the keyboard so fast they were a blur. Then, she returned the phone to her pocket and pointed at Harry.

He rolled his shoulders back one at a time, readying himself to leap into action.

"Make sure the outside light is on," she said.

Harry nodded

"Stand outside and wave them down."

Harry nodded again and disappeared toward the foyer to carry out his assignment.

"Where are the keys for the SUVs?" Griff asked. "I'll clear the driveway, so the ambulance can park there."

Raj pointed toward the kitchen with a shaky finger. "In there."

Griff gave Raj a curt nod of acknowledgement, then looked at Karla. "I'll update Rosalie and tell her to stay in the kitchen."

"Thanks," she mumbled.

Max turned her attention to Karla. "Dad's on his way. So are the paramedics."

Karla nodded, still processing everything that was happening.

"I texted him directly so the media wouldn't pick up the call on the police scanner."

"Thank you," Karla said, grateful Max had thought about the potential media circus. Reporters would pitch their tents in Bellbrook if they discovered one of the wealthiest people on the planet had lost consciousness during a murder mystery game.

"Why on earth is your father coming here?" Colin asked Max, still cradling Millie's head against his chest. Millie's fist was pressed against her mouth, and her entire body trembled, teetering on a tightrope between hope and despair.

"He's the police chief," Max replied.

"Maxine Sheridan is an officer of the law," Lynn explained. "Like father, like daughter."

"Does everyone in this town have more than one job?" Lady Olivia asked, while avoiding looking at Samir's limp body.

"You said, 'Dad' to Karla as though her father was on his way," Raj commented to Max, his face clouded with shock and confusion. "How many fathers have you summoned?"

"We have the same father," Karla explained. "Max is my half-sister."

"Oh my." Lady Olivia leaned heavily on her cane, using her free hand to fan her face.

"Sit down," Raj instructed, offering Lady Olivia his arm.

He guided her to a small armchair and steadied her as she lowered herself.

Rob was still performing CPR on Samir and seemed to have blocked out the fog of shock and fear that had engulfed the room. Either Rosemary or Thyme—Karla still couldn't tell the identical cats apart—had skulked onto Samir's thighs and proceeded to knead his stomach. Max shooed away the cat.

"I'll get these two out of here," Lynn said, scooping up the twin Siamese cats and whisking them out of the room. One cat protested with a hiss, the other with a long, low mewl.

"Put them in my room," Lady Olivia called after her.

Karla felt helpless. Rob and Max worked on Samir with urgency while the rest of them stood around, their only contribution being not to get underfoot.

"This can't be happening," Raj kept repeating under his breath. "This can't be happening." He shook his head, his gaze trained on his brother's lifeless body.

"They're here." Max took to her feet.

Karla listened for the wail of sirens but heard nothing.

"Their lights and sirens are off," Griff said, appearing out of nowhere at her side and seeming to read her mind. "They're being as discreet as possible." He took Karla's hand and dropped the keys into her palm. His hand was reassuring and warm. "Both SUVs are around the corner on Maple Street. Harry is outside on the porch."

She nodded.

"We need to clear the room," Max announced. "And I need to separate you until the police have interviewed everyone individually."

"No!" Millie wailed, pushing against Colin and freeing herself from his grasp. "I'm not leaving my husband." She shook her head. "He'll need me when he comes 'round." Her eyes pleaded with Rob. "He'll ask for me as soon as he wakes up."

Rob stopped chest compressions, glanced at her watch, then met Millie's gaze with an expression that exuded sympathy. "I'm sorry," she said softly, shaking her head.

"Noooo!" Millie's cry started as a defiant howl but ended as a defeated whimper.

Her knees began to shake and buckle. Colin caught her before she hit the floor. He supported her around the waist as she pulled toward Samir's body with outstretched arms, reaching for her husband, her mouth opening and closing but emitting no sound. Screams so loud they were silent.

The thudding of boots and a low murmur of voices echoed in the hall outside the library.

"Come, my dear," Lady Olivia stood, handed Raj her walking stick, and reached for Millie. "Let's go to the other room. Leave the professionals to do their duties."

Millie nodded in response to Lady Olivia's instruction, but her eyes were still glued to Samir on the floor. Without averting her gaze, she reached toward Lady Olivia's open arms. They held each other up as Lady Olivia steered Millie down the hall toward the sunroom. Millie kept her eyes peeled on Samir's body until it was no longer possible for her to turn her head and crane her neck enough to see him.

Max agreed not to separate Millie and Lady Olivia.

She would allow them to comfort each other while the police and paramedics did their jobs. But she dispatched everyone else to separate areas of the house. Raj and Colin were assigned to their separate bedrooms, Griff was exiled to the dining room, and Karla was banished to the adjoining lounge. Lynn volunteered to wait in the breakfast room. Karla knew Lynn had chosen the breakfast room because it would position her near Rosalie.

THE KEYS GRIFF had placed in Karla's hand dug into her palm. Despite the pain, she couldn't seem to loosen her grip on them. She sat, absorbed by her thoughts, going through the potential worst-case scenarios from Samir's death. Why did Samir die? Was it food poisoning? A heart attack? Would she lose her other VIP clients because of the negative publicity? How would she protect Samir's family from the paparazzi while they were in Bellbrook? How long could she hide Samir's death from the press? From his shareholders? From her other clients? She was vaguely aware of Griff in the next room, pacing laps around the large, cherry wood dining table, spinning his bowtie in circles on his index finger.

"Are you OK?" Dean Sheridan swooped into the lounge, and Karla jumped up from the sofa.

"I'm fine, Dad."

He gripped her shoulders and scanned her for injuries, or evidence, or something. "What happened, La-la?"

La-la, or sometimes Karla-la—in a sing-song voice—was the nickname Dean had conferred upon his eldest daughter when she was too young to remember. Growing up, she'd hated the nickname but had learned early on that if she made a big deal of it, he'd make it worse by saying it louder or turning it into a song and serenading her. So, she learned to ignore it, accept it, and—now that she was older—find comfort in the familiarity and predictability of it.

"I'm not sure," she admitted. "He collapsed and died. Rob and Max tried…" Her voice trailed off before she could finish her sentence.

"He didn't eat much supper," Griff added from the adjoining dining room. "And he looked uncomfortable. I don't think Samir was feeling well."

Dean spun at the unexpected voice. "Didn't see you there, Griff." The men exchanged nods. Dean turned back toward his daughter, completely blocking her view of the dining room.

Dean Sheridan was tall and wide. He had large hands and feet, and a big voice that boomed with authority, even in situations where he had none. As a little girl, Karla thought he was the personification of a giant teddy bear. If teddy bears had flat-top haircuts wide enough to carve a Sunday roast.

"Max'n'cheese suggested that we take your statement first, and I agree with her," Dean explained, referring to his younger daughter and colleague. Max was far less tolerant of her Dean-bestowed nickname than Karla. She *hated* being called Max'n'cheese, especially at work. The term of endearment triggered her inner, insolent child. She would roll her eyes, stomp her feet, and huff when Dean used it. He either didn't care or didn't notice. He loved his girls. Try as he might, he didn't understand them, but he loved them and was proud of them. "We're hoping you can act as a kind of liaison between us and the family. They know you, and they're comfortable with you. If you happen to observe anything that makes you suspect any of the witnesses are lying, could you use your special skill and let us know?"

Karla nodded. "Raj nods when he tells a lie." She gave her father an exaggerated nod as a demonstration. Dean flipped open his notebook and began taking notes. "Like he's trying to convince himself and the person he's lying to that he's telling the truth."

Dean looked up from his notes. "Anything else?"

"Colin never uses contractions when he lies," she discloses. "And he overemphasizes the words he would normally contract."

"Can you give me an example, La-la?"

"Like, he'll say 'I *do not* know' instead of 'I don't know.'"

Dean nodded and continued taking notes.

"You can still do that?" Griff asked from where he now sat at the dining room table. "I always figured you'd outgrow it."

"The opposite, I'm afraid," Karla replied. "Age has strengthened my weird skill and made it stronger than ever." She shrugged one shoulder. "The more I use it, the more accurate it gets."

Karla was a human lie detector. It started when she was eight years old, and Lynn had made a fleeting trip to Bellbrook to visit her and Grandma May. Karla was upset when it was time for Lynn to fly back to whatever exotic destination she had come from. To soothe her, Lynn had promised her daughter that she would "be back real soon." Karla made the connection between her mother's lies and the aggressive, prolonged eye contact she would make when telling them.

After that, she started recognizing lies with other people she knew. Almost everyone had a Tell; a tic or behaviour they exhibited when they lied. Some people had more than one Tell, depending on the severity of the lie and the person to whom they were lying. Some people had no Tells, which had duped Karla into more than one unhealthy relationship. She used to be too naive to understand that some people—like narcissists and sociopaths—don't always have Tells because they don't experience stress and guilt like other people. Therefore, they don't need a tic to relieve the discomfort that accompanies a lie. She wasn't naive anymore. She no longer trusted anyone she couldn't read.

Sometimes people became aware of their Tell and tried to suppress it, but they would end up replacing it with something else, and it didn't take Karla very long to figure out their new pattern.

Shortly after Rob finished medical school, she diagnosed Karla with ADHD. This led Rob to develop a theory to explain Karla's lie detection ability. Rob theorized that Karla's ADHD and possible SPD—sensory processing disorder—made her hypersensitive and hyperaware of the constant onslaught of stimuli and small details most people ignored with their conscious brains. Not only was she able to distinguish these small details, but she could process them fast enough to extract patterns and predict behavior. Karla's brain was like a super-fast computer with a tiny memory.

At first, Rob's theory about her brain had been a relief. Karla had often wondered why she struggled with things that seemed so simple for other people, like remembering appointments or finishing one task before starting three more. It also explained why, when Karla and her college friends downed energy drinks and double espresso shots so they could cram all night for an exam, her friends would be wired and full of energy, but Karla would relax and drift off to sleep earlier than usual.

But now, she had a different perspective. In a heartbeat, she would have loved to trade in her human polygraph skill if it meant she could relinquish her other ADHD symptoms.

She took daily medication. Most days. OK, half the days because she often forgot. How was she supposed to remember to take the medicine when she needed the medicine to remember? The meds alleviated some symptoms, but not all, and had no effect on her ability to read people's micro expressions and behaviour.

"How about Millie Khan?" Dean asked.

"I haven't spent enough time with her to figure out her Tell."

Dean's large hands gave the impression that he was writing in a miniature notebook with a tiny pen.

"Chief!" The unfamiliar voice floated into the room from somewhere else in the large house.

"I better see what they want." Dean flipped the notebook shut and slid the pen into his breast pocket. "I'll send someone to take your statement, La-la. Shout if you need me." He smiled, turned, nodded to Griff, and strode out of the room.

CHAPTER 9

HINDSIGHT IS TWENTY-TWENTY

"WHAT'S MY TELL?"

Karla flinched. For a moment, she had forgotten Griff was there. "I don't know," she replied. "I could never figure you out."

"Because I've never lied to you."

"Yes, you did," Karla retorted with a small, involuntary snort. "Last time we saw each other before I left Bellbrook." She crossed her arms in front of her chest. "And goodness knows how many weeks before that. Every time you let me believe we were leaving Bellbrook together, you were lying."

"That wasn't a lie, K." Griff stopped pacing and slingshotted his bowtie onto the dining room table. "It was a change of heart. I changed my mind that morning. Hours before we were supposed to leave."

"Admit it," Karla urged, "you never intended to leave with me. You just said it so I wouldn't get upset, and we wouldn't fight. You strung me along."

"That's not true, K. I would never do that," he

lamented. "I had every intention of leaving with you. Right up until the last minute."

"I'll have to take your word for it, won't I?"

"Ms. Bell?" The young officer looked back and forth from Karla to Griff as if he was trying to figure out which of them was Karla.

A second officer showed up and took Griff's statement at the dining room table.

Karla answered the officer's questions and waited patiently while he made notes. She told him about her professional history with Samir, and why he had come to Bellbrook for the weekend. Samir's security and publicity teams had done a stellar job. The young officer had no idea Samir was in town until he arrived on the scene and was told who had died.

Griff must not have had much to say because Karla was still answering questions when Griff and his officer left the dining room.

"Am I free to leave?" Karla asked as the officer closed his notebook and slid it into his pocket.

"Chief says you're allowed access to the scene," the officer confirmed.

"Thank you."

Karla stood and smoothed her dress with a sigh. She left the room ahead of the police officer and headed toward the kitchen. She was parched. It wasn't late, but she was tired and overwhelmed. Then, she was struck with a pang of guilt for indulging in self-pity. She might be mentally tired and emotionally spent, but imagine how Millie, Raj, Colin, and Lady Olivia felt! They had lost a husband, a brother, a best friend, and a surrogate son-in-law. They must be heartbroken. *The least I can do is put on a brave face and help them through this. Samir would have wanted that.*

"K!" Griff's voice chased her down the hall, interrupting her mental pep talk.

She stopped and waited for him to catch up.

"I'll drive Rosalie home," he offered. "She already gave her statement, and you probably have a long night ahead of you."

Karla huffed out an exasperated breath and rubbed small circles in her temples with her index fingers. "I completely forgot about Rosalie."

"Don't worry," Griff assured her. "She's having the time of her life. She fed the officers and paramedics. She said this was the most exciting evening she's had in decades. Your dad questioned her, and she gave an official statement. She's never given a police statement before. She said she can't wait to get home and cross it off her bucket list."

Being involved in a police investigation was on Rosalie's bucket list? How oddly specific.

"At least someone had a good evening," she mumbled.

"K, this isn't your fault," Griff insisted. "When Rob examines Samir, she'll find an unfortunate, natural cause of his death. Something that no one could have prevented."

"I hope so," Karla agreed.

"Ready, Griff," Rosalie said, carrying her apron over her arm like a jacket. She spotted Karla, handed Griff her apron, and threw her arms around her late best friend's granddaughter. "Come here." She engulfed Karla in her short, warm, safe arms. She smelled like molasses and unconditional love. "You poor dear. What an awful ending to an evening that started so wonderfully."

"Thank you for helping tonight, Rosalie," Karla said, breaking away from the embrace and pulling herself up to her full height. Karla wasn't tall at five feet five inches, but in heels, towering next to Rosalie made her feel like a giant.

"I'm always happy to help," Rosalie reminded her. "You have a whole town of folks who are always happy to help. Sometimes, you need to remember that."

"Yes, ma'am," Karla said.

"I'll stop at your place and pick up Gucci." It was a statement, not an offer. "Griff and I will collect his things. He can stay with me until you and Lynn are less busy."

"Thank you, Rosalie."

Rosalie pulled Karla's shoulders and forced her into another stooped hug. "Send someone to see me in the morning," she instructed. "I'll have breakfast ready for Samir's family. Something healthy and wholesome. Comfort food."

"You don't have to do that. I'm sure food will be the last thing—"

"Hush." Rosalie pointed at Karla with a stern expression. "They won't feel like eating, but they have to keep up their strength. Especially his wife. She's already skin and bones." She waved her hand in front of her face like she was erasing the words she'd just said. "On second thought, send someone to pick me up. I'll feed them myself." She turned to Griff. "I'll meet you at your truck."

Rosalie strode down the hall, accompanied by murmurs of "Hello, Ms. Howard," and "Evening, Rosalie," as she passed familiar faces in first responder uniforms.

"I remembered something," Griff said, now that they were alone. "Something I should mention to Max or Chief Sheridan."

"What?" Karla asked.

"Earlier, when we moved from the lounge to the dining room for dinner, Samir said something that, in hindsight, seems ominous."

"He did?" This piqued Karla's interest. "What did Samir say?"

"Millie and Raj were talking about how excited they were for the murder mystery game and how it's one of the family's favourite ways to spend an evening. Samir looked at me and, in a quiet voice, he said—" Griff leaned in close to Karla's exposed ear and shoulder. He smelled like whiskey and temptation. His voice was low and raspy. His breath was warm, and she resisted the urge to turn her face toward it. "Enjoy the little things, Griff, like family game night, because you never know when it will be your last one."

A shudder ran up Karla's spine, and goosebumps prickled to life on her exposed neck and shoulder. Was it the heat of Griff's breath on her skin, or the possibility that Samir Khan had predicted his own untimely demise?

He straightened his back and returned to a more

conversational, less intimate stance. "I thought he was telling me to stay grounded and grateful. You know, not to let the money go to my head. But now, I wonder if he knew something was wrong with him?"

"There you are!" Max charged toward them.

"Rosalie is waiting for me," Griff said. "See you later, Max." He touched Karla's arm, and she swore her heart paused for a beat. "See you later, K." He turned and left.

"What was that about?" Max asked.

Karla told her what Griff had said about Samir's eerily prophetic warning.

"Did he include it in his statement?"

Karla shook her head. "He said he remembered after."

Max made a quick note and thanked her for mentioning it. "You have a good rapport with Samir's family," she said. "Wanna join me while I talk to Millie?"

On the way to the sunroom, Karla spotted Lady Olivia's walking stick leaning against the hearth in the library. They stopped to retrieve it. Samir was still there, in the same spot where he collapsed. Someone had covered him with a white sheet, and a police officer was taking photos of the room, stepping carefully around the books that Samir had knocked off the shelves when he collapsed.

"Is such a heavy police presence really necessary, Chief Sheridan?" A lilt of annoyance tinged Lady

Olivia's posh accent. Her arm was around Millie's slumped shoulders as the new widow sobbed silent tears into her hands.

"The *Lady* summoned the chief," whispered a uniformed officer standing guard at the entrance to the sunroom. "She says treating the death like a crime scene is causing the widow unnecessary stress."

Karla and Max nodded.

Max thanked the officer and sent her on a break.

She asked if there was any molasses-raisin pudding left, and Max told her that Rosalie had brought extra, just in case, and she should hurry. She ran, hat in hand, to the kitchen.

"Splendid!" Lady Olivia's voice was thick with fake enthusiasm. "Father and daughters. How quaint." She gave them a fake smile and pointed toward the hall. "Perhaps I should fetch Lynn, and you can have a proper family reunion."

Lady Olivia's eyes betrayed her carefully cultivated facade. Her countenance was controlled and calm, but her eyes swirled with emotion. Under the surface, Lady Olivia was churning like an angry volcano. Karla would do whatever necessary to help Lady Olivia contain her volcanic emotions. For now.

"Actually, Lynn's being questioned in another room," Max said.

"I was being sarcastic, dear."

Max's face tightened at Lady Olivia's condescending tone.

Karla touched her sister's arm. A wordless attempt to stop her from snapping an ugly retort at the elderly, grieving woman.

Lynn and Dean were Karla's parents. They never married. They hardly even dated. Karla was the result of a casual relationship during their senior year of high school.

Dean, being someone who believed in doing the right thing and taking responsibility, proposed. Lynn declined. It was widely believed that, contrary to his insistence otherwise, Dean Sheridan proposed to Lynn Bell not out of obligation but because he was in love with her.

The feeling was not mutual.

Lynn had no intention of marrying Dean and staying in Bellbrook to raise a baby. She had Big Plans that didn't include Bellbrook, Dean, or apparently, Karla.

While Lynn traversed the globe searching for herself, Dean stayed close to home and embarked on a career in law enforcement. He was a constant presence in Karla's life. Grandma May raised her, but Dean was always around, on the periphery. Always within earshot. He was the best parent he could be at eighteen years old, hardly an adult himself. He had spent his twenties climbing the career ladder and ricocheting from one short relationship to the next. Until he met Max's mum. Having finally met someone willing to marry him, Dean raced Max's mum down the aisle within six months of their first date. Max came along soon after when Karla was eleven. The marriage fizzled, and Max's parents divorced. Max spent the school year in Bellbrook and summers on the other side of the world, in the small Japanese village where her mother grew up.

Max had worshipped her older sister, and Karla had loved being worshipped. They might be more than a decade apart in age and look like they were born on different sides of the world—both girls inherited their mothers' looks and bore no resemblance to Dean—but they shared a strong, intangible bond. They were sisters. Sisters by blood and sisters by choice.

Max relaxed under Karla's touch. "We have to treat every unexpected death as a crime scene until the coroner determines otherwise," she explained to the titled woman.

"I already said that," Dean uttered.

"Surely your procedures and protocols can wait until tomorrow." Lady Olivia gave them a terse glare. "It's not like we're going anywhere."

"Not without my husband." They all leaned in, straining to hear Millie's words. Her already quiet voice was even harder to hear when infused with emotion and sobs. "I won't leave Bellbrook until I can take Samir with me."

"Of course not," Karla agreed.

Millie reached for the box of tissues someone had thoughtfully placed on the coffee table. She plucked two tissues from the box and blew her nose. As if by maternal instinct, Lady Olivia offered her open hand. Millie dropped the used tissues onto the mound of tissues already in her mother-in-law's palm and plucked two more from the box.

"Trade you," Karla whispered, holding out Lady Olivia's walking stick.

The wood cane was surprisingly heavy. Solid. Old,

except for the modern rubber foot on the end. Karla wondered if it was a family heirloom.

"It's a beautiful cane," Karla added. "Much more character than the aluminum one Rosalie used after her hip surgery."

"This is an heirloom," Lady Olivia explained. "It's from my late husband's side of the family. His great uncle picked it up in America during prohibition." She unscrewed the handle. "I'll tell you a secret." The elderly woman leaned toward Karla. "Sometimes, when the cats are being particularly difficult to herd, I stick catnip treats in here. The smell keeps them spellbound, and they'll do whatever I say."

Lady Olivia took the cane, passing Karla a handful of damp, wadded up, used tissues in exchange.

Karla tried to ignore the damp weight in her hand. She held the wad just tight enough not to drop them.

"Stop that cat!!" Lynn's shrill voice carried through the house amid a flurry of hissing and scurrying. "Grab that kitty!"

CHAPTER 10

WHERE DID THE THYME GO?

"THAT WILL BE THYME." Lady Olivia expelled a knowing sigh. "She abhors confinement," she said, shaking her head, "and will not tolerate a closed door unless I'm in the room with her."

A breathless Lynn appeared in the doorway. "I only opened the door a crack," she insisted. "I was going to freshen their water bowl." Her chest heaved from chasing the fleet-footed feline across the hall and down the stairs. "How was I supposed to know a cat would pounce at my face?"

"Are you hurt, Mother?" Karla asked.

"Nah, I'm fine." Lynn waved away her daughter's concern, smoothing her hair toward her blonde bun. "I got out of the way just in time. It wasn't me she wanted. It was freedom."

"Found her!" Harry appeared behind Lynn, wearing oven mitts. "She's holed up in the dumbwaiter, hissing and swatting." He held up his hand

and waggled his thick silver eyebrows at the slices in the oven mitts. "She won't come out without a fight."

"Go," Millie instructed Lady Olivia. "I'll be fine. Collect Thyme before she does someone a mischief."

"Are you sure, my dear?" she asked, reaching for her cane.

"I promise you. I'll be fine?" The intonation in Millie's voice made it seem like she wasn't convinced she would be fine ever again.

"I'll stay with Millie," Karla assured the dowager.

Chief Sheridan offered Lady Olivia his arm. "I have a way with cats," he said. "And maybe I can ask you a few questions about this evening."

"Thank you, Chief." She gripped his arm while she gained purchase on her feet.

He accompanied her out of the room.

"Millie." Karla sat down on the overstuffed blue loveseat next to her. "I'm so sorry for your loss."

Millie nodded and plucked another tissue from the box. "It's unbelievable." She sniffed and dabbed her eyes. "It doesn't seem real."

"I can't imagine what you're going through," Max added.

"Try going through it twice," Millie mumbled.

It hadn't occurred to Karla that Millie was now a widow twice-over. That her first husband, Lady Olivia's late son, had died tragically in a car accident, and her second husband dropped dead suddenly during family game night.

"Perhaps, it's me," Millie said, correcting her posture. "Maybe I'm cursed?"

"You aren't cursed," Karla insisted. *Just incredibly unlucky.*

"Listen, Karla." Millie's voice was even quieter than usual. Karla leaned in and squinted to hear. "Do you think your friend Dr. Rob..." Millie paused, searching for Rob's surname.

"Mayhew." Karla filled in the blank for her.

"Right, Dr. Mayhew," Millie agreed. "Do you think she would mind checking on Mumsy, er, Lady Olivia? It must appear to be the doctor's idea. Mumsy would be outraged if she suspected I had sent her."

"I'm sure Rob would do that," Karla replied.

"Is Lady Olivia OK?" Max asked. "Has she complained about not feeling well?"

Max had her notebook and pen poised for action. Karla knew her sister was worried that whatever befell Samir might now be happening to Lady Olivia.

"She's strong as an ox." Millie's mouth twitched into a near-smile. "Samir always jokes that Mumsy will outlive all of us." She caught herself. "Joked. He always *joked*," she corrected herself, then cleared her throat.

"No one had a sense of humour like Samir," Karla agreed, recalling his fun, easygoing nature.

"I'm afraid tonight's events might trigger her, though," Millie explained. "Samir wasn't her son, but they were quite fond of each other. Samir enjoyed doting on Mumsy the way he never could with his own mother. They were close in their own special way. A motherless son and a sonless mother who took comfort in each other's existence. I'm not sure Mumsy can take another loss. You see, losing her husband, then her son was difficult. She struggled. Stopped eating. Hardly slept. Most days, I couldn't get her out of bed, never mind convince her to get dressed. It went on for months. She became dangerously frail and sickly."

"I'll speak to Rob." Karla placed her hand on top of Millie's. "We'll keep an eye on her."

"You and Lady Olivia seem very close," Max observed.

"Now," Millie commented. "We weren't always. She didn't approve when I married her son."

"I didn't know that," Karla said. "Why not?"

"Mumsy wanted her son to marry someone more aristocratic, a marriage that would redeem her in the eyes of her family. They had disinherited her for marrying a commoner."

"You might not have a title, but you check all the other boxes," Karla said. "You're kind, smart, loving, educated."

"You went to Oxford, right?" Max asked.

Millie wrung her hands in her lap. "That was where I met my first husband, Samir, and Colin. They were mates."

"What did you study?" Max asked.

"Art history?" Millie replied as though she wasn't quite sure.

"Cool," Max replied with a smile. "You must like museums."

Millie inhaled sharply and pinched the bridge of her nose.

"Maybe Rob should examine *you*," Max suggested. "How are you feeling, Millie? Physically, I mean.

Have you experienced any unusual symptoms lately?"

"Unless Rob can mend a broken heart, she won't be able to cure me, I'm afraid," Millie said. "Anyway, I'm quite certain I know what killed my husband, and it wasn't food poisoning."

"What was it?" Karla asked.

Max's pen hovered over the blank page of her notebook, and her eyes bore into the top of Millie's down-turned head.

"Samir was recently diagnosed with stomach cancer."

Karla and Max's jaws dropped. They stared at each other, then at Millie.

"Millie, I had no idea," Karla uttered.

"No one did. That was how Samir wanted it," Millie explained. "After this weekend in Bellbrook, we were heading to Germany, so Samir could get a second opinion from a German oncologist who specializes in this type of cancer."

Karla opened her mouth to speak. Her brain swirled with questions. How sick was Samir? How long had he known about his illness? Did the doctor who diagnosed him give him a prognosis?

"Millie?!" Colin's voice boomed through the house. "Millie! Where are you?" His footsteps hastened and grew louder.

"Shhh," Millie hushed. "Please don't discuss Samir's diagnosis. No one knows yet. Please let them hear it from me."

Karla nodded.

"There you are!" Colin swept into the room and made a beeline for Millie.

Karla jumped off the loveseat just as Colin claimed the spot for himself. Had she been a little slower, he would have ended up in her lap.

"I came as soon as I could," Colin implored. "I had to give the police my statement." Millie nodded.

He clutched her hand. "Can I get you anything? Anything at all?"

"We'll be right outside if you need anything," Karla said, eager to find a recycling bin for the wad of tear-soaked tissues she was still holding.

Outside the sunroom, Dean walked past, wearing a shredded pair of oven mitts and holding a hissing, swatting Thyme at arm's length. Lady Olivia ambled behind them, uttering sweet nothings to soothe the furious feline.

Max pinched Karla just under the ribs.

"Ow!"

"Cancer?!" Max hissed. "Samir Khan had cancer? We need to tell Rob."

Karla nodded. "As soon as I get rid of these tissues."

"Is it me, or is Colin Coventry a little *too* attentive to Millie Khan?"

"It's not you," Karla agreed. "I noticed it too."

"Well, it's a good thing Samir wasn't murdered," Max chuckled. "'Cuz his crush on his best friend's wife would have made Colin a suspect."

"Yes, I suppose it would." A drop of dread dripped into Karla's stomach.

CHAPTER 11

FASTER THAN A FRUIT FLY
AT A FARMER'S MARKET

Karla's to-do list infiltrated her semi-conscious brain before she opened her eyes. *Coordinate with Samir's PR team, cancel the private lighthouse tour I had booked for Samir and Millie, ask the family where they want Samir's body laid to rest, cancel the family's dinner reservation at The Pavlovian, return Rob's not-so-lucky earrings, ask Rob about the logistics of shipping a dead body, check on the food-poisoned staff…*

She reached across the bed for Gucci but found a mound of duvet where the petite pooch usually slept. "Right, you're at Rosalie's," she mumbled to the absent dog. "I forgot."

Karla padded to the kitchen, yawning and rubbing sleep from her heavy eyes. The world was dark and quiet. Sunrise was almost an hour away. The house was different without Gucci's bounding energy and constant motion. Empty. A body without a soul.

Karla had only slept a few hours. She didn't leave

the Nestled Inn until Millie, Raj, Lady Olivia, and Colin were settled—well, as settled as possible under the circumstances. Most of the police were gone when Karla had finally left.

Millie was bunking with Lady Olivia, Rosemary, and Thyme. Colin was setting up a makeshift office in the dining room and scheduling an emergency, pre-dawn video conference with the rest of TechSavvy's board of directors. Raj was pacing the halls of the large bed and breakfast like a shark patrolling the water, unable to stop swimming.

She reached into the canister on the counter where the coffee pods would have been had she remembered to stop at the store and pick some up yesterday. *Pick up coffee pods,* she added to her mental to-do list.

Karla's phone chimed, pushing the list from her mind. She reached for the phone in her bathrobe pocket and read the text from Lynn.

> There's a reporter at Déjà Brew asking
> questions about Samir.

Karla cursed under her breath.

Thirty minutes later, she was showered, dressed, presentable, and searching for her keys. Why weren't they on the hook near the door? She always kept them on the hook near the door. Found them! On the table, next to her sunglasses. She must have been too tired and too distracted to bother placing them on their designated hook.

THE EARLY HEAT wave had passed, and the early morning air was seasonably crisp. Karla could see her breath when she got out of her car on Main Street. Birds chirped and a sliver of peach sky peeked over the horizon.

"No rain today." Lynn's voice startled Karla. "My sinuses are clear as a crystal." She flared her nostrils and inhaled deeply to prove her point.

"Why are you up and at 'em so early?" Karla asked.

Lynn enjoyed a good lie-in; another trait she had passed on to her daughter.

"I went to the Nestled Inn to feed her ladyship's cats," Lynn explained. "They have a strict routine. Lady Olivia keeps them on the same feeding schedule regardless what time zone they're in."

"I forgot about the cats," Karla admitted. "Thank you for taking care of them."

"I'm just doing what any good PA would do," Lynn said with an elbow nudge and a wink. "Rob gave Millie something to help with anxiety. She and Lady Olivia were still asleep when I left. Colin had sequestered himself in the dining room, having a top-secret video meeting about Samir's company, and Rob gave Raj something to help him sleep too. According to Colin, Raj paced the place for hours."

"I was going to stop by there next," Karla said.

"I wouldn't go yet, love." Lynn opened the door and gestured for Karla to go ahead of her. "Let them sleep for a while."

"You're probably right," Karla said, stepping into Déjà Brew.

"Woohoo, Karla!" The blonde reverse-bob with caramel highlights waved to her from a centre table.

"It was The Posers who told me about the reporter who was inquiring about Samir," Lynn whispered.

Karla nodded, smiling at the table of yoga enthusiasts.

The Posers, as they were locally known, were a group of women who were always dressed in designer yoga gear, carried bags with rubber yoga mats sticking out, and never had a hair out of place. No one had ever actually seen them do yoga and, rumour had it, they weren't even members of Om Sweet Om, the local yoga studio. As far as Karla could tell, The Posers spent most days at Déjà Brew huddled around a central table, monitoring the conversations and comings and goings of their fellow residents.

"Good morning, ladies," Karla said with a wide smile. Five grins beamed at her in return. "What's this I hear about a reporter?"

"He's gone now." The brunette ponytail waved him off with a manicured hand.

"What did he want?" Karla asked.

"He said he heard a rumour that Bellbrook was hosting a wealthy tech mogul," replied the brunette ponytail.

"He asked if we *Khan* tell him if we knew which rich and famous techie had booked most of the Seascape Hotel," said the auburn bob.

"We told him his source was wrong," said the inverted blonde bob. "There are no *tech savvy* moguls in our small town." She gave Karla a sly grin.

"Then, we distracted him with a tempting tip," the

auburn bob added, checking the time on her smart watch. "He should arrive in Beaver Creek any minute." Her smile was smug.

"What's in Beaver Creek that would interest him?" Lynn asked.

"A certain *married* politician and her boy toy are enjoying a romantic getaway in a secluded love nest there," explained the ponytail.

"Really?" Lynn pulled up a chair and joined them. "Who?"

The blonde inverted bob whispered something in Lynn's ear.

"I knew it!" Lynn said, slapping the table. "With her handsome, young bodyguard, right?" The table nodded. "I've seen the sneaky looks they give each other on the news!"

"How do you know they're rendezvousing in Beaver Creek?" Karla asked.

"My sister's neighbour's brother-in-law works with a guy who plays hockey with the bodyguard's roommate." The brunette ponytail crossed her arms in front of her chest, daring them to challenge her.

"Did this reporter tell you the name of the wealthy tech mogul he was looking for?" Karla asked.

"He didn't have to," interjected the brunette pixie cut. "We all knew he meant Griff Dixon."

"Griff Dixon?" Lynn asked. "Are you sure?"

"Who else in Bellbrook would be *tech savvy* enough to create a viral app?" asked the auburn bob with a wink.

Karla grinned and let out a sigh of relief. Her shoulders dropped at least an inch.

"Don't worry, Karla," added the brunette ponytail. "We've got your back. We'll do everything we *Khan* to redirect nosy outsiders away from Bellbrook."

"We aren't going to sell out our friends and neighbours to some tabloid buffoon just so we can get our names in the paper," the inverted bob added.

Karla grinned, biting the inside of her cheek. Rosalie was right; gossip travelled through Bellbrook faster than a fruit fly at a farmer's market. In less than twelve hours, the town was abuzz with the news about Griff's new status as the wealthiest man in Bellbrook and Samir's role in his sudden wealth.

Rosalie had come up with the idea to use Griff's newfound wealth as a red herring to distract the rumour mill from Samir's presence and death in Bellbrook. Griff agreed to go along with it since he knew his anonymity had a limited life span. Rosalie concocted a story: The owners of the Nestled Inn had gone away for a long weekend while Harry and Griff tended to some maintenance work at the bed and breakfast. Harry and Griff were working there last night when Griff had an accident. Harry panicked and called 911. That's why the neighbours saw police cars and ambulances around the place. Meanwhile, Rosalie whispered in a few carefully selected ears about Griff's multi-millionaire status and how he developed and sold the Screw It! app to TechSavvy, having personally met Samir Khan. She had sent Karla a long text about it after Griff drove her home last night. Karla agreed as long as Griff was fine with it.

The Posers put two and two together and, reliably,

came up with five. They believed Griff was the rich tech mogul the reporter was looking for.

"It's getting busy here. I better get in line," Karla said to the table. "What would you like, Mother?"

"I'll come with you, love."

Standing in line, Lynn rummaged through her purse, and Karla assumed she was scrounging for change.

"Put your wallet away, Mother. I've got this. It's the least I can do after you got up early to feed the cat who tried to attack you last night. I would've made coffee for us at home, but I've forgotten to buy coffee pods every day this week."

"You need to make a list on your phone, so you capture your thoughts before you forget them." Lynn tapped her temple with her right index finger. "I'm learning how to make accommodations for your ADHD." She nodded proudly.

Since learning about Karla's lifelong ADHD struggles, Lynn had gone from denying ADHD was real to taking it upon herself to research the condition and become an armchair expert. She had recently declared herself an informed ally and activist for the neurodivergent population.

Coffee in hand, Lynn joined The Posers for more gossip about the married politician and her much younger boy toy while Karla headed to Rosalie's house to take Gucci for his morning walk.

CHAPTER 12

SOUP FOR EVERYONE

"SOMETHING SMELLS AMAZING." Karla filled her lungs with the comforting aromas. Rosalie's house always smelled like comfort food and hugs.

Gucci ran to her and pawed her knees, whining and yelping with excitement.

"Gucci poochie," Karla said with puckered lips as she placed the tray of coffee cups on a nearby table and lowered herself to the floor to greet the excited dog. "I missed you!"

"Chicken soup," Rosalie said, stirring one of two large stockpots on the stove. "I made enough for everyone at The Nestled Inn and for Rob to feed Samir's sick employees at the Seascape Hotel. She'll be here to pick it up in a few minutes."

Today, Rosalie wore a royal-blue head wrap with blue, dangly parrot earrings, and a blue-and-white house dress with matching blue slippers.

"Where did all these thermoses come from?" Karla asked, returning to her feet and noticing the collection of assorted insulated containers on Rosalie's kitchen table.

"Some are mine," Rosalie replied. "The rest are on loan from the church. They're for the soup."

"Samir's visit to Bellbrook has become a community effort," Karla observed.

"Everything in Bellbrook becomes a community effort, my dear." Rosalie stopped stirring and picked up a glass container from the nearby counter. "Toutons," she said, giving the container a gentle shake that caused her cat, Purrnest Hemingway, to rush into the kitchen from somewhere else in the house. "With homemade blueberry jam for on top."

Toutons were a local breakfast tradition. A sort of fat pancake made from risen bread dough. Usually topped with a dab of butter and something sweet.

The small cat sat at Rosalie's feet, flicking his grey tail with his eyes trained on the container of food in Rosalie's hand.

"Yummy!"

"They aren't for you," Rosalie clarified, managing Karla's expectations. "It's breakfast for Samir's family. Toutons with blueberry coulis and scrambled eggs." She smiled, and her face softened. "Of course, I made enough for you too. And Harry. And Lynn. And whoever else is there and needs feeding."

"Flat white?" Karla offered Rosalie a takeout coffee cup from Déjà Brew.

"My favourite!" Rosalie freed the paper cup from the recyclable tray. "Thank you."

Karla tugged the two smaller cups from the drinks tray. Two Catuccinos: small cups of frothed milk for

Hemi—Purrnest Hemingway—and Gucci. She placed Hemi's open cup on the nearby windowsill. The small grey tabby leapt onto the sill and started lapping up the treat, shaking her front paw during the first few sips. Karla took the lid off Gucci's treat and squatted next to him, holding the cup while he slurped out the contents.

"Thank you for taking care of Gucci," Karla said, looking at the happy terrier who had a spot of frothed milk on his nose.

"Hemi and I love having him." Rosalie had returned to her stirring duties at the stockpots. "He's good company."

"I'll take Gucci for his morning walk, then come back to collect his things," Karla suggested, already clipping his designer leash to his matching designer collar.

Rosalie nodded.

KARLA AND GUCCI walked toward the waterfront, stopping every few feet so Gucci could sniff things and pee on them.

"Colin?" Karla squinted at the tall, blurry figure loping toward them. "What are you doing here?" she called as he came into focus.

"Good morning, Karla," said Colin in his upper-crust accent. "And who is this charming fellow?" He pointed at Gucci who was straining against his leash to get close enough to touch Colin.

"This is Gucci," Karla replied. "He's my partner in

crime." She smiled. "Why are you wandering around Bellbrook? If you need anything, you only have to call or text. It'll be difficult to keep your location a secret if you're walking around town in broad daylight."

"No worries on that front," Colin chuckled. "No one ever recognizes me. I'm not the famous one. Samir was. He was the public face of TechSavvy. I'm just the guy who gets cut out of the paparazzi photos."

Did she detect a hint of resentment in his voice? Perhaps she was overthinking it. Colin had just lived through one of the roughest twelve hours of his life. He's bound to be out of sorts.

Karla chewed the inside of her bottom lip to stop herself from telling him about the reporter who was asking questions earlier at Déjà Brew. She didn't want to add to his list of concerns.

Colin's prominent Adam's apple bobbed and bulged when he swallowed. He looked exhausted. His eyes were sunk-in. They were red and puffy. Karla was willing to bet that he hadn't slept at all since he woke up yesterday.

"I needed to clear my head," Colin explained. "I just finished a rather difficult video call with the Tech-Savvy board of directors."

"That must have been a tough call for you and Raj," Karla sympathized.

Colin joined Karla and Gucci, and the trio meandered toward the water.

"For me, yes. Raj isn't on the board of directors," Colin explained. "Samir was always quite insistent that Raj not have any corporate responsibility. Raj played more of a personal advisory role in Samir's life."

"I didn't know that," Karla said. "They were always together, so I assumed Raj had a role in the company."

"Raj would love a role in the company, but Samir wouldn't allow it. They bickered about it."

This was news to Karla who had always had the impression that the brothers got along well and enjoyed each other's company.

"How did the board take the news about Samir's death?" she asked.

Colin let out a defeated sigh. "Not well, I'm afraid. To say they were shocked would be an understatement. They had a lot of questions, and I had very few answers, which they didn't like. They're used to immediate answers."

"You'll have answers soon," Karla assured him. "Rob is performing Samir's autopsy this morning."

"The sooner the better," Colin said. "The company must release a statement announcing Samir's death and my subsequent appointment as interim CEO and chairman of the board before the stock markets open on Monday morning. It's a regulatory requirement."

"You're the new CEO of TechSavvy?"

"Interim CEO," Colin corrected. "Someone has to be in charge, and I'm most suited for the job."

Karla didn't know what to say. Under less tragic circumstances, she would congratulate Colin on such a big career advancement, but congratulations didn't seem appropriate the morning after his best friend died.

"It would be ideal if we could have enough information to satisfy the gossip mongers so poor Millie won't have to deal with the press's speculations and theories about Samir's death," Colin continued. "It's bad enough that she'll be harassed by reporters everywhere she goes. Also, a confirmed cause of death will, hopefully, minimize the instability Samir's death will have on TechSavvy's stock price."

"We're working hard to keep Millie's location secret," Karla reassured him. "And I'll speak with Rob today to figure out how we can discreetly transport Samir."

"Speaking of transportation," Colin continued. "I'd like to ensure Millie is safely ensconced in their London home *before* the world finds out about Samir's death. In London, she'll be surrounded by friends and family. It will be easier to insulate her from the press and other unwanted attention. I'm planning to fly her home tonight or tomorrow at the latest. I've started making arrangements."

"Does Millie know about your plan?" Karla asked. "She was quite clear that she won't leave Bellbrook without Samir."

"*I will* make her see sense," Colin said. "I'll fly to London with Millie, Olivia, and the cats. Raj will stay behind in Bellbrook and accompany Samir's remains."

Good luck with that, Karla thought to herself as she recalled Millie's steadfastness about staying in Bellbrook until Rob released Samir's remains.

After strolling along the waterfront, Karla and Gucci escorted Colin back to the street where the Nestled Inn was located. He didn't know the area well enough to find his way back on his own. Then, Karla returned to Rosalie's house to collect Gucci's things and take him home. Rosalie was ready and waiting when Karla and Gucci returned. She had changed into a going-out outfit of royal-blue polyester trousers, matching blue t-shirt layered with a white, unbuttoned blouse, and practical shoes.

"Rob's too busy to pick up the soup," Rosalie explained. "So, you can drop me and the toutons off at The Nestled Inn, then you can deliver the soup thermoses to The Seascape Hotel."

"Got it," Karla agreed, hefting the laundry basket full of thermoses toward the trunk of her car. "I'll leave Gucci at your place until I'm done running around."

"You can leave Gucci at my place forever if you want. Hemi and I would love that."

She dropped off Rosalie and helped her, the toutons, and a few thermoses of soup get settled in The Nestled Inn's large, modern kitchen. Harry was sitting at the kitchen table, attired in his makeshift butler uniform, amusing himself, Rosemary, and Thyme by darting the red dot of a laser pointer across the white tiled floor.

"Everyone's asleep," he said. "According to Max, they didn't get settled until a few hours ago."

"I heard," Karla said, nodding.

"Did I hear my name?" Max peeked around the corner from the breakfast room.

"You're still here?" Rosalie asked in a way that sounded concerned.

"You must be exhausted," Karla agreed.

"I told her to go home." Harry raised his hands in a placating gesture. "I told her there's no point in her staying when everyone is fast asleep. I offered to call her if someone woke up and needed her."

Harry dropped the laser pointer on the kitchen table, and one of the cats let out a frustrated meow when the red dot disappeared.

"I'm the family's liaison officer," Max explained. "I *have* to be here." She checked the time on her watch. "I went home, slept for a couple of hours." She fought back a yawn. "Dad is coming to relieve me in fifteen minutes, so I can go home and sleep for a few more hours. But I'll be back this afternoon." She stretched her smile to stifle a yawn. "Colin mentioned that he ran into you and Gucci on his walk."

Karla nodded. "Good thing he did. I had to bring him back. The last thing I need is him wandering around asking locals for directions and running into the nosy reporter who's been snooping around."

"He's back now," Max told her. "He dragged himself up to his room and shut the door. I assume he's finally asleep. If he gets the urge to go walkies again, I'll try to dissuade him or at least convince him to walk with an escort."

"Thanks," said Karla with a smile.

"Lynn tidied the library when she was here earlier," Harry said. "The police released it early this morning."

"Everything is back where it belongs," Max added. "You can't tell anyone died there last night." She stifled another yawn. "I found the mop and cleaned the boot prints off the floors. Other than Samir's absence, all the evidence of his death is gone."

"Thank you," Karla said to everyone with a sigh.

"Colin gave me Griff's bowtie. He left it on the dining room table last night. I told Colin that I'd make sure Griff got it back, but maybe I should let *you* return it to him." Max's crooked grin was mischievous.

"You do it. I'll forget," Karla said, forcing her face into submission so she would have no readable reaction to Griff or his bowtie.

"You could wear it, La-la. Remember how you used to wear his hoodies in high school?" Max teased.

"No, but I might use it to strangle my annoying little sister!"

"Ladies! That's enough. You are professional women who are here in a professional capacity. Save your sibling snark for later."

"Yes, Rosalie."

"Sorry, Rosalie."

They both mumbled with their heads bowed in shame.

"That's better," Rosalie praised. She turned her attention to Karla. "Shouldn't you deliver those thermoses to the Seascape Hotel before the soup gets cold?"

CHAPTER 13

IN WHICH A MYSTERY IS SOLVED, AND A NEW MYSTERY EMERGES

KARLA STRUGGLED to balance the heavy laundry basket and hit the automatic door access button with her elbow at the same time.

"Let me get the door for you." Griff appeared next to her and pulled the door, gesturing for her to walk through.

"Thank you." She walked into the hotel lobby.

Griff ran ahead of her, turned, and opened his arms. "I'll carry that."

Karla was about to politely decline his offer, but he had already relieved her of the basket and was almost at the front desk.

He heaved the basket onto the counter and Karla dinged the bell.

"Thanks," she said.

"No problem," he replied with a grin that turned her insides hectic.

"Why are you here?"

"They want to knock down some walls and

convert a few hotel rooms into business suites," Griff explained. "The manager asked me to stop by and discuss it." He jerked his thumb behind him toward the door he had just opened for her. "I was just leaving when I saw you struggling with the door."

"It was nice of you to help," she responded. "But I would have figured it out."

He chuckled.

"What's so funny?" She hoped her voice sounded more curious than offended.

"You're so independent," he said, shaking his head. "Accepting help isn't a sign of weakness, you know."

"I know—"

Karla's defensive rebuttal was interrupted by the arrival of the front desk clerk. She apologized for the wait and had been expecting Karla because Rosalie called ahead to warn them about the influx of soup they were about to receive.

"Rosalie said you should wait," advised the clerk. "I'll have our cook decant the soup into a soup pot, then we'll wash the thermoses for you. Rosalie said the church needs the thermoses in time for their meals-on-wheels outreach program."

"Of course." Karla smiled. *How can I not wait if it means the church won't have clean insulated flasks to feed homebound parishioners?*

Griff offered to carry the thermoses into the kitchen, but the clerk insisted she was more than capable, hoisted the basket off the counter, and disappeared through a door behind the desk.

"How's Samir's family doing?" Griff whispered,

ducking his head so no one in the empty hotel lobby would overhear.

"Aside from Colin, I haven't seen them yet today," Karla replied. "Colin seemed pretty tired and over-whelmed. Listen, Griff, thank you for sacrificing your anonymity to protect Samir's family's privacy. Thanks to you letting Rosalie distract the rumour mill with the news about your app and your relationship with Samir, we've been able to run at least one nosy reporter out of town."

"It was the least I could do." Griff gave her a small, tense smile. "I feel kind of responsible, K. I mean, the only reason Samir came to Bellbrook was to meet me for dinner and murder mystery night." He exhaled hard and shook his head.

Karla gave him a sympathetic smile. "Samir's death wasn't your fault, Griff. It was no one's fault. At least he died happy, surrounded by the people he loved."

They stood together in companionable silence.

"If you have a few minutes, I have those crown moulding samples in my truck," Griff suggested, leaning his elbow against the counter.

"Sure," Karla agreed. "Let's get it out of the way. I don't want you to blame me if the entire reno job is delayed because I never chose the crown moulding," she teased.

Griff pushed himself off the counter and followed her toward the exit.

"Karla!"

Karla and Griff stopped just feet from the door.

"Wait up!"

They spun at the same time to find Rob closing in on them. She wore lilac scrubs, black running shoes, and had a large messenger bag slung over her shoulder. Her long ginger tresses were piled into a messy bun on top of her head.

"Hi!" Karla smiled.

"Hey, Rob," Griff said, then he touched Karla's shoulder, and she involuntarily stopped breathing for a breath or two. "I have to pick up the twins at batting practice, then I have to meet Harry at the manor house to discuss the wiring in the ballroom. I'll catch up with you on Monday for the crown moulding. Like we'd planned."

"OK." She smiled and he left. She turned her attention to Rob. "What are you doing here? I thought you had an autopsy this morning."

Rob sighed and shifted the messenger bag to her other shoulder. "I'm running late," she explained. "I had a long phone conversation with Samir's primary physician this morning. He's on the West Coast, so I had to wait for him to wake up and return my call." She stopped to catch her breath. "Then I came here to check on the food-poisoning patients." She touched Karla's shoulder. "It's definitely food poisoning, by the way. I got the lab results from the samples I took yesterday. My guess is they caught it from the salmon. Scombrotoxin."

"Gesundheit!"

"Very funny." Rob giggled and rolled her eyes. "Scombrotoxin, or scombroid poisoning, is a bacterial infection from ingesting improperly handled fish. It's quite rare to catch it from salmon but not unheard of."

"Will they be OK?"

"They'll make a full recovery," Rob assured her. "A few of them are already feeling better. But given what happened last night, and the fact they don't know their employer died, I've prescribed them two more days of rest and hydration."

"Thanks," Karla said, expelling a sigh of relief that at least one of this weekend's mysteries was solved, and everyone who ate the salmon would be OK.

The front-desk clerk returned with Rosalie's laundry basket and caught Karla's attention. The thermoses were much lighter empty than full.

"I'll walk with you," Rob said, pressing the automatic-door access button for them.

Rob's phone chimed, and she stopped to read the message. "It's from the lab," she said. "I took some samples from Samir last night and dropped them off as a rush job. Some of the results are already back." She dropped the phone in the pocket of her scrubs. "I'll read it when I get to the office."

"How was your conversation with Samir's doctor?" Karla asked as they walked through the parking lot. "Did he confirm what Millie said about Samir's stomach cancer?"

"He confirmed Samir had stomach cancer," Rob admitted. "But he's of the opinion that the cancer probably didn't kill him. Samir's cancer was small, contained, and not aggressive, according to his doctor. Also, it was found in the very early stages. Samir hadn't developed any symptoms yet. His doctor found it during a routine physical exam for TechSavvy's insurance provider. Because of Samir's position as

CEO and Chairman of the Board, he had frequent exams and tests to satisfy his stakeholders. It was caught very early, Karla. Earlier than most. Samir's doctor was of the opinion that, with swift treatment, Samir's prognosis would have been excellent."

"What does that mean?" Karla asked, stopping to push the button on her keychain that opened the trunk. "Maybe the doctor is wrong. Or maybe Samir developed symptoms all of a sudden. He was uncomfortable before he died. Millie was feeding him sodium bicarbonate tablets, and he wasn't eating."

"I should have more answers in a few hours," Rob said.

If the cancer didn't kill Samir, what did?

CHAPTER 14
A MYSTERY PACKAGE

ON THE DRIVE from Rosalie's house to Rob's house, Karla apologized to Gucci and explained why she was late picking him up. She had budgeted an hour, at most, to drop off the thermoses at the church, drop off the laundry basket at Rosalie's house—pick up Gucci while she was there—then drop off the earrings she'd borrowed from Rob, and take Gucci home. She had not budgeted an extra forty-five minutes to chat with a loquacious church volunteer, who then roped her into spending an additional forty-five minutes helping to print and assemble labels for the church's meals-on-wheels initiative.

"At least you had Hemi to keep you company," she reasoned to the small terrier that was watching the world pass by the passenger-side window.

"Here we are!" she declared, pulling into Rob's driveway. "Last stop before home." She made an X on her chest with her index finger. "Promise."

She unbuckled Gucci's doggy seatbelt and carried

him to the door, used the spare key Rob had given her to unlock the house, and placed Gucci on the floor just inside the door. She ran upstairs to return the earrings to Rob's jewelry box. Then she ran downstairs, phone in hand, and sent Rob a quick text.

> The earrings are in your jewelry box.
> Thanks again for lending them to me.

Nearby, Rob's computer dinged. Her laptop was open on the dining room table. Karla's text message had woken up Rob's sleeping computer. Rob's phone, computers, and tablet were connected to the same network. Which meant Karla's text would show up on all of Rob's devices. By instinct, she craned her neck to look at the screen. Her text message appeared across the top of the screen like a banner. The rest of the screen was Rob's inbox. The email with Samir's lab results was at the top of her email list. Karla could tell Rob had already read it because it wasn't in bold. She was dying to know the results, but she would never betray her best friend's trust by snooping through her email or accessing her computer without permission. No matter how tempted she was! And she was tempted. *I bet it's written in medical-speak anyway,* she reasoned with herself. *Lots of Latin and weird abbreviations. I doubt I'd understand what any of it means.*

She took a few steps closer to the laptop. It was within arm's reach now. She stood there, gnawing the inside of her bottom lip and willing her hands to stay firmly stuck to their respective hips, hoping to will away the urge to snoop. The computer went back into sleep mode, and the screen went black. Temptation averted. She let out a sigh, and her entire body softened. She reached for the device and slammed it shut.

"Let's go, Gooch!" She scooped the little dog off the sofa. "Before I do something I'll regret."

AT HOME, a grocery bag hung from Karla's front door. She wracked her brain trying to remember if she had ordered anything online. Not that she could recall.

"A mystery package! What do you think it is, Gooch?"

The little dog ran up to the bag, balanced on his short hind legs and sniffed the thing, stopping to lick his lips before sniffing it again and wagging his quill-like tail at top speed.

Karla unhooked the bag from the door and peeked inside. A box of her favourite coffee pods. With a neon yellow sticky note stuck to the top.

In case you forgot again! Can't have you falling asleep on the job. Love, Mum, with a heart drawn around the word *mum.*

Karla sighed as she unlocked the door. "I hate to admit it, Gooch, but Lynn would make an excellent PA." She hated the thought of her mother being right. "We have a lot of differences, but our differences complement each other. And, as much as I don't understand it, she has a way with people. Everyone likes her."

Karla put her keys on their designated hook, hung her coat in the closet, and set her purse in its designated spot. A routine that, if she were to deviate from it, would cost her hours of searching for the misplaced items next time she needed them. She freshened Gucci's water bowl and tossed a couple of small dog treats into his red Le Creuset dog dish. As she opened the box of coffee pods and poured them into the empty canister on the counter, her phone dinged. Then almost immediately dinged again. A foreboding chill crept up her spine. She tossed the empty coffee box in the recycle bin and grabbed her phone. A group text from Dean to her and Max, followed by Max's reply.

DEAN

Come to the Nestled Inn. Urgent!

MAX

Be there in fifteen.

Karla grabbed her keys, purse, and coat from their designated spots, said goodbye to Gucci, told him to be a good boy, and ran to the car.

UNMARKED POLICE CARS AND A WHITE, windowless van occupied the driveway. Karla parked on a side street and ran around the corner to the large Victorian house.

Police officers were coming and going from the bed and breakfast with bags and boxes. *Bags and boxes of what?* she wondered.

She rushed through the kitchen door into a scene of chaos and confusion.

Raj was criss-crossing the large breakfast room, huffing and puffing.

Millie sat at the kitchen table, an open paperback face down in front of her, in her pajamas, sobbing and covering her face with her hands. Colin stood next to her, rubbing her upper back and yelling at no one in particular that he demanded a second opinion.

A second opinion about what?

Lady Olivia, dressed entirely in black except for the pearl choker that was strangling her wattle, was using her walking stick to herd Rosemary and Thyme away from the busy front door.

Karla stumbled forward as Lynn pushed past her and into the house.

"What's going on?" Lynn demanded.

That's what I'd like to know!

"I leave for twenty minutes to take Rosalie home, and the whole place erupts in chaos?"

"We're confiscating all food and liquid," Dean replied, snapping a black latex glove onto his oversized hand.

"Confiscating it for what?" Karla asked.

"Evidence." Max pointed her gloved finger at the search warrant on the kitchen counter.

"Evidence?" Karla and Lynn demanded in stereo.

"Evidence of what?" Lynn plopped her purse and keys on the counter.

"Murder," Dean replied. "According to the coroner's preliminary findings, Samir Khan was murdered."

Karla's jaw dropped.

Lynn gasped and raised her hand to her mouth.

Murdered! By whom? Why? Questions raced through Karla's brain faster than she could catch them.

"How?" she asked her father when she overcame her speechlessness.

"Rob found poison in Samir's system. She said the poison was ingested."

What kind of poison? Who would want to kill Samir? The questions kept coming.

Dean's words only served to intensify Millie's anguish. The distraught widow was sobbing louder, hugging her knees, and rocking back and forth.

Raj's pacing became more determined, and his huffing and puffing was louder.

Colin's demands for a second opinion were more insistent, verging on forceful.

Dean instructed an officer to confiscate the garbage from the outdoor bins. "After we finish down here, we'll go upstairs," he announced. "Food, liquids, anything that could be ingested. Toothpaste, mouthwash, all of it."

Max continued bagging and tagging the contents of the fridge.

"I need fresh air," Raj blurted. "I can't be here." He grabbed a baseball cap and sunglasses from the kitchen table.

"Perhaps someone should go with you, chap," Colin suggested.

"I want to be alone." Raj donned the ball cap and sunglasses and disappeared through the front door.

Dean instructed an officer to confiscate the crystal decanters from the library, breakfast room, and dining room.

"If I don't get these two out of the way, they'll end

up under an officer's boot, or they'll escape, and I'll never see them again," Lady Olivia grumbled.

"Let me help you." Karla reached down to scoop up one cat, but the cagey kitty slipped through her hands. The other agile pussycat wove through her ankles, then ran to the floor-to-ceiling cat post in the sunroom. They thought this was a game. *This isn't the time to play tag, kitties!*

Karla chased the cats. They ran in opposite directions.

Lady Olivia cleared her throat, made a kissing sound with her puckered lips, and wrapped her gnarled, arthritic fingers around a container of cat treats. One shake was all it took. She immediately had the undivided attention of both cats.

Karla was able to gather them up as they approached their owner, mesmerized by the jar of goodies in her hand.

Lady Olivia continued to shake the jar and make smooching noises as she hobbled down the hall with her walking stick.

Karla followed, her arms full of cats.

Lady Olivia led them into the library and stopped at the bookcase on the far wall. The bookcase was a Murphy door which camouflaged a small service elevator to the second floor. Lady Olivia stepped into the small compartment.

The elevator was tiny enough to make even the smallest person feel claustrophobic.

"We'll be fine." Lady Olivia gave Karla a small smile. "You can put them down. They won't run. They'd follow me off a cliff to get their paws on these treats." She gave the jar another shake, and Rosemary and Thyme struggled to free themselves from Karla's grasp. Lady Olivia gestured with her eyes for Karla to place the cats on the floor. "I'll secure them in my room where they won't be in the way. You stay here." She raised her eyebrows and glanced toward the kitchen. "One of us needs to control the chaos."

Karla did as instructed and released the cats. They hopped onto the elevator without once averting their eyes from the jar of treats.

"Good kitties," Lady Olivia praised her feline companions as the elevator door closed.

Karla closed the Murphy door and rushed back to the kitchen.

"Rob will arrive soon to talk to the family about her findings," Max said.

"Raj will want to be here for that," Colin added. "I've tried texting him, but he left without his phone." He nodded to the abandoned cell phone on the kitchen table.

He won't be able to call for help if he gets lost. Unless that's the point. What if Raj left his phone behind because he doesn't want anyone to find him?

"I'll find him," Karla said.

"I'll stay in case anyone needs anything," Lynn offered. "And I'll call Harry to go out looking too. He went to the manor house to meet Griff about the wiring or something."

"I'm coming with you." Max slipped off her latex gloves and stretched her fingers in the open air. "Bellbrook PD is in charge of security while Samir's security team is sick."

Karla and Max headed for the door. Just as Max followed Karla onto the porch, Lynn appeared behind them. She shut the door and nudged them toward a quiet corner of the yard.

"Why don't I call Rosalie and tell her you're looking for Raj," Lynn suggested. "In a matter of minutes, everyone in town will have their eyes peeled for him."

Karla looked at Max for guidance.

"Lynn, the more people find out Samir and his entourage are here, the more difficult it will be for us to protect them," Max said. "Our police force isn't very big. We can't afford for anyone to find out. The town would be filled with paparazzi, fans, and haters."

"Everyone already knows they're here," Lynn said in a tone that implied it would be foolish to believe otherwise.

"Are you serious, Mother?" Karla asked. "Why didn't you tell me?"

"I assumed you knew, love."

"How would I know that?"

"Why else do you think The Posers helped run that nosey reporter out of town? They practically told you they knew." She scoffed, seeming not to believe her daughter hadn't figured it out. She tossed her hands in the air in frustration. "They said the reporter asked if they *Khan* help him find a tech billionaire?" She stared at Karla, waiting for her to catch up.

It dawned on Karla; the vague nuances she'd ignored at Déjà Brew earlier. Wow. She was really off her game when she was under-caffeinated. "There are no *TechSavvy* app developers in Bellbrook," she mumbled the recollection out loud, shaking her head. "I can't believe I missed it."

"You've had a rough few hours, La-la," Max sympathized, hugging her sister's shoulders.

"Someone died in front of you, you haven't slept much, you're running around like crazy trying to keep everyone comfortable. Don't beat yourself up."

"Max is right, love. You're handling this really well. Don't be so hard on yourself," Lynn agreed, squeezing her daughter's hand. "Now." She cleared her throat and adopted a more professional stance and tone of voice. "Is it all right if I call Rosalie and tell her about Raj?"

Karla swallowed, dreading the thought of asking for help and the vulnerable feelings that would go with it. *Asking for help is not a sign of weakness.* Griff's voice in her head rumbled through her entire body.

"You can trust us, love. We've got your back."

"Fine." Lynn and Max let out simultaneous sighs when Karla agreed. "I'll trust your judgement." *I hope I don't regret it.*

SO MANY SUSPECTS, SO LITTLE TIME

THE SISTERS DROVE toward the water in Max's unmarked police car. According to Max, "We don't get a lot of missing people in Bellbrook, but when we do, they always seem to gravitate toward the water. Same with missing pets too."

Max drove slowly while Karla scanned the area for signs of Raj.

It was a seasonal, early spring day. The streets were dotted with Bellbrookians soaking up vitamin D, waving and smiling at one another as they walked their dogs, pushed strollers, or raked up the leftover leaves and twigs that had been buried under a blanket of snow for months. Neighbours separated by mani-cured hedges chatted and laughed.

"You seemed shocked when Dad announced that Samir was murdered," Max observed. "Rob didn't give you a heads-up?"

"No." Karla shook her head. "It was a total surprise."

"Me too," Max said. "We have until Monday morning to solve this. Then it becomes public knowledge, and the whole world will descend on Bellbrook looking for answers."

Karla sighed and gave her sister a tense smile. "Then we better figure out who killed Samir before Monday."

"Do you think Raj ran out of the house because he was upset?" Max asked. "Or because he has something to hide?"

"Both options occurred to me," Karla admitted. "I mean, look at his behaviour since his brother died. He's been pacing non-stop like a caged animal and giving off this stoic yet super intense energy. I can't tell if he's angry, sad, or what."

"He couldn't get out of the house fast enough when Dad announced that Samir had been murdered," Max added.

"I hope he's OK."

"He can't have gone far. He left his phone and passport behind. He wasn't planning to stay away very long."

"What if he left his phone and passport behind on purpose?" Karla asked, absently fidgeting with Raj's phone in her lap. "What if he doesn't want to be found because he's guilty and on the run, or so grief stricken that he's planning something drastic?"

"We'll find him, La-la. I feel it in my bones."

"He had a motive, you know," Karla admitted, scanning people as she searched for Raj's black Tech-Savvy ball cap.

"Everyone in the house had a motive," Max

responded. "Samir was a billionaire. His death means that his wife, brother, and best friend will inherit fortunes."

"Raj had another motive."

Karla told Max about Colin's disclosure that Raj and Samir had argued about Raj's desire to work at TechSavvy and Samir's refusal to give him a role in the company.

"Did Colin mention *why* Samir didn't want his brother to work at TechSavvy?"

"Not really," Karla replied. "He said something about Samir needing Raj as more of a personal advisor than a business associate."

"If Raj killed Samir, it wouldn't necessarily result in him getting a job at TechSavvy," Max pointed out.

"No," Karla agreed, "but it would end the arguments."

"Raj is definitely a suspect," Max admitted, "but so is everyone else who had access to the Nestled Inn and Samir in the hours before he died."

Karla gasped with comprehension, turning her attention away from the street and onto Max. "That includes us!"

Max nodded without taking her eyes off the road. "You, me, Rob, Lynn, Harry, Rosalie, Griff, we're all suspects. So are the sick staff at the Seascape Hotel. Everyone who had access to either Samir or the Nestled Inn before Samir died."

The magnitude of Max's statement hit Karla like a Mack truck. The people Karla loved—her family— who had selflessly stepped up to help her when her career depended on it—were now embroiled in a murder investigation because of her. This was her fault. In that moment, Karla knew that she would solve Samir's murder, or die trying, if that's what it took to clear their names.

"We're the least likely suspects," Max continued.

"Obviously," Karla mumbled, gulping down a swallow and rubbing the pit in her stomach.

"First, we'll focus the investigation on Samir's inner circle, the handful of people he was closest to. Then if we eliminate them, we'll move to his next closest circle, his staff. If we eliminate them, then we'll focus on the locals." Max nodded with confidence. "But I'm sure it's someone in his innermost circle. It almost always is."

"Someone staying at the bed and breakfast is a killer?" Karla mumbled.

"That's my guess," Max said.

They continued in silence, Max rolling slowly through the waterfront neighbourhood and Karla keeping her eyes peeled for Raj until Karla's phone startled them out of their hyperfocussed states.

"It's Rosalie," Karla said. "The Posers found Raj. He's at The Pavlovian."

Max maneuvered a smooth but too-fast, three-point turn, pressed her foot on the accelerator, and sped toward the local pub, going at least twenty over the speed limit.

THE STALE, dark pub was a stark contrast to the bright, fresh day outside. It took Karla's eyes a few moments to adjust to the sudden change.

Except for a few regulars lined up on barstools along the hand-carved, dark wood bar, the pub was empty. The musical stylings of ABBA filled the otherwise quiet space. The TV over the bar was muted and tuned to the twenty-four-hour sports channel. The wooden tables and booths were spotless and shiny, dotted with a mishmash of unused beer mats ready for the masses that would retire to the pub for a quick pint this evening after dinner.

"I put him in the back." The publican approached Karla and Max, wiping his hands on his black beer-branded apron. "It's dead in here—pardon the pun—but I didn't want to risk an outsider recognizing him. I heard about the reporter at the cafe." He put his hands on his hips and raised his dark eyebrows. "We're all being extra careful."

Does everyone in this town know about Samir?

"Thanks, Kwame," Max said.

Kwame Pritchard had owned The Pavlovian Pub for the better part of twenty years. He and his family lived upstairs and took turns working behind the bar. When the pub was busy, it was all hands on deck with Kwame, his wife, and their two grown children all working together. Like most Bellbrook businesses, The Pavlovian Pub was a family-owned and run establishment.

"No problem." Kwame's smile was sympathetic and sincere.

Coming home to Bellbrook had been a good daily

reminder for Karla that the world was full of kind, sincere people, and weirdly, most of them somehow seemed to live in Bellbrook.

Heavy wooden saloon doors separated the back room from the rest of the pub. Kwame usually reserved this room for private parties or crowd over-flow on The Pavlovian's busiest nights. It was a large room with randomly scattered tall pub tables and high stools.

In the far corner sat Raj, alone and still wearing his ball cap and sunglasses in the dimly lit, unoccu-pied room. He was the embodiment of gloom. His chin hung low to his chest, his shoulders were slumped forward, and his face hovered inches from the rim of his half-full pint glass, like he was gazing into a crystal ball. Two empty pint glasses sat on the table near his left hand. Though he only took up one stool, his presence filled the room like a sad, lonely fog.

"You left this behind." Karla slid Raj's forgotten cell phone across the table and took up residence on the stool across from him.

"Thanks," he muttered, ignoring the phone.

"Raj, why don't we take you back to The Nestled Inn?" Max suggested. "Rob is on her way over there to discuss her preliminary findings and answer questions."

"I have all the answers I need." Raj picked up the pint glass and tipped the amber liquid into his mouth. He swallowed and smacked his lips. "I know who killed my brother. I don't know how, but I know why."

"Who was it?" Karla asked.

Raj opened his mouth to respond but was interrupted by the squeaky swing of the saloon doors.

"Here we are," Kwame announced, lifting a glass off the tray he was balancing with his left hand. "Cranberry-ginger ale for our on-duty Officer Sheridan." He handed the glass to Max. "And Diet Coke for Karla."

"Thank you, Kwame," Karla said as he placed the drink and a cocktail napkin in front of her and collected Raj's empty pint glasses.

She had forgotten how welcoming it felt to never have to place your order because someone already knew what you wanted.

"Thanks, Kwame," Max said as the publican backed out of the room through the swinging doors.

Karla and Max sipped their drinks, staring expectantly at Raj.

"Well?" Max urged. "You said you know who killed Samir and why they did it."

"Isn't it obvious?" Raj asked, swirling the remaining liquid around the inside of his glass. "It was Colin."

"Colin?" Karla and Max couldn't hide their simultaneous shock.

"Why would Colin kill his best friend?" Karla asked.

"How would Colin benefit from killing his boss?" Max asked. "TechSavvy could go under without Samir. Colin wouldn't have a job, and his shares in the company would be worthless."

Raj drained the rest of his ale and slammed the empty glass onto the table.

"Some things are more valuable than jobs or money," he said.

"Like love?" Karla asked.

"Precisely," Raj agreed. "As long as my brother had a breath in his body, Colin had no chance with Millie."

"But with Samir out of the way, Colin can be Millie's knight in shining armour," Karla thought out loud, recalling Colin's plan to fly Millie back to the UK and shelter her from the oncoming media storm that Samir's death would trigger. *He told me Raj would stay here. Is he trying to isolate her, like some kind of twisted Beauty and the Beast scenario?*

"Colin is in love with Millie?" Max's drink now rested on the table while she flipped open her note-book and began scrawling notes.

Raj nodded.

"Does Millie feel the same about Colin?" Karla asked.

"No," Raj replied with a hint of a chuckle. "Millie was devoted to Samir. They were kindred spirits. But Colin has loved Millie since the day they all met her at Oxford."

"They all?" Max asked.

"Samir, Colin, and Millie's first husband," Raj clarified. "They were together when they met Millie. Colin fell for her right away, but she only had eyes for her first husband. Even after they got married, Colin still loved her. He never hid it well. He can barely keep his eyes off her or maintain his composure when she's in the room."

"We kind of noticed," Karla admitted.

"Colin must have taken it pretty hard when Samir and Millie got married," Max theorized.

"Samir and Millie's marriage was a daily reminder to Colin that Millie didn't choose him. Again." He removed his baseball cap, ran his fingers through his short black hair, then replaced the cap. "Millie and Samir were always together, and I mean always. They were together day and night. The only other people Samir spent that much time with was me and Colin."

"Whenever Colin saw Samir, he would also see Millie," Karla summarized.

"Their happy, loving relationship was always in Colin's face," Max paraphrased.

"Not anymore," Raj pointed out.

"Do you know if Samir ever confronted Colin about his feelings for Millie?"

"Samir trusted Colin implicitly," Raj explained. "He also trusted Millie. Regardless of whether he knew how Colin felt, he trusted them." He picked up the empty pint glass and gave it a swirl as though it might magically refill itself. When that didn't work, he set it on the table with a sigh. "I daresay, Samir trusted Colin more than he trusted me."

"I'm sure that's not true," Karla reassured him.

"Then why did he trust Colin with TechSavvy instead of me? Why does Colin get all the responsibility and glory, and I get nothing but a big fat trust fund and instructions to 'enjoy myself' and 'do whatever I've always wanted to do?'" He shook his head with narrowed eyes. "I'm sure Colin was conspiring against me. I'm sure he convinced Samir not to hire me. He wanted me out of his way. He was always jealous of our relationship. Colin wanted to have Tech-Savvy and Millie all to himself."

"Did you and Samir argue about your role?" Max asked between jotting notes.

"Yes," Raj admitted. "But more often lately. For the past couple of weeks, Samir had been transferring even more responsibility to Colin. Why?" Raj raised his hands, palms up and shrugged. "Colin has enough to do. I asked Samir to let me shoulder some of the responsibility, let me contribute. I'm a hard worker. I worked three jobs to put Samir through school and earn the seed money for TechSavvy. I'm capable. But my brother wouldn't budge. Toward the end, he outright refused to discuss it anymore."

Karla wanted to tell him that Samir's decision to transfer more responsibility to Colin likely had nothing to do with his confidence in either Colin or Raj and more to do with Samir's recent cancer diagnosis. She refused to believe that the timing of both events was coincidental, but instead, she said, "That must have been frustrating for you."

"Raj, did you kill Samir?" Max asked out of nowhere.

Karla sucked in a breath and braced herself, expecting Raj to explode at the accusation.

"No," he replied matter-of-factly. "I loved my brother," he added with an exaggerated nod. "I would never hurt him."

CHAPTER 16

TWO QUESTION MARKS

RAJ SAT in the front seat next to Max. Still wearing his ball cap and sunglasses, he was silent on the drive to The Nestled Inn except for the occasional sniffle and throat clearing.

When Karla noticed him slipping a hand behind the dark lenses of his sunglasses to wipe his eyes, she handed him a pack of travel tissues from her purse.

Karla sat in the back seat, her mind racing with potential scenarios and suspects. Raj had confirmed that he had a motive to kill Samir—their disagreement about Raj's role at TechSavvy. Raj obviously had strong feelings about the situation, but could he have felt strongly enough to kill his brother? Karla wanted to believe Raj when he told her and Max that he did not kill Samir, he loved his brother, and would never hurt him, but his exaggerated nod made it difficult for her to accept that he was telling the truth. Raj only used his Big Nod when he lied. But what did he lie about? That he didn't kill Samir? That he loved his brother? That he would never hurt him? All of the above?

Colin was a strong suspect, too, if Raj was right about him wanting Millie and TechSavvy all to himself. He had arranged a meeting with the board of directors before Samir's body was even cold and was promoted to Samir's position. While Colin might not have had the relationship he wanted to have with Millie, murdering Samir would have eliminated his biggest obstacle, as well as created a scenario where he could swoop in and comfort her through her tragic loss. But if Colin murdered Samir, why did he demand a second opinion when Dean announced that Samir's death was murder? Was he hoping the opinion of a second coroner would be different or at least create enough reasonable doubt to derail the murder investigation?

Max pulled up in front of the bed and breakfast and parked behind Rob's car, which was still running. Rob must have just arrived.

Max and Raj walked toward the house, and Karla loitered by the car, waiting for Rob to finish gathering her things and exit her vehicle.

"Murder?" Karla asked when Rob closed the car door. "Are you sure?"

"Positive," Rob replied as she joined Karla, and they ambled toward the house. "Samir Khan was poisoned."

"I can't believe it."

"I know," Rob commiserated. "I wasn't expecting it either. I thought this would be an open-and-shut case of death by natural causes."

Lady Olivia waved from the wicker rocking chair on the front porch. "Just getting my daily dose of fresh air and vitamin D." She wasn't quite smiling, but she closed her eyes and turned her face toward the sun with an almost-smile.

An officer carrying a large plastic bin came out of the front door and toward them. "Use the side door please, ladies," he said as they stepped aside so he could pass. "We're trying to keep the front door clear for police business."

"Of course."

"Sure."

They responded even though the officer was already out of earshot.

They walked around to the kitchen door at the side of the house.

Karla was about to open the door and hold it for Rob, whose hands were full, when she spotted them. She released the door handle and raised her index finger to her lips.

"*Shhh*," she mouthed, then pointed to the two semi-circular benches that surrounded the fire pit in the back garden.

Rob's gaze followed Karla's finger.

There, on the semi-circular bench sat Colin and Millie. They were straddling the bench, facing each other, and sitting in close proximity. Their spines were curved like question marks, their foreheads and knees touching. Colin was clutching Millie's hands. Their eyes were closed. It was a private moment. Karla felt like she was invading their privacy by watching them. There was something so intimate about the way they sat together in comfortable silence. She wondered what that would be like.

"Do you think Millie knows Colin is in love with her?" Rob whispered.

"I'm not sure," Karla whispered in reply, "but I intend to ask."

"She must know," Rob reasoned. "I just met them yesterday, and Colin's feelings for her are as obvious to me as the noses on their faces."

"Sometimes it's easier to recognize these things when they happen to other people. We tend to lose perspective of our own lives."

"You would know."

"What's that supposed to mean?" Karla hissed.

"Nothing," Rob replied with a side glance that hinted that Karla should know exactly what she meant without being told. "How's the manor house renovation coming along?" She smirked. "Seen Griff lately?"

Karla loved being back in Bellbrook, surrounded by the people who saw *her* and not just another face in the crowd, but she also hated being back in Bellbrook where she couldn't just *be* another face in the crowd. Feelings were harder to conceal in a small town where everyone knew everyone else. Eager to end the uncomfortable conversation, she yanked the door open and gestured for Rob to go ahead of her into the house.

While Rob proceeded to the dining room, Karla spied on Colin and Millie through the kitchen window. They hadn't moved. Colin's back was to her, but she could see Millie's face, and her eyes were still closed. *I wonder how Samir would feel about his best friend and his widow being so comfortable together?*

What if Millie felt the same way about Colin as he felt about her? What if they conspired to kill Samir together? Was the tablet that Millie had dropped in Samir's water last night really a sodium bicarbonate tablet or something more sinister? With Samir out of the way, they would be financially secure for the rest of their lives. Murdering Samir would be faster and less expensive than a long, drawn-out, contentious divorce. Colin would get to keep his job at TechSavvy, and they wouldn't have to deal with the negative publicity that would accompany their scandalous affair. *If there even is an affair.*

"Rob's ready." Dean's voice startled Karla back to the here and now. "She wants everyone to gather in the dining room."

She turned to reply, but he had already moved on to the sunroom where she heard him make the same announcement to Raj.

"Where are Millie and Colin?" Lynn's voice carried throughout the house. "Has anyone seen Millie and Colin? Good gracious, I hope we haven't lost them. We've only just found Raj." Her padded footsteps sped up as she neared the kitchen. "We need to put tracking devices on these people," she murmured as she passed by.

"Millie's in the garden," called Lady Olivia. "Colin might be with her." Each rhythmic *thunk* of her walking stick hitting the hardwood floor was louder than the one before it until it *thunked* right behind Karla.

Did she get a new cane? It sounds different than it did this morning.

"There they are," Karla chirped, pointing at Colin and Millie outside the window. "I was just going outside to get them." She smiled.

"Allow me." Lady Olivia upended her walking stick and pointed the rubber tip into the air. The windows rattled as the tip of the cane rapped on the pane of glass.

Lady Olivia returned her walking stick to its regular position and gave it an extra tap on the floor for good measure.

"Is that a different cane?" Karla asked. "It looks the same but sounds different."

"You have a good ear," said Lady Olivia in a tone that almost sounded like praise. "I changed the rubber tip." She lifted the tip and tapped it again on the floor. "They wear out so quickly nowadays. Disposable, just like everything else in our throwaway society."

The kitchen door opened. Millie entered the house first with Colin holding the door for her.

"Rob is waiting in the dining room," Karla advised them.

THE ROOM WAS silent as Rob explained how she determined Samir's cause of death and manner of death. Samir's cause of death was myocardial infarction—heart attack—caused by sudden, erratic changes to his blood pressure and heart rate putting too much strain on his heart. The manner of death was ingestion of a mystery poison that caused Samir's erratic blood pressure and heartbeat.

"What kind of poison was it?" Colin demanded.

"I've asked Dr. Mayhew not to disclose that information," Dean replied. "We know what poison we're looking for but, for now, we'd like to keep it between us."

"Between you and Dr. Mayhew?" Raj asked, confused.

"Between us and the killer," Dean clarified.

A blanket of tension draped itself over the quiet room. Everyone exchanged shifty glances as they realized the person sitting next to them might be Samir's killer.

"We're almost finished, Chief." Max poked her head into the dining room. She always called Dean, "Chief" when they were at work. "We just have one more room," she continued. "But two angry, hissing cats won't let us in."

"That would be my room," Lady Olivia said, pushing her chair away from the table and reaching for her cane. "I'll manage the cats while you take care of business."

"I'll help you," Karla offered, already on her feet.

CHAPTER 17

A SPLASH OF GIN, SOME TONIC, AND A WEDGE OF LIME

HAPPY TO SEE THEIR OWNER, Rosemary and Thyme were charming, purring fluffy balls of delight when Lady Olivia opened the door.

She sank into the large easy chair in the corner, and both cats leapt onto her lap. One kneaded her black skirt, and the other rubbed the side of its face against her cheek.

"Are these the only liquids you have, Lady Olivia?" Max asked, holding up a few bottled toiletries in each gloved hand.

"Yes," Lady Olivia replied. "I don't buy into this anti-aging, Photoshop world we live in." She *harrumphed*. "They can keep their lotions and potions. The key to a healthy complexion is simple," she informed Max and Karla. "Plenty of fresh English countryside air and lots of water—occasionally with a splash of gin, some tonic, and a wedge of lime."

Max handed the confiscated toiletries to another

officer, who tagged, photographed, and bagged the items in the adjoining washroom.

Both cats were now coiled together and sleeping in Lady Olivia's lap, their furry bodies rising and falling in unison with each synchronized breath.

"Would you be a dear and hand me my book?" she asked, staring at Max and gesturing to the nightstand beside the canopy bed.

Max reached for the Agatha Christie novel and handed it to Lady Olivia.

"Thank you," she said, accepting the well-read paperback with curled corners and a dried water ring on the front cover.

"I hate to wake my girls when they're sleeping. If I'm going to be stuck here, I may as well amuse myself and try to figure out whodunit before Poirot."

"You seem to have a tight bond with your cats," Max pointed out. "They don't warm up to anyone else like this." She raised her eyebrows and pointed with her eyes at the sleeping kitties.

"Well, we've been through a lot together," Lady Olivia explained, stroking the purring cats. "I've had Rosemary and Thyme since they were just small kittens. They were a gift from Millie after my son died. She had hoped their presence would comfort me, and they might give me a reason to get out of bed every day." Her smile was thin and tight-lipped. "She was correct on both counts."

"It sounds like you and Millie helped each other cope after your son died," Max said.

"Millie did most of the helping and coping, I'm afraid," Lady Olivia explained. "I fell apart after he died and, at the time, didn't care if I ever put myself back together." She sighed. "Now we're the opposite," she continued. "Millie is falling apart, and it's my turn to help her piece herself back together."

"Are you saying Millie is more upset about Samir's death than she was when her first husband died?" Max's handy dandy notebook was already open, her ballpoint pen scrawling the date across the top of a fresh page.

"Millie was quite distraught when my son died," Lady Olivia insisted. "But in a different way than she is with Samir."

"Different how?" Karla asked.

"Well, this time she's not telling everyone she killed her husband."

"Millie told everyone that she killed her first husband?" Max asked.

"I thought your son died in a car accident," Karla demanded. "A single vehicle crash and he was the only occupant in the vehicle."

"That's precisely how he died," Lady Olivia confirmed, "yet Millie blamed herself, nonetheless."

"Why?" asked Max.

"Millie believed that, had it not been for her, he wouldn't have been driving that night. You see, they'd had another disagreement…"

"*Another* disagreement?" Max interrupted. "Did Millie and your son have a lot of disagreements?"

"Unfortunately, yes," Lady Olivia admitted. "You see, they had one of *those* relationships. The impassioned kind. They were always either arguing or making up. There was no in-between. It was quite dramatic and, frankly, exhausting for those of us who had to watch."

"And they argued the night your son died?" Karla asked, refocusing the conversation and trying to get to the part where Millie blamed herself for killing her first husband.

"Yes," Lady Olivia confirmed. "I wasn't there, but apparently, it was a doozy of a disagreement! Millie became so angry that she left their London flat and drove to their country home to 'get some space.'" She used air quotes around the last three words. "My son died following her."

"Oh, my," Karla said with a small gasp. "That's… I'm so sorry for your loss." She shook her head and swallowed. "I can't imagine."

"But Samir's death is different," Lady Olivia continued. "Their relationship was much more mature, less dramatic. Samir and Millie had a kind, patient love. The sort of mature love Millie and my son never had time to develop. Millie and my son were young and immature when they got married." She waggled her crooked, knobbly index finger. "I told them to wait, but they wouldn't listen. The arrogance of youth." She rolled her eyes. "But by the time Samir and Millie found each other, they were both mature and had outgrown their youthful impetuousness. They had a more stable dynamic."

"I understand Millie and Samir had lost contact for a while but reconnected at your son's funeral," Max urged.

"That's right," Lady Olivia confirmed. "Samir was busy building TechSavvy. Other than Colin, he had lost touch with most of his mates from school. But he and Colin came to my son's funeral. They reconnected with Millie, and Samir stayed in touch. Months later, they started dating and got married soon after."

"It must have been difficult for you to see Millie happy again," Max suggested. "With someone who wasn't your son."

"Not at all," Lady Olivia insisted. "Millie was young and full of life. Should I have expected her to spend the rest of her life lonely and sad? Longing for a man she'll never see again, like me? Anyway, I liked Samir. He always made me feel welcome and treated me like family. He was a motherless son, and I was a childless mother. We filled a void in each other. He was a good man, and I harboured no ill feelings toward him."

"Do you know if anyone else harboured ill feelings toward him?" Karla asked.

"Lots of people in the business world weren't very fond of him," Lady Olivia replied. "There were a few former employees he didn't see eye to eye with, and some mentally unstable activists who hate billionaires."

"Anyone closer to home?" Max asked.

"How close to home?"

"Someone who lived with Samir or worked inside the home."

"Well, he and Raj had been butting heads lately, but Raj would never hurt Samir. He practically raised Samir after their parents died. And Colin gets along with everyone. He and Samir always agreed on everything."

"Did Samir know how Colin feels about Millie?" Karla asked.

"We don't discuss that," Lady Olivia said sharply. "It's the proverbial elephant in every room Colin and Millie occupy at the same time."

"So, neither Samir nor Millie have ever mentioned Colin's feelings toward her?"

"Never." The elderly lady shook her head. "At least, not to me. As far as I know, everyone pretends not to notice."

"Do you think Millie has romantic feelings for Colin?" Karla asked.

"No." Lady Olivia's tone and demeanour were emphatic. "Millie loved Samir. She only had eyes for him." She squinted and gave Max and Karla skeptical side glances. "Are you suggesting Colin killed Samir so he could woo Millie?"

"Among other reasons," Max mumbled. "He's been in love with her since they all attended Oxford together. That's a long time to be tortured by watching the woman you love marry two other people."

"You mean since Samir, Colin, and my son attended Oxford together," Lady Olivia corrected.

"I thought they all met Millie at Oxford at the same time," Karla said.

"They did," Lady Olivia confirmed, "but Millie wasn't a student. She was an employee."

"Was she part of a student-work program?" Max asked.

"No," Lady Olivia replied. "She worked in facilities management. I believe her title was 'custodian.' She worked in the Art History department if I recall."

Karla was certain that Millie had told her and Max that she had attended Oxford as a student. If she lied about this, what else had Millie lied about? As she replayed the conversation from the night before in her mind, Karla distinctly recalled Millie's voice saying she studied Art History at Oxford. She gasped.

I know Millie's Tell!

CHAPTER 18

A PERFECT MURDER
WEAPON

KARLA SQUIRMED IN HER CHAIR, then rose to her feet, bugging her eyes at Max.

Picking up on Karla's urgent body language, Max excused them from Lady Olivia's room, telling her that they had imposed upon her enough, were thankful for the background information, and would now leave her and the cats to read and nap in peace.

"What happened in there?" Max whispered as they hustled down the hall. "You made your flat-iron face."

"My what?" Karla asked.

"The face you make when you worry that you left your flat iron turned on."

"I didn't use my flat iron today," Karla said, reassuring both of them that she couldn't possibly have left the appliance plugged in or turned on. "I figured out Millie's Tell." They came to a halt at the top of the stairs and looked at each other. "She intonates her lies? Like this?"

Realization washed across Max's face. "Like when she said she studied Art History?"

Karla nodded. "Exactly like that."

Max scribbled in her notebook.

"Why would Millie lie about her education?" Max asked. "It doesn't make sense to lie about something that's so easy to confirm."

"I don't know why she lied," Karla replied. "But we should ask her and find out what else she might have lied about."

"I thought Millie just had horrible luck," Max admitted. "I mean, how many people get widowed twice before their thirty-fifth birthday? But I'm starting to wonder if bad luck had anything to do with it."

They descended the stairs in silence until Max asked, "Do you know if there are eye drops in the house? You know, the over-the-counter drops for red, tired eyes?"

"Not that I've seen," Karla replied. "I have a bottle in my medicine cabinet at home. You're welcome to them. Use your spare key and let yourself in." Karla jerked her head toward the sunroom, indicating that Max should follow her there. She closed the French doors behind them.

"Last night, Millie dissolved a tablet in Samir's water glass," Karla disclosed to her law enforcement sister. "I mentioned it to Rob. We assumed it was a sodium bicarbonate tablet, but given the circumstances, now I'm not sure."

"We don't think the tablet killed Samir," Max told

her. "The poison we're looking for is called tetrahydro-zoline, and it's a liquid."

"Tetra-hydro-zoline." Karla rolled the new-to-her word around her mouth like a peppermint candy as she tried to commit it to memory.

"Dad said I could tell you, but you can't tell anyone else," Max said. "The poison is a holdback. Only the killer knows what poison they used—"

Max's phone chimed, interrupting her explanation. As she read the screen, the French doors opened behind them.

"Can I come in?" Rob asked, poking her head inside the room.

"Of course," Karla gestured for Rob to join them. "Max was just telling me about tetrahydrozoline," she said, quite pleased with her smooth pronunciation of the long word.

"I have to leave," Max announced, pocketing her cell phone and closing her notebook. "Dad took a team to the Seascape Hotel to interview the staff and confiscate liquids. They need help." She was already moving toward the door. "I'll be back as soon as I can. Text me if something comes up."

Karla and Rob assured Max that everything would be fine in her absence.

"How much did Max tell you about tetrahydrozo-line?" Rob asked.

"She said it's a clear liquid," Karla replied.

"Tetrahydrozoline is a vasoconstrictor," Rob explained. "It constricts blood vessels which slows or blocks blood flow, depriving the organs of oxygen. The heart must work harder to supply blood and oxygen to the organs. If the heart works too hard, it fails."

"That sounds awful," Karla sympathized, wondering how painful this was for Samir. "How did the killer get their hands on such a deadly poison?"

"It's available at most pharmacies and grocery stores," Rob explained. "It's the main ingredient in over-the-counter eye drops, the kind for itchy, dry eyes."

"Those eye drops are made of poison? This explains why Max asked me about eye drops. I assumed they were for her, but she must have been asking because of the case."

"It's only poisonous if it's misused or ingested."

"What does it taste like?" Karla asked. "Would Samir have noticed that his food or drink tasted strange?"

"Odourless, colourless, and tasteless. It's also fast-acting. As little as a few drops could have killed him. Tetrahydrozoline is a perfect murder weapon."

"What about the discomfort we observed before his death?" Karla asked. "Samir was clearly having issues several hours before he died."

"It's possible the killer poisoned Samir more than once," Rob theorized. "When the first dose only made him sick, the killer tried again until they achieved their desired outcome."

A shiver ran up Karla's spine at the thought of someone intentionally and methodically poisoning Samir, watching him suffer, and doing it again anyway.

"Millie might not have killed Samir with a bicarbonate of soda tablet, but she's still a suspect," Karla said. "I figured out her Tell. She lied about Oxford." She told Rob how Millie's voice intonated when she lied and how, according to Lady Olivia, Millie wasn't at Oxford as a student but as a custodian in the Art History department.

"Why did she lie?" Rob wondered aloud. "What else could she have lied about?"

"That's what I'd like to know."

Somewhere down the hall, the rumble of deep, agitated voices interrupted their conversation. They left the sunroom to find the source of the loud kerfuffle.

"I will not hand over my phone or laptop!" Colin shouted, his eyes wide and intense. "Do you under-stand the magnitude of what you're asking? I run the largest tech company in the world." He tapped the back of his smartphone. "This phone is the property of TechSavvy International. It's an access point to sensi-tive, classified information. There are people who would *kill* for access to this phone."

He was right! One of TechSavvy's competitors could have killed Samir to gain an advantage in the marketplace he dominated. *We're supposed to be elimi-nating suspects, not discovering new ones!*

"We're asking for everyone's internet enabled tech-nology, sir, not just yours. Mr. Khan surrendered his phone and computer immediately upon request."

"Raj's phone doesn't contain any sensitive corpo-rate information," Colin lamented. "He doesn't work for TechSavvy."

"We're only interested in your search history, sir.

Nothing else," the officer explained. Karla recognized this rookie officer. He was the officer who had questioned her the night before. The new guy who had recently moved here from somewhere else. "We can access the information without your cooperation, but it will take longer. Withholding your devices will prolong the investigation that, as you keep reminding us, needs to be solved as fast as possible."

Millie appeared next to Colin and extended her hand, offering the officer her cell phone. "I have nothing to hide," she said. "If it will help find the monster who murdered my husband, please keep my phone as long as necessary. I don't have a laptop. I share my husband's. It's on the nightstand in our bedroom. I'll gladly provide the password."

The officer accepted Millie's phone with a thankful smile.

"Please, Colin." Millie placed her hand on his arm, and Colin's body visibly relaxed under her touch. "We promised we would do whatever possible to aid in the investigation."

Karla could barely hear Millie's soft words.

"Fine." Colin relented and handed the officer his phone. "But if ANY corporate secrets are exposed, I'll know who to blame, and I will have you FIRED!" he added through clenched teeth in a voice that was, in Karla's experience, uncharacteristically fierce for mild-mannered Colin Coventry.

The officer accepted the phone, nodded his thanks, and left.

"Thank you," Millie said, rubbing the sleeve of Colin's sweater.

"I need to get to the Seascape Hotel," Colin announced. "The police chief is questioning the servants and searching their belongings. They know something has happened. I need to tell them about Samir and remind them about the non-disclosure agreements they signed when they were hired. I'm determined to keep Samir's murder under wraps until we're forced to disclose it on Monday."

"I'll see if Harry can drive you," Karla said, already texting him.

Harry texted back right away.

"He'll be here in five minutes and says he's available to drive you for the rest of the day."

Colin looked at Millie, his mouth turned down into a thin frown, his eyes full of concern.

"I'll be fine," Millie insisted. "I have Mumsy, Raj, and Karla to fuss over me. Take your time visiting everyone. Reassure them that the police will arrest Samir's killer and hold them accountable."

Colin squeezed her shoulder and left the lounge, turning toward the kitchen.

"It will be good for him to get out of here for a while," Millie commented with an exhausted sigh as she moved her paperback off the leather sofa cushion and sank into it. "Colin and I could both use a break from his incessant attentiveness."

"It's obvious he cares about you very much," Rob observed.

"Yes," Millie acknowledged. "Colin is a devoted friend. I have no doubt his intentions are as good as they are suffocating."

"Was he this attentive toward you before Samir

died?" Karla asked, hoping the mention of her late husband's name wouldn't trigger a fresh batch of tears for the grieving widow.

"No," Millie replied. "Samir was a very dedicated husband. Whenever I needed comfort or consolation, Samir was right there. Always. There was no room for Colin."

Until now. Karla barely managed to stop the words from escaping her mouth.

Could Millie's exasperation at Colin's attention be an act? Was she pretending to tolerate Colin's fussing to give Karla and Rob the impression that she didn't have romantic feelings for him? Did Millie kill her husband to create room in her life for Colin?

"How long have you known that Colin Coventry is in love with you?" Karla asked, exiling the elephant in the room once and for all.

Shock flashed across Millie's face. Was she shocked at the revelation or shocked someone dared to speak the forbidden words aloud?

After an awkward silence, during which, Karla presumed, she was debating with herself about whether to lie or tell the truth, Millie replied, "Since the day we met."

"You met at Oxford, right?" Rob asked. "I hear it's an interesting story. You met Samir, Colin, and your first husband at the same time?"

"That's right," Millie confirmed. "I met both loves of my life in the same moment."

"What did you study at Oxford?" Rob asked without a hint of suspicion.

"Didn't Karla tell you?" Millie asked, gesturing to Karla.

"I didn't," Karla said. "I couldn't remember whether you studied art or history." She tilted her head. "Which was it again?"

"Art history?" Millie mumbled, then smiled.

"We heard that you didn't study at Oxford," Rob said. "We heard you worked there."

"In the facilities management department," Karla added. "As a custodian."

"Actually, I worked in the Art History department," Millie admitted. "I was in charge of keeping the department clean and well supplied. The lecturers allowed me to attend lectures whenever I wanted." She shrugged one delicate shoulder. "I'm at least as educated as an Art History graduate. Probably more."

"Why did you lie?" Karla asked.

"Because it was easier," Millie confessed. "When a woman marries above her social status, society labels her as a money grubber. A gold digger. Do you know what nickname the Oxford snobs bestowed upon me when I started dating my first husband?"

Karla and Rob shook their heads.

"Wisteria," Millie said in a voice that would be considered loud for her. "Because I was fragrant, decorative, and a vigorous climber of social ladders."

"Ouch!" Karla said.

"If that's what people thought of me when I married the son of a dishonoured aristocrat, can you imagine the vicious names they would have called me for marrying a billionaire entrepreneur?"

"No," Rob said. "I can't imagine that kind of judgement or scrutiny."

"Me neither," Millie agreed. "So, when a reporter interviewed Samir and me after we got married, misinterpreted the story of our first meeting, and errantly reported that the four of us attended Oxford together, Samir and I decided not to correct it." She shook her head. "I suppose the publication couldn't be bothered to fact-check the article." She shrugged one shoulder again. "So, it became commonly misreported that I had attended Oxford." She shook her head again. "I have never said the words myself. I have never directly lied. Neither did Samir. He was clever like that."

"But you lied by omission," Karla argued. "Every time you heard it and didn't correct it, you contributed to the lie and helped it get bigger."

"We have different definitions of what constitutes a lie."

Karla nodded, feigning agreement. "If that were true, you wouldn't have a Tell, and I never would have caught your lie. The only reason you have a Tell is because, subconsciously, you know you're lying and have feelings about it."

"What do you mean, a Tell?" Millie inquired.

Karla explained to Millie about her special skill of distinguishing patterns in peoples' behaviour and detecting lies.

"Yes, now that you mention it, I recall Samir saying something about your uncanny ability to get to the crux of most matters."

"Does Colin love you enough to kill for you?" Karla asked.

"Colin could never kill anyone," Millie said. "He has a gentle, sensitive soul. He's not cutthroat enough to harm anyone."

"He was cutthroat enough to shout at the officer who asked for his phone," Rob reminded her. "And he wasn't very gentle or sensitive when he threatened the man's job."

"That's not what I mean," Millie clarified. "Colin would never harm someone he loves."

"Maybe he didn't love Samir," Karla challenged. "Or maybe he loves you more than he loved Samir."

"Stop trying to trick me into implicating Colin! It couldn't have been Colin. He loved Samir like a brother."

"Speaking of brothers," Karla took advantage of the easy segue to ask her next question. "Raj admitted that he and Samir argued frequently before his death. Do you know what they argued about?"

Raj and Colin had already confirmed what Raj and Samir had argued about, but Karla wanted to hear Millie's explanation. She hoped that Millie's version of events would be from Samir's point of view since she had likely heard about it from him.

"Raj always wanted a role at TechSavvy, but Samir refused to hire him."

Finally, something everyone agrees on.

"Why did Samir refuse to hire him?"

"I have no idea," Millie said, shaking her head. "Samir and I shared everything. We had no secrets, but the only thing we didn't discuss was TechSavvy.

Aside from Raj, I was the only person in Samir's world who wasn't affiliated with the company. When we were alone, TechSavvy didn't exist."

"I think you might have answered the question without realizing it," Rob interjected. "You said that you were the only person in Samir's life, aside from Raj, with no affiliation to TechSavvy." She looked at Karla. "Maybe Samir didn't want Raj to become another person he would have to discuss TechSavvy with."

Karla nodded. "Millie and Raj were his TechSavvy-free havens."

"After Samir found out about the cancer, he began delegating more responsibility to Colin," Millie continued. "Raj noticed and intensified his campaign to work at TechSavvy."

"Didn't Colin and Raj wonder why Samir was handing more responsibility to Colin?" Karla asked.

"Yes," Millie confirmed. "Samir told everyone that he wished to spend more time with me. No one suspected it was a lie." Millie sighed. "Anyway, Samir was frustrated that Raj wouldn't let it go. Samir lost his temper during one of their exchanges and said something insulting to Raj." She held up her hands in a placating gesture. "I don't know what Samir said that insulted Raj. He didn't tell me, and I didn't ask. Raj responded by slapping Samir across the face. After that, they didn't talk for two days which is forever for those two. Then, they forged a delicate truce. Raj apologized for slapping Samir, and Samir made Raj promise never again to mention working at TechSavvy."

"Raj slapped Samir?" Karla couldn't believe her ears. She'd already forgotten most of whatever Millie said after, *Raj responded by slapping Samir across the face.*

"Caught ya," Karla mumbled to herself, recalling Raj's exaggerated nod when he told her and Max that he "would never harm Samir." If he'd lied about that, he could have also lied about killing him.

CHAPTER 19

REVITALEYES

"Sorry to interrupt," Lynn said after she knocked. "I'm making a list to replace the confiscated items." She held out a pad of paper and a pen. "Would you like to add anything to the list, Millie?"

Rob excused herself to get back to work while Millie added a few items to the bottom of Lynn's list.

She handed back the pad and pen with a small smile and quiet, "Thank you, Lynn." She brought her first two fingers to her temple. "I feel a headache coming on." She excused herself to go upstairs and lie down.

Lynn jotted *headache tablets* to the bottom of the list, then tore it from the pad. "Here, you'll have to go." She thrust the list at Karla. "Her ladyship fell asleep reading and just woke up. She wants me to draw her a bath, feed the cats, and arrange her clothes for after the bath."

"Listen, Mother," Karla said, taking the list and folding it in half. "Thank you. You've been incredible

413

this weekend. I couldn't have pulled this off without you. You really came through for me when I needed you."

"That almost makes putting up with her grumpy ladyship worthwhile," Lynn teased with a wink. "Almost."

Lynn hugged her daughter; Karla let her and even hugged back.

KARLA WANDERED the aisles of Pharmasaurus Rx, Bellbrook's local pharmacy, collecting toiletries and beauty supplies to replace the items Dean and his officers had taken as evidence.

"Toothpaste for sensitive teeth," she muttered, reading from the list Lynn had given her. She scanned the shelves of toothpaste, wondering which brand she should get. She let out a sigh and added three different brands to her basket. "One of these must be the right one."

"Do you always talk to yourself?"

Karla let out a small gasp, surprised by the voice.

"Only when I want to have an intelligent conversation." She added a bottle of mouthwash to her basket. "If you're following me, I'm heading to Paradise Aisles next," she teased.

"I'll meet you there," the officer joked with a chuckle.

"You're the new guy, right? Bellbrook PDs new cybercop?"

"IT specialist," the officer corrected. "Cybercop sounds like I'm part robot."

"How are you liking Bellbrook?"

"I've only been here a week, but it's been a busy, interesting week," replied the officer. "First, I attended the scene of a billionaire's murder, then I interviewed the police chief's daughter. Next, I get to read the texts and emails of one of the most famous families in the world."

"Never a dull moment," Karla replied. "You can't tell from the outside, but Bellbrook is a busy place. It's also friendly, welcoming, and full of kind people." She dropped a bottle of moisturizer into her basket. "You'll get used to running into the same people all the time."

"One of the many quirks of living in a small town," quipped the officer. "Stocking up?" He pointed his chin at the mountain of items in her basket.

"No," Karla replied. "I'm replacing the items that the police confiscated from the Nestled Inn. What brings you here?" she asked, changing the subject.

"Allergy meds." He held up a small white paper bag with the store logo on the front—a cartoon dinosaur waving his tiny hand and wearing a white lab coat with a red *Rx* on the lapel.

"Seasonal allergies?" Karla asked, continuing down the aisle and stopping in front of the shelves of body wash.

"Pollen," Cybercop said with a nod. "The pollen is terrible this week. Is it always this bad in Bellbrook?"

"I'm not sure," Karla replied. "I don't have allergies."

"You're lucky." Something vibrated on the officer's

uniform. He clutched the pocket where the vibrations seemed to come from. "I gotta go, Karla. See you later."

"Bye," she said as he disappeared around the corner.

She placed four bottles of body wash in her basket, then shifted it to her other arm.

"What's next?" she mumbled.

She knitted her brows together, unable to believe what she was reading. "Revitaleyes?"

Revitaleyes was a popular brand of eye drops for dry eyes.

She set her basket on the floor and squinted at the handwriting. Aside from the items that Millie had added to the list, all the items were in Lynn's distinct, flourished handwriting. Who asked Lynn to add Revitaleyes to the list?

This is too easy, Karla reasoned with herself.

Surely the killer wouldn't be this obvious. Like Max said, "The killer knows what poison they used." But the killer must realize that the police have figured out which poison killed Samir. Karla shook her head. This must be a weird coincidence.

Unless… what if the killer was restocking because they were planning to kill again? But who were they planning to kill? Why?

She pulled out her phone.

KARLA

Who asked you to add Revitaleyes to
the shopping list?

She waited, staring at the screen and willing the three dancing dots to appear that indicated Lynn was typing a response.

Nothing. Lady Olivia must be keeping her busy.

Karla hurried through the rest of the store, picking up the remaining items on her list. She was surprised when the pharmacy had the paperback novel Millie had requested. Until that moment, Karla had never noticed that Pharmasaurus Rx had a small book section stocked with a handful of current best sellers. She had been reading e-books for so long that she forgot how it felt to hold a paperback. It was comforting. The unread pages smelled like rest and relaxation. It was like hugging an old friend. She made a mental note to get herself to the Bellbrook library next week and borrow an actual physical book.

"Karla!"

Karla scanned the parking lot, looking for the source of Harry's voice.

"Over here!" he called, running toward her from across the street.

"Hi," she said as his long strides closed the gap between them.

"I just dropped off Colin at the Nestled Inn." Harry came to a halt in front of her. His head tilted with concern, and his bushy silver eyebrows furrowed as he searched her face for something. "I called out to you three times. Couldn't you hear me?"

"Sorry," she said, closing the trunk of her car. "I'm so distracted today. Samir's death is all I can think about."

"Dean and Max will figure out who killed him," Harry reassured her.

"I'm sure they will," Karla agreed. "But Samir will still be dead, and my company's name will forever be associated with his murder. He was one of my highest profile clients."

"No one will blame you. You had nothing to do with Samir's death. Neither did Just Task Me!"

Karla wished she was half as confident as Harry sounded. She forced a smile to show Harry that his attempt to comfort her was successful, even though it wasn't.

"Last night, I asked Griff why, despite becoming a multi-millionaire, he kept working at Fixin' By Dixon. He said he liked his job, and his employees relied on the company to support their families."

"Sounds like Griff," Harry agreed.

"I feel the same way," Karla admitted. "I love my job. I'm good at what I do, and I have employees all over the world who rely on Just Task Me! to feed their families." Karla swallowed when her voice hitched on the last word. "How would I live with myself if my ruined reputation put their livelihoods at risk?"

"Oh, Karla." He wrapped a strong but gentle arm around her shoulder, his careworn face etched with compassion and concern. "Like you said, you're great at your job. Whatever the reaction to Samir's murder, I have no doubt that you'll find a way to spin it so you look like a hero."

"Thanks, Harry." She gave him another forced smile. Her phone dinged. She checked the screen and exhaled loudly. "I lost track of time," she said.

"Kwame is texting to remind me to pick up the cod au gratin from The Pavlovian in thirty minutes." Karla had forgotten Kwame was catering dinner for the Nestled Inn tonight. Tonight would have been Samir's chef's night off, and she had arranged for the family to have dinner at The Pavlovian. Given the circumstances, Kwame offered to prepare their meal for takeout, so they could eat at home and not venture out into the world if they weren't ready. She recalled how eager Samir had been to sample the local cuisine.

"That's great!" Harry said, rubbing his hands together like she was picking up his dinner. "Kwame's cod au gratin is—" He brought his index finger and thumb to his lips and did a chef's kiss. "The Khans will love it."

"I still have to walk and feed Gucci, then go to Paradise Aisles before I drop everything off at the Nestled Inn," she continued. "I can't do all that in thirty minutes," she said with a sigh.

"I'll take care of Gucci," Harry offered. "He's my favourite little buddy!"

"I've already asked you to be a butler and a chauffeur," Karla said. "I can't ask you to be a dog walker too."

"Let me help," Harry insisted. "Gucci and I love to hang out."

"I can't ask you to do that," Karla argued.

"You didn't ask, Karla. I offered." This was the same tone Harry would use when Karla was little, and he would warn her not to wander too close to the road or too near the fireplace. A tone she'd always felt compelled to heed.

"Are you sure you don't mind?"

"I have to drive past your cottage to get to my cabin," Harry reasoned. "I was planning to visit the manor house, anyway," he explained. "The tilers finished the kitchen today, and I want to check their work. I can stop by and pick up Gucci. He can walk with me and Clancy to the manor house, I'll check on the job site, then I'll walk Gucci home and feed him."

Clancy was Harry's faithful Irish Wolfhound. He wandered the estate grounds as though he were the groundskeeper, not Harry.

Karla thanked Harry and reminded him where the spare key was hidden.

He reminded her he already knew because he'd hid it there.

She told him where to find Gucci's leash and gave him thorough instructions on feeding the food-motivated terrier.

Her phone dinged again.

"No rest for the wicked," Harry teased as he turned to leave.

Karla watched Harry run across the street toward his beat-up, much loved, old white pickup truck as she pulled her phone out of her pocket. It was a text from Lynn. She had forgotten that she was waiting for Lynn's reply about who added eye drops to the shopping list.

LYNN

Raj.

Despite knowing Raj was a suspect, the revelation

that he could actually be Samir's killer still came as a shock. Her phone dinged again, distracting her from her thoughts.

LYNN

Why?

Not wanting to alarm Lynn or break her promise to Max about keeping the eye drops secret, Karla had to think on her feet.

KARLA

Does he want regular or extra strength?

LYNN

He didn't specify. Should I ask him?

KARLA

No, don't bother him. I'll get both. Thanks!

It was far easier to lie in a text message than in person. Karla had no intention of buying eye drops. If Raj was the murderer and had tasked her with restocking his preferred murder weapon, he would be disappointed.

CHAPTER 20
TWO TRIPS IS FOR SISSIES

KARLA HEAVED both armfuls of shopping bags onto the counter in the Nestled Inn's large kitchen. She let out a long breath, rubbed her sore hands and wrists, and savoured her victory. She had challenged herself to carry all the bags from the car in one trip. *Two trips is for sissies,* she had told herself as she loaded each hand and wrist with more bags than she could comfortably carry.

Ignoring the purchases from Pharmasaurus Rx and Paradise Aisles, Karla focussed on the insulated bags from The Pavlovian. Her priority was to serve supper while it was still hot.

"Where's Harry?" Lynn asked, taking in the sea of shopping bags strewn across the quartz countertop. "He said he'd be back to help with dinner. We're short staffed now that Rob and Max are working on Samir's murder."

"Harry's on Gucci-duty," Karla replied. "Look at the cute selfie he sent me." She showed Lynn a selfie of

Harry posing cheek to cheek with Gucci and Clancy. "I swear, Gucci is smiling. Aww, he loves Harry."

"Of course he's smiling, and of course he loves Harry," Lynn agreed. "Harry always gives him meat. What's not to smile about?"

"He gives Gucci meat?" Karla asked.

"Only every time he sees him," Lynn confirmed. "Slips him a bit of that homemade jerky he keeps in the glove box of his truck."

"Rosalie asked Harry to drive her and her friends to their garden club meeting tonight, so I don't think we'll see him until tomorrow."

"I forgot about that," Lynn said, collecting dishes from the cupboards and piling them on the kitchen table. "It's the Petal Pushers first meeting of the season. Rosalie can't miss it. She's the club president."

Lynn set the dining room table, and Karla plated the food. Kwame had outdone himself. She wondered if he had made the dessert himself or ordered it from the local bakery. Either way, everything looked and smelled delicious. Karla's stomach grumbled, a loud reminder that it had been hours since she'd eaten anything.

They called the family for supper.

Raj, Colin, and Millie filed into the dining room and took their seats. Lady Olivia followed, the rhythmic *thunk* of her walking stick piercing the sad silence.

Karla served the red lentil-chickpea-tomato soup, then retreated to the kitchen where she could watch the family without being obvious.

"Your head must be quite chilly, Raj," Lady Olivia's

tone and smile were steeped in dry sarcasm. "Otherwise, I'm sure you would remove your hat at the dinner table."

Did Colin just roll his eyes? Karla glanced at the ceiling above Colin's head. There was nothing out of the ordinary, nothing she thought would have grabbed his attention.

With a slight sneer, Raj removed his cap and hung it on the back of his chair. He did not, however, remove the dark sunglasses he had been wearing all day.

Aside from occasional compliments about the soup and remarks about how much Samir would have enjoyed it, the first course was quiet. Millie and Raj hardly touched their soup except to stir it and blow on each spoonful longer than necessary.

After the first course, Lynn swept in and removed the soup bowls. Karla followed, serving plates of the main course—cod au gratin with zucchini fritters and coleslaw.

There wasn't much eating. The guests mostly shuffled forkfuls of food around their plates.

Colin's gaze landed on the empty chair at the head of the table where Samir had sat the previous evening and enjoyed his last meal. He blinked fast several times in a row, cleared his throat, and refocused his attention on his plate.

Raj didn't avert his gaze once. Though it was hard to be sure with those dark sunglasses.

Lady Olivia indiscreetly slipped small pieces of cod to Rosemary and Thyme who were poised at attention at her feet.

Millie stared at her plate like she was trying to muster the energy to tackle it.

It was the most joyless meal Karla had ever witnessed. Needing a break from helplessly watching the family's grief, she distracted herself by putting away the groceries and other purchases until it was time for her and Lynn to collect the dinner dishes and serve dessert—pavlova covered in fresh berries.

"Why don't you take a break," Karla suggested to Lynn as they scraped plates and loaded the dishwasher. "You haven't had much of a break since yesterday."

"I don't mind, love," Lynn chirped with a smile. "I like to keep busy." She made a jazz-hands gesture. "You know what they say about idle hands."

"It doesn't take two of us to clean the kitchen," Karla insisted.

"Fine," Lynn conceded, wiping her hands on her black apron. "I'll take these toiletries upstairs and put them away, then I'll scoop the litter box, and maybe sneak in a short break in Lady Olivia's big comfy easy chair." She tapped her phone in her pocket. "I'm dying to start the new smutty book I downloaded on my reading app. Millie suggested it. Did you know she's an avid reader? That easy chair is an eyesore, but it does look comfortable."

"I won't tell her if you won't," Karla promised with a smile.

Lynn took the bags of toiletries and headed upstairs.

Karla heard the shuffling of chairs and people in

the dining room and poked her head into the doorway.

"Can I get anyone coffee or tea?" She smiled.

"Tea, please," everyone replied slightly out of sync.

Karla directed them to the sunroom and told them she would bring the tea in a few minutes.

They hardly touched their supper. Maybe I can tempt them by serving a plate of Rosalie's Hermit cookies with the tea.

"One slice or two, La-la?"

Dean's voice shocked Karla back to the present.

"Dad! How long have you been here?" Her eyes lit up at the sight of the Dough-Re-Mi pizza box on the kitchen table. "Is that pizza?"

"I just arrived," he said, handing her a plate. "I got your text about the Revitaleyes, and I was on my way here when Lynn texted to tell me you haven't eaten. She said you like pizza with pesto, spinach, mushrooms, zucchini, tomatoes, and goat cheese." He opened the box and lifted a slice. "So, I turned around and got pizza."

"That's my favourite," Karla confirmed, shocked that anyone aside from Rob and Max knew her regular pizza order, especially Lynn.

Always the multi-tasker, Karla held a slice of pizza in one hand and used the other to gather tea supplies and condiments, arranging them on the wooden tray. She gripped the slice between her teeth when she needed both hands to rinse the teapot. She ate a second slice while the water boiled, and the tea steeped in the pot.

She left the pizza in the kitchen when she delivered the tea tray to the sunroom.

"Shall I be Mother?" Millie offered as Karla left the room, closing the French doors behind her.

A phrase Karla hadn't heard since her grandmother died.

She returned to the kitchen, her thoughts focussed on a third slice of pizza.

"Excuse me, Karla?"

Karla spun, holding a slice of pizza, quite inelegantly, in her mouth.

"Raj," she mumbled, without letting the pizza slice fall.

Dean slid the plate under her chin so she could dispose of the slice.

"What can I get you?" she asked, dropping the slice onto the plate.

"I was wondering if you picked up the Revitaleyes I requested?" he asked, fidgeting with his baseball cap, which he gripped in front of him.

If Raj had killed Samir, then had the nerve to ask her to pick up more of his favourite murder weapon, surely he wouldn't have been brazen enough to ask her about it in front of the police chief, would he? That would make him either arrogant or stupid, and Raj had never struck Karla as either.

"It was out of stock." Karla closed the lid of the pizza box to avoid eye contact with anyone while she fibbed. "I'll go to another store after supper."

"Thank you, Karla. I appreciate it."

"If there's something wrong with your eyes, I can call Rob and ask her to look at them," Karla offered.

"No need." Raj waved his hand like he was erasing an invisible chalkboard. "I would hate to bother her when she's working on my brother's murder."

"It wouldn't be a bother, Mr. Khan," Dean said, stepping forward.

"It's fine," Raj insisted. "It's just seasonal allergies."

"Let's see," Dean challenged, his eyes narrow.

With more than a little hesitation, Raj removed his sunglasses.

Karla brought her hand to her mouth to stifle the gasp that tried to escape.

Dean winced and looked away for an instant.

Raj's eyes were bloodshot, swollen, veiny, and somehow appeared both raw and weepy at the same time. His nose was swollen too. The skin around his eyes was puffy and red.

"That looks pretty serious." Dean put aside his cop voice and spoke to Raj in the gentler, more paternal tone he reserved for school visits and community events. "Could be a nasty case of conjunctivitis."

"It's not," Raj said. "I haven't slept... I-I've cried almost non-stop... I didn't realize the pollen would be so bad in Bellbrook," he stammered with a hint of panic. But he didn't do the exaggerated nod that would indicate he was lying. "I thought I packed a bottle of eye drops, but I can't find them. I think your officers confiscated them."

"The Bellbrook police department doesn't have your eye drops," Dean revealed. "We didn't find any eye drops during our search."

"Then I must have left them on my nightstand in LA."

Still no exaggerated nod.

"Cybercop has allergies too," Karla said to Dean. "He said the pollen is terrible this week." She hoped Dean would interpret her nod as she intended—an indication that she believed Raj was telling the truth.

"Max is stopping by later," Dean said. "I'll text her and ask her to bring you a bottle of Revitaleyes."

"Extra strength if they have it."

"For sure," Dean said, his meaty thumbs flying across the screen of his phone.

"Raj," Karla said as he turned to leave. "Would you like a cool compress for your eyes?"

"That would be great. Thank you."

Karla gestured for Raj to sit down. She found a clean, white, dish towel in the pantry and soaked it in cool water.

"May I ask you a question, Raj?" Karla asked as she wrung out the cloth until it stopped dripping.

"Of course," Raj replied, rubbing his right eye with his fist and further irritating his situation.

"Is it true that you hit Samir during a recent argument?"

Dean snapped to attention, pocketing his phone and pulling out his notebook and pen.

"You had a physical altercation with Samir?" Dean asked.

Raj nodded.

"Why didn't you tell us?" Dean demanded. "Did you think we wouldn't find out? We always find out."

"It was not my proudest moment," Raj defended. "I am not an angry man. I am not violent. Until last week, I had never touched anyone in anger. Ever."

"Did he hit back?" Dean interjected. "When you hit Samir, did he retaliate?"

"No, of course not," Raj replied as if it were the only possible answer. "Samir would never strike anyone. Especially me."

"What did Samir say before you slapped him?" Karla asked.

"I don't remember." Raj gave one deep nod, then covered his eyes with the cool compress.

"He's lying," Karla mouthed to Dean, who nodded in acknowledgement.

"Were you arguing because Samir was giving Colin more responsibility at TechSavvy?" she asked.

"Yes," Raj admitted, resting his head on the cold compress in his hands, with his elbows on the table. "He said he wanted to spend more quality time with Millie, and Colin was eager to take on more responsibility."

"Did you believe him?" Karla asked.

Raj removed the compress and raised his head to look at her. "Of course I believed him. Why wouldn't I?" he asked. "Samir would never lie to me. Besides, he loved Millie. He was always looking for ways to spend more time with her. And Colin was always hovering around, looking to take on more and more at TechSavvy. I tried to warn Samir that Colin was trying to take over TechSavvy. But he refused to listen to me."

"Is that why you hit him?" Dean asked. "Because Samir wouldn't believe you about Colin having bad intentions with TechSavvy?"

"Sort of," Raj admitted. "I accused Samir of turning a blind eye while Colin fleeced him and pushed him out of the company he built. I also accused him of giving Colin more responsibility to spite me. To rub my face in the fact that he wouldn't hire me."

"I see." Dean flipped the page in his notebook and continued scrawling notes.

Raj returned his face to his hands and held the compress against his eyes.

If Raj had believed Samir was using Colin to rub Raj's face in the fact that he didn't have a role at TechSavvy and never would, how did Colin interpret Samir's actions? Did he also assume that he was a pawn in Samir's power struggle with Raj? How did Colin feel about taking on extra work so Samir could devote more time to the woman Colin loved? Karla knew Samir wasn't assigning Colin extra work to irritate Raj, but Raj and Colin didn't know that. They didn't know that Samir's sudden desire for more work-life balance was motivated by his recent cancer diagnosis.

Raj lifted his head again to flip over the cool compress. "Look, I was fine with Samir wanting to spend more time with Millie, though I don't know how that would be possible. They were already together practically twenty-four hours a day. But I don't think Colin was thrilled about it. Samir got the glory of being the founder and CEO of TechSavvy, and he got Millie. What did Colin get? More work and longer hours at the office." He looked up at Dean. "You're questioning the wrong suspect."

"I think we should clear up a few things," Colin said from the doorway behind Dean.

CHAPTER 21

BIG VOICES AND BIG CLUES

"How long have you been standing there?" Raj demanded.

"Long enough," Colin replied, stepping into the kitchen. "You struck Samir?" Dumbfounded, he scanned Raj as though he were seeing him for the first time. "You actually hit him?"

"I'm ashamed of what I did," Raj admitted. "But it was your fault." He stood up and raised his voice. Karla had never seen this side of Raj—aggressive and emotional. His trembling hands piqued her curiosity about the explosive emotions bubbling just below his surface. Could these emotions have erupted into a rage that caused him to kill Samir? "If you hadn't tried to replace me as his brother, steal the company that he built, and lust after his wife, Samir and I wouldn't have had anything to argue about."

"I *am not* guilty of any of the things you're accusing me of," Colin said with a dismissive scoff. "You're paranoid."

432

"Liar!" Raj's outburst caught the attention of Millie and Lady Olivia. Millie was already in the doorway behind Colin, and Lady Olivia's walking stick *thunked* toward the kitchen at a pace Karla hadn't thought the elderly lady capable of. "You killed my brother because he was in your way."

Like they were watching a tennis match, everyone's heads turned toward Colin, awaiting his rebuttal.

"You delusional fool," Colin mocked with a sneer, shaking his head. "When the world finds out about Samir's death, TechSavvy's shares will tank. The markets will be in chaos. I wouldn't be surprised if, twenty-four hours from now, the shares are worthless. He was the founder and visionary. Samir *was* TechSavvy." He poked himself in the chest. "I've invested all my wealth in TechSavvy shares. Why would I risk making them worthless by killing Samir?"

Oblivious to the tense situation around them, Rosemary and Thyme leapt onto the counter and slinked their way toward the window over the sink, snaking their nimble bodies around the coffee and tea canisters.

"You convinced Samir to exclude me from Tech-Savvy," Raj accused, ignoring Colin's question. "You wanted to be the only person Samir could rely on. You alienated him from me. You made yourself indispensable to TechSavvy and to Millie, then you got rid of him," Raj concluded by making a dramatic sweeping motion with his hand.

"Samir wouldn't hire you because he respected you." Colin sucked in a deep breath and softened his tone. "Raj, you worked three jobs to support Samir through school and raise the money to start Tech-Savvy. He was grateful for the sacrifices you made. In return, he wanted to give you financial security and a life of leisure. He wanted you to enjoy life and never have to work again."

"Why didn't he tell me that?" Raj asked, his irritated eyes filling with a fresh supply of tears. "If only he had told me... none of this would ha..." His voice cracked and trailed off before he could finish his sentence.

"Samir was a proud man," Colin explained. "He knew you were a proud man too, and he was afraid you would be offended and see it as a handout."

Raj jabbed his index finger toward Colin. "You still had a motive!" He shifted his pointer to Millie. "Her!"

Colin closed his eyes and pinched the bridge of his nose with his thumb and index finger. "Fine," he admitted in a defeated tone. "You're right, I love Millie. I always have. Because I love her, I want her to be happy. Samir made her happy. Killing Samir would have hurt Millie. Therefore, I would never have done it. Not to mention my own selfishness. Samir was my best friend. He was the brother I never had. I would never have hurt him." He waggled his finger toward Raj. "You, however, hit him! If either of us is a likely suspect in his murder, it's you! You argued with him constantly in his final weeks, and now we find out you have a history of violence against him."

Raj took an imposing step toward Colin.

"Let's settle down, gentlemen," Dean bellowed,

using his authoritative voice. "Trading accusations will only make the situation worse."

"We wouldn't be trading accusations if you did your job and found out who killed my brother!"

"I'm confident that an arrest for Samir's murder is imminent." Dean oozed confidence, but Karla knew he was lying by the way he lifted his chin higher than normal and looked down his nose at Raj when he spoke.

"You have no clue who killed Samir," Colin challenged. "That's what the cops on TV always say when they have no leads or no suspects." He squeezed his brows together and went cross-eyed looking at his own nose. "An arrest is imminent," he said in a voice and demeanour intended to mimic Dean.

"Do you even have a suspect?" Raj implored.

Yes, Karla thought to herself, *multiple suspects, and all of them are currently in this kitchen.*

"Yes," Dean replied to Raj. "We know how Samir died. Now we're working on linking the manner of death to the suspect." His chin was so high it was almost parallel with the floor.

Lady Olivia slammed the tip of her cane against the floor. The loud *thunk* made everyone stop and stare at Lady Olivia and Millie in the doorway.

"Enough!" Millie stepped past Colin and positioned herself between him and Raj. "Samir's motivation for giving Colin more responsibility at TechSavvy had nothing to do with Raj, and his refusal to hire Raj was not because of Colin! You both think highly of yourselves!" Shock and awe filled the room. Shock that Millie had found her Big Voice and awe that she seemed to have insight into her late husband's actions that no one else in his inner circle had been privy to.

She turned to Colin. "Samir needed you to be his eyes and ears at TechSavvy because he knew he would have to take a leave of absence soon." She turned to Raj. "And he couldn't hire you because he needed you to be available for emotional support because he was terrified."

"Why?" asked Lady Olivia, *thunking* her cane to the nearest chair so she could sit down. "Why was Samir terrified? Why would he need to take time away from work?"

"Because Samir was ill, Mumsy," Millie said in that too-calm, too-steady voice people used when they delivered bad news. She joined her mother-in-law at the kitchen table. "He would have had months of treatment ahead of him."

Everyone listened in stunned silence as Millie explained how Samir's recent routine physical exam did not have the routine outcome he had expected. Instead of the doctor issuing him a clean bill of health and submitting a short, uneventful report to Tech-Savvy's board of directors like he always did, the doctor had ordered more tests to investigate anomalies in Samir's lab results. Samir had asked the doctor to delay sending the report to the board of directors until he had sought a second opinion. Until he had a more confident prognosis of his condition.

"This is why Samir cleared his schedule to fly to Germany tomorrow," Millie said in conclusion. "He had an appointment with a doctor in Hamburg who specializes in the specific cancer he had."

"Cancer?" Colin sounded as stunned as he looked. "I can't believe it. Samir was always healthier than a butcher's dog."

"Why didn't he tell me?" Raj collapsed into his chair and sank his head into his hands. His shoulders heaved with silent sobs.

Colin placed a supportive hand on Raj's shoulder. "I could tell something was bothering him," he admitted. "I assumed it was work. I thought he just needed a break. I told him a week in Hamburg with Millie was just what he needed. I even teased him about playing hooky." He shook his head. "I'm such an insensitive idiot."

"You didn't know, Colin. Don't blame yourself." Millie gave him a tight-lipped smile. "He didn't want anyone to know yet. He didn't want you to worry."

"That fool! How dare he suffer in silence and not let any of us know what was going on," Lady Olivia mumbled, dabbing her eyes with a black handkerchief she unfurled from the cuff of her black blouse.

"How ill was he, Millie?" Colin asked, steadying himself with both hands on the back of Raj's chair.

Millie cleared her throat and opened her mouth to reply, but Lady Olivia planted her walking stick firmly on the tile floor and leveraged it to pull herself to her feet. "If you'll excuse me," she rasped, more breathless than usual. "I feel the sudden urge to lie down."

Karla, Dean, Millie, Colin, and Raj rushed to assist her.

"No, thank you." She waved off the simultaneous offers of support. "I'll be fine once the shock wears off." She inched toward the threshold, then pursed her lips and made a smooching sound that caused Rosemary and Thyme to leap off the counter and run ahead of her, out of the kitchen, and down the hall.

"Are you sure, Mumsy?" Millie asked. "Perhaps you shouldn't be alone."

"Being alone is precisely what I need right now," Lady Olivia retorted, squeezing Millie's hand. "I'll be fine." She winked. "Don't worry about me."

Millie nodded and Lady Olivia followed her cats down the hall.

"I should go with her," Millie said, grappling out loud.

"You heard her, Millie. She wants to be alone," Colin said.

"You don't understand," she pleaded. "You weren't there when her son died. What if Samir's death brings back all those feelings, and she goes back to that horrible, hopeless place?"

"Colin's right," Raj said, his voice shaky and thick with emotion. "You know how Lady Olivia is. She doesn't like to show her emotions. Give her some privacy. If she needs anything, she'll let us know. She's hardly the type to suffer in silence."

"Lynn is upstairs," Karla interjected. "If Lady Olivia needs anything, Lynn will take care of her."

"Fine," Millie agreed with a long inhale. "I'll give her a few minutes, then I'll check on her."

"Why don't you all return to the sunroom," Karla suggested. "I'll brew a fresh pot of tea."

After a series of mumbles and nods, Millie, Colin, and Raj returned to the sunroom. The French doors rattled closed behind them.

"OK, La-la," Dean said as Karla lobbed Raj's compress into the laundry room all the way across the kitchen. "Who lied and what did they lie about?"

"I think Colin and Raj were honest. They each believe the other killed Samir," Karla revealed. "Millie was honest about Samir's health issues. Lady Olivia didn't say much, but I haven't figured out her Tell. I think she might be one of those brutally honest people who doesn't care about offending anyone."

"Colin and Raj are so busy accusing each other, neither of them suspect Millie could be the killer."

"You think Millie killed Samir?" This was the first time Dean had named a suspect out loud. "Why?"

"Statistically, it's usually the spouse," Dean reasoned. "Also, Millie stands to inherit a fortune from her late husband. Samir's death will make her one of the wealthiest women on the planet."

"Millie could have secured her financial future by divorcing Samir. She didn't have to kill him," Karla countered. "They didn't have a prenup. She would have walked away with a sizable chunk of Samir's fortune." A confidential fact Karla had discovered by accident when she helped plan their destination wedding years earlier.

"Murder is faster than divorce, La-la," Dean argued. "And less public. Millie is a private person. She doesn't embrace the spotlight like Samir did. She prefers to fly under the radar, so to speak. A divorce would make their marital problems public. The media attention would be intense, and she'd have to tolerate constant speculation and rumours. Not to mention that, with all the money and fancy lawyers that Samir had access to, he could have delayed a divorce settlement for years." He scratched the top of his head. "The killer tried to make Samir's death look like natural causes," Dean continued. "If Rob's post-mortem exam hadn't been so thorough, the killer would have gotten away with it. Another coroner might've just blamed complications from Samir's recent cancer diagnosis and closed the case. Aside from Samir's doctor, Millie was the only person who knew about Samir's cancer. Maybe she hoped his diagnosis would camouflage his murder."

Karla thought about this for a moment. Millie was quick to tell Max—who would obviously tell Rob—about Samir's cancer right after he died. Was that part of her plan? Was she hoping that revelation would influence Rob's conclusion about how Samir died? Karla didn't like this possibility. She wanted to believe that Samir and Millie's love story was the real deal.

"But Millie and Samir loved each other. They were happy together. If there were problems in their relationship, surely Lady Olivia, Colin, or Raj would have noticed, considering how much time they all spent together and how close-knit they were."

"Everybody has secrets, La-la. Some people just hide them better," Dean reminded her. "Take Samir's cancer diagnosis, for example. He and Millie managed to keep it from the rest of the family for weeks." He shrugged his broad shoulders. "Maybe they had other secrets." He shook his head. "The only two people who ever truly know what happens inside a marriage are the people who are married."

Karla nodded in reluctant acknowledgment that Dean could be right.

Having fulfilled his mission of questioning Raj about the Revitaleyes and delivering pizza to his hungry daughter, Dean left, grumbling about mountains of evidence and reports to sift through.

Karla delivered a fresh pot of tea and a restocked plate of Rosalie's Hermit cookies to the sunroom, then turned her attention to cleaning the kitchen and dining room, which were still messy from dinner.

She wiped down the surfaces and swept the floors. Then Karla separated the compost, recycling, and trash into piles and took all of it to the wooden trash corral just outside the kitchen door.

Inside the trash corral—a large, wooden shed with double doors wide enough to wheel the bins in and out on trash day—the bins were open and empty, untouched since the police had confiscated their contents hours earlier. She dropped the compost into the compost bin and locked the raccoon-proof lid. Then she tied up the bag of trash and placed it in the trash bin. "The last thing we need is critters making a mess all over the place," she muttered as she ensured the large saucer-style lid was locked in place. She dropped the recycling into the blue plastic recycling bin and lifted the flip-top lid to close it. Something was stuck to the underside of the lid. A slip of white paper fluttered in the breeze coming through the open double doors. Karla reached for it, but the breeze beat her to it, and the slip of paper flew out of her reach and fluttered to the ground a few feet away. She lunged at the thing, but a gust of wind carried it away again just as she was about to trap it under her black Dr. Martens loafer.

Karla chased the slip of paper out of the trash corral and along the side of the house as the breeze carried it toward the driveway. The sun had already set, and Karla feared, if it blew out of the narrow range of light provided by the motion-activated lights, she would lose sight of it for good. "Stay still," she ordered the slip of paper under her breath. "Stop blowing," she instructed the wind. Every time she got close enough to pounce on the mysterious slip of paper, a wind gust came along and blew the elusive thing in a different direction. "This is how it must feel to be a cat chasing a laser pointer." It blew toward the black SUV parked in the driveway, finally coming to a stop against one of the large black tires. "Gotcha!" Karla declared as she reached down and grabbed it. "You must've been left behind when the police took the trash."

She smoothed the slip of paper and moved under the light. It was a receipt. The ink was faint. There was a pink stripe along the side, and a small spot of something dark and sticky where the receipt had been stuck to the underside of the lid. "The ink and the paper both needed to be replaced when this was printed," she murmured as she trained her eyes on the faint text. The date on the receipt was almost two weeks ago. It was from a nationwide chain drugstore in Los Angeles. "Such a long receipt for only a few purchases," she muttered. The receipt was almost the length of Karla's arm, but only a small section of it actually displayed the items the purchaser had bought. The rest of the receipt was devoted to personalized rewards, coupons, and new product suggestions. "What a waste of paper." She squinted hard at the section of the receipt that displayed the purchases: a paperback book and two bottles of extra-strength Revitaleyes.

CHAPTER 22

THE GAME IS AFOOT

KARLA GASPED and fisted the receipt so hard her knuckles ached, and her fingernails dug into her palm.

She glanced at her dark surroundings as potential theories raced through her brain. *Wait, where's the other SUV? Weren't there two black SUVs parked in the drive-way?* Still gripping the receipt and ignoring the accompanying pain of her nails digging into her palm, she ran halfway down the driveway, far enough to scan the road around The Nestled Inn. *No SUV. Huh! Maybe Harry has it? He would have used one of the SUVs to drive Colin to and from the Seascape Hotel earlier. No, it can't be Harry. When I ran into him outside Pharmasaurus Rx, he was driving his pickup truck. Did he park the SUV some-where else?* She unlocked her phone and sent Harry a text.

KARLA

Where did you park the SUV when you dropped off Colin?

Karla raced back to the house. She used her phone's camera to take a photo of the receipt, carefully folded the long slip of paper, secured it in a small resealable sandwich bag, and tucked it into the front pocket of her high-waisted, black cigarette pants.

She tapped her nails on the counter and organized her thoughts about the clue she had just found.

Lynn's words echoed in her head. "Did you know Millie is an avid reader?" Did the receipt belong to Millie, or did the killer frame Millie by purchasing the paperback along with the eye drops? Why would the killer frame Millie? Why implicate a grieving widow?

If the Revitaleyes on the receipt was used to kill Samir, where were the bottles of eye drops now? Did the killer decant the poisonous liquid into something less conspicuous before they travelled from LA to Bell-brook? Were the small bottles of eye drops hidden somewhere?

"Hey, Sis!" The sound of Max's voice and the kitchen door startled Karla back to reality. "Dad asked me to drop off a bottle of Revitaleyes for Raj."

"He's in the sunroom," Karla said. "But wait!" She made a stop gesture with one hand while she retrieved the receipt from her pocket with the other. "I found this in the trash corral after dinner. You guys must have missed it when you confiscated the trash earlier."

Max opened the sandwich bag, slid out the paper, and unfolded it until it reached its full, unnecessary length. She scanned the receipt, searching for its significance.

Karla watched Max's eyes widen and her jaw slacken when she found the clue.

Max raised her eyes to Karla without raising her head. "Whose receipt is this?"

"I think it belongs to Millie."

"Why?" Max asked, her expression skeptical.

Karla explained how, just a few hours earlier, she had picked up a paperback for Millie at Pharmasaurus Rx.

"Pharmasaurus Rx sells books?" Max asked.

"I know." Karla nodded. "I had the same reaction. They have a small but current book section near the magazines." She produced the shopping list from her purse and showed Max where Millie had added the book title near the end of the list. "Millie's an avid reader," Karla continued. "She recommended a book to Lynn, and whenever I see her, she's either holding a book, or there's a book somewhere nearby."

"I hear what you're saying," Max agreed, "but anyone could have purchased this book. Even if this is the book Millie is currently reading, it doesn't mean she purchased it." She held up the factory-sealed bottle of extra-strength Revitaleyes. "Raj uses eye drops. Millie could have asked him to purchase the book." She slid the receipt back inside the sandwich bag, sealed it, and slipped it into her pocket. "Or they could've sent a servant to the store to make these purchases. Billionaires probably don't run their own errands."

"Millie, Raj, and Colin are in the sunroom," Karla said. "Let's ask them who this receipt belongs to."

The French doors rattled and clamoured when Karla burst into the sunroom.

Startled, Raj almost spilled tea all over his lap.

"Where is everyone?" Karla asked.

Raj placed a napkin on the coffee table, then set his teacup on top of it to soak up the tea ring from the small splash of tea that escaped from the cup when Karla barged in.

"It's just me, I'm afraid."

"Here are your drops, Raj." Max placed the Revitaleyes on the coffee table.

"Thank you," he said, already unsealing the package.

Max pointed to the paperback resting on the arm of the overstuffed blue sofa. "Is that Millie's book?"

"Yes," Raj replied. "She tends to leave a trail of books wherever she goes." He took off his sunglasses and tipped the bottle into one eye, then the other.

"Did you purchase that book for her, Raj?" Karla asked.

"No," Raj said, blinking fast. "Millie does her own shopping. I never visit stores. I just tell the housekeeper what I need and, like magic, it appears."

Millie does her own shopping!

"Have you ever asked Millie to purchase Revitaleyes for you when she goes shopping?" Max inquired.

"No," Raj repeated. "Like I said, I tell the housekeeper and stuff just appears."

"Where is Millie?" Karla asked.

"She wanted some fresh air," Raj explained. "She said she was going for a walk. Colin offered to accompany her, since our usual security people are sick. She told him she wanted to be alone. He told her it wasn't a good idea, especially with Samir's killer still wandering around. Millie got irate, told Colin he was suffocating her, and stormed out."

"Where did she go?"

"I have no idea."

"Where's Colin?" Max asked.

"He followed her," Raj replied with a shrug.

"Is Lady Olivia still lying down upstairs?" Karla asked.

"Who knows?" Raj waved his hand like he was swatting a fly. "She probably lied about going upstairs to lie down so she could sneak outside for a smoke."

"A smoke?" Karla and Max asked in stereo.

"Lady Olivia smokes?"

"Not officially," Raj replied. "It's one of the many things everyone knows but no one talks about. Like Colin's permanent crush on Millie." He picked up the teacup, took a small sip, then returned it to the napkin, setting it exactly on top of the tea ring.

"Don't leave the house," Max instructed in a stern voice.

"I won't." Raj held up his hands in a surrender gesture.

Karla and Max exited the room with far less dramatic flair than she entered, closing the French doors behind them as gently as she could.

"Did you see the title of the book?" Karla whispered as they strode down the hall. "It's the same book that's on the receipt."

"It's circumstantial," Max reminded her. "It doesn't mean the receipt belongs to Millie." She pulled the sandwich bag out of her pocket. "But I have an idea." Max took a photo of the portion of the receipt with the loyalty reward information. "I'll send this to Cybercop and ask him to find out whose name is on the loyalty points."

"Brilliant."

"When did Millie and Colin leave?" Max wondered aloud.

"If I was in the house when they left, I would have heard them. I've only been in the kitchen, and it's near the front door," Karla said. "When those French doors rattle, you can hear it through the entire house." She checked the time on her phone. "They must have left about ten minutes ago when I was taking out the trash."

Karla and Max tried to phone and text Millie and Colin. Neither of them answered. Then they remembered they had both surrendered their cell phones to Cybercop to help with the investigation.

"Maybe Lynn knows where they went," Karla said, heading toward the stairs.

"Lynn is still here?" Max asked, chasing her sister upstairs.

"Yes," Karla replied. "She went upstairs after dinner to put away a few things and have a rest."

Lady Olivia's bedroom door was closed. Karla knocked. No answer.

She opened the door. The room was unoccupied, except for Lynn snoozing in the easy chair and exhaling soft, muffled snores.

"Where is she?" Karla asked, scanning the room and running into the attached washroom. "Where is Lady Olivia?"

"What? Who?" Lynn stretched and rubbed her eyes. "What's wrong, love?"

"Lady Olivia is supposed to be here. She came upstairs to lie down," Karla explained, checking the closet. "Where is she?"

"I must've fallen asleep," Lynn said, sitting up straight and rubbing the back of her neck. "This chair isn't much to look at, but it sure is comfy."

Karla searched frantically for a clue to Lady Olivia's whereabouts. She dropped to her knees and lifted the ruffled bed skirt to look under the bed. Four luminescent eyes stared back at her. One of the cats hissed a warning. She dropped the ruffled bed skirt and returned to her feet.

"She wouldn't go far without her cats, love," Lynn pointed out. "I haven't seen her. I was reading my book"—she held up her phone as proof—"and I guess I dozed off."

"Maybe Lady Olivia came in to lie down, saw Lynn, and went somewhere else," Max theorized.

"The cats followed her upstairs," Karla recalled, nodding. "She must have let them in here, then closed the door."

"We should check the other rooms," Max said. "Lynn, do us a favour. Keep an eye on Raj and call me if he tries to leave the house. Also, call me if either Millie or Colin show up."

"Millie and Colin are missing too?" Lynn asked. "Rich people sure like to wander, don't they?" She shook her head and clucked her tongue.

They checked Millie's room, Colin's room, Raj's

room, and the two unoccupied rooms. No sign of Lady Olivia.

"Maybe she's with Millie and Colin," Karla suggested.

"Possibly," Max agreed. "If she had a cell phone, we could call her."

"They've only been gone for ten to fifteen minutes. How far could they have gone?" Karla asked. "Especially if Lady Olivia is with them."

Max unlocked her phone and started typing. "I'll text Dad. He'll dispatch officers to search for them."

"Good idea," Karla said. "I'll check the backyard and the front of the house."

Karla raced downstairs, through the kitchen, and outside. She walked around the outside of the house calling for Millie, Colin, and Lady Olivia. No reply.

She walked to the bottom of the driveway and searched the surrounding area.

"Which way did you go?" she asked herself, unsure which direction to start searching.

Max caught up with her. "Dad has everyone searching," she said. "I've also called Rosalie and asked her to put the word out."

"What if they were kidnapped?" Karla panicked. "What if something terrible has happened to them? What if Samir's killer has them?"

"I'm sure they're fine," Max reassured her. "Like you said, how far could they have gone on foot in fifteen minutes?"

Karla's phone chimed inside her pocket. "Maybe that's them!" She pulled it out and read the text.

HARRY

> I parked it in the driveway. Behind the other SUV. Why?

Karla held out her phone so Max could see the screen. "I don't think they're on foot."

They looked at the empty spot in the driveway where the second SUV should have been.

CHAPTER 23

THEY ALWAYS GO TOWARD THE WATER

KARLA HURRIED BACK to the house and ran into the kitchen. She checked the hooks on the back of the pantry door. There was only one set of keys for the SUVs. There should have been two. She rushed back to the driveway to tell Max.

"The keys are gone," she confirmed to Max who had her face buried in her phone.

"These armoured SUVs have LoJack technology," she said. "The vehicle can be remotely located and disabled."

"How do we do that?"

"I'm texting Samir and Millie's head of security, but he's not texting back." Max let out a low, frustrated grumble.

"Maybe Cybercop can figure it out," Karla suggested.

"I can't find him either," Max complained. "He still hasn't acknowledged my text or call about the loyalty account on the drugstore receipt." She dropped her hand at her side in frustration. "Where is everyone?" she asked through clenched teeth.

"They must be out searching for Millie, Colin, and Lady Olivia," Karla reasoned.

"Get in." Max unlocked her patrol car and ran to the driver's door.

"Where do we even start searching?" Karla asked, buckling her seatbelt.

"The water," Max replied. "They always go toward the water, remember?"

They drove in silence with no sirens or flashing lights. Max drove and Karla searched the streets and sidewalks but found no sign of the missing people or the SUV.

Max's phone chimed.

"Who is it?" Max asked.

"It's a text from Samir's head of security," Karla said. "It's a group text to you and Dad."

"Read it."

"I have located and disabled the SUV. It's in a parking lot at the bottom of Ocean Avenue."

"That's the waterfront," Max pointed out. "I told you they always go toward the water."

Max turned on the patrol car's lights and sirens and sped toward Ocean Avenue.

They squealed into the parking lot at the same time as Dean. They surrounded the SUV with their patrol cars, parking in such a way that the armoured vehicle wouldn't be able to leave, even if the security guy hadn't disabled it.

Red and blue flashing lights illuminated the dark

parking lot as Max exited the car and approached the black SUV.

"These stupid tinted windows are too dark," she complained, trying to look inside. "The doors are locked," she said, circling the vehicle and tugging on the handles.

The vehicle was abandoned, and there was no sign of the missing heirs.

"We'll have to search the trails," Dean announced. "Other officers are on the way to help, but we'll have to start without them."

Bellbrook's waterfront park had a trail system. Kind of like a two-lane highway, except these trails were built for people instead of cars and trucks. There were two parallel trails that meandered the shoreline. The trail closest to the water was for walkers, and the next trail was for bikes and rollerblades and such. The trails were separated by a grassy expanse that, in the warm months, featured ice cream stands, paddleboat rentals, picnic tables, food trucks, a playground, and other waterfront attractions.

"La-la and I will take the walking trail," Max said.

"What is going on?" demanded a familiar British accent. "Why won't this key unlock the car?"

"Colin!" Karla was torn between wanting to hug the man and wanting to clip him round the ear. "Are you OK? Where have you been?"

"We're fine," Colin replied as though it were a silly question. "We've been here, of course." He gestured behind him. "Millie wanted to see the ocean."

"We would have arranged for an escort to accompany you," Dean chided. "It's dark. Your cell phones are still with our cyber investigator. You don't know your way around, and in case you've forgotten, there's a killer on the loose."

"It was a last-minute excursion," Millie piped up from behind Colin. "Unless the killer followed us, we were perfectly safe." She shrugged. "I kept an eye on the mirrors and made sure we weren't followed. It was a real adventure."

"Raj said you went for a walk," Max said.

"I wanted to go for a walk," Millie explained. "Colin insisted on accompanying me—"

"For safety's sake," Colin interrupted.

"We decided to drive to the waterfront and walk by the water," Millie concluded. She looked at Karla. "We were going to tell you when we went into the kitchen to collect the car keys, but you weren't there."

They couldn't leave a note?

"I was taking out the trash," Karla replied. "Is Lady Olivia with you?"

"No," Millie replied. "She went upstairs to lie down, remember?"

"And you haven't seen her since?" Dean asked.

Colin and Millie shook their heads.

"Is something wrong?" Millie asked. "Is Mumsy OK?"

Ignoring Millie's question, Dean proceeded to further lecture Colin on all the reasons, from a safety perspective, his and Millie's impromptu field trip was a bad idea.

Max turned on her flashlight and approached Millie. She produced the sandwich bag from her uniform pocket.

"Millie, is this receipt familiar?" She pulled out and unfolded the receipt. When Millie reached for it, Max pulled it back just out of reach. "Sorry, you can't touch it."

Clever, Karla thought. *If Max had let her touch the receipt, then forensics discovered her fingerprints on it, Millie could argue that her fingerprints were there because Max had handed her the receipt.*

"I've never seen it before," Millie said. "But that's the brand of eye drops that Raj uses. You should ask him."

"Who gave you the book you're currently reading?" Max asked.

"I ordered it online," Millie said.

"But it's on this receipt," Max argued.

"I can show you the online order confirmation if you'd like," Millie said. "I ordered it about a month ago."

Max encouraged Millie to recall where she was at the time and date the receipt was issued. While Millie contemplated her whereabouts two Tuesdays ago at 1:17pm, Karla's phone chimed, and she moved aside to read the text.

Lynn: Lady Olivia is fine. She's here. She was in the elevator when you were looking for her. She joked that the elevator is old and slow, like her.

Lady Olivia made a joke?

Karla acknowledged the text with a **thanks** and a thumbs-up emoji.

"Lady Olivia is at The Nestled Inn," Karla said, interrupting Max and Millie's conversation. "She's fine."

"Why can't I unlock this bloody car?!" Colin demanded, pressing the button on the remote.

"We had the vehicle remotely disabled," Dean explained. "For your safety. We weren't sure if you left of your own accord, or if you'd been taken against your will."

"Well un-disable it," Colin demanded.

Max's and Dean's phones chimed simultaneously. Max glanced at the screen and gasped. Everyone looked at her expectantly.

"It's cybercop," she said. "He found out whose loyalty points are on the receipt."

CHAPTER 24
A SPARK OF GENIUS

THEY TRAVELLED IN TWO VEHICLES. Karla and Max rode in Max's patrol car, and Dean, Colin, and Millie rode in Dean's car.

Max slammed the car into park and had jumped out before Karla finished lurching forward from the sudden stop. "Stay here, don't come inside," she said before taking off toward the house.

"Max! I'll secure the suspect, you secure the other two occupants and escort them to safety," Dean ordered, running to the front door.

"Got it!" Max yelled, rounding the corner toward the kitchen door at the side of the house.

Karla got out of the car.

"Now what?" Millie asked.

"Now, we wait," Karla said.

After thirty seconds that felt like thirty minutes, Max appeared at the front door. She ushered both occupants outside, down the steps, and toward the patrol cars at the bottom of the driveway.

"No," Millie wailed as she saw them appear. "I can't believe it." She cried and brought her hand to her mouth "Where is —" Colin wrapped his arms around Millie and pressed her face into his sweater, muffling the end of her question.

"Where's Dad?" Karla asked.

"He can't locate the suspect," Max said. "I'm going back to help him search. Stay here. Backup is on the way."

"Are you OK?" Karla asked, giving Lynn a quick head-to-toe glance.

"I'm fine," she reassured her daughter. "The timing could have been better, though. I was just getting to the smuttiest part of the book."

They watched the house as Dean and Max searched inside. The house was dark except for the occasional strobe of light from Max or Dean's flashlight.

"How do they expect to find anything in the dark?" Colin asked.

"They should turn on the lights," Raj concurred.

A single spark of light appeared on the wrap-around porch.

"If they turn on the lights as they go, it'll give the killer the upper hand." The flame from the lighter briefly illuminated Lady Olivia's face. "They don't want to make themselves easy targets for a psychotic killer."

The light disappeared, replaced by the dim orange glow of a burning cigarette.

"Why?" Millie pushed Colin away and lunged toward the porch. Lynn stopped her by grabbing her arm. Karla took her other arm to assist in restraining the fuming widow. "Why did you kill my husband?"

"Why would you accuse me of killing your husband?"

"We know it was you, Lady Olivia," Karla said. "We have proof."

"What sort of proof?" the widow asked, taking a drag of her cigarette.

"We found your receipt for the murder weapon," Dean replied, appearing from the kitchen door beside the house. "You shouldn't have used your loyalty points at the drugstore."

"Who says *I* used them?" Lady Olivia challenged. "Anyone could have taken my loyalty card from my purse, used it to implicate me in Samir's murder, and put the loyalty card back before I realized it was missing."

"But that's not what happened," Max said, appearing beside Dean. "Cybercop just texted me a video clip from the drug store's video surveillance. We have video footage of you purchasing the eye drops and the paperback on the same date as the receipt, at the same time and location of the receipt."

"You killed Samir with a paperback and some eye drops?" Raj asked. "How?"

Max explained that tetrahydrozoline was the main ingredient in products like Revitaleyes, and Rob had figured out Samir's death was caused by ingesting tetrahydrozoline.

"What did Samir do to you?" Colin demanded.

"Nothing," Lady Olivia admitted. "I was actually quite sad that he had to die."

"Then why did you kill him?" Millie demanded.

"So you would know how it felt to lose the only man you ever loved!" Lady Olivia snapped. "So you would feel what I felt and suffer how I have suffered!"

"You wanted Millie to feel how you felt when your husband died?" Colin asked, confused but trying to follow along.

"You don't understand! You're an emotional imbecile!"

Karla understood. The pieces came together in her brain like a jigsaw puzzle. She recalled Lady Olivia's response when Max had asked if it had been hard to see Millie happy again, with someone other than Lady Olivia's son. She'd said, "Should I have expected her to spend the rest of her life lonely and sad? Longing for a man she'll never see again, like me?" Karla assumed Lady Olivia was referring to the loneliness, sadness, and longing she'd felt after the death of her husband, but she meant her son.

"You know how difficult your son's death was for me," Millie pleaded. "Why would you make me suffer that unbearable loss again?"

"Because you didn't suffer enough!" The elderly lady sneered as she lowered herself into the wicker rocking chair on the porch. "If it weren't for you, my son would still be alive," she continued. "With any luck, he would have realized the massive error in judgement he made when he married you, and he would have been happily married to someone else by now. Someone worthy of him."

Everyone on the driveway gasped.

"If my son hadn't tried to follow you that night, he

wouldn't have skidded off the road and over an embankment. He would still be alive! His death was your fault."

Millie trembled under Karla's touch. Her knees wobbled. Was she shaking from weakness or anger?

"How did you do it?" Karla asked. "How did you sneak the eye drops into Samir's food and drink?"

"It was easy." Lady Olivia took another deep inhale from her cigarette and dropped the butt on the porch, grinding it with her practical, black, skid-resistant, slip-on shoes. "I slipped them into his water bottle on the plane. Everyone else was asleep. None of you noticed. I'd hoped he would die before we landed."

"But that didn't kill him," Karla pointed out. "It obviously caused him some discomfort, but he didn't die until after dinner. Rob said he was poisoned just a few hours before he died."

"When I realized that I hadn't given him enough to kill him, I gave him more. At first, I was going to leave it and try again in a few days, maybe on the plane to Germany. But when the staff fell ill with food poisoning, I was encouraged to try again. I'd hoped that the coroner would simply attribute Samir's death to the same illness that caused the servants to get sick. I slipped the drops into his drinking glass before dinner, during cocktail hour. Everyone else was distracted by the arrival of Karla and that Griff fellow. It only took a few seconds." She hooked a crooked finger in the cuff of her blouse. "I hid the bottle of eye drops up my sleeve." She gave them a self-satisfied grin.

"Where are the eye drops now?" Karla asked.

Lady Olivia tapped her gnarled index finger alongside her nose. "That's for me to know."

"I hope you enjoied that cigarette, you old battleaxe!" Colin shouted. "It'll be the last one you smoke outside of prison."

Lady Olivia responded with a smug sneer.

"If you wanted Samir to die, why were you so distraught when Millie told us he had cancer?" Raj demanded. "You cried. I saw you."

"First of all, I had nothing against Samir," Lady Olivia said, letting out a puff of smoke. "In fact, I was quite fond of him and impressed by his vivacity and spirit. I didn't want to kill him, but it was the only way to punish Millie. To avenge my son's death. When I found out Samir had been diagnosed with cancer, I realized that I had missed an opportunity. Had he disclosed his diagnosis earlier, I would have postponed my murderous plan and let nature take care of it. Instead, I'd already done the deed. The authorities had figured out it was murder, and it was a matter of time before I was discovered."

"The tears weren't for Samir. They were for you," Karla summarized.

"If you say so." Lady Olivia smiled.

"Did the police miss the receipt in the trash corral, or did you plant it there to frame either Millie or Raj for the murder?"

"Preferably Millie," Lady Olivia admitted. "I purchased the book because I knew it was the same title that Millie had recently purchased for herself. I disposed of it in a trash bin outside the drugstore. Earlier today, after the police had finished searching the house, and Karla had left to run errands, I gave Lynn a few tasks to keep her out of the way while I snuck outside and planted the receipt in the trash corral." She smirked. "I stuck it to the underside of the lid with a dab of blueberry coulis from the toutons Rosalie had made for breakfast." She pointed her arthritic finger at Karla. "I knew you would find it. You notice things. You're like me."

I'm NOTHING like you. Karla bit her tongue, fearing if she spoke the words out loud, the elderly killer would clam up and stop answering questions.

The dowager chuckled and unscrewed the handle of her walking stick. Then she tipped it until a new cigarette slid out. She brought the cigarette to her mouth and lit it.

"The walking stick!" Karla shouted. "The eye drops are in the walking stick!"

Lady Olivia's face paled. Shock washed over her face, replacing the smug expression that had been there a moment earlier.

"When the police searched the house, you took the cats upstairs to keep them out of the way. You wouldn't let me go upstairs with you. Next time I saw you, your walking stick sounded different. You told me it was because you had replaced the rubber foot, but that was a lie, wasn't it?"

Max was on the porch now and snatched the walking stick from Lady Olivia's grip. She unscrewed the handle and dumped the contents of the cane onto the wooden porch. A handful of cigarettes, a spare lighter, a few cat treats, and two bottles of Revitaleyes.

Everyone gasped.

"Samir was right about you, Karla Bell. You are clever." Lady Olivia winked. "We have more in common than you think."

"No, you don't," Lynn protested. "Don't you dare insinuate that my daughter has anything in common with a psychopathic, unhinged killer!"

Max helped Lady Olivia to her feet and cuffed her hands in front of her. Then, she helped the frail woman down the porch steps, and they slowly made their way to Max's patrol car.

The dark driveway and porch were lit up with flashing blue and red lights. Police cars lined the street and officers stood on the lawn, awaiting instructions from Dean.

As Lady Olivia passed Millie, she turned and said, "I don't have much, dear, but I do have almost one million drug store loyalty points. I'd like you to have them."

Karla thought Millie was either about to spit at or launch herself at Lady Olivia. She and Lynn placed supportive hands on the young widow.

"She's not worth it," Lynn whispered close to Millie's ear.

CHAPTER 25

A CHOSEN ASSISTANT

Two Days later

"Wait up!" Lynn called as she closed her front door. "I want to come with you and see the progress."

Karla and Gucci stopped and waited for Lynn to catch up.

"You can help choose the crown moulding," Karla said as they walked toward the manor house. "I always struggle when there are too many options."

"I talked to Griff about that," Lynn said. "I told him about the relationship between analysis paralysis and ADHD. He said he'd narrow down the options to three."

"Please stop reading ADHD books," Karla said, rolling her eyes. "I've been managing my symptoms forever."

"I know, love, but if we can make it easier, we should."

"That sounds like something a good assistant

would say," Karla commented as she stopped and waited for Gucci to finish sniffing the base of a tree.

"Are you saying I would make a good assistant?" Lynn asked. "Are you offering me a job?" She could hardly contain the excitement in her voice, and her demeanour became more buoyant.

"Let's see how it goes," Karla said. "How about a three-month trial, so we can make sure the arrangement works for both of us?"

"I already know we'll both love it! Three months from now, you'll wonder how you ever functioned without me."

When they arrived at the manor house, Gucci greeted everyone as though they were his long-lost best friends despite seeing them on almost a daily basis. Karla caught Harry in the act; he slid a small piece of beef jerky from his pocket and slipped it to Gucci on the down-low. She pretended not to notice and let them revel in the secrecy.

Griff and Harry gave Karla and Lynn a tour, showing them the various stages of progress for each part of the renovation.

Just as Lynn had said, Griff provided three crown moulding options.

"If you don't like any of these, I have three more in my truck," he said.

"Actually, I think I like this one." Karla pointed to the second option.

"Me too, love," Lynn concurred. "It's the sleekest, most elegant choice."

Griff reached to collect the samples and brushed Karla's arm. "Excuse me," he said with a wink.

Her heart sped up, and warmth spread across her face and chest. "No problem." She cleared her throat.

"I spoke with Colin before he, Millie, and Raj boarded their plane," Griff commented. "I gave them my condolences."

"I'm sure they appreciated the gesture," Karla said.

"Colin said they were grateful for everything you did for them," Griff said. "He said you went above and beyond to make them comfortable and to help find Samir's killer. He said they would never forget the kindness and discretion of everyone in Bellbrook."

"I can't take all the credit," Karla gushed. "I couldn't have done it without Max, Lynn, Rob, Harry, you, Rosalie, Kwame… even The Posers. It was a community effort."

"But you were the leader." He grinned. "And you're amazing."

A hundred butterflies fluttered in Karla's belly when he grinned at her.

"I've been reading online articles about Samir's death," Harry interjected, holding out his phone. "Millie mentioned you when she released her official statement." He handed Karla his phone with the news article on the screen.

"We are in shock at the sudden, tragic death of my darling husband, Samir Khan," Karla read aloud. "His innovations and generosity have made the world a better place and improved the lives of so many. His legacy and vision will live on through the Khan Family Charitable Foundation. Special thank you to our dear friend, Karla Bell, and her friends and family for their support and kindness during this horrendous upheaval. We ask that you respect our privacy at this time while we mourn our painful loss."

Karla dabbed her eyes and cleared her throat. "I don't know what to say."

"I told you no one would blame you or your company for what happened to Samir," Harry said, offering her a dingy rag. She politely refused and wiped her eyes with the knuckle of her index finger.

"I guess this is why Just Task Me's head office has been fielding calls from potential new clients since Samir's death became public," Karla said.

"I told you so," Harry said with a smirk.

"Raj has already touched base about arranging a huge fundraiser for the new charitable foundation," Karla added. "He's thinking it could be an annual event to be held on Samir's birthday."

"Raj?" Lynn asked. "I thought Raj didn't work for TechSavvy."

"He doesn't," Karla confirmed. "But when Millie decided to set up a charitable foundation in Samir's memory, she asked Raj to help. The charitable foundation is separate from TechSavvy. She offered Raj the role of Executive Director. Raj will donate his salary back to the foundation, so he won't be paid. He wants to do it on a volunteer basis. He gets to stay busy doing something he loves, and they still honour Samir's wish that Raj never has to work again."

"I think Samir would have approved," Lynn said.

"Me too," agreed Griff.

"But who will run TechSavvy now that Samir is gone?" asked Harry.

"The board plans to install Colin as the new CEO

and chairman of the board," Karla replied. "TechSavvy will continue as usual but without their founder and visionary. The stock price plummeted when Samir's death was made public yesterday, but Colin says he's confident it will rebound."

"Are we keeping you awake, Lynn?" Harry asked cheekily when Lynn covered a yawn with the back of her hand.

"You're not keeping me awake," Lynn retorted, "but Rosemary and Thyme are doing their best to keep me awake from dusk till dawn."

"How are they settling in?" Karla asked.

After Lady Olivia was arrested, she was concerned about what would happen to Rosemary and Thyme now that she would be locked away for the rest of her life. Millie used the cats as leverage. She agreed to find the cats a new home, together, in exchange for Lady Olivia's confession and guilty plea—avoiding a painful, public trial. If Lady Olivia didn't confess and plead guilty, Millie swore she would separate the bonded cats and place them in shelters on opposite sides of the world. Millie was lying, of course. She had no intention of punishing the cats for their owner's transgressions. She'd already offered the cats to Lynn, who snapped up the opportunity to adopt them. Apparently, Lynn and the cats had developed a rapport while Lynn took care of them.

"They're still living in a different time zone," Lynn explained. "But I'm slowly adjusting their routine. Soon, they'll be on the same schedule as the rest of us." She yawned again. "Max dropped off one of their scratch posts from the Nestled Inn, so they'd have something familiar while they get used to their new living situation. She said Millie donated the other scratch post to the local animal shelter and donated the not-so-easy chairs to the local nursing home."

"How was Max?" Karla asked. "She and Dad have been so busy with paperwork that I haven't seen them since Lady Olivia's arrest."

"She told me to tell you that you were right about the rubber foot," Lynn said. "She combed through the evidence that the police confiscated from The Nestled Inn, and there was no rubber tip in any of the trash they'd confiscated. Lady Olivia lied when she told you that her cane sounded different because she'd changed the rubber foot. The cane sounded different because Lady Olivia had hidden the two bottles of Revitaleyes inside." Lynn snapped her fingers. "She also said to tell you that they found Lady Olivia's drug store loyalty card in her wallet, and it matched the loyalty reward number on the receipt."

Karla's phone dinged. It was a text from Rob.

"Everything OK?" Griff asked.

"Rob and I were supposed to have lunch together today, but she had to cancel," Karla said. "She was contacted by authorities in England. They've asked her to review Lady Olivia's late husband's autopsy report. Initially, his death was attributed to a heart attack but, based on some comments Lady Olivia made after her arrest, they believe she might have killed him."

"Maybe Lady Olivia is a serial killer." Lynn shuddered.

"Hey, Lynn, are you available to help me choose a

paint colour?" Harry asked. "Now that the Khans have left Bellbrook, and everything is back to normal, I thought I might finally paint my kitchen this weekend."

"I'll have to check with my new boss and make sure she doesn't need me," Lynn replied.

"Your new boss?" Harry asked, furrowing his bushy silver eyebrows.

Lynn told Harry and Griff about her new job as Karla's PA.

"It's a temporary arrangement," Karla reminded Lynn. "We'll see how it goes for three months and take it from there. You might not like being a PA. Sometimes, you'll be so busy that you barely have time to breathe, and other times, you'll have so much free time that you'll think you might die from boredom."

"Don't say that!" Lynn chided. "No one else is going to die. Not from boredom or anything else."

Touch wood.

Click here to read an exclusive bonus scene from Rage Before Beauty.

LOST AND DROWNED
A Bellbrook Murder Mystery
Book 3
REAGAN DAVIS

COPYRIGHT

FOREWORD

Dear Reader,

Despite several layers of editing and proofreading, occasionally a typo or grammar mistake is so stubborn that it manages to thwart my editing efforts and camouflage itself amongst the words in the book.

If you encounter one of these obstinate typos or errors in this book, please let me know by contacting me at Hello@ReaganDavis.com.

Hopefully, together we can exterminate the annoying pests.

Thank you!

Reagan Davis

CHAPTER 1
THE AQUAHOLIC

THE DAY of the murder

Karla inhaled a lungful of salty sea air and fixed her eyes on the hazy grey-blue horizon line in the distance. The blurry boundary between ocean and sky that she could see but never touch, chase but never catch. Elusive. Limitless and untouchable. She loved that horizon line. It was her favourite part of the ocean. It drew her eye more than the waves, and even more than the whales that sometimes surfaced in the distance.

"Thanks for the lift," she said to her sister, Max. "The dealership said my car should be ready this afternoon."

"I don't mind driving you around," Max said, adjusting one of the many zips and pockets on her police vest. "Besides, it's not every day I get to see a yacht up close."

The Aquaholic wasn't exactly close. It was too big to dock near shore, so it sat anchored out in the ocean, a man-made floating refuge. There was nothing discreet or understated about it. The ship was massive, white, and covered with mirrored windows that gleamed in the sun. The points of light reflecting off the water made the vessel sparkle like a diamond in a jewellery store.

"It's a mega yacht," Karla corrected. "My client was quite specific that it's a mega yacht."

"What's the difference?" Max slid her aviator sunglasses from the top of her head to her eyes, staring at the enormous ship. "A yacht's a yacht, right?"

"Size," Karla explained. "Apparently a mega yacht is bigger than a regular yacht."

"It's always about size," Max said with a sigh and a headshake.

The sisters laughed.

"Here's my ride." Karla nodded toward the yacht tender that was cruising toward them. "I'll be onboard for about an hour," she said, checking the time on her phone.

"Text me when you're ready, and I'll pick you up."

Karla strode down the long pier to meet the tender. She turned and waved to Max.

Max waved back but didn't turn to leave.

Karla knew Max wouldn't leave until she had safely boarded the small watercraft, and it had sped away from the pier. Watching, protecting, helping, they were part of Max's nature. She couldn't stop herself.

"G'day!" The well-tanned, uniformed man had a deep voice with an Aussie lilt. "Welcome aboard." He extended his hand to help Karla step aboard the speedboat.

"Thank you." She slung her bag over her shoulder and gave him one hand while she used the other to lift the hem of her long sundress. A loose, flowy, maxi wrap-dress with an all-over floral pattern. "I'm Karla Bell." She smiled and stepped onto the boat, glad she'd opted for flats instead of the stiletto sandals she usually wore with this dress. "It's nice to meet you."

"Captain Henry Peterson." The man returned the smile.

Captain Peterson was a conventionally handsome man, tall and lean with a well-tailored white captain's uniform. His chiseled face was clean shaven, and a hint of salt and pepper hair peeked out from beneath his captain's hat. His deeply tanned skin made his teeth appear unnaturally white and exaggerated the smile lines around his mouth and eyes. Karla guesstimated he was about fifty years old and, judging by the thick band of gold on his left ring finger, married.

"Does the ship's captain usually ferry guests back and forth from the yacht?" Karla asked.

"No," Captain Peterson replied. "But everyone else was busy, and Mr. Casey said to treat you like a VIP." He gave her a quick grin. "No luggage?"

"I'm not staying," Karla shouted over the boat's motor and surrounding sea sounds.

"Well, Mr. Casey had a deluxe cabin prepared for you, in case you change your mind," bellowed Captain Peterson as he navigated away from the pier and aimed the boat toward The Aquaholic.

"That's very kind of him," Karla shouted over the

ocean waves crashing against the bow of the speed-boat. "But I only live about ten minutes from here." She steadied herself against the back of her tan leather seat with one hand and held her wide-brimmed sun hat in place with the other. The front of the brim curled and flapped against the headwind like it was trying to take flight. "And I have a dog. His name is Gucci. I hate to leave him." She wasn't sure if the captain didn't hear her or didn't care.

Karla stepped off the tender and boarded the yacht. She had barely finished thanking Captain Peterson when a tall, professional woman with a leather planner, cell phone, and the confident urgency of a Type-A personality whisked her away.

"Lovely to see you again, Karla." said the woman without breaking her brisk stride. "Welcome aboard. Am I correct that this is your first time visiting us on The Aquaholic?"

"Nice to see you again, as well, Caitlin." Karla smiled and did an awkward trot-jog to catch up to the rushing woman. Caitlin's long, willowy legs took longer strides than Karla's ever could. "Yes, this is my first time aboard. It's even more magnificent in person."

Caitlin Lopez was, in Karla's opinion, one of the most organized and efficient people who had ever lived. Coming from Karla, who prided herself on organization and efficiency, that was quite a compli-ment. Caitlin was the embodiment of productivity from her no-nonsense chin-length tonal-brown bob to her ever-present leather-bound planner, and her fitted lilac power suit that featured crisp walking shorts in lieu of a skirt or pants. Karla had been tempted, more than once, to let Caitlin discreetly know that, should she ever find herself between jobs, Karla would love to hire her as a concierge at Just Task Me! But Caitlin had been Damien Casey's executive assistant for twenty years. She seemed content and well-compensated, so it was unlikely that she'd be interested in a concierge position. Why change jobs when she got to live on a luxury yacht and travel the world?

They hurried along narrow corridors and turned several corners before climbing a few steps and emerging onto a large white deck that was decorated like an outdoor living room.

"Have a seat." Caitlin gestured with her phone hand to the cushioned furniture arrangement near the outdoor bar. "Can I offer you a drink? We have a fully stocked bar, and we make our lemonade and iced tea fresh throughout the day."

"I would love an iced tea. Thank you," Karla said graciously.

Caitlin gave a terse nod to the crew member behind the bar.

He sprang into action, scooping ice into a large tumbler he had produced from somewhere beneath the bar.

"Mr. Casey will be with you shortly," Caitlin advised. "In the meantime, if you need anything, the deckhand will help you."

"Thanks, Caitlin." Karla smiled and removed her sunhat. She smoothed her hands along her blonde hair, ensuring no flyaways had escaped from the low, sleek chignon during the short, blustery speedboat ride.

Caitlin left the deck and disappeared down the steps that led to the underbelly of the enormous yacht.

The deckhand placed Karla's iced tea on the table next to her on top of a custom cocktail napkin branded with the yacht's name, The Aquaholic, in a cartoonish blue font that resembled ocean waves.

She thanked him, and as she reached over to pick up the insulated tumbler, Damien Casey strode onto the deck flanked by his daughter, her fiancé, and an air of superiority.

Damian Casey was an average-sized man with an above-average presence. He took up most of the air in every room he entered, even when that room was a wide-open deck in the middle of the Atlantic Ocean. He looked like an advertisement for nautical casual wear, dressed in a pair of white walking shorts with a brown leather belt and coordinating brown leather deck shoes. His signature Cuban cigar was in his right hand—unlit—and he had another at the ready in the breast pocket of his loose fitting, light blue button-down shirt. His shirt sleeves were rolled up to his elbows, and the shirt was mostly unbuttoned, revealing a thick patch of chest hair that was much darker than the shaggy sand-coloured hair on his head.

"Good afternoon, Karla." His southern drawl elongated the last syllable of each word. "Welcome aboard my humble abode." He smiled and raised his dark sunglasses, nesting them in his hair. "If you need anything to make your visit more comfortable, you just let me know." He stepped forward and extended a hand.

"That's my line," Karla teased, standing up and shaking her client's hand. "I'm here to make *your* life as easy as possible."

Karla's concierge business, Just Task Me! specialized in catering to the whims and fancies of affluent clients like Damien Casey. People whose exclusive lifestyles were highly visible but inaccessible to all but an elite few. Most of Karla's clients ran Fortune 500 companies, were self-made tech millionaires, celebrities, or aristocratic types with generational wealth. However, Damien Casey was none of the above. He'd never run a company, as far as Karla knew. He'd never innovated anything techy, entertained anyone, or inherited his wealth. Damien Casey was a lobbyist. Without ever running for public office, he had politicked his way into a lucrative and successful career in foreign affairs and international politics. His ability to socialize, influence, and broker alliances had made him a very wealthy, very well-connected man. Karla chose to ignore the rumours of blackmail, manipulation, and influence peddling that seemed to follow Damien Casey around like a bad smell.

"This is my daughter, Saskia." He placed the unlit cigar between his teeth and gestured to his daughter.

"We've met online," Karla shook Saskia's hand. "It's wonderful to meet you in person, Saskia."

"Daddy, Karla and I have been exchanging emails and video calls while she helps me and Ben find the perfect wedding venue," Saskia explained to her father.

Saskia did not have the same southern drawl as Damien. In fact, she had no discernible accent at all. Her father was from the American deep south, and her mother was a 1990s German-born supermodel-turned-socialite and recovering addict, who now divided her time between New York and London. Damien and Saskia's mother never married. Saskia was the product of a short, tumultuous relationship that ended with a highly publicized custody battle and tell-all book written by her former nanny. Damien won the custody battle, of course. Damien Casey always got what he wanted. Saskia was raised by him, a team of the best nannies money could buy, and the most prestigious all-girl boarding schools on the East Coast.

Saskia was a mix of both her parents. She had inherited her mother's angular bone structure and thick dark hair, as well as her father's light amber eyes and charisma.

"This is my fiancé, Ben Underwood." Saskia stood aside, making room for Ben to step forward.

"Nice to meet you, ma'am." He extended his hand and gave Karla a thousand-watt smile.

"Please, call me Karla."

"Yes, ma'am." He chuckled. "I mean yes, Karla."

Ben was more reserved than his photogenic fiancée and her charismatic father. He was attractive for someone his age.

Having just turned forty, men Ben's age—mid-to-late twenties—had fallen off Karla's radar, but she could still appreciate his fit physique, youthful glow, short, trendy black frohawk, dark smouldering eyes, and the two days of stubble that adorned his chin. Ben had been an up-and-coming football star, but an unfortunate career-ending knee injury sidelined his career early on.

"I can't wait to visit the venue." Saskia stretched out on a chaise lounge, kicked off her black wedge heels, and caught the deckhand's eye, wordlessly indicating that she would like a drink. Her gauzy white cover-up was transparent enough to make out the silhouette of the black cut out swimsuit underneath.

Ben sat on the chaise next to her, and Damien joined Karla on the generous loveseat.

Without taking their orders, the deckhand delivered a tray of drinks and served each of them.

"So, tell me about this venue," Damien said, then ran the length of his unlit cigar under his nose, inhaling its essence.

"Well, Bellcroft is my ancestral home," Karla began.

She gave her clients a brief history of Bellcroft and its local significance. Bellcroft was the name of the estate, composed of a sizable plot of oceanside property, a large manor house—the potential wedding venue—two small cottages—Mirabel and Bellflower—and a gamekeeper's cabin in the woods.

"And no one else has ever been married there?" Saskia asked. Again. Like she did every time she discussed wedding venues with Karla.

"No one in living memory," Karla clarified. "My grandparents and great-grandparents were married on the grounds, but to the best of my knowledge, the estate hasn't hosted any other weddings. Certainly not in the past sixty years."

"It's very important to Saskia that she and Ben get married somewhere special," Damien explained as he opened a plain wooden box on the coffee table and pulled out a box of matches. "She's a bit of a trendsetter, you see. She likes to be first." Damien struck a match and held the foot of the cigar close to the flame, rotating it as he toasted it.

Karla nodded as the proud father boasted.

Saskia Casey had turned trendsetting into an empire. Thanks to the phenomenon known as social media, Saskia Casey™ was a luxury lifestyle brand. She had a PR team, glam squad, a team of stylists, a manager, and an agent. Saskia commanded a six-figure appearance fee for showing up at trendy nightclubs and star-studded after-parties. She was a social media influencer. Millions of followers around the globe—mostly young women—followed her every move and obsessed over her every post, endeavouring to copy her style, hoping to experience a teeny bit of Saskia's champagne-wishes-and-caviar-dreams lifestyle for themselves. Luxury brands competed to give her free samples and financial endorsements in exchange for a staged photo or short video of her using their products. When Saskia Casey endorsed a product, that product went viral and became The Next Big Thing.

"Will your wedding planner be joining us for the tour?" Karla asked.

Damien brought the smoldering cigar to his mouth and started puffing it, drawing the flame from the match toward the tip of the cigar.

"No." Saskia gave Ben a sideways glance. "We're

not sure we want to continue using the wedding planner," she elaborated. "We're hoping, if we choose Bellcroft as the venue, that you would consider planning our wedding. After all, you found the venue and you know the local area. The wedding planner had months to find our dream venue and couldn't do it, but you came up with the perfect location right away."

Karla's insides quivered with possibility. Saskia and Ben's high-profile wedding would be a huge opportunity for so many Bellbrook businesses. The florist, the hotel, the local inn, restaurants, everyone would benefit from the over-the-top event. Not to mention Bellcroft itself. Over the past several months, Karla had sunk her entire net worth into renovating the dilapidated manor house. Her plan was to earn back the money by renting out the oceanside estate as a destination event venue. Saskia and Ben's wedding would be The Event of The Year. If they selected Bellcroft as the venue, Saskia's followers would line up to host events there. Bellcroft would become the new It Place.

Damian puffed away on his cigar. Plumes of smoke circled him like a smoky wreath.

"If you'd like, Ms. Bell, I can have your bag delivered to your cabin," the deckhand piped in after watching Karla shift her designer tote bag to avoid any cigar ash or tobacco smell from infiltrating it.

"It's kind of you to offer, but I'm not staying aboard overnight," Karla explained. "I don't need a cabin. I live nearby, and I have a dog—"

"But you already came aboard and checked in." The deckhand screwed up his face in confusion. "I delivered your luggage myself. You ordered a Cobb salad for lunch. I delivered it to your cabin. You thanked me from inside."

"That wasn't me." Karla shook her head. "You must be confusing me with another guest."

"We don't have any other guests," Damien interjected. "Are you sure you didn't come aboard earlier today, Karla?"

"Positive," Karla insisted.

"Then whose luggage did the deckhand deliver? Who ordered the Cobb salad for lunch?"

Karla shook her head and shrugged.

"It sounds like we have ourselves a mystery to solve," Damien blew out a trail of white smoke. "Where's Caitlin?"

CHAPTER 2

A MYSTERIOUS STOWAWAY

CAITLIN APPEARED on deck as though she had been waiting for Damien to summon her. Karla gave the deckhand a quick sideways glance. Did he press a magic button under the bar that had summoned her, or did Caitlin have weirdly impeccable timing?

"It's possible we have an interloper on board," Damien informed his executive assistant. He urged the deckhand to fill her in about the luggage and Cobb salad he delivered to the mystery occupant in Karla's cabin.

"That's right," Caitlin agreed with the deckhand's version of events. "Karla's assistant boarded The Aquaholic this morning. She said she was dropping off luggage and prepping the cabin ahead of Karla's arrival." She opened her leather planner and flipped to a specific page. "She said her name was Jennifer."

"Jennifer?" Karla questioned. "I didn't send anyone. The only people who know I'm here are my sister, Max, and my mother, Lynn." Lynn also happened to be Karla's assistant, but she didn't mention that. Lynn couldn't have boarded The Aquaholic since she was at Shearlock Combs having her roots touched up, getting lowlights, and having her eyebrows shaped; a ritual that would have taken all morning. "I don't even know anyone named Jennifer."

"Did you speak with Jennifer?" Damien asked, enthralled by the mystery.

"Briefly," Caitlin admitted. "We rode to The Aquaholic together. She was waiting at the dock when the tender picked me up this morning. I had been ashore picking up a few things and exploring the town. The driver wasn't expecting her, so when she told me she was Karla's assistant, I gave permission for her to board."

"You should have called me," Karla interjected. "I would have given you a guided tour."

"That would have been lovely," Caitlin said. "From what I saw, Bellbrook is a beautiful, cozy little town, but my phone was ringing off the hook, and I was too distracted to really enjoy myself." She shrugged one shoulder. "So, I gave up and came back to my office." She went on to explain how she texted the crew member who had shuttled her to the shore, requesting that he pick her up. When she arrived at the dock to meet him, Karla's imposter assistant was already there with two large hot-pink, hard-side rolling suitcases she claimed belonged to Karla.

"I don't have pink luggage. My luggage is silver. And why would I bring two large suitcases for an overnight visit?" Karla added as further proof that she was not involved with the mystery woman's actions. "What did Jennifer look like?"

"Mid-twenties," Caitlin replied. "Trendy hair that's shaved on one side and long on the other. She was wearing a white tank top and a long, loose bohemian-style blue skirt. She had tattoos across the top of her chest and both shoulders. Lots of earrings and big, pink sunglasses. Oh, and she had a purse, a large brown leather satchel." She held her hands apart to illustrate the size of Jennifer's satchel. "It looked vintage, it had a nice patina."

"She doesn't sound familiar," Karla said, shaking her head.

Everyone else shook their heads and mumbled in agreement. They didn't recognize the description either.

"When we boarded The Aquaholic, I showed Jennifer to Karla's cabin," Caitlin continued. "I told her I would have the luggage delivered shortly. The next crew member I encountered was the deckhand. He delivered the luggage."

"I left it in the hall." The deckhand nodded in agreement. "I would've taken it inside, but when I knocked, she said to leave it outside the door. Then awhile later, she called the kitchen and ordered a Cobb salad. I delivered it. She thanked me from inside the room and told me to leave the tray outside." He looked at Karla. "I assumed, since it was your cabin, that you had ordered the salad."

"Well, someone ordered the damn salad," Damien concluded, rising to his feet and giving his cigar a puff. "And I'm sure as heck gonna find out who."

"Oooh, a mysterious stowaway," Saskia said, nudging her fiancé Ben in the ribs. "My followers will love this!" She futzed with the settings on her phone, leaned into him, held her phone at arm's length, tilted her head, puckered her lips, and took a selfie.

Following Damien's lead, they all stood up. Everyone except the deckhand followed Damien in a single-file line as he left the deck.

"Karla, wait!" Saskia grabbed Karla's hand. "A quick selfie for my followers?" she asked.

"Sure," Karla replied.

"Make a face like we're solving a mystery." Saskia formed a small *o* with her mouth, pressed her manicured index finger against her chin, and looked upwards and to the right as though she were performing mental gymnastics.

Playing along, Karla laid her hands on her cheeks and made her best *Home Alone* face.

Saskia snapped the pic, then they hurried to catch up with Damien, Ben, and Caitlin.

THEY GATHERED in huddled silence around the cabin door.

Damien knocked.

No answer.

He knocked again, louder this time.

The group collectively held their breath and cocked their ears toward the door, listening for sounds of life on the other side. Nothing.

"Maybe Jennifer already left," Saskia whispered.

"Every time the tender leaves or returns to The Aquaholic, the trip is logged and so are the passengers. The only tender that has left the yacht since Jennifer and I boarded is the boat that picked up Karla from shore," Caitlin said.

All eyes turned to Karla.

"No one got off the boat when it arrived to pick me up, and I was the only person aboard for the ride back," she informed them. "Well, me and Captain Peterson."

Damien cleared his throat. He knocked again and shouted, "Hello! Anyone there?"

Silence.

Ben squeezed the door handle and gave it a gentle push. "Locked," he said.

"Caitlin, find a key," Damien instructed.

"Already on it," she replied, tapping her phone screen.

Moments later, Captain Peterson rounded the corner toward them.

"I texted the steward, not you," Caitlin protested.

"He's busy meeting with the chef," Captain Peterson replied. "I thought it best not to keep you waiting."

"Thank you, Peterson," Damien said.

The small crowd parted to make room in the narrow hallway for the captain.

He unlocked the door and stepped back.

Damien squeezed the handle and cracked open the door just enough to poke his head inside. "Hello?"

Karla strained and stretched her neck, but the door

wasn't open enough for her to get a glimpse inside the cabin.

Saskia squeezed herself between the door and her father. "Jennifer? Are you in there, Jennifer?"

Silence.

Damien opened the door the rest of the way and stepped inside. He strode to the other side of the cabin.

Saskia and Ben followed him.

Caitlin gestured for Karla to go ahead of her. Captain Peterson stayed just outside the door.

The room was dark; the curtains were drawn, and the lights were off.

Damien threw open the heavy white curtains, and sunlight flooded the room.

The cabin was larger and more luxurious than Karla had expected. She ignored the momentary pang of regret that she'd declined Damien's offer to spend the night. Aside from the dark wood floors, everything was white. White walls, furniture, linens, and accessories. There was even a white vase of white roses on the small round table in front of the window.

There was no doubt someone had been there. A half-eaten Cobb salad sat abandoned on the writing desk across from the bed. The bed was made, but the white linens were creased and rumpled as though someone had been lying there. The decorative pillows had been disturbed.

One large bright-pink, hard-side rolling suitcase lay, unopened, on the luggage rack beside the dresser. A pair of flip flops were neatly stowed underneath.

"Where is she?" Saskia asked no one in particular.

Ben checked the small closet. "Empty," he said.

Caitlin set her planner on the nightstand and pocketed her phone, then lowered herself to her hands and knees to look under the bed. "Nothing under here."

Captain Peterson stood in the doorway with his feet hip width apart and his arms crossed in front of his chest, as though poised to stop the intruder should she suddenly pop out and make a run for it.

Damien opened the sliding door and stepped out onto the narrow balcony, peering over the railing.

What if she went overboard? Karla kept the thought to herself, not wanting to jump to hasty conclusions or panic her clients with worst-case scenarios.

Karla found herself butted up against a door. She opened it and slipped into the ensuite washroom. It was small and efficient but still well-appointed and elegant. The room was narrow, spanning the same width as the deep soaker tub under the window on the far wall. Light streamed through the window. A puddle of water next to the tub caught Karla's eye when the sunlight reflected off it. Karla inched closer to the deep tub. It was full of water, almost to the top. Something floated there, just below the surface.

Karla's heart thumped hard. Her throat dried up, and she forced a swallow. Every cell in her body warned her not to look inside the tub. She ignored her body's warnings and took cautious, slow steps toward the tub.

"Caitlin, Peterson!" Damien's muffled voice came from the next room. "We need to organize a search. There's an unknown woman wandering around the ship."

"I don't think she's wandering," Karla called from the edge of the tub where she watched the woman's arms floating on the surface of the water with her body just below. Her voluminous blue skirt billowed on the surface and her dark hair drifted, obscuring her face. Her leafy tattoos were varying shades of green.

Damien appeared a few feet behind her. Karla moved aside to give him an unobstructed view of the tub.

"Is that—?"

Karla nodded.

"Is she?"

Karla nodded again. "She's dead."

CHAPTER 3

KARLA BELL-DIXON

"YOU DID GOOD, LA-LA," Dean praised his eldest daughter. "You prevented the witnesses from further contaminating the crime scene, and you separated everyone until we could question them individually." He winked. "You'd make a great cop."

"Thanks, Dad," Karla said. "I'm still shocked they listened to me. Damien Casey has never struck me as someone who obeys orders."

"You did exactly what Max'n'cheese and I would have done," Dean added, beaming with pride.

"Please don't call me that at work." Max paused long enough from photographing the inside of Jennifer's cabin to roll her eyes at Dean.

"Sorry, Officer Sheridan," Dean replied, calling his youngest daughter by her professional name.

Police Chief Dean Sheridan was Karla and Max's father. Although he was a consummate professional, when it came to his daughters, he sometimes blurred the boundary between his professional and personal life. This was understandable, considering his youngest daughter Max was an officer under his command.

Karla didn't mind Dean calling her La-la. He had called her that as long as she could remember. It had gone from annoying and slightly embarrassing when she was young, to comforting and familiar now that she was older. Max was eleven years younger than Karla; a fact that Karla sometimes forgot because Max had always seemed so much more mature and responsible than other people her age. She knew Max would reach the same milestone eventually and grow to embrace—or at least tolerate—her Dean-bestowed nickname, Max'n'cheese.

"I'll take your statement first, La-la." Dean opened his notebook to a blank page and clicked the top of his ball-point pen. "That way, you can observe the rest of the witness interviews and act as a liaison for us. If you happen to have any insight into whether everyone is telling us the truth, that would be very helpful and appreciated." He scrawled the date across the top of the empty page. The notebook and pen appeared doll-house-sized in Dean's massive hands.

"I only know Damien's Tell," Karla told her father. "I haven't spent enough time with the other witnesses to know their Tells yet."

"What's Damien's Tell?" Dean asked, pen poised to write.

"He narrows his eyes and turns his head ever so slightly to the side while making intense eye contact with the person he's lying to." Karla demonstrated the Tell as she spoke.

A Tell is a subconscious, involuntary action that people do when they lie. They don't realize they're doing it. It's usually subtle and sometimes lasts only a microsecond. It's the body's way of releasing the guilt and discomfort that accompanies a lie.

Since she was a little girl, Karla had been able to identify and isolate patterns in people's behaviour and recognize their individual Tells. Her personal motto was never to trust anyone until she figured out their Tell. But that wasn't always easy because not everyone had a Tell. Some people, like sociopaths for example, don't feel guilt or shame when they lie and therefore don't need a Tell. Some people have multiple Tells. They might have one for small white lies and another for bigger lies. Or they might have specific Tells for specific people. Some people are brutally honest and don't need Tells.

"But you might figure out Tells for the other witnesses, right?" Dean asked.

"If I spend enough time with them," Karla replied.

"Tell me what happened La-la."

Karla told Dean everything that happened from the moment she stepped onto the yacht tender until he and Max came aboard The Aquaholic from their police boat.

"Does Jennifer have a surname?" Dean asked when Karla had finished recounting her story.

Karla shrugged in reply. "Caitlin Lopez might know. She's the one who told us Jennifer's first name."

"Is Caitlin the witness who spoke with the deceased?"

Karla nodded.

Dean scanned the cabin and sighed. "Well, we'll start with her fingerprints," he said. "If Jennifer is in our system, we'll find her full name, and from there we can contact her next of kin to notify them."

"And you'll be able to figure out why she was here and why she pretended to be my assistant," Karla added.

"There's literally nothing in this cabin that points to Jennifer's identity," Max said, having switched from photographing the cabin to searching it with purple-gloved hands. "Where's her wallet?" she asked, rifling through the contents of the suitcase on the luggage rack.

"Her wallet could be inside the leather satchel she was carrying," Karla recalled. "Caitlin said she specifically noticed it because it looked vintage and had a nice patina."

"Well, it's not here now." Max tossed her purple latex hands in frustration.

"Neither is the second suitcase," Karla remarked, scanning the room for the missing luggage.

"Are you sure there's supposed to be two suitcases, La-la?" Dean asked.

"Both Caitlin and the deckhand who delivered the luggage to the cabin said Jennifer boarded the yacht with two bright-pink hard-side suitcases," Karla replied. "She told Caitlin they belonged to me. I remember commenting that I would never bring two large suitcases for an overnight visit. I'm an efficient packer."

She had to be. Karla's concierge job often had her

jetting across the planet to fulfill some urgent request or other from her demanding clients.

"She must have more luggage," Max concurred, removing each item from the suitcase to photograph it. "This one is full of clothes, but no outfits. Only tops. Tank tops, t-shirts, a sweater, a hoodie, a denim jacket, and a bunch of slinky lingerie, but no practical underwear." She turned to face her sister and father. "So, unless Jennifer was planning to wear the same blue boho skirt and flip-flops but change her top and only wear slinky, lacy foundation garments that offer zero support, something's missing."

"Also, there are no toiletries in the washroom," Karla pointed out. "Her deodorant and such must be in the other suitcase with the rest of her clothes."

"Well, if two suitcases and a brown leather satchel came on board, they must be here somewhere," Dean theorized.

"Unless…" Max raised her eyebrows and shifted her gaze to the balcony door.

"I had the same thought," Karla confessed. "I worried Jennifer had gone overboard when we first entered the cabin and couldn't find her."

"It's *possible* the rest of Jennifer's luggage went overboard," Dean added, "but I don't think it's likely."

"Why not?" Max asked.

"Because this cabin faces shore. It's a beautiful summer day. The waterfront is full of locals and tourists enjoying the weather. Droves of people have visited the waterfront to see The Aquaholic since it arrived yesterday. It's not every day a state-of-the-art mega yacht drops anchor so close to our waterfront park. It's kind of become a tourist attraction. People are taking photos of it. Also, hard-side luggage floats before it sinks. Even if no one saw it fall, someone could have easily seen it floating around."

"So, if someone had tossed Jennifer's other suitcase off the balcony, there's a good chance someone would have seen it," Karla surmised.

"If the luggage is still on this ship, we'll find it," Dean said with confidence. "My officers are searching every square inch of this yacht."

"Assuming the killer got rid of the luggage, they wouldn't have thrown it overboard because they wouldn't have wanted to draw attention to it until they made their escape," Max added.

"Killer?" Karla asked. "You think Jennifer was murdered?" She screwed up her face in confusion. "But the door was locked. If Jennifer was murdered, and the killer locked the door when they left, that means the killer had a key to the cabin."

"It might not be murder," Max reminded her. "But if Jennifer did this intentionally, she didn't leave a note." Max shrugged. "It could have been an accident or a medical episode." She let out an exasperated sigh. "When we discover the deceased's identity, we'll be able to find out if she had any underlying health issues that might explain her sudden death."

It wouldn't explain her missing belongings though, Karla thought to herself.

"We can't say for sure yet that it was murder, La-la," Dean said. "But every death scene is a crime scene until the coroner confirms the cause of death."

Karla picked up on Dean's *yet*. Reading between the lines, she knew Dean suspected Jennifer's death was murder, but he was waiting for the coroner to confirm it.

"Speaking of the coroner, where is Rob?" Karla checked the time on her phone and noticed seventeen text message notifications from Lynn. *I'll have to deal with those later*, she thought, locking the screen.

"She'll be here any minute," Dean replied. "The yacht tender is picking her up from shore as we speak."

"Damien Casey is being as cooperative as possible," Max said. "He offered us exclusive use of his yacht tender and driver. So, we have that and our police boat at our disposal." Max eyed something on the floor suspiciously. "What's this?" She crouched down. "There's something half hidden under the bed." She popped up again, clutching Caitlin Lopez's dark leather planner in her purple-gloved hand.

"That's Caitlin's planner," Karla said. "She must have dropped it in all the confusion when we discovered Jennifer's body."

"I almost missed it," Max said. "It was camouflaged against the dark wood floor."

"Caitlin must be freaking out looking for it," Karla added. "I'd be frantic if I misplaced my planner. It's like an extension of my brain. It's more reliable than my memory."

"Are you sure it belongs to Caitlin, La-la?"

"One hundred percent."

"Are you sure Caitlin brought it with her into the room?" Dean asked.

"Is there any chance it was already in the room when you guys arrived?" Max clarified.

Karla thought back to the events on the deck before they came to the cabin. "It was with her when we entered the cabin. I remember her opening it on the deck earlier to search for Jennifer's name."

Max popped the clasp on the planner and opened the cover. "Let's see if she wrote anything else about Jennifer, shall we?"

Karla repositioned herself beside Max, so she could look at the planner pages for herself.

The first page had Caitlin's name, contact information, and a note offering a reward for the planner's return should someone find it.

Max flipped through the calendar pages which were covered in notes and annotations, some highlighted and some crossed out, underlined, or circled. It was beautifully chaotic, not unlike Karla's own planner. An archive of a busy life. She flipped to the notes section at the back of the planner. The first page was covered in doodles. Mostly Caitlin practicing her signature as *Caitlin Casey* in fancy handwriting, sometimes with hearts drawn around the pretend signatures.

"This reminds me of when you were in high school, and I opened your notebook and found out you had been practicing your signature with Griff's last name," Max teased with an impish grin. "Mrs. Griffin Dixon." She pinched her thumb and index finger together and pretended to write in the air. "Karla Bell-Dixon."

The streak was over. It had been two weeks since

anyone had mentioned Griff's name to Karla. Two blissful, peaceful weeks. With Griff out of town on a family vacation until the end of the month, and with the renovation work on the manor house at least ninety-percent complete, Karla had, for the first time since returning to Bellbrook, managed to put her handsome, charming, and funny former high school sweetheart, Griff Dixon, out of her mind. Until now. *Thanks a lot, Max.*

"Shut up, Max'n'cheese!" Karla shoved Max with her hip.

"Hey, don't call me that at work." Max returned her sister's hip check.

"Girls." Dean's voice was deep and authoritative. "Focus." His phone chimed, and he checked the screen. "Rob's here," he said. "She just boarded the yacht."

"Are Damien Casey and Caitlin an item?" Max asked, looking at a two-page spread of Caitlin's doodles and variations of her signature as Caitlin Casey.

"Not that I'm aware of," Karla replied. "Caitlin has been Damien's executive assistant for about twenty years. They live on the yacht together much of the year."

"Most assistants don't live with their employer," Dean pointed out.

"Max, why don't you return Caitlin's planner and take her statement."

Max nodded.

"La-la, go with her as our liaison and let us know if you believe Ms. Lopez's version of events."

"THANK GOODNESS!" Caitlin exclaimed when she opened her cabin door to find Max and Karla standing there. "I think I left my planner in the other—"

Max held up the planner. Caitlin stopped talking mid-sentence. Her shoulders dropped, and she let out a sigh of obvious relief.

"It was on the floor next to the bed," Max said.

"I put it on the nightstand," Caitlin explained. "It must have fallen in all the confusion. It was quite crowded in there with all of us."

"I'd like to ask you some questions about what happened," Max said, handing Caitlin her prized possession.

"Come in." Caitlin stood aside so Karla and Max could step inside her cabin.

Karla placed her sun hat on the small table just inside the door and set her tote bag on the floor next to it.

Max's phone chimed. She checked the screen, then pocketed her phone, ignoring the notification.

Caitlin's cabin was identical in layout to the cabin where they had found Jennifer's lifeless body. Except Caitlin's cabin was on the other side of the ship with a beautiful, endless ocean view, and was more personalized than the elegant white cabin Karla and Max had just left. Family photos dotted Caitlin's walls and dressers. Her floral bedding and personal items strewn about the space made it feel homier and less formal than the elegant all-white cabin where Jennifer died.

"Did you look inside my planner?" Caitlin asked. "There's sensitive, confidential information in there." She opened the book and flipped through it, as if to satisfy herself that the contents were still intact. "I know I shouldn't keep sensitive information in here, but sometimes I just jot things down in a hurry before I forget. I'm not always near a computer." She looked at Karla. "You know how it is."

"Yes, I do." Karla smiled.

"I leafed through your planner when I found it," Max admitted. "At first, I thought it might have belonged to the deceased."

"Right." Caitlin nodded. "Have you found out who she is, and why she was here?"

"Not yet," Max replied. "I was hoping you might know more about her. It seems you were the only person who spoke with her face to face."

"Only for a moment," Caitlin clarified. "She was waiting at the dock when I arrived to meet the tender. She introduced herself as Jennifer and told me she was Karla's assistant. The way she said it sounded like I should have been expecting her. She said Karla had sent her to drop off luggage and prepare the cabin for Karla's arrival." Caitlin shrugged. "I had no reason not to believe her."

Max's phone chimed again. She checked the screen, shot the device an annoyed look, and switched off the sound so it would only vibrate instead of ring and chime.

"Tell me everything, starting with the moment you saw her on the dock," Max instructed, her pen and notebook poised for action.

Caitlin told Max the same story she had told earlier on the deck. She mentioned Jennifer's two pieces of luggage and a large brown leather purse. She described Jennifer's hair, sunglasses, earrings, and tattoos. Caitlin recalled with detail the outfit Jennifer wore; the same outfit she was wearing when they discovered her body floating in the bathtub.

"That's it?" Max confirmed at the end of Caitlin's story.

Caitlin shrugged. "I wish I knew more."

"Where did you go after you escorted Jennifer to her cabin?" Max asked.

"I was working until Karla arrived," Caitlin replied. "Damien and I are *very* busy right now. He has several projects on the go."

"So, you were in your office?" Max asked.

Caitlin nodded.

Karla was trying to focus on Caitlin, to determine her Tell, but got distracted every few minutes by Max's vibrating cell phone.

"Do you live aboard The Aquaholic year-round?" Max asked.

"Pretty much," Caitlin confirmed. "I go where Damien goes, and he spends six to nine months of the year aboard his yacht."

"Floating around the world must complicate your personal life," Karla suggested, hoping to create a smooth segue into discussing Caitlin's relationship status.

"How do you mean?" Caitlin asked.

"I mean, it must be difficult to maintain relationships when you're always moving around and far away from land."

"I'm married to my career," Caitlin said. "Damien is very generous with giving me time off and *very* accommodating when I want to spend time with my family." She gestured to the family photos that adorned her desk. "He's a *very* generous employer. I make a point of flying out to visit my sister and her family at least every other month. And sometimes, Damien flies them here for a vacation. My niece and nephew love The Aquaholic, and they adore Damien. He often makes time to take them fishing or tubing so I can spend quality time with my sister. We're only a year apart, and we're very close."

"Karla and I are very close too," Max said, "even though we're eleven years apart."

"Oh." Caitlin looked back and forth from Max to Karla quizzically. "You two are sisters? I never would have guessed."

"Same dad, different moms," Karla explained.

Caitlin nodded as though this made sense.

No one ever guessed that Karla and Max were sisters. On the surface, Dean's genes were nowhere to be found. Aside from sharing the same 5'5 height and foot size, Karla and Max looked like they were born on opposite sides of the world. Both women were near clones of their mothers. Max's brown eyes and dark straight hair were the opposite of Karla's green eyes and blonde wavy hair. They even inherited their mothers' mannerisms. And Max was bilingual thanks to spending every summer of her childhood in her mother's hometown in Japan.

"OK, but other than your sister," Karla said. "How do you maintain *other* personal relationships when you move around so much?"

"Other personal relationships?" Caitlin's confused squint made it clear that she didn't understand what Karla was alluding to.

"Are you and Damien..." Max's voice trailed off before she finished her question, but the insinuation was clear. She was asking if Caitlin and Damien had a romantic relationship.

"No." Caitlin was emphatic. "Our relationship is strictly professional. Damien would *never* date an employee. He knows better. Scandals like that destroy careers like his." She let out a small huff. "Besides, I'm not his type," she added under her breath.

"Damien has a type?" Max asked.

"Maybe," Caitlin shrugged one shoulder. "I dunno."

"You've known Damien for almost two decades," Karla challenged. "You spend more time with him than anyone else, including his daughter. You know everything about him. I'm sure you've noticed what type of woman Damien Casey finds attractive."

"He keeps his personal relationships low profile," Caitlin admitted. "When Damien is dating someone, it's practically a secret. He doesn't like the people he works with to know too much about his personal life. Except for me, of course. He tells me." She looked around as though she was making sure there was no one else in the cabin, eavesdropping on their conversation. "He doesn't even introduce his lady friends to Saskia unless it's really serious."

"Was Jennifer his type?" Max asked.

"Are you suggesting Jennifer came aboard The Aquaholic because Damien invited her?" Caitlin demanded, her volume increasing with each word. "That she was here for a secret rendezvous with him?"

"No," Karla replied, hoping to deescalate the offense Caitlin displayed on her employer's behalf. "We need to investigate every possible reason Jennifer could have snuck aboard, no matter how unlikely."

"Maybe you sent her," Caitlin accused, pointing at Karla. "After all, she said she was *your* assistant. How did she know your name? How did she know you were going to be here today? How did she know Damien had prepared a cabin for you?"

"I didn't send her," Karla said. "I've never seen her before. Whoever Jennifer is, she's not from Bellbrook, and she doesn't work for Just Task Me!"

"Well, she's not Damien's type," Caitlin defended. "First, she's too young. Damien prefers women his own age. Second, I've never known him to date someone so… so… trendy. The earrings, the tattoos, the half-shaved head, they aren't Damien's style. He prefers classy, professional, politically connected women who he can have intellectually stimulating conversations with."

Could Jennifer have been politically connected?

"If Damien and Jennifer were friends, I would know about it. Part of my job is protecting Damien's privacy and keeping his name out of the tabloids. I facilitate his dates, meetings, getaways, and even smooth over his break ups."

"Can you think of any reason Jennifer might have snuck aboard?" Max asked. "Even if you think it's far-fetched, I'd still like to hear it."

Caitlin shrugged one shoulder and shook her head in a way that made Karla wonder if she was having an internal debate about whether to say something out loud. "It's possible that maybe Jennifer was a jersey chaser?" Her voice was barely a whisper.

"A what?" Max asked, her pen hovering over the notebook page.

"A jersey chaser," Caitlin repeated. "It's a crude name for football groupies."

"You think Jennifer might have snuck aboard for Ben?" Karla asked.

"It's possible," Caitlin replied. "He was a professional football player, and now he's famous because of his relationship with Saskia." She let out a soft chuckle and snort. "Saskia puts their entire relationship on social media. Ben is a good-looking guy. We've had previous issues with women going to extreme lengths trying to get near him."

"Thanks," Max said. "We'll look into it."

Sensing that they had overstayed their welcome, Max thanked Caitlin for her statement and for helping with their inquiries.

Karla hoisted her tote bag over her shoulder as Caitlin thanked them for returning her planner.

"You didn't ask her about the doodles," Karla whispered to Max after they left Caitlin's cabin.

"Caitlin's feelings for Damien are only relevant if Jennifer was murdered," Max reasoned. "It's likely Jennifer's death was an accident or something. And I didn't want to upset her. You saw how defensive she got when we asked if she and Damien were a couple. If I'd mentioned the doodles, she probably would have shut down the conversation and thrown us out of her cabin."

"I noticed how defensive she was too," Karla said. "She's quite protective of him."

Could Caitlin Lopez be protective enough of Damien Casey to kill for him?

"WHAT'S GOING ON?" Max asked. "Why are you guys out in the hall instead of inside the cabin?"

"Clark is in there," Dean replied, jerking his head toward the cabin door.

"We're staying out of his way while he does his thing," Rob elaborated. "He's finishing his search of the ship."

K-9 Constable Clark was Bellbrook PD's police dog. He was a three-year-old Belgian Malinois and local celebrity, often making appearances at community events, and local schools.

"We haven't found the missing luggage yet, but if it's on this ship, Clark will find it," Dean said with certainty.

Max and Dean wandered down the hall while she debriefed him about her and Karla's conversation with Caitlin.

"Do you have any SPF in there?" Rob asked, nodding at Karla's tote bag. "I was expecting to work inside today, not in the middle of the ocean on a sunny day."

"I've got your back, my fair-skinned friend." Karla rummaged through her bag for the travel size bottle of sunscreen she remembered putting in there this morning. "Keep it," she said, handing her best friend the small tube. "I have plenty, and you need it more than me."

Karla used sunscreen for its anti-wrinkle, anti-aging benefits, not because she was prone to burn. In fact, Karla had never had a nasty sunburn. She was one of the lucky ones whose skin broke out in a sun-kissed glow. Rob, on the other hand, was an alabaster redhead with skin so sensitive it turned an angry shade of red within minutes of exposure to the sun's rays. Growing up, Karla had spent many summers rubbing SPF into her best friend's back at the beach. She sometimes felt guilty when her friend would suffer tender burns and her skin would peel, while Karla's biggest sun-related inconvenience was an occasional tan line under her jewellery.

"What do you think about Jennifer?" Karla asked

as Rob slathered sunscreen on the back of her neck and the exposed parts of her arms, protecting her clusters of red freckles from the harmful UV rays.

"It's a head scratcher," Rob admitted, adjusting her long ginger ponytail so it wouldn't stick to her lotioned neck. "It could be a medical episode. I'll know more once she's on my exam table. I don't observe any obvious signs of foul play or trauma. Dean said there are items missing from the room, and they can't find anything to identify her, so even if her death isn't suspicious, the circumstances surrounding it are."

Karla nodded and, before she could ask Rob if, in her professional opinion, Jennifer could have been murdered, the cabin door opened.

"All clear, Dr. Mayhew," said Clark's handler.

"Thanks," Rob smiled. "May we pet Clark?"

Dr. Robyn Mayhew was Bellbrook's resident family doctor and moonlighted as the town coroner on an as-needed basis. Like Karla, she immediately loved every dog, cat, and other domesticated animal she met.

"Sure," replied the handler.

Rob and Karla took turns scratching Clark between the ears and telling him he was a good boy. The large dog lapped up the attention, panting happily and thrashing his tail with glee.

Karla's phone vibrated inside her purse. She stopped petting Clark to check it. Twenty-seven messages from Lynn.

"Lynn's trying to reach you," Max called from down the hall. "She's texted me eleven times asking where you are."

"Something must be up," Karla said, furrowing her brow at the notifications on her phone. "I should get back to shore and find out what she wants." She looked at Dean. "Am I allowed to leave?"

Dean nodded. "I'll ask the tender driver to take you back to shore."

"Actually, I'm taking Clark back on the police boat if you need a lift," the handler offered.

Dean nodded his approval.

"That would be great," Karla replied. "Thank you."

CHAPTER 5

NOT JUST A PRETTY FACE

LYNN WAS PACING on the dock and checking her phone when the police boat arrived. Gucci, tethered to her by his Fendi leash and collar, obediently paced alongside.

Karla stepped onto the wooden dock and crouched to greet her petite pup. To her dismay, but not her surprise, Gucci charged right past her and straight toward Clark. The adorably dishevelled small terrier sniffed Clark's enormous paws and jumped to sniff his alert ears while Karla thanked Clark's handler for the ride.

"C'mon, Gooch!" Karla took the leash from Lynn and gently tugged Gucci away from the patient object of his attention. "Let's go," she urged.

"Thank you for taking care of Gucci," Karla said to her mother as they made their way toward the parking lot.

"According to your schedule, you should only have been aboard The Aquaholic for an hour. Then you were supposed to give Saskia and Ben a tour of Bellcroft."

"We had to postpone the tour until tomorrow," Karla said.

"Lucky for you, we're supposed to have this amazing weather all week," Lynn said, gesturing to the blue, sunny sky. "It would be a shame if Saskia and Ben had to tour Bellcroft in the rain." She stopped walking, pressed one nostril closed and inhaled deeply, then pressed the other nostril closed and inhaled again. "Crystal clear," she declared. "No rain for at least four days.

"That's a relief." Karla was grateful for her sunglasses because they hid her eye roll.

Lynn believed her body had barometric superpowers. She swore her sinuses could predict rain, and her left hip could predict snow. As far as Karla knew, Lynn's sinuses and hip had never been wrong, but she still didn't like to encourage her mother's meteorological quirk.

"You've been aboard the yacht all afternoon. If we don't hurry, we'll be late for dinner at Rosalie's house."

"I forgot about dinner at Rosalie's," Karla said, suddenly aware of the hollow rumble in her tummy. "With all the excitement, I missed lunch."

"Why?" Lynn asked. "What happened? Everyone in town is saying police officers and Rob have been going back and forth between the shore and the yacht."

"All I can say is someone snuck aboard, and some luggage is missing."

"That doesn't explain why Rob is there," Lynn pressed. "Is she there as a doctor or a coroner? Did someone get sick?" She studied Karla's face for a hint of reaction. Nothing. "Did someone die?"

"I'm not at liberty to say anything," Karla replied.

"But—" Lynn continued.

"Why did you send me a gazillion texts?" Karla asked, interrupting her mother and changing the subject. "You know I turn off my phone when I'm with a client. Max said you texted her a dozen times when you couldn't reach me."

"It was an emergency," Lynn insisted. "Just Task Me's website crashed from too much traffic. The phone line at your main office went down because it was overwhelmed with incoming calls, and you've gained over ten thousand new social media followers in the past three hours. It was crazy."

Karla stopped dead in her tracks. Gucci kept walking until he ran out of leash, then turned to see what was holding them up.

"Were we hacked? What happened?" Worst-case scenarios swirled through Karla's brain.

"Saskia Casey happened," Lynn replied. "She posted a selfie of you and her. It went viral and blew up the website, phone line, and Just Task Me's social media accounts." She made a mock explosion with her hands, complete with sound effects.

Lynn had a knack for hyperbole, so Karla checked for herself in case Lynn was exaggerating.

"Haven't you seen it?"

"No, I haven't." Karla pulled out her phone and unlocked the screen. She scrolled through the dozens of notifications from Lynn and stopped on a notification from the car dealership. "Shoot! My car isn't ready. They're still waiting for the part to arrive. It won't be ready until tomorrow at the earliest."

"Don't worry, love," Lynn reassured her. "I'll drive you wherever you need to go until you get your car back."

"Thanks, Mother." Karla hated to be a burden; relying on other people went against her fiercely independent nature.

She opened the social media apps on her phone and searched for Saskia's profile.

There it was. The photo Saskia took of her and Karla on the upper deck of The Aquaholic. Saskia's contemplative face and Karla's shocked expression with the caption, *Off to solve a mystery with the world's best wedding planner. The case of the mysterious stowaway.* Followed by six mystery and wedding related emojis. Saskia tagged Just Task Me's social media account. Karla checked Just Task Me's social media page. Twelve thousand new followers today so far. And hundreds if not thousands of comments on her most recent posts.

"Wow," Karla said. "I knew Saskia had a powerful social media presence, but I didn't realize how dedicated her followers are."

"They're beyond dedicated. They're rabid," Lynn corrected. "Did you know they call themselves Saskians? They have groups and websites devoted to obsessing over her and copying her style. Since she posted that photo of you and her, Saskians all over the world want to hire you to plan their next big event or get details about Saskia and Ben's upcoming nuptials."

"She hasn't even approved the venue yet," Karla said. "Imagine how busy we'll be after the wedding when she posts photos and videos from the big day."

They arrived at Lynn's car, and she unlocked the doors using the remote on her keychain.

"I'll have to miss dinner," Karla lamented as she positioned herself in the passenger seat with Gucci on her lap.

"You can't miss dinner," Lynn argued. "Rosalie will be devastated. She went to a lot of trouble. You know how much she looks forward to feeding us. You have to come."

"Mother, my website and phone lines crashed. That has to be my priority."

Lynn took her hand off the gearshift and flicked her wrist dismissively. "I took care of the website and the phone lines," she said. "And I've reposted Saskia's social media post on Just Task Me's account. I've already started sorting through the hundreds of comments in case any of them are actual, good leads for new clients."

"Seriously?" Karla didn't even try to hide the shock in her voice. "How did you know what to do?"

"A good assistant is resourceful and always figures out what to do." Lynn shifted the car into reverse and eased it out of the parking spot. "I contacted your IT guy about the website. He worked his magic, and the website is back. He's monitoring it, so hopefully it won't crash again. I called your office manager at the head office about the land line. She called the phone company. They fixed it within a couple of hours."

"Wow. Thank you, Mother." Karla let out a relieved sigh. "Hiring you might be one of the best things I've ever done."

"I told you I'd be a brilliant assistant." Lynn grinned and used her *I told you so* voice. "I'm not just a pretty face, you know." She gave her daughter a sly side-eye and playful wink. "You didn't just inherit your looks from me. You inherited your brain, too."

Karla couldn't deny the resemblance. They had the same wavy blonde hair, but Lynn's was longer than Karla's shoulder-length bob. Their facial features were nearly identical, except Karla had green eyes, a combination of Lynn's blue eyes and Dean's hazel eyes.

"I inherited some of Dad's qualities too," Karla added in Dean's defence.

"You inherited his strong moral compass and his empathetic nature," Lynn agreed. "I'm just relieved you didn't inherit his flattop haircut."

Karla bit her lip but laughed despite herself.

GUCCI RAN into the house and disappeared down the hall, no doubt in search of his favourite feline friend, Purrnest Hemingway, lovingly called, Hemi.

Rosalie Howard's house was always the perfect temperature and always smelled like home cooking and unconditional love. The lady herself always smelled like Ponds cold cream and total acceptance.

Her antiques-crowded house struck the perfect balance between cozy and welcoming.

Karla went into the kitchen and rearranged the jam-packed fridge to make space for the wine she and Lynn had brought for dinner.

"Grab a knife and slice these cucumbers." Rosalie placed a cucumber and cutting board on the kitchen table, next to where she was pitting an avocado.

"Yes, ma'am," Karla replied, doing as she was told.

"Lynn, you're on red onion duty," Rosalie advised. "Thinly sliced, please."

"Whatever you say, Rosalie," Lynn said, joining them at the kitchen table.

The three women chatted, chopped, sliced, and laughed while they assembled the heirloom tomato salad with couscous that would be their side dish.

"It's a beautiful evening," Rosalie observed. "I thought we could eat alfresco."

"That sounds wonderful," Lynn agreed. "I can't think of a better view than your beautiful garden, Rosalie. We should take advantage of the long days and warm evenings while they last."

Whining and meowing at the back door interrupted their relaxed conversation.

"Gucci and Hemi want to go outside," Rosalie announced, pushing her chair away from the table.

"I'll go," Lynn insisted, standing up first. "You stay here."

"It's fine. I need to take the chicken off the rotisserie anyway," Rosalie argued, pointing toward the backyard where her gas barbecue lived.

"I think I can carry a chicken from the backyard to the kitchen," Lynn said.

Rosalie shot her a dubious look that suggested otherwise.

"Fine," the octogenarian reluctantly relented. "There's a serving plate on the table by the back door."

Lynn washed the onion residue off her hands and headed toward the backdoor, assuring Gucci and Hemi that their release into the backyard was imminent.

"It's nice to see you and Lynn getting along so well," Rosalie commented as she shook up the mason jar of lemon juice, olive oil, and fresh chopped cilantro that would dress their salad.

"We've come a long way," Karla admitted with a sigh. "Our relationship is far from perfect, but we've grown closer in the past nine months than the rest of the forty years I've been alive."

"May would be thrilled," Rosalie said with a wide smile. "There's nothing she wanted more in the world than for you and Lynn, the two people she loved most, to take care of each other after she left." She squeezed Karla's hand and wistfulness twinkled in her brown eyes.

Grandma May didn't leave. She died. But Rosalie always used a euphemism that sounded less harsh than death. They were best friends. Grandma May and Rosalie saw each other almost every day of their lives for over sixty years. If they couldn't see each other in person, they spoke on the phone. They spent so much time at each other's houses that they wore a path in the ground between their back doors. The path that

Karla ensured was left untouched when she renovated Grandma May's cottage. The path that she walked with Gucci every day. Rosalie and Grandma May were so close that until she was six, Karla thought Rosalie was her grandmother too. She was not, but only in the biological sense of the word. Rosalie, Lynn, and Karla had helped each other through their matriarch's death last fall, clinging to each other while they learned how to live with the Grandma May-shaped holes in their hearts.

"I still catch myself unlocking my back door every morning so May won't have to knock," Rosalie said, smiling sadly and gazing in the general direction of nostalgia.

"Chicken's here!" Lynn crooned in a sing-song voice as she swept into the kitchen. "Three chickens might be a bit much for one meal, Rosalie."

"Nonsense," Rosalie said, rising to her feet. "I'm sending both of you home with leftovers for yourselves, Max, Dean, and Rob. I hear they've had a hectic day on the water. They'll need a hearty meal."

Does anything happen in this town that Rosalie doesn't know about? Karla wondered.

Feeding the people she loved was Rosalie's love language. Her overflowing fridge, freezers, and pantry were physical manifestations of her overflowing heart.

"Lynn, you set the table," Rosalie instructed. "Karla, you carry the chicken and the salad. I'll bring the wine and the bread."

Standing at the counter, carving and plating the slow-cooked rotisserie chicken seasoned with herbes de Provence, Rosalie Howard stood a hair under five feet tall in her purple rubber gardening clogs, light blue pants with an elasticized waistband, and purple t-shirt that said, *I love gardening from my head to my tomatoes.* Her earrings always matched her outfit. Today's earrings were daisy studs with purple petals and light-blue centres.

Despite her diminutive stature, Rosalie Howard was an unstoppable force in the Bellbrook community. Her opinion was widely sought after and highly regarded on many local matters. She was president of the local gardening club, and organized more community events than Karla could count. She didn't let her age—she was eighty years young—stop her from doing anything. Ever. Rosalie's dark skin was care-worn, and her once dark hair was more silver than not, but when she laughed and her dimples appeared, Karla could catch a glimpse of the young woman she once was.

DINNER WAS DELICIOUS. Birds singing in the trees accompanied their meal, and Gucci and Hemi lurked at their feet, hoping someone would drop scraps. Karla, Lynn, and Rosalie took turns pitying the persistent pets and snuck them bits of chicken under the table. The chicken was tender and moist, and the salad was seasonal perfection. The food fed their bodies, and the good company and conversation fed their souls.

"I think I'll have a bit more of everything," Lynn announced, reaching for the salad bowl. "It's so delicious."

"Save room for dessert," Rosalie warned. "I made blueberry squares."

"Mmm, blueberry squares are my favourite," Karla mumbled with a mouth full of salad.

"I'm glad to hear it," Rosalie responded. "I made an extra batch for each of you to take home."

Rosalie has spent more time cooking today than I have in my entire life, Karla mused to herself.

"I've been meaning to mention," Karla said, picking up her wine glass and touching Lynn's hair. "Your hair looks amazing. I mean, it's always perfect, but it seems a little extra perfect today."

"Thanks, love." Lynn smoothed her long blonde locks behind her ears and pushed her hair behind her shoulder. "Jennifer did a fabulous job."

Jennifer?!

CHAPTER 6
JENNIFER-LEILA

"Jennifer?" Karla asked, flabbergasted that this name had come up again. "I thought Ava was your hairdresser?"

"Ava's on maternity leave, love," Lynn explained. "She's due to have the twins any day now."

"Right, I forgot," Karla said.

"Jennifer is filling in for her. I was nervous, at first, about trusting someone new with my hair, but Ava trained her and highly recommended her." Lynn smoothed her tresses again. "I'm happy with the result."

"What does Jennifer look like?" Karla asked.

"Why?" Lynn asked, tilting her head and squeezing together her professionally shaped brows.

"Remember, I told you that someone snuck aboard The Aquaholic?"

Lynn nodded.

"I heard about that," Rosalie said. "Apparently some luggage went missing too."

"That's right," Karla confirmed. "Well, the intruder called herself Jennifer."

"Oh well, it couldn't be my Jennifer," Lynn theorized. "I was in her chair all morning and when I left, she said she had back-to-back appointments all afternoon." She gazed into the distance and swirled the last bit of wine in her glass. "I hope it's not the same Jennifer. I'd hate to lose another hairdresser."

"What does Jennifer look like, Lynn?" Rosalie refocussed Lynn on the topic at hand.

"She's quite young," Lynn replied. "Taller than me, but not by much. Long dark hair with highlights and long bangs that cover her eyebrows. She's chatty and friendly with a lot of energy."

"That doesn't match the description of the person who infiltrated The Aquaholic." Karla sighed. "I guess Jennifer is a pretty popular name."

"What did the other Jennifer look like?" Rosalie asked.

"Dark hair that's shaved on one side and long on the other," Karla recalled. "Lots of earrings, and"—she swept her hand across her chest from one shoulder to the other—"an intricate tattoo that stretches across her chest and throat from shoulder to shoulder."

"Vines?" Lynn asked. "Are her tattoos green vines that start on each shoulder, meet in the middle, and wrap around her neck like they're choking her?"

"Yes!" Karla slapped the table, amazed by the accuracy of Lynn's description. "You know her?"

"She sounds like the tourist I met at Shearlock Combs today," Lynn replied. "But her name wasn't Jennifer, it was Leila."

"Maybe Jennifer and Leila are the same person," Rosalie suggested. "If she trespassed onto someone's yacht, she might have lied about her name so she wouldn't get caught."

"For all I know, she lied when she told me her name was Leila," Lynn pointed out. "It's not like I checked her ID or anything."

"Did you speak to Leila?" Karla asked.

"Oh, yes!" Lynn replied. "We sat next to each other and had a nice long natter. I was waiting for my high-lights to marinate, and she was getting a mani-pedi."

"What did you and Leila talk about?" Rosalie asked, pouring herself another glass of wine and settling into her chair, prepared to consume Lynn's response like the juicy gossip it was.

"This and that," Lynn replied. "She said she was in town for a few days to meet up with her boyfriend. Apparently, he travels for work, so they only get to see each other every few weeks. He flies her into which-ever town he's in, and they spend time together before he leaves again."

"Did she tell you where she's staying?" Karla asked.

There is only one hotel in town, The Seascape, and one bed and breakfast, the Nestled Inn, but Jennifer-slash-Leila could have stayed in one of the many vaca-tion rentals that had popped up in Bellbrook over the past few years.

"She said she's got an ocean view room at the Seascape," Lynn replied. "She went on and on about how excited she was to see her boyfriend. She's completely smitten with him. She told us she brought so much lingerie on this trip that it filled almost an entire suitcase."

It sure did, Karla thought to herself, recalling the suitcase Max had searched that only contained tops and sexy lingerie.

"Did she mention her boyfriend's name or what he does for a living that brought him to Bellbrook?" Karla asked.

"She wouldn't tell Jennifer and me his name. She said he works in an environment with sensitive information and a lot of security, so they have to be discreet when they get together." Lynn drained her wine glass and placed it on the table. "She wanted to take him out to dinner tonight and asked us to recommend a restaurant with a romantic ambience and good food. Somewhere local so they could enjoy a bottle of champagne and not have to worry about driving back to the hotel."

"Where did you suggest?" Rosalie asked.

"La Truffe Noire," Lynn replied. "It's the nicest restaurant in town, and it's the most intimate. We told her to tell the maître'd that Lynn and Jennifer sent her and recommended table five." She looked at Karla. "It's the best one in the restaurant. Corner table with windows on two sides overlooking the ocean."

Comprehension fluttered in Karla's belly.

"Did you introduce yourself to Leila? Did you say, 'My name is Lynn?'"

"I don't think so," Lynn replied, shaking her head. "We started talking, and she said, 'My name is Leila.' Then Jennifer, who was putting in my foils, said 'We're Lynn and Jennifer, it's nice to meet you.'"

The flutter in Karla's belly grew bigger and spread to her chest.

"Did you tell her what you do for a living?"

"I might have mentioned it," Lynn admitted. "We were talking about The Aquaholic and how big and modern it is. Jennifer googled it and found out it's worth over ten million dollars. Then she said she'd love to see what it looked like on the inside." Lynn gazed sheepishly at her hands wringing in her lap. "And… I might have mentioned… that you're Damien Casey's private concierge, and I'm your assistant, and you were visiting the yacht to meet with your client and… He even offered you a cabin so you could stay the night, but you declined because you live close by and don't like to leave Gucci overnight if you don't have to."

Lynn's voice was so quiet and her words became so fast as she spoke, Karla could barely keep up with her confession.

"Mother, you know we never discuss clients with anyone who doesn't work for Just Task Me!" Karla admonished. "One reason Just Task Me! can attract VIP clients is because of our reputation for discretion."

"I know, love, and I'm sorry! It won't happen again, I swear." Lynn made an X across her heart with a French-manicured index finger. "They were so impressed by the yacht, and they caught me up in the moment…"

"Let's talk about this later," Karla said, pulling out her phone and texting Max and Dean.

"Because Jennifer introduced herself and Lynn at the same time, Leila mixed them up. She thought the hairdresser's name was Lynn, and my mother's name was Jennifer. It was an honest mistake," Karla summarized, drying the glass food container that had held Dean's serving of chicken and salad.

Dean positioned his fork on the edge of his plate, knitted his brows together as he connected the mental dots, then said, "So you're suggesting the deceased's name isn't Jennifer, it's Leila, and she introduced herself as Jennifer because she mixed up Lynn and Jennifer when she met them together at Shearlock Combs. She thought Lynn was Jennifer, and Jennifer was Lynn, and therefore your assistant's name was Jennifer, not Lynn."

"Right." Karla nodded with enthusiasm as she snapped the lid onto the empty food container.

"It's plausible." Dean nodded and shovelled the last forkful of chicken into his mouth.

"This explains how she knew my name, that I had a meeting with Damien onboard the yacht, and why she claimed to be my assistant," Karla continued. "If I'm right, that's one mystery solved." She placed the clean, dry container on the table by her front door so she would remember to return it to Rosalie. "But we still don't know *why* she snuck onto the yacht."

"Whether her name is Jennifer or Leila—her fingerprints aren't on file," Dean revealed. "Her description doesn't match any missing person's reports for our department or the surrounding area. Max'n'cheese is at the station now widening the search." He washed down his meal with a tall glass of water, having declined Karla's offer of beer because he was working late on the mysterious woman's death.

"Caitlin and Lynn both said Leila didn't have a noticeable accent, and she mentioned nothing about where she lived," Karla agreed, clearing Dean's plate and taking it to the dishwasher.

"Wherever she's from, someone must be missing her by now." Dean scooped up Gucci from the floor, flipped him onto his back, and cuddled him like a baby. The small terrier looked downright tiny nestled in Dean's bulky arms and hands but was happy for the belly rubs, stretching out to give Dean access to as much of his furry belly as possible.

"She told Lynn she was staying at The Seascape. Also, she might have a reservation tonight for table five at La Truffe Noire," Karla added.

"Those are good leads, La-la," Dean praised. "Well done." He sighed and placed Gucci on the floor, then pulled out his notebook, and opened it on the table in front of him. "I'll send an officer to Shearlock Combs first thing tomorrow to talk to the staff there. Maybe she paid with a credit card or told them some identifying information." He jotted notes as he spoke. "I'll follow up with The Seascape Hotel and La Truffe Noire tonight after I visit Lynn and take her statement." He jerked his head sideways toward the cottage next door where Lynn lived.

Karla and Lynn lived in side-by-side twin cottages on the grounds of their ancestral home, Bellcroft. Karla lived in Mirabel, the cottage where Grandma May had lived and where Karla had grown up.

Lynn lived in Bellflower, the cottage next door. Karla had both cottages gutted and renovated after Grandma May's death. On the inside, Mirabel no longer resembled Karla's childhood home, but she still found comfort in being there.

"Since you still haven't officially identified Leila, I assume Clark didn't find her missing suitcase or purse on The Aquaholic?"

"There's no sign of the missing items," Dean confirmed. "At this point, we're assuming someone tossed them overboard, and no one witnessed it." He shook his head. "But if that's the case, there should be video footage of the luggage falling into the water."

"There are security cameras on the yacht?"

"Not inside," Dean clarified. "There are only two cameras inside the yacht. One pointed at Damien's office door, and one pointed at Caitlin's office door. Damien considers the rest of the yacht his personal residence and won't allow cameras. But there are several cameras on the outside of the yacht, and one of those should have picked up the falling luggage."

"Unless whoever disposed of the luggage is familiar with The Aquaholic's security details and knew about a blind spot where the cameras wouldn't capture the luggage," Karla suggested.

"If there's a blind spot, we haven't found it, La-la." He sat back in the chair and rubbed his hand across his grey flattop. "Max'n'cheese noticed something interesting when she was processing the suitcase we found in the cabin. There were no tags on any of Jennifer-

Leila's clothing. Someone had cut them all out. Why do you suppose someone would do that?"

Karla shrugged one shoulder. "Maybe she had sensory issues? Tags can be itchy and annoying."

"Maybe."

Dean's nod gave Karla the impression that he wasn't convinced sensory issues could be the reason.

"You're not convinced?" she asked.

"It's possible, La-la, but considering Damien Casey's job, reputation, and connections, we have to be open to the possibility that Jennifer-Leila was working on someone's behalf."

"Like a spy or something?"

"Maybe." Dean's nod was more convincing this time. "Someone could have sent her to find out information about Damien Casey, or maybe even to hurt him."

"She could also be a rabid Saskian," Karla countered. "Or a jersey chaser. Or a deranged mega yacht enthusiast."

"You're right." Dean held the backs of his hands against his shoulders in a placating gesture. "I'm just saying, until we figure out the dead woman's identity and why she was in that cabin, we must consider every possibility. Even the most unlikely ones."

Karla gave Dean an insulated bag with heaping servings of Rosalie's chicken and salad for Max and Rob. He promised to deliver both containers tonight. As he left to interview Lynn, he asked Karla not to be too hard on her mother for discussing Just Task Me! business with strangers in a salon.

"She's so proud of you, La-la. She loves to brag

about your accomplishments," Dean pleaded in Lynn's defence. "And she's excited that you're letting her work with you. She's trying to make amends. To be a better mother and for you to get to know each other better."

"OK, Dad, I'll keep it in mind."

"Also, because of Lynn's indiscretion, we have two solid clues that could lead us to Jennifer-Leila's true identity, the hotel room and the restaurant reservation."

Karla had always been in awe of Dean's lack of animosity toward Lynn. He seemed to harbour no ill will toward the woman who declined his proposal, had his baby, left their baby with her mother, then disappeared from their lives for almost forty years. Granted, Lynn had been eighteen years old and overwhelmed, but forty years was a long time to avoid your responsibilities and not own up to your mistakes.

"I'm not going to fire her, Dad." Karla rolled her eyes.

"I'm glad to hear it."

Dean kissed his daughter's forehead, said goodbye to his granddog, and trudged across the shared lawn to Lynn's cottage.

CHAPTER 7

A TOUPEE IN A TORNADO

THE DAY after the murder

Karla's phone was already chiming and vibrating before she'd even opened her eyes. While she slept, news about the mysterious woman's death flew through Bellbrook faster than a toupee in a tornado. Dean and his officers had kept the situation quiet as long as they could, but there was no disputing the locals who, with their own eyes, had seen Rob and her coroner's assistant removing the deceased woman's bagged body from the police boat and loading it into the back of the town's white, unmarked coroner's van.

With a lack of any actual facts to guide them, the people of Bellbrook were using their collective imagination to conjure explanations for her presence on the yacht and her mysterious death. She snuck aboard to burgle the wealthy occupants. She was an international spy who snuck onto the yacht to plant covert surveillance devices and monitor Damien's top secret political meetings and conversations. She was an obsessed Saskian. She was stalking Ben. She was Damien's mistress. As she and Gucci walked their regular morning route, Karla scrolled through her phone, hoping someone had suggested a theory that hadn't already occurred to her. They hadn't.

Karla's phone chimed with a message from Rob.

ROB

Time for a quick coffee?

KARLA

I always have time for my best friend!

ROB

Déjà Brew? Fifteen minutes?

I can walk to Déjà Brew in fifteen minutes, Karla challenged herself. *It'll be my daily cardio.*

KARLA

Meet you there.

"Good morning, Karla," Harry bellowed as he emerged from the thicket with his Irish wolfhound, Clancy.

"Good morning, Harry." Karla smiled, and Gucci tugged on his red leather Valentino leash and collar with silver studs, desperate to get close enough for Harry to pet him and within sniffing distance of his friend, Clancy.

"I thought you'd left for the day," Harry said. "Your car's not here."

"It's not fixed yet," Karla explained, rubbing Clancy's furry grey head. "The dealership is still waiting for a part. Hopefully it'll be ready today."

"I'm heading into town if you need a lift," Harry offered, crouched down to Gucci's level with the excited pup resting his front paws on Harry's knee for balance, bouncing on his hind legs, and wagging his tail like a fan.

"It's fine," Karla said. "I don't mind walking, but thank you. There's no need to interrupt your day."

"It's not an interruption, Karla," Harry insisted. "I offered because I want to do it." He furrowed his thick silver brows and shook his index finger at her. "We've talked about this. You don't have to be so self-sufficient. Accepting help is not a sign of weakness," he lectured. "When people offer to do something for you and you decline, you deny them the opportunity to do something nice for someone else and to feel good about it."

Harry was right, and Karla hated it. She had lived in the city for so long that she had gotten used to being independent. Old habits died hard. She had embraced the anonymity that the busy city provided and took pride in not asking for help. But now that she was back in Bellbrook, where even the most mundane task was turned into a community effort, she struggled to relax her high standards of independence, cede a bit of the control she loved to have, and accept that cooperation was a way of life here and helping was as much for the helper's benefit as it was for the person receiving the help.

"Thank you, Harry, I appreciate the offer." Karla smiled. "I just need to drop off Gucci at home first."

"Perfect," Harry replied with a triumphant grin. "I'll take Clancy home, grab my keys, and pick you up in a few minutes." Harry looked at Clancy who had loped away to sniff and pee on a nearby tree. "C'mon Clancy!" He let out a shrill whistle and scratched his bushy silver beard. "Let's go."

Harry and Clancy disappeared into the trees toward his cabin.

Harry Kincaid had lived in the gamekeeper's cabin on the Bellcroft estate his entire life. He was the same age as Lynn and Dean; the three of them had gone to school together. Harry took over the gamekeeper position from his father, who had taken it over from his father before him. Being Bellcroft's gamekeeper was kind of Harry's family business. Except Harry had never married or had children. There were no more Kincaids waiting in the wings to inherit the gamekeeper position when Harry was ready to retire.

Karla didn't like to think about Harry retiring. She couldn't imagine Bellcroft without him. He was as much a part of Bellcroft as the manor house, the trees, and the ocean. Karla had never known Bellcroft without Harry, nor had she known Harry without Bellcroft. Harry wasn't family in the traditional sense, but he was the only doting uncle Karla had ever known. He had been part of her everyday life growing up. Harry doted on her like the favourite niece he'd never had. Every week, he had joined Grandma May, Karla, and Rosalie for Sunday dinner. He'd built a treehouse for Karla and Rob in the woods on the estate. And a tree swing. In the winter, he had made a small skating rink for her and her friends in Grandma

May's backyard. When she was little, Harry had often walked her to and from school, teaching her about the trees and local wildlife that also lived on the estate grounds. When she'd been old enough to walk by herself, he'd sometimes snuck her a secret five-dollar bill so she and Rob could get ice cream or candy after school. "But don't spoil your dinner," he warned as he slipped her the folded bill, "or your grandmother will tear a strip off me."

THE INSIDE of Harry's beloved old white pickup truck smelled like motor oil and fake pine. Karla resisted the urge to tear the pine-tree-shaped air freshener from the rear-view mirror and toss it out the window as they drove. The cracked leather bench seat was scorching from the heat of the summer sun, even though it was still quite early in the morning.

"You already knew she was dead, didn't you?" Harry shouted to be heard over the sound of the wind rushing past their open windows.

Karla nodded. "Dad asked me not to say anything," she explained.

"Who was she?" Harry asked, his thick head of silver hair blowing in the breeze. "Why was she there?"

"No one knows," Karla admitted. "It's a mystery."

Karla told Harry how they had discovered the deceased woman's body inside a locked cabin and how some of her luggage had disappeared. She knew Harry wouldn't say anything. Karla trusted him implicitly. Along with Max and Rob. She could tell him anything in confidence. She told him how the dead woman conned her way aboard the yacht by pretending to be Karla's assistant.

"Don't be too harsh on Lynn," Harry said, echoing Dean's pleas from the night before. "She's trying her best to build a relationship with you."

"So everyone keeps saying," Karla mumbled.

"She just gets a little carried away sometimes," he reasoned.

They pulled up in front of Déjà Brew.

"I'm going to the garden centre to check on the river rocks I ordered for the path through the cutting garden," Harry informed her. "They were supposed to be delivered yesterday. Then I'll tidy up and meet you there when you bring your client to view the venue."

"Thanks, Harry." Karla didn't have to tell Harry how important Saskia and Ben's tour was. He knew this was their big chance to make Bellcroft a successful event venue again and earn back the money they had invested in renovations. "She's so excited to visit Bellcroft. I get the feeling that, if she likes what she sees, it's a done deal, and Saskia and Ben will book their wedding with us."

"I knew you'd make Bellcroft a huge success." He winked with a knowing grin. "I couldn't have made a better investment."

When Karla found out she had inherited Bellcroft from Grandma May, she knew she had inherited a money pit. The main building was derelict, having spiraled into a state of disrepair after Grandma May ran out of money to maintain the mansion over three decades ago. Karla had to decide whether to sink her entire net worth, and then some, into repairs and renovations, or to subdivide the large estate and sell the oceanside manor house. Desperate to hang on to her family's ancestral home, Karla devoted all her resources to restoring and renovating the historical building and re-landscaping the grounds. Eager to support the venture and restore the estate to its former glory, Lynn contributed her inheritance from Grandma May to the renovation, and Harry donated what Karla suspected was most, if not all, of his retirement savings. She'd tried to talk him out of it, but Harry was adamant he wanted to help gentrify the estate and insisted he could afford it because he had never paid rent—living rent free in the gamekeeper's cabin was a benefit of his position.

Karla unbuckled her seatbelt and thanked Harry for the lift. As she tugged the door handle to open the truck door, Harry said, "Just shoot me a text when you need a lift back to Bellcroft, and I'll pick you up."

"Thanks, Harry," Karla said, fighting the instinct to decline his offer. She didn't need another lecture before she'd had her first cup of coffee.

CHAPTER 8

G'DAY LADIES

"Over here." Rob stood and waved her hand over her head.

Karla smiled, made a beeline for Rob, and slid into the small two-person booth in the corner of the bustling cafe.

"Americano with a dash of simple syrup." Rob slid a steaming mug of coffee toward her.

"Thank you." Karla smiled, grateful for a best friend who always knew her order. "It's busy here today." She wrapped her hands around the wide mug and lifted it toward her mouth.

"Nothing gets Bellbrookians out and about like an unsolved murder."

"Murder?" Karla froze, the mug almost touching her lips. "Leila was murdered?"

"You haven't heard?" Rob asked, leaning in closer and lowering her voice to a whisper. "I assumed Dean or Max would have told you."

"I haven't spoken to them yet today," Karla said.

"They worked late last night, caught a few hours' sleep, and were back at work by the crack of dawn." Rob stifled a yawn. "I worked late with them. Thank goodness Josie is at her dad's this week."

Josie was Rob's nine-year-old daughter. Identical to Rob but smaller in scale and wiser than most adults. Rob and her soon-to-be-ex-husband shared fifty-fifty custody, an arrangement that Rob was still struggling to get used to.

"Are you sure Leila was murdered?" Karla understood that murder was a possibility, but she had clung to the hope that Rob would discover the dead woman had an underlying medical condition, or she had suffered some sort of fatal and unfortunate accident near the bathtub. "How do you know?" Karla asked, then finally took her first sip of coffee, swallowed, and inhaled deeply, savouring the moment the first drop of caffeine touched her soul.

"I haven't completed the full autopsy," Rob said as a professional disclaimer, "but there's enough evidence so far to suggest her death was homicide."

Karla leaned in until their heads were almost pressed together above the centre of the small table. "Like what?" she whispered.

"First, we found hairs on the bed that, upon initial examination, match the hairs on Leila's head." She looked around to make sure no one was eavesdropping. "I'm just waiting for the lab to confirm that they came from the victim."

"So, at some point, Leila was on the bed," Karla concluded, remembering the rumpled white duvet cover and disturbed accent cushions. "That doesn't mean she was murdered, right? Maybe she just rested on the bed for a few minutes. To be fair, the bed looked really inviting. I wouldn't blame her for being tempted to try it out."

"There was evidence of conjunctival and facial petechiae," Rob added.

"What's that in non-doctor speak?" Karla asked, sipping her Americano.

"Red, pin-prick sized spots that occur when tiny capillaries in the eyes and face rupture due to increased pressure on the veins in the head because something has obstructed the airways," Rob explained.

"She had red spots on her skin from the small veins in her head and eyes bursting under the pressure of being suffocated?" Karla paraphrased. *What a painful, terrifying way to die.* She placed her mug on the table as a wave of nausea roiled in her belly.

"Or strangled," Rob said. "But in this case, I suspect the petechial hemorrhage was likely caused by suffocation."

"How can you tell the difference?"

"I retrieved fibres from Leila's throat," Rob disclosed in the quietest whisper possible. "I'm waiting for the lab to get back to me, but I'd be willing to bet the fibres from Leila's throat will match the fibres from one of the pillows on the bed."

"Someone smothered her with a pillow?" Karla asked, matching her friend's volume.

Rob nodded. "I'm doing the autopsy as soon as we finish our coffee," Rob said, "but I don't expect to find water in her lungs." She sat upright and sipped her iced coffee. "But I will look for any other fibres that she may have inhaled while her killer suffocated her. The cause of death is a hold back," Rob explained. "Dean wants the public to believe that the police think she died by drowning. He's hoping the true cause of death will help the police find the killer."

"Got it." Karla nodded. "So, you suspect she died on the bed and someone moved her dead body to the bathtub?"

"Dead people can't move themselves," Rob replied with a half shrug.

"Why move the body?" Karla asked. "Why didn't the murderer kill her in the bathtub, if that's where they wanted us to find her, or just leave her on the bed? The killer had to take extra time to move her. Every extra moment they spent at the crime scene increased their chance of getting caught in the act."

"I don't think this murder was premeditated," Rob surmised. "It seems more like a spur-of-the-moment murder. A crime of passion or panic or something. It's like the killer panicked when Leila died and staged the scene, hoping investigators would presume it was suicide or an unfortunate accident."

They sat in silence. Karla sipped her coffee, processing the information Rob had just divulged.

"Why didn't the killer toss the body over the balcony?" Rob wondered aloud. "It would have delayed finding her and possibly destroyed some of the evidence."

"There are cameras," Karla explained. "According to Dean, there are cameras covering the outside of the yacht. Cameras that would have captured Leila's body going overboard. He thinks the killer knew about the cameras. That's why he was so certain Leila's missing luggage was somewhere on the yacht. It would have been difficult to get it off the yacht without being caught on camera or seen by someone."

"Good morning, ladies."

Suddenly, four women clad in yoga leggings and tank tops surrounded their small corner table.

"Good morning," Karla and Rob responded in stereo.

"Is it true you were on the yacht yesterday, Karla?" asked the brunette ponytail who, judging by her position in the middle of the group and her confident posture, was The Head Poser.

"Yes," Karla admitted. It wasn't like she could lie. Lots of people, including The Posers, would have seen her climbing on board the yacht tender yesterday, then disembarking the police boat hours later.

The Posers were a group of alleged yoga enthusiasts who, as far as Karla could tell, spent most of their time occupying the centre table at Déjà Brew, monitoring the comings and goings of their fellow townsfolk and discussing other people's business. They always wore yoga gear, had rolled up yoga mats poking out of their backpacks and gym bags, yet no one had ever actually seen them at Om Sweet Om, the local yoga studio. Regardless of their methods, their information was almost always accurate, and they had been known to use their powers for good when necessary to quash harmful and inaccurate gossip.

"Did you see her?" The blonde reverse bob leaned

in, eager to hear Karla's response. "The dead woman," she clarified. "Were you there when they found her?"

"Sort of," Karla admitted, trying to answer the question without giving away too much information for fear of compromising the police investigation. "I can't talk about it," she explained. "You know, client confidentiality, police confidentiality, so many confidentialities."

"Did you meet her before she died?" asked the pixie cut with frosted tips. "Did you speak to her?"

"Look at the time!" Rob announced, checking her smartwatch and interrupting the conversation before Karla could answer the curious Poser. Every day, Rob changed the band on her smart watch to match her scrubs. Today she wore olive-green scrubs with an olive watch band. "I have to go." She stood up, forcing the Posers to take a step back from the table.

"Me too," Karla announced, following her best friend's lead.

"You're so close, even your outfits match," pointed out the brunette shoulder-length shag. "Did you two coordinate your outfits on purpose?"

Karla looked at her sleeveless, muted olive blouse tucked into a pair of slim darker olive-green cigarette pants that ended just above her ankle, and her strappy gold stiletto sandals, and realized that she and Rob looked like a sample card for shades of olive-green paint.

"Total fluke," Karla assured The Poser.

The Posers suddenly became distracted, perking up like curious meerkats and forgetting all about Karla and Rob's matching wardrobe choices. They whispered to each other, pointing excitedly to something, or someone, outside.

"There he is!" The blonde reverse bob bounced on the balls of her feet and grabbed the brunette ponytail by the arm.

"He's back," observed the brunette ponytail, narrowing her eyes.

"He's so handsome!" said the brunette shoulder-length shag.

"Who?" Rob asked, straining to look through the window at what, or who, had The Posers in a tizzy.

"The tall, good-looking Australian guy," replied the brunette shoulder-length shag cut. "He's come in here three days in a row now. He's one of the yacht people. He usually wears a white uniform like Richard Gere in *An Officer And A Gentleman*."

"That scene where Richard Gere sweeps Debra Winger off her feet in the factory…"

"Captain Peterson?" Karla mumbled, peering through the window, squinting to see through The Posers' reflections in the clean glass.

"Who?" demanded the brunette ponytail. "What did you say his name was?"

"I'm not sure," Karla muttered, uncertain if the man who had The Posers swooning was the same man who drove her to The Aquaholic yesterday and unlocked the cabin where they'd found Leila's body.

It *could* have been Captain Peterson, but it was difficult to tell for sure. His back was to the window, and he wasn't wearing his crisp white captain's uniform—the only outfit Karla had ever seen him in. Instead, he wore a pair of slim, straight leg khaki pants, a royal blue short-sleeved golf shirt and brown leather sandals. He was tanned enough to be Captain Peterson. He was the right height, build, and had similar short, neat, salt-and-pepper hair. His head was bobbing and his hands were gesticulating, but his body blocked whomever he was conversing with.

"He's come in here every day since The Aquaholic arrived. This will be his third visit to Déjà Brew," said the blonde reverse bob. "He always orders a doppio and a cup of ice water to go." She stared at the man's back with a mischievous glint in her eye. The corner of her mouth twitched slightly upward. "Then as he leaves, he looks right at us, smiles, winks, and says, 'G'day, ladies,' in his hot Aussie accent." She fanned herself.

"Yesterday, he looked at our yoga mats and said, 'I bet you ladies are flexible, aren't you?' I almost fainted," added the pixie cut with frosted tips amid a fit of giggles.

"I wouldn't mind showing him how flexible I am," purred the brunette ponytail.

"Stop!"

"You're baaad,"

"Me too!"

The other posers gushed in response, giggling and playfully swatting their flirty friend.

"He can't be *that* cute," Rob argued. "I mean, no one is *that* hot."

Captain Peterson turned his head and looked toward the cafe.

"Never mind." Rob nodded. "I was wrong. He looks like he just fell out of an issue of GQ magazine."

"He's the captain of The Aquaholic," Karla confirmed.

The reverse blonde pouted. "That means he's leaving soon. I was hoping he'd be around a while."

Captain Peterson turned back to his unknown conversation partner and shifted his weight. He held a crumpled paper bag in his hand. He nodded to the nearby garbage pail, lined up his shot, and lobbed the bag into the can. Karla heard whomever he was speaking to cheer when the bag made it into the basket.

Hey, I know that laugh! Karla thought.

Captain Peterson was fidgeting with his wedding band when he stepped to the side and pivoted his body just enough that, instead of his back, Karla could now make out his profile—and the person to whom he was speaking.

"Lynn?" Rob blurted, pointing out the window. "Is he talking to Lynn?"

"Mother?" Karla couldn't believe her eyes.

"Way to go, Lynn." The brunette ponytail gave Karla's mother an impressed nod.

Lynn laughed, tossing back her head, and flicking her hair behind her shoulder with one hand, while *almost* placing her manicured fingertips on Captain Peterson's tanned, muscular forearm with the other. Was Lynn flirting with a client? Not that Captain Peterson was a client, but he was the employee of a client which, as far as Karla was concerned, crossed the same professional line. *I guess we need to discuss professional distance.*

CHAPTER 9
OOPSIE DAISY

"I WASN'T FLIRTING, LOVE," Lynn defended herself against Karla's accusation. "I was being polite to a tourist. He stopped me and asked for directions." She gestured vaguely around them. "Bellbrook is a summer tourist town, in case you've forgotten." She shook her index finger at Karla. "Tourism is the backbone of our local economy, remember? The last thing Bellbrook needs is online reviews claiming the townsfolk are rude and unhelpful."

Karla only had Lynn's side of the story to consider since Captain Peterson had disappeared by the time Karla had woven her way through the busy cafe and made her way to the sidewalk outside.

"Directions to where?" Karla crossed her arms in front of her chest and tapped the toe of her stiletto sandal on the sidewalk.

"He was looking for a florist, love," Lynn replied with a small huff. "He wants to send flowers to his wife. She has a big presentation at work or something, and he wants her to know he's thinking about her even though he can't be there."

"He works for Damien Casey," Karla whispered, "which means he's practically a client of Just Task Me!. We don't fraternize with clients or their employees. Ever."

"I told you, love, we weren't flirting." Lynn seemed downright exasperated with the accusation. "He asked if I could recommend a local florist that could send flowers internationally. I recommended Oopsie Daisy." She pointed toward the local florist. "In fact, when he told me he worked on The Aquaholic, I introduced myself as a Just Task Me! employee and offered to take care of his order for him." She shrugged her right shoulder. "May as well. I'm going to Oopsie Daisy, anyway." She held up her cell phone. "He texted me his wife's name, address, and the message he'd like to include on the card." She pocketed her phone. "Her favourite flowers are white or blush ranunculuses. I always thought they were called Persian Buttercups, but Captain Peterson says they're called ranunculuses." She shrugged. "He would know, I guess. He says he and his wife have a garden full of them."

"From inside Déjà Brew, it looked like you were flirting."

"No one was flirting," Lynn insisted. "Trust me, if Captain Peterson was flirting, he wouldn't have spent five minutes waxing lyrical about his wonderful wife. He wears a wedding ring, for goodness' sake. Just because a man is ruggedly handsome and speaks with a sultry Australian accent doesn't mean I can't control myself. What kind of woman do you think I am?"

The truth was, Karla didn't really know what kind of woman Lynn was. They had spent so little time together that Karla and Lynn hardly knew each other at all. She knew Lynn rarely stayed in one place longer than a few months. She knew Lynn had mentioned a new boyfriend practically every time she phoned or sent a postcard to Grandma May. She knew Lynn had handed over Karla to the loving care of Grandma May when she was just a few months old, left Bellbrook, and almost never looked back. And thanks to Rosalie and Harry's constant reminders, she knew that when Karla was born, Lynn had been a terrified, over-whelmed eighteen-year-old girl trying to cope as best as she could under tremendous stress.

Karla relaxed her stance and added, "I'm sorry if I got it wrong." She gave Lynn a small, apologetic smile. "I guess I'm still uneasy after yesterday when you told Leila and Jennifer more than you should about The Aquaholic and my professional connection to Damien Casey."

"I promised you that won't happen again," Lynn reminded her. "And it won't."

"Why are you going to Oopsie Daisy?" Karla asked. "You said you were going there, anyway, before Captain Peterson asked about a florist."

"I thought I'd pick up flowers for the manor house," Lynn replied. "We want the venue looking its best for Saskia and Ben's private tour today. After the florist, I'm heading to Rosalie's house to pick up a charcuterie board, blueberry cheesecake bites, and a few other nibbles she made to help Saskia and Ben feel welcome."

"Good idea," Karla commended. "Saskia has chosen a palette of muted fall colours for the wedding. I'll text you a link to her mood board."

"I'll check what muted fall colours the florist has in stock." Lynn nodded.

Karla and Lynn said goodbye, and Lynn headed toward the florist farther up Main Street.

"Are you OK?" Rob asked.

Karla turned to Rob, having forgotten that her best friend had followed her outside.

"Yes," Karla replied. "I'm fine. But I suspect Lynn might be growing bored with Bellbrook's small-town lifestyle. It wouldn't surprise me if she hitched her trailer to the next visiting cowboy and rode out of town."

"I'm not so sure," Rob disagreed. "Lynn seems to have different priorities now. She's trying really hard to build a life here and build a relationship with you."

"Time will tell," Karla said, hoping to end the conversation.

"Besides, if anyone was flirting, it was probably him. You heard The Posers talking about how friendly he was with them and that comment he made about how flexible they were." Rob checked the time on her watch. "I have an autopsy to perform," she reminded Karla.

"I'll walk with you," Karla offered.

They strode down Main Street, soaking up the mid-morning sun and pausing occasionally to look in a store window, or smile and say hi to a friend or neighbour.

"Karla!"

Karla and Rob stopped, searching for the source of Karla's name.

"Woohoo! Karla!"

Caitlin Lopez jogged toward them, impressively fast for someone wearing heels.

"I'll call you after I finish the autopsy," Rob mumbled.

"Good luck," Karla said, unsure if those were the appropriate words of encouragement for a doctor about to perform an autopsy.

Rob continued walking, and Karla waited while Caitlin's long strides closed the gap between them.

"You left this in my cabin yesterday." A breathless Caitlin thrusted the wide-brimmed sun hat toward Karla.

"Thank you," Karla said, taking the hat. "You didn't have to deliver it. I would have been happy to pick it up next time I visit the yacht."

"It's sunny today," Caitlin reasoned. "I thought you might need it."

"Thank you." Karla smiled. "I appreciate it."

"No problem," Caitlin said. "I came to shore with Captain Peterson. This town is so small that I figured there was a good chance we'd bump into each other." She shrugged. "If I didn't run into you, I would've taken it back to The Aquaholic and asked Saskia or Ben to give it to you at Bellcroft later."

"You and Damien aren't coming to Bellcroft with them?" Karla asked.

"We'd love to," Caitlin replied, "and Damien wishes he could be there too, but something came up at work, and now we have back-to-back video meetings all afternoon."

"I'm glad we bumped into each other," Karla said. "I wanted to apologize for yesterday. Max and I didn't mean to offend you when we asked if you and Damien were more than colleagues. Max's interest was purely professional. And I want you to know that, had your answer been different, I wouldn't have judged you or betrayed your confidence."

"Thank you, Karla," said Caitlin as they strode along Main Street, heading towards the waterfront. "Since we're exchanging apologies, I'm sorry for suggesting you were responsible for bringing the dead woman on board. I know now that she was just pretending to be your assistant. Max visited the yacht this morning with an update. It turns out you and Leila didn't know each other, and she lied about her credentials to get on board."

"I wasn't offended," Karla said. "None of us was sure what to think. The whole situation was weird and scary."

"Damien trusts you, and I trust Damien's judgement," Caitlin said. "You've always been discreet and reliable, and that's good enough for me." She sighed and appeared to steel herself for what she was about to say next. "For the record, Damien and I have a strictly professional relationship. We're friendly and sometimes enjoy each other's company outside of work, but we've never been intimate. I'm *very* happy just being his friend."

"You've never been tempted?" Karla asked. "Damien's good looking. Smart. Charming. He gives off strong alpha-male energy. And you guys spend months at a time together on his gorgeous yacht."

"Not tempted," Caitlin retorted with a chuckle. "I'm a *very* big believer in keeping my personal life separate from my professional life." There was a brief pause before she added, "So you didn't ask about my relationship with Damien because of anything Max might have seen when she flipped through my planner?"

Karla hated lying. The twinge of shame when she did it made her whole body uncomfortable. As far as Karla was concerned, withholding information was just as much a lie as actually saying something untruthful. Like not admitting that Max wasn't the only person who saw the contents of Caitlin's planner, and not confessing that Karla herself had been peering over Max's shoulder and saw pages of doodles where Caitlin had practiced signing her name as Caitlin Casey, with hearts and multiple variations of her pretend signature.

"If Max had questions about something in your planner, she would have asked." Karla watched her feet as she spoke to avoid eye contact with Caitlin. "I'm relieved we didn't upset you," she continued, directing the conversation away from Caitlin's planner. "I have a lot of professional respect for you, and I'd hate to offend you."

"You didn't offend me," Caitlin insisted. "I was in shock. Finding an intruder, dead, in my home, up the hall from where I sleep, freaked me out. I've never found a dead body before."

"It would freak out anyone," Karla reassured her.

"And I was frantic with worry about Saskia. I wanted to go to her cabin and make sure she was OK, but there was a cop in the hall who made everyone stay inside their cabins until the police finished interviewing everyone and collecting evidence."

"Why were you frantic about Saskia?" Karla asked.

"Did you read the unauthorized biography that Saskia's former nanny wrote?"

"The one that came out when Saskia was little?" Karla clarified. "The one that was released after Damien won the custody battle? I read it years ago but hardly remember it."

Karla had only been working for Damien for a few years. She had read the book as research but couldn't remember most of it. Damien had neither contributed to the book nor sanctioned it, so she placed little credibility in the accuracy of its details.

"During the height of the custody dispute, Saskia found her mother floating in a bathtub," Caitlin reminded her. "She survived, but only because Saskia and the nanny got to her just in time."

Karla stopped dead in her tracks. "I'd forgotten about that," she said, recalling the passage from the book. "It was true?"

Caitlin nodded.

Saskia had been six years old. She'd been spending a week at her mother's Manhattan penthouse as per the temporary custody arrangement issued by the judge presiding over the custody case. The nanny had left the penthouse to pick up young Saskia from a nearby birthday party. While she was gone, Saskia's mother washed down an assortment of prescription and non-prescription painkillers with a few shots of tequila. She then thought it would be a good idea to take a bath. It wasn't. Saskia and the nanny returned to the penthouse just in time to save the woman's life. According to the nanny's version of events, it was Saskia who found her mother floating in the bathtub. Miraculously, Saskia's mother survived and agreed to go to rehab. Again. She spent the next several years in and out of various rehab facilities, all at Damien's expense. Damien's legal team had used the incident to arrange an emergency court hearing where the judge awarded full physical custody of young Saskia to Damien.

"That event traumatized Saskia," Caitlin revealed. "I had only worked with Damien for a few years at that point, but I remember how the bathtub incident affected her. That girl was haunted by what had happened. She was like a different child after. Before she left to visit her mother, Saskia was her usual energetic, fun, playful self. When she came back, she was different. She hardly slept and had nightmares when she did. She was sullen and anxious. She clung to Damien like she was scared she'd never see him again if he left the room. The nanny had to teach her to use the shower because she trembled and cried if Damien or the nanny tried to coax her into a bath." Caitlin looked over her shoulder, then leaned in, and whispered, "One time, I found her floating her doll in a sink full of water. She'd hold it under the water, then pull it out, and save it. She would do this for hours."

"Oh, my!" Karla said. "I've never heard about any

of this. It wasn't in the book, and I don't recall hearing about it in the press."

"It wasn't," Caitlin said. "Damien and the nanny were protective of Saskia. Damien did everything he could to keep Saskia's struggle out of the media. Even the nanny didn't include the aftermath in her book. Everyone thinks Damien loved the media attention around the custody battle. They think he used the court of public opinion to poison gossipmongers against Saskia's mother, but he didn't. Damien hates the press. Always has."

"But Saskia's livelihood depends on the media," Karla pointed out. "She uses the paparazzi to her advantage. She's one of the most photographed celebrities in the world."

"Damien hates it," Caitlin claimed. "He thinks the media exploits his daughter, and he thinks her fans—The Saskians—are dangerous. But he's a good, loving dad. He supports Saskia's choices regardless of how he feels about them. He doesn't confide in many people, but he confides in me, regularly, about how much he hates the media and Saskia's fans."

Could he hate them enough to kill them? Karla asked herself. What if Leila was paparazzi or a crazed fan who snuck aboard the yacht to get close to Saskia? Could Damien have found her and become so enraged at the breach of privacy and decency that he killed her to protect his daughter?

The women resumed their lazy pace along Main Street.

"Have you spoken to Saskia?" Karla asked. "Did

finding Leila's body in the bathtub trigger her past trauma?"

"I spoke to her last night, and I saw her at breakfast this morning. She was a little quieter than normal but seemed fine. She didn't see the body," Caitlin revealed. "Everyone else saw it except her. Damien and Ben took turns comforting her and keeping her away from the bathroom. Damien told us not to discuss it in her presence. He's afraid the details might upset her and bring back memories of her mother. We've all complied. No one wants to upset Saskia. But just because she didn't see it doesn't mean it didn't affect her. One good thing that has come from this is that Saskia and Ben have stopped arguing. He's being super attentive and doting on her now."

"Saskia and Ben had been arguing?" Karla asked. "They seem so affectionate and in love. What were they arguing about?"

"Same old argument they always have," Caitlin replied. "Girls throw themselves at Ben and Saskia gets jealous."

"Why would she be jealous?" Karla asked. "Saskia is gorgeous, famous, and it's obvious Ben adores her."

"I love Saskia and I love Ben," Caitlin reasoned. "I don't want to say anything negative about them. They're great people, but they've had relationship issues, just like any other couple."

"What sort of issues?" Karla pressed.

"Ben's a bit of a flirt," Caitlin disclosed. "Girls approach him all the time when he's out in public. They take selfies with him and try to insinuate they know him better than they should. Fans send him flirty messages and intimate photos on social media. Saskia is a pretty confident woman, but early in their relationship, Ben cheated, and she still struggles with it. Sometimes, she accuses him of cheating. He gets angry. She reminds him why she's insecure. He tells her to get over it and threatens to cancel the wedding if she can't trust him."

"I had no idea," Karla said, stunned at how dramatic life on the yacht seemed to be. If Caitlin was telling the truth, it certainly wasn't the peaceful, idyllic life of leisure that Damien had led her to believe. "Do you think Ben cheats on Saskia?"

"No." Caitlin's response was confident and without hesitation. "Ben loves Saskia, but he gets frustrated because he's not as comfortable as her with living in the spotlight. She's monetized their relationship, and he doesn't like that. Their life together appears perfect and easy, but creating that illusion is a full-time job."

"Maybe today isn't the best day to look at wedding venues," Karla thought out loud. "Maybe I should call Saskia and offer to reschedule. You know, give her some time and space to deal with what happened on the yacht yesterday."

"No! Don't do that!" Caitlin protested. "Saskia *needs* to find a wedding venue. They're getting married in three months. This wedding is a huge media event. Saskia and Ben have contractual obligations. She has secured sponsors, sold rights to the first interview and first photos, and world-famous fashion designers have donated their time to design the dresses and suits in exchange for the publicity. This wedding *must* happen. Her image and reputation depend on it. Saskia Casey is proud, like her dad. Her image means everything to her, and she would do anything to preserve it."

Would Saskia Casey kill to preserve her image? Karla wondered to herself. If Leila had sneaked aboard for a secret rendezvous with Ben, or even if she was just hoping to meet her celebrity crush in person, could that pressure, so close to the wedding, have been enough to push Saskia over the edge of reason? Did Saskia kill Leila in a fit of jealous rage and leave her in a tub of water just like she had found her mother twenty years earlier?

CHAPTER 10

KISSES AND AFFECTION,
NOT BARKS AND BITES

KARLA MADE a point of always arriving everywhere before her clients and never making them wait. Therefore, she and Gucci arrived at the manor house before Saskia and Ben. The walk wasn't long, but the midday summer sun was hot, leaving both Karla and Gucci parched by the time they reached their destination.

"You should have sent me a text," Lynn said when she saw her panting daughter and granddog. "I would've picked you up."

"It was time for Gucci's midday walk, anyway," Karla replied, relishing the central air conditioning and focussing on the silver lining in her car situation.

Karla's car still wasn't ready. The dealership had sent her a wordy apologetic text message along with a guarantee that it would be ready tomorrow and, to compensate for the inconvenience, offered a free maintenance visit when it was time to install the snow tires and winterize her car.

"Saskia and Ben aren't here yet." Harry stated the

obvious as he placed a bowl of water on the kitchen floor for Gucci. "Do you usually bring Gooch when you meet with clients?" he asked, rubbing the terrier's small head and slipping him a piece of homemade jerky from his pocket. "I left Clancy at home. I didn't know this was a dog friendly meeting."

"Gucci's here by special request," Karla replied. "Saskia has seen him during our video chats and wants to meet him in person. She even sent a text message reminding me to bring him." She found a drinking glass in the cupboard and poured herself a glass of cool water from the dispenser built into the stainless-steel commercial fridge. "The place looks incredible," she said before gulping down half the glass.

"Thanks, love," A hint of a blush peeked through Lynn's perfectly applied makeup. "The theme was simple elegance. I used Saskia's mood board for inspiration."

"Saskia will love it." Karla smiled.

Rosalie's creative, albeit larger than necessary, charcuterie board, platters of various sweet treats, a bottle of champagne—in a chiller—and several stemless, crystal champagne glasses adorned the large white quartz kitchen island. Lynn had stocked the small beer fridge in the butler's pantry with Ben's preferred brands. Simple yet striking floral arrangements adorned the kitchen table, island, and various accent tables through the main floor.

It wasn't long before Ben and Saskia pulled up in two chauffeur-driven black, electric SUVs.

The first SUV carried Saskia, Ben, and a huge bodyguard who looked too big to fit in the vehicle. He positioned himself next to the passenger door, standing at attention with his feet hip width apart, his hands clasped in front of him, and his shoulders squared. He was like a human statue. His serious expression didn't move, and Karla couldn't tell what he was looking at behind his mirrored aviator sunglasses.

The second SUV carried the head of Saskia's Social Media Strategy Team, Saskia's head stylist, and four outfit changes, complete with shoes and makeup.

"Welcome to Bellcroft." Karla beamed as she greeted them.

"Is this Gucci?" Saskia ignored Karla's welcome and focussed on the excited terrier who was pulling on his leash, whimpering and desperate to reach his new best friend. "He's even more adorable in person." Saskia crouched down, and her voluminous maxi skirt billowed around her. Not understanding about expensive designer clothes, Gucci trampled all over it, trying to reach her face and give her kisses. Saskia didn't mind. She seemed to love Gucci as much as he loved her. She turned her head and looked up at her fiancé. "We should invite Gucci to the wedding, babe!"

"As a guest?" Ben sounded mortified at the idea. He pressed his back against the SUV as though, if he moved a muscle, Gucci would attack him. He would, but with kisses and affection, not barks and bites.

"Actually," Karla said, "he has a little tuxedo. He wore it last Halloween."

Saskia gasped and inspiration twinkled in her amber eyes. "We could have a tux made for him," she suggested. "To match the groomsmen." She looked at

Ben again. "He could go from table to table during the reception, greeting the guests. Like a little host. What do you think, babe?"

"I think we should tour the venue first," Ben suggested, creeping sideways until he ran out of car to press himself against, then slinking past Gucci before running into the house.

"Does Ben have allergies?" Karla asked Saskia. "Gucci is hypoallergenic."

"He's not allergic," Saskia explained with an eye roll. "He's scared. He's terrified of dogs. When Ben was growing up, his grandmother had a mean miniature schnauzer that would always corner him and growl."

"Oh," Karla said. "That's too bad." *It's a good thing Clancy isn't here. Ben would be downright terrified of the huge hound.*

"It's devastating," Saskia corrected. "I've always wanted a dog. Since I knew dogs existed. My dad would never let me get one because we travel so much and spend so much time at sea. I would've asked my mother, but she could barely look after herself, never mind keep a pet alive." She sighed, gave Gucci a final head-to-tail stroke, returned to standing, and straightened her skirt. "I guess I'll never have a dog. Ben is too terrified of them. He was a sweaty, anxious mess the whole time that police dog, Clark, was sniffing around The Aquaholic yesterday."

Interesting, thought Karla. *Was Ben a mess because he was afraid of Clark or because he was afraid of what Clark might find?*

The social media strategist and stylist were

wandering around the front of the mansion, whispering among themselves, pointing, and snapping photos on their cell phones.

"They're scoping out potential locations for photoshoots," Saskia explained, gesturing to her employees. "And, if it's all right with you, we might take a few staged photos today to tease my followers leading up to the wedding?"

She phrased it as a statement, but Saskia's voice intonated at the end like it was a question, so Karla nodded her approval. "Maybe you should see the rest of the estate first," she suggested.

The tour went well. Saskia loved every room more than the one before it. Her excitement about getting married at Bellcroft was palpable. She was full of ideas and enthusiasm about Bellcroft's potential to be the best wedding venue ever. By the end of the tour, she had decided that the bridal party and groomsmen would stay at the manor house in the days leading up to the wedding.

"What about our parents, babe?" Ben asked.

"My dad will stay on his yacht." Saskia shrugged. "Your parents can stay with him, and we'll book every hotel room in town for everyone else."

Ben nodded. He hadn't said much during the tour but seemed pleased that his fiancée was happy. He kept a constant, watchful eye on Gucci and maintained a safe distance from the excitable pup.

By the time the tour was over, Saskia had decided they would host the rehearsal dinner in the dining room and invite the immediate family to a special breakfast the morning after the wedding.

They would hold the reception in the ballroom, and the doors to the huge patio would be open so the party could spill outside. Karla made notes about securing a tent and heaters because October nights this close to the ocean could be chilly and unpredictable.

Her strategist pointed out that the outbuildings would be perfect command centres for the media outlets who had purchased the rights to photograph and video parts of the ceremony and reception. The stylist had a few concerns about lighting.

"Send me a list of your requirements," Harry said in his role as project manager for the massive renovation project. "When our contractor, Griff, gets back to town at the end of the month, we'll see what we can do to accommodate them."

There was that name again. Karla knew Griff hadn't left town for good, but she had hoped his absence would be an out-of-sight-out-of-mind situation. She had looked forward to not being distracted by him for a while. So much for that.

"Other than the beautiful gardens and the patio, are there options for good outdoor photos?" the social media strategist asked.

"Wait until you see the waterfront," Karla said with a knowing grin. "Follow me."

Karla led Saskia, the stylist, and the social media strategist to the private waterfront behind the manor house.

Saskia was speechless until she wasn't. "This is it," she declared. "This is where I want Ben and I to exchange our vows. Right here next to the water."

The stylist and strategist jumped in to manage

Saskia's expectations about weather, tides, and other unknown variables that might disrupt her plan. Their quick intervention and coordinated effort gave Karla the impression that managing Saskia's expectations was, perhaps, the biggest part of their jobs.

"Would you mind if we took some photos near the water?" Saskia asked. "I want to hype up my followers with a few photos of the venue as the wedding gets closer."

"Sure," Karla replied.

The stylist and strategist left them and rushed to retrieve Saskia's wardrobe changes, makeup, and hair products from the car.

"Changing my look gives the illusion that we took the photos at different times," Saskia explained to Karla. "This way we have enough photos for several days, and my followers think each photo is new."

"You and Ben should come back tonight and tour the estate after dark," Karla said as she and Saskia ambled back toward the house with Saskia holding Gucci's leash. "It's beautiful when it's lit up. You'll get some great nighttime photos."

"That's a good idea," Saskia agreed. "My dad can come with us. He wanted to come this afternoon, but Caitlin scheduled a bunch of meetings." She rolled her eyes and let out a frustrated huff. "Apparently, some-thing urgent came up."

"I heard," Karla said. "I offered to reschedule the viewing again, but Caitlin didn't think it was a good idea. She said how disappointed she and Damien were that they couldn't be here."

"I bet she did," Saskia muttered. "That's what she wants you to think."

"Why would she lie about wanting to visit your wedding venue?"

"Caitlin saw an opportunity to get my dad all to herself and took it," Saskia replied. "With me and Ben off the yacht, and a bunch of the crew taking time off to visit the town, they're practically alone on The Aquaholic. Caitlin loves having all my father's attention. It wouldn't surprise me if those urgent meetings were suddenly cancelled or rescheduled at the last minute."

Is this why Caitlin had been so insistent that Karla not postpone today's tour? Was she really worried about how close the wedding was, or did she want Damien to herself? Karla was getting the impression that Caitlin and Saskia didn't have the warm, friendly relationship that Caitlin had led her to believe.

"May I ask a personal question?" Karla asked when they stopped so Gucci could sniff a rock.

Saskia nodded. "Shoot."

"Are Caitlin and Damien a couple?"

"She wishes!" A small snort escaped when Saskia tried not to laugh. "My dad doesn't see Caitlin as a romantic option, and it drives her crazy," Saskia said. "Caitlin Lopez has been in love with my father for as long as I can remember. He's too oblivious to see it, but to everyone else it's as obvious as the cigar in his shirt pocket and a bit sad." As they neared the house, Saskia handed Gucci's leash back to Karla. "She uses me to get to him," Saskia revealed. "I like Caitlin, but she tries too hard to be my friend, my mother-figure, whatever she thinks will impress my dad."

"Is it possible that Caitlin wants to be your friend and mother-figure because she likes you? I mean… she's known you since you were little," Karla suggested in Caitlin's defense.

"You don't know Caitlin very well, do you?" Saskia's tone suggested that Karla didn't know Caitlin at all. "She's clever and calculating," Saskia continued. "She hates other women having access to my dad. Sometimes I feel like she's jealous of *me*, and I'm his daughter. I'm surprised she's so friendly with you. She must not think you're a threat. I bet she told you she's 'married to her job and *very* happy just being Damien's friend.'"

Saskia's impression of Caitlin was dead on, like she had practiced mimicking her father's executive assistant.

"Word for word," Karla replied absently, her mind replaying the interactions she had with Caitlin on Main Street earlier that day and aboard the yacht the previous afternoon.

"She also mentioned how generous Damien is as an employer. Apparently, he invites Caitlin's sister to visit the yacht and even spends time with her sister's kids so Caitlin and her sister can spend time together."

"Caitlin's sister hasn't visited The Aquaholic in ages," Saskia said, shaking her head. "They fought about something a couple of years ago, and as far as I know, Caitlin has only seen her sister, niece, and nephew at a couple of family events since then."

I know Caitlin's Tell!

"Have you ever noticed that there are no female crew members on The Aquaholic?" Saskia asked, interrupting Karla's revelation.

"Now that you mention it," Karla replied, wracking her brain to recall whether she had encountered a female crew member during her visit.

"It's not a coincidence, you know," Saskia said. "Caitlin is responsible for hiring. She only hires men. Less competition for my dad's attention."

"Maybe women are underrepresented in the yacht industry," Karla hypothesized, still hoping to redeem Caitlin with Saskia.

"I'm pretty sure that's not the reason," Saskia said dismissively. "She also sabotages his relationships. She's the reason he's alone. If he's interested in a woman, she makes it too difficult for him to spend time with her. She books meetings that coincide with their dates, she makes travel arrangements that keep him away from whoever he's interested in." Saskia looked Karla in the eye. "If Caitlin Lopez can't have my father, no one can. But my dad doesn't see it, and even if he did, he's so dependent on her that he probably couldn't do anything about it."

Did Caitlin kill Leila? Jealousy is a powerful motive. Maybe Leila was a special friend of Damien's, and Caitlin found out.

"She was pretty worried about you after we found the body yesterday," Karla said as a segue. "If you need to talk to someone, a professional, I can arrange it. No one else would need to know, if that's what you want. Just say the word and I'll make it happen."

Karla knew Rob could recommend someone qualified and discreet.

They stopped walking as they reached the door to the house.

"Thank you, but there's no need to worry," Saskia retorted. "I'm fine." She shrugged one shoulder. "I know everyone is waiting for me to have some kind of breakdown because the dead woman was in the bathtub, like when I found my mother twenty years ago, but I'm fine. Finding that Leila woman was nothing like finding my mother. I'm older now. More mature. I can handle it better. Also, my mother was floating face down and wearing a bathrobe, Leila was face up and fully dressed. It wasn't the same at all."

How do you know what Leila's body looked like? Karla wondered to herself but didn't ask out loud. Didn't Caitlin say that Saskia never saw Leila's body? Didn't she say that Ben and Damien were sure to keep her away from the bathroom? Didn't she also say that Damien had asked everyone not to discuss the details with Saskia for fear of triggering her past trauma? Did someone who was at the scene go against Damien's wishes, or did Saskia see Leila's lifeless body first-hand? But how could she when Damien and Ben had tasked themselves with keeping her away from the bathroom? Could Saskia have seen Leila's body earlier? Was Saskia the reason Leila was floating in the tub?

CHAPTER 11

HAPPY SPOUSE, HAPPY HOUSE

BEN WAS RELIEVED to find out his presence was not required at Saskia's impromptu seaside photo shoot. He was also relieved when Saskia asked if Gucci could be in the photos with her. Apparently, the distance between the manor house and the waterfront was sufficient for Ben to relax and not be on high alert for Gucci's sudden movements.

"My followers will love Gucci," Saskia gushed as she picked him up and cuddled him close to her face. "And the Versace bikini I'm planning to wear for the first shoot matches Gucci's Versace collar and leash! It's too perfect! He's like a mini-me!"

Euphoric at the coincidence and still snuggling Gucci, Saskia disappeared into a nearby powder room where her stylist and strategist had set up an impromptu dressing area.

"Would you like to visit the waterfront, Ben?" Karla asked. "We can make it there and back before Saskia and Gucci get there for their photoshoot."

"No thank you, Ma'—Karla. It's not necessary. If Saskia's happy, I'm happy."

"Happy spouse, happy house, amirite?" Harry teased.

"Yes you are, sir—I mean Harry."

"Where's Lynn?" Karla asked.

"She took a bottle of water to the bodyguard," Ben replied.

"He's still standing there." Harry jerked his thumb toward the front of the house. "He hasn't moved a muscle. I've been watching him through the window. He's a human statue."

"I got a nod out of him," Lynn announced, sweeping into the kitchen. "He didn't move though, so I just put the water on the hood of the SUV. He's sweating. There are beads of sweat on his forehead, and he won't even move to wipe them."

"He's fine," Ben assured them. "That's just how he is."

This seemed acceptable as everyone nodded.

"Where's my granddog?" asked Lynn, searching around her feet for the pup who was usually so happy to see her that he would attack her knees whenever she entered the room.

Karla told Lynn about Gucci's photo shoot with Saskia down by the water.

Lynn volunteered to join them in case anyone needed anything, grabbed a few bottles of water and a small bowl for Gucci, zipped them into an insulated bag, and left.

While Karla was showing Saskia the waterfront, Ben and Harry bonded over Ben's short athletic career.

"Karla, did you know that in his rookie year, Ben rushed the ball 330 times for 1,601 yards and nine touchdowns?"

"Really?" Karla asked, nodding and hoping she looked sufficiently impressed. "That's amazing." She had no idea what the numbers meant. "That must have been a record?"

"Oh, it was," Harry replied on Ben's behalf. "He also caught 40 passes for 305 yards and scored on three receptions."

"Wow," Karla said, understanding nothing that Harry had just said. "That's incredible." *Right?*

"Thank you," Ben replied, equal parts proud of his achievements and embarrassed that Harry was making such a big deal of them. "I'm not the only former athlete on The Aquaholic," Ben said, directing the conversation away from himself. "Captain Peterson was a lock for Queensland County."

"Rugby," Harry explained for Karla's benefit. "He played professional Rugby in Australia." He opened two cans of beer and handed one to Ben.

Karla nodded. "I didn't know that."

"I'm sure he told Lynn all about his athleticism when he flirted with her earlier," Harry muttered under his breath before taking a swig of beer.

Is Harry jealous? Based on things she'd overheard growing up, Karla had always suspected that Harry had a crush on Lynn when they were in high school, but it never occurred to her that Harry still had feelings for her mother.

"They weren't flirting," Karla defended. "Mother

was helping him with something. Besides, how did you hear about it?"

"Can't keep secrets in this town, Karla," Harry reminded her, then took another swig of beer.

"The hedge trimmer is here," Harry said, lifting his chin toward the window. "I need to have a word with him." He placed his beer can on the counter. "The hedges were way too short last time." He looked from Karla to Ben. "Excuse me. I'll be right back."

"It looks like Saskia and I are getting married at Bellcroft," Ben announced, filling in the silence left by Harry's departure. "This is the most excited she's been about any venue, and we've visited dozens of potential venues on four continents since we got engaged."

"Which venue was your favourite?" Karla asked.

"They're all the same to me," Ben admitted. "This wedding business is exhausting, and I can't wait to get married so it will be over." He laughed. "But seriously, as long as Saskia gets the wedding of her dreams, I'll be happy wherever we get married."

"She wants to come back tonight," Karla said. "The estate is beautiful at night with the gardens and the manor house lit up. She wants Damien to see it too." She sighed. "I hope he likes it as much as Saskia."

"Damien Casey will say and do anything to make his daughter happy," Ben said in a reassuring tone. "I'm sure he'll love Bellcroft, but even if he doesn't, he wouldn't say anything that might dampen Saskia's enthusiasm about it."

"Are you and Damien close?" Karla asked. "Caitlin mentioned how you worked together yesterday to comfort Saskia when we found you-know-who in the you-know-what." She was purposely vague, just in case someone was nearby.

"Are sons-in-law ever close to their fathers-in-law?" Damien asked, answering her question with a question.

"Some are, yes," Karla replied. "How about you and Damien?"

"We're friendly, but not friends, if you know what I mean."

Karla nodded, understanding exactly what Ben meant. There was a difference between being friends and being friendly.

"The only thing we really have in common is Saskia," Ben continued. "We both love her and always put her first. Beyond that, we don't interact much. Saskia says he likes me, but I feel like he just tolerates me, so she'll be happy. He has a way of making me feel... inadequate. Like I don't belong in the same room as him. It's hard to explain." He swished the beer around inside the can. "Let's just say, in Damien Casey's opinion, no one would be good enough for his daughter. She could marry Prince Charming, and he'd still think she settled."

"Did something happen between you?" Karla asked. "Do you think there's a reason Damien might not like you?"

"It was something that happened when Saskia and I first got together," he said, shaking his head dismissively.

"I'd heard you cheated on her," Karla said cautiously, hoping she didn't just offend the future son-in-law of one of her biggest clients.

"I never cheated," Ben insisted with more emotion than Karla had ever witnessed from him. "Yes, that girl and I had a fling, but it was before Saskia and I even met. That girl sold her story and her photos of us to a tabloid, and the tabloid insinuated the photos were recent. They weren't. I hooked up with that jersey chaser months before I ever laid eyes on Saskia."

"Does Saskia know that?" Karla asked.

"I've told her," Ben said in a tone that sounded defeated. "I showed her my text messages with that girl to prove that we'd stopped texting two months before Saskia and I met." He sighed. "It doesn't make sense, but Saskia is insecure. On the outside, she's confident and self-assured, but deep down, she worries people don't like her, and she's afraid that everyone will leave her."

I can't imagine why, Karla thought to herself sarcastically. *Her mother left her repeatedly because of addiction, and her father sent her to boarding schools for most of her childhood and left her in the care of nannies when she wasn't at school.*

"There's nothing I wouldn't do for Saskia," Ben claimed. "I love her more than anything."

Would you kill for her? Karla wondered. *Or would you kill with her?*

What if Leila had snuck aboard The Aquaholic to rendezvous with Ben, Saskia found out, and Ben killed Leila to prove his love and devotion to Saskia? Or maybe they killed her together. Or... what if Saskia killed Leila, and Ben helped cover up the crime?

"Did Saskia see Leila's body in the tub?" Karla's

whisper was so quiet that Ben had to lean in and put his ear near her mouth.

"No, she didn't," he insisted, shaking his head as he leaned away. "I know for a fact that she didn't see *the body.*" He mouthed the words *the body.*

"She described it to me," Karla challenged. "In detail."

Ben shook his head harder. "Damien and I made sure she didn't see that scene. He even texted everyone after and told us not to talk to her about the details. He was afraid she would freak out."

"Did Saskia ask you about it?" Karla asked. "Did she ask you to describe the scene in the washroom?"

"Yes," Ben admitted.

"Did you tell her?"

"Do you think I'd be stupid enough to defy Damien Casey?" It was a rhetorical question.

CHAPTER 12

TECHNICAL DIFFICULTIES

KARLA INHERITED her propensity for punctuality from her father, Dean. Neither of them could stand being late and went out of their way to always be on time, or better yet, a little early. Karla wasn't sure what motivated Dean to strive for perpetual promptness, but anxiety was her motivation. The thought of being late filled her with a nagging mental and physical unease that she would do anything to avoid. So, she did not complain, and was a tad relieved, when she and Dean arrived at the dock fifteen minutes before the yacht tender was due to pick them up.

"Thanks for driving me to the marina, Dad," Karla said as she unbuckled the seatbelt and opened the door of Dean's patrol car.

"No problem, La-la. I have an appointment with Damien Casey on The Aquaholic, so I was coming here, anyway."

"About the murder case?"

"Strangely, no," Dean replied. "He wants to talk

about security for Saskia's wedding. He's worried the Bellbrook Police Department doesn't have the resources or experience to handle such a large, high-profile event."

"I can help set him straight."

"Thanks, La-la. But I think I can handle him." Dean locked the patrol car, and they walked toward the dock where the tender was supposed to pick them up. "Why are you going to the yacht?"

"Dinner," Karla replied. "Saskia and Ben invited me. They want to discuss the wedding, then I'm taking them back to Bellcroft for a nighttime tour."

Standing on the dock, waiting for the tender to pick them up, Karla replied to emails on her phone while Dean paced. He paced one side of the dock, then the other, all the while keeping his eyes peeled on the water sloshing below.

"Looking for something?" Karla asked, knowing full well that Dean was scoping the area for a sign of Leila's missing bags.

"Leila's missing luggage is really gnawing at me," Dean admitted. "I've had divers search around the yacht and dispatched marine officers to search the water. We've even asked the fishing boats to keep their eyes open for anything suspicious. It's like the luggage just disappeared into thin air." Dean brought his fingertips together and made a mock *poof* with them.

"The ocean's pretty big, Dad," Karla said, trying to console him. "Maybe the luggage sank and hasn't resurfaced yet. Or maybe the wind changed and carried it in a different direction."

"We should have found something by now," he

muttered. "Something's not right with this situation, and I can't stand not knowing what."

"Did you follow up with La Truffe Noire and The Seascape hotel?" she asked, hoping to refocus her father on the more productive parts of the investigation.

"There was no reservation at La Truffe Noir," Dean said. "The maître'd said the restaurant was fully booked last night. This is one of their busiest months. Last night's reservations were booked weeks in advance. He said he would've known if there had been a last-minute cancellation and someone else filled it. Also, none of the reservations for a table for two included a woman named either Leila or Jennifer. I even asked him to check for a reservation in Lynn's name in case the dead woman pretended to be someone else again."

"So the restaurant was a dead end," Karla sympathized.

"Yeah," Dean agreed. "It would've been great if she had booked a table and given them her and her boyfriend's names for the reservation."

"She might have paid Shearlock Combs with a credit card," Karla suggested hopefully.

"Cash," Dean said, shaking his head.

"What about the hotel?"

"She had a room at The Seascape," Dean confirmed. "But she didn't have a reservation. She showed up yesterday morning and took the only room they had available. The clerk remembered her because he told her how lucky she was to get a room this time of year, without a reservation. Lucky for her, a guest had to check out early and left the night before."

"Did you search her hotel room?"

Dean nodded. "Yes, but we found nothing useful. Just her fingerprints, and the fingerprints of a few hotel employees. The hotel's security cameras captured her arriving with her luggage—two bright pink rolling suitcases and a large, brown, crossbody bag, just like everyone said. The cameras also captured Leila leaving at a time that coincided with her visit to Shearlock Combs, returning after her visit to the salon, then footage of her leaving the hotel with her luggage a short time later, presumably to sneak aboard The Aquaholic. She didn't check out, but she took all her luggage. Was she planning to leave for good? Or was she planning to come back but was permanently delayed?" Dean wondered aloud with a shrug. "We may never know."

"Leila must have provided a credit card when she registered," Karla said. "You can't stay in a hotel without giving them a credit card number to keep on file."

"Can you believe their computer was down when she checked in?" Dean closed his eyes and shook his head in disbelief. "'Technical difficulties,' the hotel manager called it. I call it a comedy of errors. The clerk who registered her was a summer student. He's new and didn't know how to process a credit card without the computer, so he didn't take it. He told her they would call her room and ask for her credit card information when the computer system was fixed."

"Oh my," Karla said. "That's too bad."

"That's what the hotel manager said. He also said the correct procedure was to photocopy Leila's ID and credit card, input them into the system when it started working again, then destroy the photocopies. But the clerk didn't know that, and they were short staffed yesterday, so they never got Leila's credit card. They also require guests to provide details about their vehicles, so I'd hoped to get the make, model, and plate number, but she arrived by cab. She told the clerk she came straight from the airport. I've assigned an officer to contact cab companies and try to track down the car that picked up Leila from the airport. It's like searching for a needle in a haystack." He let out a heavy breath.

"But they confirmed her name was Leila?" Karla asked.

"Yes," Dean replied. "She checked in as Leila Grant and gave them her cell phone number."

"That's a significant lead."

"It's a burner," Dean said, dashing her hope. "She probably picked it up at a convenience store somewhere and used it on a pay-as-you-go basis." He looked at Karla and squinted into the sun behind her. "Why would Leila have a burner phone?"

"Maybe because of her boyfriend?" Karla suggested. "Leila told Lynn and Jennifer that she and her boyfriend had to be discreet during their visits because his job involves security, or something, and he needs to stay below the radar."

"Whose radar?" Dean asked, exasperated. "She also told Lynn and Jennifer that her boyfriend was only in town for a few days. For all we know, he's already gone." Dean used the toe of his huge black police shoe to kick a leaf from the dock into the water. "Max mentioned you figured out Caitlin Lopez's Tell."

Karla nodded. "She uses the word, very, and exaggerates it *very* much. Now that I know her Tell, it's *very* easy to tell that she lied to Max and I about her feelings for Damien and, for whatever reason, lied to us about her relationship with her sister. Basically, Caitlin is in love with Damien and no longer has a close relationship with her sister."

"Interesting." Dean's notebook was out, and he made notes as Karla spoke.

"I think I figured out Ben Underwood's Tell too," she continued. "His is interesting and less common than the usual Tells. He avoids lying by either changing the subject or answering a question with another question."

"Can you give me an example, La-la?"

"When I asked him if he disobeyed Damien, which I suspect he did, he replied with, 'Do I look stupid enough to defy Damien Casey?' He also did it when I asked him if he and Damien were close. They're not, by the way, but Ben says they have an understanding based on their mutual love for Saskia."

The tender's arrival interrupted their conversation. Dean flipped shut his notebook, clicked his pen, and returned them to his pocket.

This yacht tender was identical to the one that took Karla from shore to ship yesterday, except this one had white leather upholstery instead of tan.

"Is this a different boat?" she asked the deckhand

who was driving. "The tender that picked me up yesterday had white leather seats."

"Good eye," said the young deckhand. "The Aquaholic has two tenders in this size. The only difference is the upholstery colour."

"There are two yacht tenders?" Dean asked in his authoritative cop voice. "I was only aware of the one Damien offered to let us use. No one mentioned another one." He looked at Karla. "I don't think Clark searched it."

The deckhand shrugged at Dean's comment, shifted the speedboat into gear, and steered it away from the dock.

Karla lurched when the boat moved. She grabbed the back of the white leather bench seat for support. *I should sit down before I fall and break a heel or a hip.* She used the seatback to steady herself as she maneuvered to the front of the leather bench seat. As she lowered her weight onto the seat, it shifted beneath her. Something wasn't secure. The seat cushion wasn't flat. She stood to adjust the seat and noticed it was sticking up at a weird angle. She lifted the cushion to figure out what was causing the issue and hopefully fix it. To her surprise, the bench seat was an actual bench. The seat lifted to allow for hidden storage inside. Peering through the narrow gap between the bench seat and the base, Karla glimpsed something pink and shiny. *No!* she thought to herself. *It can't be!* She cracked open the bench just enough to glimpse its contents. *Bingo!*

"Dad."

Dean's back was to her. He couldn't hear her over

the rushing water smacking against the side of the boat and the wind in their ears.

"DAD!" Karla shouted, tugging on the back of his size XL black Bellbrook PD golf shirt.

Dean turned.

She pointed at the bench cushion. When Dean fixed his focus on the upholstered white leather, she opened the bench to reveal a hot pink hard-side rolling suitcase that was just a hair too tall to allow the lid to close properly.

Dean's jaw dropped, and his eyes widened. He looked at Karla, then back at the poorly hidden luggage.

"What the h—" A seagull swooped low between them, its squawk drowning out the last syllable of Dean's sentence.

CHAPTER 13
AN UNEXPECTED OFFER

By the time they arrived at the yacht, Dean had already sent text messages summoning officers to process the recovered luggage and perform a thorough search of both yacht tenders.

"I knew it," Dean said, staring at his phone screen with crinkled brows. "Clark didn't search either tender."

"Welcome back." Caitlin's smile disappeared when she saw the open bench seat on the boat. She blinked fast, and her jaw dropped. "Is that?" She looked from Karla to Dean. "Is that the dead woman's missing luggage?"

"It appears so," Dean replied.

"Has it been there this whole time?" she asked.

"Your guess is as good as mine," Dean said with a sigh.

Caitlin shook her head. "But she and I rode to The Aquaholic on the other tender. Jennifer, Leila, whatever she's called was never on this tender." She turned her attention to her cell phone. "I'd better let Damien know what's happening."

Dean offered Karla his hand as she stepped off the boat and onto the yacht. "La-la, can you tell Damien that I'll contact him to reschedule our chat? I'll have to stay here and guard the luggage until my officers arrive to process it."

"Sure, Dad," Karla replied, then looked at Caitlin. "Didn't you mention something about a log where the crew records the names and times for everyone who comes and goes from The Aquaholic?"

"The tender logs." Caitlin nodded.

"I'm going to need those logs, please," Dean said.

"Of course," Caitlin replied and gave the deckhand a curt nod.

Dean fidgeted, shifted his weight, and stared at the luggage like it was taunting him.

Karla could sense his frustration about having to wait to open the bags until his officers arrived, and they could examine the evidence methodically, following protocols.

"Here you go, Chief Sheridan." The deckhand handed a black notebook to Dean.

"This is it?" he asked. "Everything on this yacht is state of the art. I was expecting the logs to be online or something."

"We're kind of old school in some ways," Caitlin explained.

"It's for both tenders," the deckhand explained. "Each tender used to have its own log, but one of them was full, and no one replaced it, so now we record everything for both tenders in one book."

Dean opened the notebook and flipped to the last few pages. Karla stood next to him, scanning the logs of departures and arrivals.

"There are missing entries," Karla exclaimed.

"I think you'll find these logs are accurate and up-to-date," Caitlin disputed. "Damien is a stickler for accurate record keeping."

"According to The Posers, Captain Peterson has visited Déjà Brew three times in the past three days," Karla said, pointing to the entries for the past two days.

"That's right," Caitlin agreed. "I went with him. We really like that little coffee place in town."

"Those trips aren't recorded here," Karla said.

"Are you sure?" Confusion clouded Caitlin's face as she sidled up to Dean's other side and scanned the open notebook over his arm. "You're right. My trips ashore aren't logged at all." She reached around Dean's large arm and flipped back a few pages. "No one has logged my arrivals or departures for weeks." She gave the deckhand an accusatory scowl.

"We aren't as diligent with the tender logs as we used to be," admitted the deckhand. "Most of us forget to fill them in." He shrugged. "It's mostly just family and crew members coming and going from the yacht. We try to be sure and log outsiders who visit, but aside from that, we've gotten pretty lazy with the logs."

"They're useless," Dean declared, shutting the notebook.

"Anyone could have snuck aboard." Caitlin pointed out.

"Not with all the cameras that are mounted to the outside of the ship," Dean reminded her. "We've analyzed the security footage from the outside cameras, and no unknown boats or people approached the yacht around the time of the murder."

"Are you suggesting one of us is the killer?" Caitlin asked, wide eyed.

Had Caitlin seriously not considered the possibility that the killer could be someone who worked and lived aboard the yacht? Or was this her attempt to make Dean believe she was too naïve to commit murder?

"The killer is not aboard this ship," Damien's elongated southern drawl arrived two steps before he did. "I trust everyone who lives and works on The Aquaholic. Most of them have been loyal employees for many years. They're like family." He brought the stub of his cigar to his mouth and took a long pull.

"That's right," Caitlin said, positioning herself next to her boss. "On top of that, we employ the services of a *very* expensive security company. They do *very* thorough and *very* frequent background checks on all the crew and staff."

"How thorough?" Dean asked.

"*Very*," Caitlin reiterated.

Dean shot Karla a knowing look, then said to Caitlin, "I'd like to read their most recent report."

"Of course," Caitlin said. "I can email it to you next time I'm near my computer."

"Mr. Casey, remind me again where you were yesterday before you met with Karla on the upper deck?" Dean asked.

"I was in my office." He turned his head slightly to the right and made side-eye contact with Dean. "I was discussing wedding details and seating arrangements with my daughter. It's all she wants to talk about these days." He chuckled and brought the cigar stump to his mouth. "I swear I've told your officers this a hundred times already. This is why I'm skeptical that your little police department has what it takes to handle the demands of a wedding as big as Saskia's." He puffed the cigar again.

Karla gave Dean a discreet headshake.

"I don't believe you," Dean challenged.

"Excuse me?" Damien straightened his spine and puffed out his chest. "Why on earth not?"

"First, your daughter's fiance, Ben, also claims he was with her all morning. But in her statement, Saskia claims she was alone in her cabin yesterday morning while you were at work, and Ben was at the onboard gym."

Who was lying, Damien, Ben, or Saskia? Are Damien and Ben lying to give Saskia an alibi? Ben said that he and Damien have a common interest in always protecting her.

"*Pshaw.*" Damien dismissed the evidence. "Saskia is easily confused, Chief. Yesterday was rather traumatic for her. I'm sure you understand how she might have mixed things up in her mind."

"Second, Karla doesn't believe you, and if she says you're lying, you're lying."

"Karla?" Damien pivoted his body and glared at her. "Please explain."

"You do this when you lie," Karla said, turning her

head slightly to the right and giving Damien the side-eye.

"Poppycock," he said with a nervous chuckle. "That's not evidence. That's nonsense." He huffed and held out his finished cigar butt. The deckhand hurried over to take it from him.

"Prove it," Caitlin challenged with her hands on her hips and one arched brow. "What do I do when I lie?"

"You exaggerate the word *very* when you lie," Karla continued, proving her point. "In fact, you hardly use the word *very* at all, except when you lie."

Damien gave Caitlin a scrutinizing stare, nodding. "Now that you mention it, you're right about Caitlin." He narrowed his gaze and changed his focus to Karla. "How did you figure that out?"

"Karla's a human lie detector," Dean explained, but it sounded more like a brag. "I've never known her to be wrong."

"I might not have been wrong about whether someone is lying," Karla clarified, "but I can't determine everyone's Tell. So sometimes, I can't say for sure that they're lying. I might have a hunch that someone is lying, but unless I can figure out their Tell, I don't have a specific behaviour to support my hunch."

"How?" Damien asked again, laser-focussed on Karla. "I need to understand *how*."

"The short version is, I have a knack for noticing people's *very* small micro expressions and patterns." She added the *very* on purpose, hoping it might lighten the mood. It didn't. In fact, it seemed to irritate Caitlin, who rolled her eyes at the reference. "I also have the ability to recognize patterns quickly and isolate behaviours that don't match someone's established patterns."

"Dr. Mayhew suspects that Karla's special gift is a byproduct of her ADHD and SPS."

"Dad!" Karla hissed under her breath so he'd stop discussing her neurodivergence.

"Sorry," Dean mouthed to his daughter.

"Fascinating." Damien put his arm around Karla's shoulder. "Tell me more," he urged, guiding her away from the tenders and deeper into the yacht.

"Damien!" Caitlin called, jogging after them. "The senator is waiting for your response to his email. We need to go over the reply I drafted."

"The senator will have to wait, Caitlin," he said over his shoulder. "This is more important."

CHAPTER 14

IF LOOKS COULD KILL

As they walked, Karla told Damien about Rob's theory that Karla's ADHD, combined with her suspected Sensory Processing Sensitivity made her hyperaware of even the smallest stimuli, and how she could process it in a short amount of time.

"Basically, my brain is like a super-fast computer with a tiny memory," she said with a half laugh.

"Are there lots of people like you?" Damien asked, leading them to the upper deck where they had met for iced tea the previous afternoon.

"I don't know," Karla replied. "I've never met anyone else who can detect lies, but it's not something I usually talk about."

"So, your special skill is a secret?"

"Not exactly," Karla replied. "I just don't disclose it to everyone I meet. It seems to make people uncomfortable."

"I'm not uncomfortable," Damien assured her with a sly grin. "In fact, I'm quite intrigued."

He pulled the unlit backup cigar from his shirt pocket and slid it under his nose, inhaling its aroma, then slipped it back into his pocket.

Damien might not have been uncomfortable, but Caitlin sure was, judging by the way she kept shifting her weight, gnawing on her upper lip, and tapping her toe at least a hundred times per minute.

"I'm glad." Karla smiled. "By the way, my dad is going to want to look at the footage from the security camera outside your office."

The table was set for supper. Damien pulled out Karla's chair. She sat down, and he gently pushed her toward the table.

"No problem," Damien agreed, then looked at Caitlin. "Make sure Chief Sheridan has full access to whatever he needs to aid in his investigation."

Damien's demeanor had changed. He was calmer than usual, intensely focussed on Karla, and his voice was slower with an almost singsong quality. He wanted something from her.

"Yes, Damien." Caitlin didn't look up from her planner when she answered him.

Damien sat across from Karla and Caitlin sat next to him. The deckhand took their drink orders.

"I want you to come and work for me, Karla," Damien said out of nowhere, with the nonchalance of someone commenting on the weather.

"What?!" Karla and Caitlin blurted in stereo.

"You can't be serious, Damien." Caitlin's gaze shifted furiously back and forth between Karla and Damien.

"As serious as a heart attack."

The corner of Damien's mouth twitched into a crooked grin, and he maintained intense eye contact with Karla in a way that made her feel vulnerable and small.

She resisted the urge to cross her arms in front of her chest and draw back in retreat. Instead, swallowing hard, she took in a deep breath, pulled herself to her full seated height, and met Damien's stare with her own.

"Damien, I'm flattered—"

"Karla already has a job," Caitlin blurted, interrupting Karla's response. "She runs a successful concierge business."

"I'll pay you more than you earn now, and you won't have to deal with any of the hassles and demands that come with entrepreneurship," Damien cooed, ignoring Caitlin's protest.

"Uh—"

"Her family is here," Caitlin insisted, interrupting Karla's attempt to object on her own behalf. "And Bellcroft." Caitlin let out a frantic huff. "She has a dog for goodness' sake. Karla can't just abandon her life to work for you."

"Name your price," Damien offered, ignoring Caitlin's arguments against the idea. "I'll pay whatever you want. You'd live on The Aquaholic. You'll have a private cabin, and you can even bring that little dog of yours. The one Saskia can't stop talking about. What's his name? Armani?"

"Gucci," Karla said. "My dog's name is Gucci."

"I can hire people to help look after him. You and Gucci can travel the world and get paid handsomely for the privilege." Damien leaned forward and narrowed his gaze. "Someone with your unique skill set would be invaluable to me, Karla." He laced his hands together on the table in front of him. "You see, there's a lot of bullshitting in politics, pardon my language, and your unique skill set would give me, and my clients, a considerable tactical advantage. Do you understand what I'm saying?"

"I think I get the gist." Karla nodded.

"You would work exclusively for me. No one else," he clarified. "But working for me has its perks. You'd have the luxury of time. Enough time to do whatever you want. We'd work closely together, of course. You would have to accompany me to meetings and functions, but aside from that—"

"Perhaps we should table this discussion until after dinner." Caitlin slammed shut her planner and tucked it next to her on the chair. Her jaw was so tense, the muscles were twitching. "Saskia and Ben will be here any second, Damien, and you know how Saskia feels about you discussing business when she's trying to talk to you about the wedding."

As if on cue, Saskia and Ben arrived on the upper deck.

"I was hoping you'd bring Lynn and Gucci," Saskia said with an exaggerated pout.

Ben's body stiffened at the mention of Gucci. He scanned the deck for any sign of the spirited terrier.

"Gucci and Lynn couldn't make it, I'm afraid." Karla watched Ben's body return to its pre-Gucci relaxed state.

"She brought Chief Sheridan instead," Damien

teased. "They found the dead woman's missing luggage, and now our floating paradise is being turned into a crime scene. Again."

"Is that police dog here?" Ben asked, eyeing everyone suspiciously. "The big scary one that sniffs everything?"

"Not yet, but I'm sure he'll grace us with his presence soon," Damien replied, then brought his daughter and her fiancé up-to-date on the details of the recently discovered baggage.

As Damien finished updating Saskia and Ben, the deckhand delivered the salad course. A simple mix of locally grown seasonal ingredients including leafy greens, Cabot tomatoes, sweet onions, corn, cucumber, and radishes mixed with a honey Dijon vinaigrette dressing.

Glowering at Karla, Caitlin stabbed a piece of radish and tore it off the fork with her teeth.

If looks could kill... thought Karla. *Maybe Saskia was right about Caitlin preferring not to have other women around to compete for Damien's attention. What if Leila had been the centre of Damien's attention, and Caitlin killed her to make sure Leila could never upstage her again?*

The summer salad was a scrumptious prelude to the main course of porcini-crusted filet mignon on a bed of mashed garlic potatoes with a confetti of oven-roasted grape tomatoes, leeks, and shitake mushrooms drizzled with a port wine reduction sauce.

Saskia turned the conversation to her and Ben's upcoming wedding. Karla gratefully immersed herself in wedding talk as a distraction from Caitlin's onslaught of icy glares and her aggressive use of the steak knife and fork.

Saskia was telling Damien about her plan to host the bridal party and groomsmen at the manor house in the days leading up to the wedding when her phone chimed several times in a row.

"Excuse me," Saskia said to her dinner companions. "This might be the dress designer. I've been waiting for her to get back to me about designing wraps or shrugs for the bridesmaids' dresses. Something the girls can slip over their shoulders if they get chilly at the reception." Saskia set down her fork and picked up her cell phone. As she read the screen, her serene, relaxed expression morphed into one of fear and panic. "Oh no! The sponsors are getting cold feet!" she declared, scrolling faster. "They've heard rumours that Ben and I are involved in a police investigation into a mysterious death. Apparently, they can back out of our contract because of it. The magazine and TV show that bought the rights to cover the wedding are considering backing out too." She looked at Ben, her eyes wide with fear and confusion. "This is a disaster! What are we going to do?"

"It's OK, babe." Ben took Saskia's phone out of her hand and placed it face down on the table, then wrapped his hand around hers. "We don't need a bunch of sponsors and media coverage to get married," he reassured her. "The day is about us. The other stuff doesn't matter."

"Doesn't matter?" Saskia shouted, yanking her hand away from Ben's, her wide eyes brimming with unshed tears and horror. "What's the point of getting married if I can't share it with my followers?!" She grabbed the white linen napkin from her lap, slammed it onto her plate, and ran from the table in tears, disappearing down the stairs.

Ben motioned to follow her.

"Sit down, Son," Damien instructed.

Ben froze, half standing, half sitting.

"You know what she's like," Damien said. "If you chase after her, she'll just push herself further away. Give her time to calm down."

Ben paused, torn between his instincts and his future father-in-law. Upon choosing to heed Damien's advice, he returned his backside to his chair, pushed his plate away, and took a long sip of wine.

"Perhaps you should go after her, Damien," Caitlin suggested.

"Last time I chased after Saskia, she slammed her cabin door in my face and called me a name I will not repeat in polite company," Damien replied, cutting a piece of steak and bringing it to his mouth.

"Should I go?" Caitlin asked.

"You're the last person who should go," Damien counselled with his mouth full. "She's still mad at you for scheduling those meetings that prevented me from visiting Bellcroft with her today."

"Those meetings weren't my fault," Caitlin defended. "How was I supposed to know they'd be cancelled at the last minute?"

Saskia was right! She predicted those meetings would be mysteriously cancelled at the last minute, leaving Caitlin and Damien alone on the yacht. Did the meetings ever exist, or did Caitlin invent them as a ruse?

"Why don't I check on Saskia?" Karla offered, hoping to diffuse the tension. "When I first started Just Task Me! I planned quite a few weddings. I've had some experience calming down anxious brides." She smiled.

"Of course you have," Caitlin muttered, rolling her eyes. She pushed a piece of shitake mushroom around her plate with her fork, then stabbed it a few times for good measure.

"Are you sure you don't mind, Karla?" asked Damien. "I hate to draw you into our family drama."

"I'm happy to help," Karla replied, pushing herself away from the table.

CHAPTER 15

THE STINK EYE

KARLA FOUND Saskia on a smaller deck, one level below the upper deck she'd run away from.

"There you are," Karla declared. "I've been looking everywhere for you."

Saskia was on the floor, hugging her knees to her chest and resting her back against a large white deck box Karla assumed was for storing the lounge cushions when they weren't in use.

"May I join you?" Karla asked.

Saskia said nothing but shifted over to make room in her hiding spot for Karla.

They sat in silence, staring at the vast expanse of ocean and sky in front of them. Saskia occasionally sniffled and dabbed her tears with the hem of her cream-coloured linen tunic.

Karla handed her a stack of paper napkins she had picked up while hunting for the hiding social media star.

"You didn't have to come after me," Saskia finally said.

"It was me or Caitlin," Karla teased.

For a microsecond, amusement tugged at the corners of Saskia's mouth, and she almost smiled. "In that case, thank you for coming after me."

"No problem," Karla said.

"Why was Caitlin giving you the stink eye during dinner?" Saskia asked as she dabbed the corner of her eye with a napkin.

"You noticed?" Karla asked. "I wasn't sure if it was real or if I was imagining it."

"It was real." Saskia nodded. "I'm familiar with that stare." She let out a half chuckle. "I've been on the receiving end of Caitlin Lopez's stink eye more than once."

"Damien offered me a job," Karla revealed. "An opportunity to live on the yacht and work closely with him and his clients."

"Oooh, I wish I'd been there to see Caitlin's face when she heard that!"

"It was awkward," Karla said. "Neither of us was expecting it." She nudged Saskia's shoulder with her own. "You were right about Caitlin, by the way. She's possessive of Damien and doesn't like it when he pays attention to other women. You're very insightful."

"It doesn't take much insight when Caitlin makes her feelings for my dad so obvious." She nodded. "I think you'd like living and working here. My dad's world is pretty cool," she added. "You'd always live in the most luxurious accommodation. You'd meet the world's most powerful people, and you'd never have to worry about paying a bill again. He and Caitlin take care of everything for everyone who works for him." Her face lit up like she had just had an epiphany. "You and I could hang out all the time. I spend a lot of time with my dad, so I'm here a lot." She hooked her arm through Karla's. "I'd have to convince Ben to get therapy for his fear of dogs, but it would be fun to have you and Gucci around. We could be like sisters." For the first time since Karla had found her, Saskia smiled.

"I have a sister," Karla reminded her.

"Right. Officer Max." Saskia nodded. "And Chief Sheridan is your dad, right?"

Karla nodded. "Lynn is my mother, Dr. Rob is my best friend, and Harry is my surrogate uncle. Bellbrook has a pretty tight hold on me."

"I get it," Saskia said. "If Lynn was my mother, I wouldn't want to leave either. When we were taking pictures at Bellcroft earlier, she lectured me about not using enough sunscreen. And between shots, she chased us around the beach with bottles of water, reminding us to stay hydrated."

"Lynn means well, but she can be a little overbearing," Karla said. "I'm sorry if she crossed a line."

"Not at all!" Saskia insisted. "I loved it! It felt nurturing, you know?" She fidgeted with the balled-up napkin in her hand. "I'm not used to maternal attention."

"Me neither," Karla said quietly. "Until recently, Lynn and I hardly knew each other. We'd only seen each other a handful of times until last year when we both came back to Bellbrook for my grandmother's funeral. Lynn left town when I was a baby. She travelled the world while my grandmother raised me."

"Wow," Saskia sympathized. "I didn't realize we had so much in common. After the bathtub incident, I only saw my mother a couple of times a year, and those were chaperoned visits. I don't think she had any maternal instincts. I could've been sunburnt from head to toe and completely dehydrated, and my mother wouldn't even have noticed. The only people who ever cared about me were people my father hired. Nannies, tutors… even you. The only reason you're here is because my father retains your company's services."

"That's not true," Karla argued. "If I didn't want to plan your wedding, I wouldn't have agreed to. The reason I started my own business instead of working for someone else was so I would have complete control over who I work for and what jobs I accept. I'm here because I want to be. I like you, Ben, Damien"—she paused for effect— "and even Caitlin."

"I hope you accept my dad's job offer," Saskia said. "It would be nice to have someone around who likes me for me. Not because my dad is paying them or because I'm a B-list social media celebrity."

"Damien loves you for who you are. It's obvious every time he talks about you," Karla reminded her, "and Ben adores you."

"I know," Saskia admitted. "Ben is too good for me. He's so pure. It's only a matter of time before he realizes he can do better and leaves me."

"I doubt it," Karla reassured her. "Ben loves you so

much he doesn't care what kind of wedding you have as long as you get married."

"Aside from Ben, my followers are the most loyal, consistent people in my life. Their approval means everything to me. If I can't share our wedding with them, I may as well not invite anyone." She sighed. "If my sponsors back out, we may as well cancel the whole thing and just elope somewhere on the down-low."

"Is that what you want?" Karla asked, hoping the answer would be a resounding no. "Do you want to ditch the big wedding and elope with Ben somewhere private? I can make that happen."

"No," Saskia replied, much to Karla's relief. "I want the huge wedding I've always dreamed about. This wedding means everything to me."

"It means a lot to me too," Karla admitted. "This is Bellcroft's first big event in almost sixty years. Everyone in Bellbrook has a vested interest in Bellcroft succeeding."

Saskia shrugged. "I guess if my sponsors pull out because of this murder investigation, I could ask my dad to help foot the bill…"

"Let's not get ahead of ourselves," Karla said, cutting off Saskia midsentence. "When the police solve this murder, it will clear your name and Ben's. Your sponsors won't have any reason to pull their support."

"I wish I could help your dad and sister with their investigation," Saskia said. "I swear, Karla, I do not know who Leila was or why she was here."

"Is there any chance she was a Saskian?" Karla asked. "Or a jersey chaser?"

"I don't think so." Saskia shook her head. "I delay my social media posts," she explained. "It's a security measure to protect my privacy. I won't post any of the pictures we took in Bellbrook until after we leave. That way, the Saskians don't know where I am in real time."

"But yesterday you posted the selfie you took of us on the upper deck," Karla reminded her.

"It was a generic yacht photo with nothing but sea in the background. It could have been taken anywhere, anytime," Saskia reasoned. "Besides, that was right before we found the body. Leila was already dead. It's not like she recognized where I was because of that photo and snuck aboard."

"Everyone in town knows you're here, Saskia," Karla pointed out. "The Aquaholic doesn't exactly blend into its surroundings."

"Well then, I guess she could have been a Saskian," Saskia conceded. "But I didn't kill her. There's no way I would ever drown someone."

Does Saskia really believe that Leila drowned? Or is she going along with public opinion because saying otherwise would prove she was the killer?

"What about Ben?"

"He's a big, tall, powerful man," Saskia admitted. "But he's a gentle giant. He won't even swat a fly. He makes me do it. He closes his eyes during the gory scenes when we watch a movie. There's no way Ben could kill someone and lie to me about it."

"How did you know what Leila's body looked like?" Karla asked. "Damien and Ben said they kept you away from the scene.

"Who said I saw the body?" Saskia asked defensively, tilting her head.

"You did," Karla reminded her. "Earlier today at Bellcroft. You said Leila's death was nothing like finding your mother in the bathtub because the position of her body and outfit were different."

"Oh, yeah, I guess I did say that." Saskia squeezed her eyebrows together. "But I never saw Leila's body."

"Someone described it to you?"

Saskia nodded.

"Ben?"

Saskia nodded again.

"But Damien instructed everyone not to discuss it with you."

"Trust me, when it comes to Ben, I have more influence than my father," Saskia said.

Enough influence to convince him to kill for you?

"You really think you can save my dream wedding if the police find the killer?" Saskia asked, bringing the conversation back to her wedding.

"I promise to do everything in my power."

Karla asked Saskia to put her in touch with the sponsors and media companies.

Saskia texted her their contact details.

"Leave it with me," Karla said, hoping she sounded more confident than she was. "I'll help them see how valuable this publicity will be for them, and what a big mistake it would be if they backed out now."

"Thank you." Saskia gave Karla a small, closed-mouth smile and rose to her feet. "I feel much better."

"Are you ready to go back upstairs?" Karla asked as Saskia offered her a hand and pulled her to her feet.

"Right after I stop by my cabin and wash my face," Saskia replied. "I'll meet you up there?"

"Sounds good."

Saskia opened her arms, and Karla reciprocated. After a short, tight squeeze Saskia pulled away and asked, "You're not going to accept my dad's job offer, are you?"

"Probably not," Karla admitted. "I've only been back in Bellbrook since last year and didn't realize how much I missed it. I'm not ready to leave again."

"I wouldn't leave either if I were you," Saskia said as they walked toward the stairs. "Let me give you some advice. Don't tell my dad yet. When he hears the word *no* he takes it as a challenge."

Is it possible that Leila said no to Damien? Did he make her an offer, then kill her when she said no?

"He'll assume you're trying to negotiate a better deal," Saskia continued, interrupting Karla's internal dialogue. "My dad thinks everything and everyone is negotiable. He loves the chase, and his perseverance will drive you nuts. Tell him you're thinking about it, then don't tell him your answer until we're about to lift anchor and sail away. It'll be easier for you."

If I decline Damien's offer, could I end up like Leila?

CHAPTER 16

ALIBIS AND BOWLING ALLEYS

"LA-LA!" Max jogged down the hall to catch up. "Dad said you were here! How's dinner?"

"Probably cold by now," Karla replied. "But it was delicious until I left."

"Why did you leave?" Max asked.

Karla tugged Max's sleeve and led her to a quiet corner. Speaking in hushed tones, she told her sister about Damien's job offer, Caitlin's less than enthusiastic reaction, Saskia running away, her search for the missing social media star, and their conversation on the lower deck.

"You've been as busy as Dad and me," Max commented.

"What have you and Dad found out?"

"We went through the suitcase you found hidden on the boat."

"Tell me!" Karla whisper-yelled.

"We found Leila' purse. The killer crammed the brown leather satchel inside the suitcase."

"That's all of Leila's luggage accounted for, right?" Karla asked.

Max nodded. "We also found a burner phone with the same phone number Leila used to check into The Seascape Hotel," Max began. "It was only ever used to call and text one number."

"Whose?" Karla asked.

"We don't know." Max shook her head and rolled her eyes. "The number she was communicating with seems to be another burner phone. But their texts were pretty spicy." She wiggled her eyebrows. "No photos though. Just text messages."

"I bet she used that phone to communicate with her boyfriend," Karla hypothesized.

"That's what we think too," Max concurred. "Dad's getting the cyber cop to trace the burner phone. Hopefully he'll find out where and when she bought it."

"Did you find her ID?" Karla asked. "Did you find out where she lived? Can you contact her family?"

"That's the weird part," Max revealed. "The contents of Leila's satchel contained the usual stuff you'd expect. Portable phone charger, hand sanitizer, make-up, a couple of random pens, granola bars, and her wallet. But the wallet was empty. No driver's license, no credit cards, no bank cards. Nothing with Leila's name or photo. There was no ID in her suitcase either. But she must've had a passport because she told the hotel clerk she flew here."

"Do you think the killer kept her ID?" Karla asked. "Like a twisted trophy or something?"

"I don't know what to think," Max admitted. "But Dad says he might have to call in the feds."

"The feds?!"

"Shhh," Max hushed, looking over her shoulders to make sure they were still alone.

"Why the feds?"

"He suspects Leila might have been some kind of operative," Max revealed in a voice so quiet that Karla had to move her ear closer to her sister's mouth. "Damien Casey's political connections, Leila's missing ID, the lack of tags on her clothes, that she lied to access the yacht, and he thinks the spicy texts between Leila and her mystery boyfriend could be some kind of code."

"Code?"

"He thinks they could be instructions to Leila from her handler but disguised as intimate messages. Dad thinks it's possible that someone sent Leila here to spy on Damien, or worse."

"He suspects Leila came here to *kill Damien?*" Karla mouthed the last two words. "But that wouldn't make sense. Why would a covert operative travel with so much luggage? And don't people like that usually blend into their surroundings? Leila had tattoos, trendy hair, and fluorescent pink luggage." She shook her head. "No, I don't believe anyone sent Leila here to assassinate Damien."

"We can't rule it out," Max said. "Damien Casey has just as many political enemies as he does friends."

"If Dad calls in the feds, I'm screwed," Karla whispered, her heart pounding against her ribs like it was trying to escape. "You've heard him complain about how slow and inefficient federal investigators are. The feds will take forever to solve Leila's murder. Rumours that Saskia and Ben are involved in a murder investigation are already threatening the wedding. If the feds show up, it'll confirm the rumours." She squeezed Max's hand. "I need this wedding, Max. I've invested everything I have into renovating and restoring Bellcroft. Half the businesses in town are relying on me to make it a successful event venue again. Saskia's wedding will either make or break me."

"I don't want the feds sniffing around either," Max admitted. "Dad says they'd only help. Act as consultants. But we all know they'll use their authority to take over the case. I'll talk to Dad and try to stall him," she offered. "I'll tell him you're still talking to the witnesses and getting new information and remind him that if he calls in the feds to 'help'"—she put air quotes around *help*—"they won't let you, a civilian, anywhere near the investigation, and we'll lose your insight."

"I should get back to the upper deck," Karla said, checking the time on her phone. "The others will wonder where I got to."

"One more thing," Max said in her normal voice before going back into whisper mode, "we reviewed the footage from the cameras outside Damien and Caitlin's offices. Saskia never entered Damien's office yesterday. Damien lied. He wasn't in his office all morning, either. He left with plenty of time to kill Leila. Same for Caitlin. She was alone in her office for a brief time before she went into town, but after she returned to the yacht with Leila, she never went back to her office. Since there are no other cameras covering the inside of the yacht..."

"No one has an alibi," Karla said, finishing Max's sentence. "Saskia admits she was alone in her cabin, Ben and Damien both lied about being with her, and Caitlin lied about being in her office." Karla sighed and dropped her shoulders in defeat. "Any of them could be the killer."

"Or all of them," Max pointed out. "Or some of them. We can't rule out anyone who was on the yacht from the time Leila arrived until you found her floating in the tub."

"I'll text you and Dad if I discover anything else," Karla said.

"Me too," Max agreed. "I'm going to interview the crew again tonight. Maybe you could observe the interviews and let me know if you pick up on any lies?"

"Of course," Karla said. "I'll do anything to help solve this mystery and get Saskia's wedding back on track."

They agreed Max would text Karla when she was ready to begin the second round of interviews.

"THERE YOU ARE!"

Karla was about to climb the stairs to the upper deck when Damien approached her from behind.

"Here I am." She smiled.

"We thought you got lost," he said in his slow, southern cadence.

"I'm not lost," Karla assured him. "Just distracted. I ran into my sister after I spoke with Saskia."

"We thought maybe you were giving yourself a tour of your future home," Damien retorted with a grin. "I'd be happy to show you around The Aquaholic. Wait till you see our media room and on-board gym. We even have a bowling alley—"

"I appreciate the generous offer, Damien," Karla said, interrupting his sales pitch, "but I'll need some time to think about it. I don't make life-changing decisions quickly."

"Of course," Damien responded. "Take all the time you need. If there's anything I can say or do to help you decide, let me know." His hand hovered so close to the small of Karla's back that she could feel heat radiate from it as he guided her away from the stairs. "How was your conversation with Saskia?" he asked quietly. "I've been worried about her non-stop since that dead woman turned up in the bathtub."

"She's coping," Karla replied, not wanting to breach Saskia's privacy by recounting their entire discussion. "Yesterday shook her up, but she seems more distressed about the sponsors' threats to back out of the wedding."

"She doesn't need sponsors," Damien declared with a muffled snort. "If they back out, I'll make sure Saskia still has the wedding of her dreams."

"She might not *need* sponsors, Damien, but she *wants* them. It's important to her."

"What can I do?" he asked. "How can I fix this for my daughter?"

Karla told Damien about her plan to reach out to

the sponsors and convince them to wait a while longer before abandoning Saskia and Ben's wedding. Then she told him about her plan to help the police solve the murder before Dean had to call in the feds to help.

"I agree with you and Max." Damien nodded. "The last thing we need is a bunch of federal agents sticking their noses where they don't belong. Using their authority to sniff around The Aquaholic and my business."

"That's why I've agreed to help them," Karla said. "Max is planning to re-interview the crew tonight. She asked me to observe and let her know if I detect any lies."

"Someone on this yacht must know more than they're letting on about Leila," Damien agreed. "Karla, you have my full support and permission to access anything you need to help solve this murder."

"Thank you, Damien," Karla said. "Since I'm needed here for the interviews, I've arranged for Lynn, my mother and assistant, to meet you at Bellcroft for the night tour. Saskia said she was fine with it. I made sure Gucci won't be there, so Ben can relax and enjoy the tour this time."

"That's fine with me," Damien said. "Let me know what else I can do to help move this investigation along."

"It would be helpful if you told the truth about where you were yesterday between leaving your office and greeting me on the upper deck."

"I told you that I was working in my office all morning." He did not tilt his head and look at Karla from the side of his face, but he adjusted the always-present unlit cigar in his shirt pocket. She wondered if he was consciously forcing himself to abandon his old Tell, now that it was public knowledge, and was unconsciously replacing it with a new one.

"Except you weren't," she challenged. "The police reviewed the footage from the camera outside your office. You left mid-morning and didn't return all day. You had plenty of time to kill Leila."

"I did not kill that woman," Damien protested. "I didn't kill anyone."

"Then tell the truth about where you were so the police can verify your alibi and eliminate you as a suspect. The more suspects they can eliminate, the faster they'll figure out who the killer is."

"Fine." Damien sucked in a long breath and blew it out. "I was at the gym for about an hour and a half. Usually, I go first thing in the morning, but yesterday a few early overseas calls disrupted my routine, so I went later. I use one of those interactive exercise bikes. It has a computer screen, and I can summon a live trainer whenever I want. The computer keeps track of my progress and workout statistics. The police will be able to verify that I was there and even speak to the trainer. After that, I had a shower in my cabin and ordered lunch from the kitchen. I had an open-faced chicken sandwich smothered in gravy. You can ask the chef. He took my order. You can also ask the deckhand who delivered it."

Without an exact timeline of his morning, it was impossible for Karla to determine whether Damien would have had the time to squeeze in a murder between the gym, his shower, and lunch. That would be a puzzle for Max and Dean to figure out.

"Why did you lie to the police?" Karla demanded.

"Because according to my daughter, whom I love dearly, her fiancé was in the gym all morning."

"Good!" Karla declared. "You and Ben can verify each other's alibis."

"Except we can't."

After a moment of confusion, Karla realized what Damien wasn't saying.

"Ben wasn't at the gym, was he?"

Damien shook his head.

If Ben wasn't with Saskia, and he wasn't at the gym when Leila was murdered, where was he?

CHAPTER 17

HERE, THERE, AND EVERYWHERE

"IF I ADMIT I was at the gym but didn't see Ben there, it will essentially point the finger of suspicion at my future son-in-law and break my daughter's heart at the same time." Damien shook his head. "I will not break my daughter's heart, Karla."

"Would you rather she married a potential murderer?" Karla whispered.

"Ben Underwood is not a murderer." Damien laughed at the notion. "He doesn't have the gumption."

"What does that mean?" Karla asked, frustrated that Damien wasn't taking Ben's status as a murder suspect seriously.

"Ben isn't capable of murder." Damien chuckled. "A few weeks ago, he refused to get out of the car because there was a puppy on the sidewalk. Twenty feet away. It was on a leash." He shook his head. "That boy sat in the car for fifteen minutes, shaking like a shirt in a hurricane until the puppy's owner moved along. It was a small dog, Karla." Damien pinched his thumb and index finger together until there was just a sliver of space between them. "Tiny."

"Do you like Ben?" Karla asked, crossing her hands in front of her chest and locking eyes with her client. "Do you want him and Saskia to get married?"

Damien reached for his unlit cigar, twirled it in his pocket twice, then stopped.

Was he about to lie but chose to tell the truth instead?

"Ben wouldn't have been my first choice for Saskia," Damien admitted. "In my opinion, she needs a strong partner. Someone with enough fortitude to challenge her impulsivity and not give in to every single demand she makes."

It was not lost on Karla that Damien was guilty of the same traits he found lacking in Ben. As far as Karla could tell, Damien didn't challenge his daughter's spontaneous tendencies and gave her whatever she wanted, whenever she wanted it.

"Ben might not be my first choice for son-in-law," Damien continued, "but Saskia loves him, so I've welcomed him into the family with open arms." He pulled the unlit cigar from his shirt pocket and slid it under his nose, sniffing it. "If Ben Underwood is a murderer, I'll eat my cigar." He clenched the stogie between his teeth as he grinned.

"Well, isn't this cozy?" Caitlin's voice oozed sarcasm. "We were wondering where you two had disappeared to." She closed the distance between them and scanned Karla and Damien from head to toe, then back again. "We're waiting for you so we can have dessert. Chef made bruléed cardamom cheesecake topped with pistachio bark and candied kiwi slices."

"Sounds wonderful," Damien said, rubbing his tummy. "We should head upstairs and enjoy it."

Karla's phone dinged. "I have to run," she said, checking the screen.

MAX:

About to interview the crew. Meet me
on the quarterdeck.

"What a shame," Caitlin said with less sincerity than a wet rag. "We'll be sure to save you a piece." She plastered a fake smile on her face.

Karla replied to Max's text with a thumbs-up emoji and slid the phone into her pocket.

"Go!" Damien encouraged. "The faster we solve this, the better."

"I MIGHT BE the captain of this ship, but I'm not the boss," Captain Peterson claimed in his Aussie accent. "I work for Mr. Casey. He signs my very generous pay cheque, and in exchange, I do what he says."

"Were you aware that certain security protocols, like the tender logs, were not strictly adhered to?" Max asked, scribbling in her notebook.

"We've become more lax with the logs recently," he admitted.

"Was everyone lax? Or just certain crew members?"

"Whoever drives the tender logs arrivals and

departures," Captain Peterson explained. "Since several of us take turns driving, I suppose it's fair to say that we've all been lax." He fiddled with his thick wedding band, slipping it up his finger, over his middle knuckle, spinning it, then sliding it back into place.

Karla found the shiny object distracting and had trouble focussing on the conversation when he fidgeted with it. *Stupid ADHD*, she thought. The ring was a fusion of deco and industrial design. It was wide, spanning the entire distance between Captain Peterson's bottom and middle knuckles. It was gold, and the hammered texture created dozens of tiny dimples that reflected the light.

"Is driving the tender a scheduled task?" Max continued her line of questioning. "Are crew members assigned specific days and times that they drive people to and from The Aquaholic?"

"No," Captain Peterson replied. "It's decided on an ad hoc basis. I assign whichever crew member is available when someone needs to be dropped off or picked up." He shrugged one shoulder. "If no one is available, I'll do it. Mr. Casey and Ben are both experienced boaters. It's not uncommon for them to drive themselves to shore and moor the boat until they drive it back."

There was a pause in the conversation while Max brought her notes up-to-date.

Captain Peterson waited, spinning his wedding ring and bouncing his knee.

"We're being more diligent with the logs now," he added, filling the silence. "Earlier today, I met with the crew and reiterated the importance of maintaining thorough records of everyone who boards and leaves The Aquaholic. It's important to me, and to Mr. Casey, that everyone on board feels safe."

"Did anyone tell you they felt unsafe?" Max asked, looking up from her notebook to meet Captain Peterson's gaze.

He shook his head.

"Do you feel unsafe?"

"I didn't," he said slowly, seeming to choose his words carefully. "But I admit, finding the dead woman in the guest cabin left me shaken." He shifted awkwardly in his seat and crossed his ankles, bringing an end to his knee bouncing. "I figured if I was anxious, then others probably are too."

More silence while Max made notes.

"Why are you here?" Captain Peterson asked, looking at Karla.

"She's helping us with our inquiries," Max replied on Karla's behalf without looking up from her notebook.

"I met your mother earlier," he said, smiling at Karla. "Lynn, I believe she's called?"

"That's right," Karla said, nodding. "She mentioned running into you outside Déjà Brew."

"The resemblance is remarkable," he commented. "I stopped her because I thought she was you. When I realized she wasn't, I asked her if she was your sister."

"They get that a lot," Max muttered.

"Lynn was really helpful," Captain Peterson continued. "I only wanted directions to a florist, but she insisted on taking the information and ordering the flowers for me." He smiled and unlocked his phone, tapping the screen a few times, then turning it toward Karla and holding it out so she could see it. "My wife received them about an hour ago. She loved them. Lynn did great. Be sure to thank her again for me, will you?"

"Of course," Karla said. "It's a beautiful arrangement. I'm glad your wife liked them."

"It's not the same as being there in person, but at least she knows I'm thinking about her." He gave the photo one final, wistful smile, then locked his phone, and placed it on his lap.

"Does your job keep you away from home a lot?" Karla asked.

"For months at a time," Captain Peterson replied. "Sometimes I get quite homesick. I miss my wife, our dogs, and my garden. Gardening is a horrible choice of hobby when you spend most of the year in the middle of the ocean." He smiled and his gaze drifted away. "Mr. Casey is great, though. He pays to fly her here, or he'll hire a freelance captain to fill in so I can go home for a visit. We'd love to see each other more often, but her career keeps her anchored to our hometown." His half-hearted smile told Karla that Captain Peterson missed his wife and wasn't thrilled with their separate living arrangements.

He slid his wedding band up and down his finger again.

"Your ring is lovely," Karla complimented. "I've never seen one like it. It's so unique."

"Thank you." Captain Peterson slipped off the ring and pinched it between his thumb and forefinger. "It was custom made. My wife and I designed it togeth-er." He performed an impressive steeplechase flourish, rolling the metal band across the backs of his tanned fingers from his index to his pinky, and back again. "I never take it off. Ever." He let out a half laugh. "Except when I fidget with it. But it's always with me."

Karla couldn't take her eyes off the thing but also couldn't figure out why she was so mesmerized by it.

"Mr. Casey is a great employer. He takes great care of his employees," Captain Peterson continued, pointing his chin at Karla. "I hear you might join us on board permanently."

"Where did you hear that?" Karla asked. "I only found out a couple of hours ago."

"Caitlin mentioned it when she came up here earlier to schedule a tender to take Mr. Casey, her, Saskia, and Ben ashore to tour the wedding venue after dinner this evening."

"Damien sounds like a generous employer," Karla said, steering the conversation back to Captain Peter-son's employer. "You're the second person who has mentioned that he often pays to fly family and friends to visit. No matter where you are in the world."

"Who else mentioned it?" he asked.

"Caitlin was telling us yesterday that Damien flies her sister, niece, and nephew to visit the yacht," Max replied.

"Not only that," Karla added, "but he helps look after the kids so Caitlin and her sister can spend time together."

"He used to," Captain Peterson responded. "Damien used to fly them out quite often, but it's been at least two years since Caitlin's had an onboard visit from anyone."

More proof that Caitlin lied about her relationship with her sister. But why? Was she trying to make Damien look good? To make it seem like such a generous employer couldn't possibly be a murderer? That someone who entertains kids so their employees can have a break would never kill someone?

"Who do you think killed Leila?" Max asked out of nowhere.

"Not anyone aboard The Aquaholic," replied the captain without hesitation. "If Leila could sneak aboard the vessel, someone else could too."

"Where were you yesterday between returning to The Aquaholic from your morning coffee run and discovering Leila's body?" Max asked, her gaze boring into the captain.

"I was here, there, and everywhere." Captain Peterson gestured vaguely around him. "I spent most of my time on the quarterdeck. But I also met with the chef briefly, spoke with a few crew members, ran into Mr. Casey and spent a few minutes discussing logistics." He shook his head. "I keep telling Mr. Casey that we need onboard surveillance cameras. Not in the private areas, but in the communal areas. If he'd listened to me and installed them, I'd be able to prove where everyone was, wouldn't I?"

Karla and Max couldn't argue with that logic.

"Did Mr. Casey explain why he's hesitant to install surveillance cameras?"

"He's fussy about his privacy, and he worries his adversaries could hack into them." Captain Peterson replied. "He swears it's not because he has anything to hide."

If he has nothing to hide, why was Damien so against installing cameras for his and his family's safety?

CHAPTER 18

THE BARKING LOT

TWO DAYS after the murder

"An extra large?" Karla's eyes lit up at the sight of the huge to-go cup with the Déjà Brew logo emblazoned on the side. "Either you're an angel in lilac scrubs, or you somehow knew I didn't sleep last night." She smiled.

"The extra-large is my way of apologizing," Rob said, handing Karla the vanilla cold brew of iced coffee. "I'm sorry I didn't phone you yesterday after the autopsy. When Leila died, I had to switch from family-physician-mode to coroner-mode and reschedule a bunch of patients. I tried to see as many of them as I could yesterday after I finished the autopsy. By the time I got home, it was late, and I was exhausted. Then I video-called Josie at her dad's house to talk about her day and say goodnight. After that, I fell asleep until an hour ago."

"You have nothing to apologize for," Karla insisted, cracking the lid on her coffee and savouring the caffeinated aroma. "Bellbrook is lucky to have such a dedicated doctor. Josie is lucky to have such an awesome mother, and I'm lucky to have such an amazing best friend."

"Where's Gucci?" Rob asked, using her hand as an impromptu visor to block the early morning sun as she scanned The Barking Lot, Bellbrook's dog park, for the fast terrier. "There he is!" Her finger followed the speedy pup as he zoomed past them in pursuit of a black and white border collie.

They stood in comfortable silence, watching the border collie's owner throw a frisbee. The border collie took off in pursuit of the flying disc, and Gucci took off in pursuit of the border collie.

"This will tire him out," Rob said, smiling at the rushing dogs.

"Nothing tires him out. He's made of perpetual energy," Karla responded, then savoured the refreshing first mouthful of caffeine as it coated her throat and stomach.

They wandered to the fenced perimeter of the dog park.

"So… why didn't you sleep last night?" Rob asked, examining Karla's face with that I'm-a-trained-medical-professional look in her eyes.

"Couldn't stop thinking about Leila's murder," Karla admitted. "We have a ship full of suspects and can't eliminate any of them." She sipped her iced coffee. "On the upside, Saskia's wedding sponsors have agreed to give the police forty-eight hours to solve the murder and clear Saskia and Ben's names. After that, they're pulling their sponsorships."

"So, you have a forty-eight-hour deadline to save the biggest wedding in Bellbrook history," Rob paraphrased.

Karla nodded.

"If anyone can do it, you, Max, and Dean can."

"I wish I had your confidence," Karla commented between sips.

"I have enough confidence for both of us," Rob said as they sat on a nearby bench shaded by an old maple tree. "I also have a theory about how Leila died. She did not die by drowning." Rob leaned in and lowered her voice. "She was already dead when the killer submerged her in water. And I found more fibres in her throat and lungs. The fibres matched one of the pillows on the bed. Combine that with the hairs we found on the bed that matched Leila's hair, and in my opinion, Leila's killer smothered her on the bed."

"So, we're looking for someone strong enough to move her from the bed to the bathtub," Karla surmised.

"Leila was a petite woman," Rob added. "It wouldn't have been too difficult for most adults to move her such a short distance. I can't tell if the killer carried or dragged her from the bed to the tub. But Dean and Max think the killer was inside the cabin for quite a while. If the killer had enough time to move the body and remove some of her luggage, they would've had enough time to drag her to the bathtub."

"I think the killer put Leila in the empty tub, then filled it with water," Karla theorized. "There was a small puddle of water near the tub when we found her." She recalled how the sunlight streaming through the window had made the wet floor glisten. "But not as much water as you'd expect from dropping a hundred pounds of dead weight into a partially filled tub."

"That makes sense. Also, the killer probably would have been soaking wet if they'd placed the body in a full tub of water. It would have been harder for them to move around the yacht undetected if they were drenched," Rob agreed, pulling her foot onto the bench and turning her body to face Karla. "It could've happened like this"—she handed her coffee to Karla—"Leila and the killer had an altercation. The killer pushed her onto the bed and suffocated her with a pillow." Rob held her hands in front of her like she was smothering an invisible person with an invisible cushion. Her long, ginger ponytail shook as she applied pressure to the pretend pillow. "When the killer realized Leila was dead, they panicked. For whatever reason, possibly believing that the bath water would wash away evidence of the crime and create the illusion that Leila's death was accidental, the killer carried or dragged Leila to the bathtub, plugged the drain, and turned on the water."

"I see where you're going," Karla said, nodding. "While the tub filled with water, the killer tidied the bed and the cabin to conceal evidence of their struggle, went through Leila's stuff, and removed her ID to slow down the investigation... or because they're psychologically twisted and wanted a souvenir."

"By the time the killer returned to the tub to turn

off the water, it was starting to overflow and some of it had sloshed onto the floor," Rob added.

"The killer turned off the water, closed the washroom door, and left the cabin with one of Leila's suitcases after cramming her purse inside," Karla continued. "Somehow, they transferred the luggage from the cabin where Leila died to the boat tender." She bit her lip, deep in thought. "There are lots of maintenance carts and food carts on the yacht," she continued. "The killer could have used a cart to move the luggage and covered it with a blanket or something."

"They probably would have moved the other suitcase too, and disposed of all the luggage, except you found the body and called the police before they had a chance," Rob concluded.

"Where's Leila's ID?" Karla wondered aloud. "It wasn't on the yacht or with the rest of Leila's belongings."

"The police missed the suitcase and purse the first time they searched," Rob reminded her, then sipped her coffee. "Maybe they missed her ID, too. The killer seems to know the ship well. They knew how to get the luggage from the cabin to the tender without raising suspicion and had access to everything they needed to attempt to conceal their crime." She looked at Karla. "It was the perfect way to hide the missing luggage," Rob said. "The tender was so busy ferrying police and investigative equipment back and forth that it was never searched. Police officers literally sat on the missing luggage while complaining they couldn't find it." She shook her head. "I bet the killer laughed the entire time."

"You're right. Leila's killer hid her luggage in plain sight. A brazen move by the murderer," Karla agreed. "Everyone would have assumed the tender was searched and cleared since the police were using it." She swirled the remaining coffee in her cup.

"Do we think the killer did it on purpose?" Rob asked. "Did they make sure the police took the yacht tender with the luggage so it would have a better chance of being overlooked during the search?"

"But it was Damien who insisted on giving the police full access to the yacht tender to help with the investigation. Dad and Max were impressed with how generous and cooperative Damien was." Karla froze. "But if your theory is right, that would mean Damien hid the luggage, which would mean Damien killed Leila." Her throat tightened, and something curdled in her stomach.

Rob said nothing, raising her eyebrows and gulping the rest of her iced coffee.

CHAPTER 19

CYNOPHOBIA

"Ooh, look at that gorgeous set of wheels," Rob said as they left The Barking Lot and made their way toward Rob's car. "It's my dream car, and it's even my favourite colour." She gestured to the royal-blue Maserati in the parking lot outside the dog park.

Karla was crouched down, holding Gucci's portable water bottle while he took a drink. She looked over at the blue sports car just as someone with a distinct, trendy frohawk slid down the driver's seat until their head disappeared below the steering wheel.

"I think that's Ben Underwood," Karla said, squinting at the luxury car.

"The same Ben who's engaged to Saskia?" Rob asked. "I haven't met him."

"He's a nice guy, but his alibi is so fishy it should come with a side of chips and tartar sauce." Karla explained how Damien disproved Ben's alibi by admitting he had been at the gym the morning Leila was killed but didn't see Ben there.

"Did anyone on the yacht tell the truth about their alibi?" Rob asked.

"Why is Ben here, and where did he get a car?" Oblivious to Rob's question, Karla tugged Gucci's leash and changed direction, walking toward the Maserati. "The Barking Lot is a strange destination for someone who's terrified of dogs," she mumbled to herself.

"Why is he hiding from us?" Rob asked, jogging to catch up to her determined friend and dog. "He slid down as soon as we saw each other."

"He might not be hiding from *us*," Karla explained, coming to a stop a few spots away from the shiny blue sports car. "I think he's hiding from Gucci. Ben is terrified of dogs. He might've panicked when he saw Gucci getting closer."

"Gucci's small, and he's on a leash," Rob pointed out, skeptical. "Ben is inside a car. Gucci can't get to him."

"I know, but phobias aren't always logical." Karla extended her hand with the leash handle toward Rob. "Would you mind? Ben might not talk to me or even roll down the window if Gooch is nearby."

"Sure," Rob said, shrugging and taking the leash. "I have to get to work. I'll drop Gucci off at your place on the way."

"Thanks," Karla smiled. As Rob walked away, she shouted, "Gucci and I appreciate it. Oh, don't forget—"

"I know," Rob called back. "Fill his bowl with fresh water and three ice cubes."

"Thank you!" Karla waved, smiling.

Karla waited until Rob and Gucci were inside her car and out of sight. Then she approached the blue car and rapped her knuckles on the driver's side window.

Ben slid up into a seated position. He strained his neck, pressed his nose against the window, and searched the pavement around Karla's feet.

"He's. Not. Here," Karla emphasized each word so Ben could read her lips. "Gucci's not here," she said, shaking her head and waving her hands in a cancellation gesture, hoping he'd understand.

Ben inched the window open. "Where is he?" His voice was cautious.

"My friend took him home," Karla replied.

Ben opened the window the rest of the way.

"Nice car," Karla commented.

"Thanks." Ben stroked the top of the steering wheel. "It's a rental. Caitlin arranged it."

"What brings you to the dog park, Ben? Are you lost?"

"No," Ben replied, then sucked in a long breath. "I'm here on purpose." He exhaled slowly, closing his eyes and counting to four under his breath, then took in another big lungful of air.

"Are you doing a breathing exercise?" Karla asked.

Ben nodded during his slow exhale and wiped his palms on the thighs of his navy-blue sports shorts.

"Are you OK?"

"I think so," he said with the same cautious voice he used to ask where Gucci was.

"Should I phone Saskia?"

"No!" Ben's voice was loud, and his eyes were

wide. "Please don't tell Saskia you saw me. She thinks I'm somewhere else."

"So, lying to your fiancé about your whereabouts is part of your normal routine?" Karla crossed her arms in front of her chest, tilted her head, and arched her brows.

"No, of course not," Ben retorted defensively. "Why would you think that?"

"Well, you lied to her about your whereabouts when Leila was killed, and you lied again today." She uncrossed her arms and forced her face and shoulders to relax. "What's going on Ben?"

"It's called exposure therapy," Ben replied. "It's part of my surprise wedding gift for Saskia. I'm getting help for my cynophobia."

"Sign-o-phobia?" Karla asked, trying out the new-to-her word.

"It means I have a phobia of dogs," Ben explained. "I'm getting help so I can surprise Saskia on our wedding day with a puppy. She's always wanted a dog."

"I see," Karla said. "And part of your exposure therapy is visiting the dog park?"

"Yes," Ben replied. "First, we—my therapist and I —talked about dogs. Then we looked at pictures of dogs. Next, we watched videos of dogs. Now, I'm observing them in person. Soon, I'll graduate to being in the presence of a leashed dog, and eventually, I should be able to handle myself around an unleashed one. My therapist says that exposing myself to dogs in a safe, controlled environment will help me break the patterns of fear and avoidance I've been relying on since I was little. She says each exposure will decrease my overall anxiety, and I'll get used to being around dogs."

"Wow, Ben." Karla brought her hand to her heart. "This might be the sweetest, most thoughtful gift ever. Saskia will be so touched and happy."

"I hope so," replied the former football player. "It would be awful if I spent months torturing myself for nothing."

"It won't be for nothing," Karla assured him. "Just yesterday, Saskia mentioned that she's always wanted a dog. You're going through so much to make her dream come true."

Surely someone this thoughtful and selfless couldn't be a murderer.

"It's hard." Ben's shoulders slumped, his frown weighing down his face. "I hope I can do it. It's the most difficult thing I've ever done. I don't want Saskia to find out because, if I fail at this exposure therapy thing, it'll devastate her."

"You're doing great," Karla reassured him. "Yesterday at Bellcroft, you got out of the car while Gucci was on a leash. You walked past him. That's huge. I heard that a few weeks ago you couldn't even get out of the car because there was a dog on the sidewalk. You've made significant progress."

"Yeah, that's what my therapist said too." He didn't sound convinced.

"Is this where you were the morning Leila was killed?" Karla asked. "Were you at the dog park practising your exposure therapy? This car is a real eye-catcher. Someone would have noticed if you were here. The police can verify—"

Ben shook his head. "I wasn't here," he said. "This is my first visit to the dog park. The morning Leila died I was on the yacht. I can prove it."

"How?"

"Get in and I'll show you." Ben unlocked the car and patted the black leather passenger seat.

Karla moved toward the passenger side of the car, then hesitated. With the utmost discretion, she used her phone to snap a pic of the Maserati's rear license plate and sent it to Rob with a quick text message.

Karla: Getting into this car with Ben. Also, I've shared my location with you, just in case.

With some of her anxious hesitation relieved, Karla continued around the car and climbed into the passenger seat.

"Where are we going?" she asked as Ben backed out of the parking spot.

"Do you want me to prove I didn't kill Leila?" he asked, narrowing his eyes on the road.

Answering a question with a question was Ben's Tell. He preferred to avoid lying by avoiding the question or changing the subject. Was he merely answering her question with a question, or was he avoiding lying to her because he didn't want her to know where he was taking her? What if this was a setup, and Ben's true motivation for visiting The Barking Lot was to lure Karla into this fancy car, so he could kill her and prevent her from exposing him as a murderer?

Did I just lock myself in a car with a killer?

CHAPTER 20

ANKLES ARE TRICKY

BEN PULLED into a parking spot at the marina.

The drive had been quiet. When Karla had tried to engage Ben in conversation, he muttered one-syllable responses and kept his stare laser-focussed on the road. He was exuding a level of intensity Karla had never sensed from him before, and it made her nervous.

"Are we going to The Aquaholic?" Karla asked, getting out of the low car. "Is someone coming to pick us up?"

To catch up to Ben, Karla jogged delicately in her sand-coloured, open-toe canvas wedge shoes. She stopped just short of the dock.

"Yes and no," Ben replied without breaking his stride toward the yacht tender. "Yes, we're going to The Aquaholic, and no, we aren't getting picked up." He was halfway down the dock already and moving like they were in a race. "I drove myself to shore. I'll drive us back."

"Oh," Karla said, hoping her voice wasn't as shaky as the rest of her. "OK."

Watching Ben approach the sleek speedboat, Karla recalled yesterday evening, when Captain Peterson mentioned that Damien and Ben sometimes drove the tenders themselves to get to and from the yacht. That meant it could have been Ben who hid Leila's luggage on the tender. Maybe he was planning to transport the rest of her luggage to the tender too, then drive himself out to sea, and dispose of it. But they thwarted his plan when they discovered Leila's body and called the police. What if that was his plan now? What if Ben was using his alibi to coax Karla onto the speedboat, so he could drive her out to sea and dispose of her? After all, it was Karla who had convinced Damien to admit that Ben had lied about his alibi. Maybe he planned to eliminate her before she found proof that he was Leila's killer.

"Are you coming?" Ben called from the boat.

"Be right there!" Karla smiled, terrified that if she got on the speedboat, she would never stand on Bell-brook's beautiful shore again.

Approaching the dock, and desperate to stall for time, Karla pretended to roll her ankle. She was careful to choreograph her fall in such a way that her above-the-knee, button-down, short-sleeved, chambray dress wouldn't expose anything it shouldn't.

"*Ooof.*" She landed on the pavement and let out a gasp loud enough to get Ben's attention.

"Are you OK?" Ben leapt off the boat and jogged down the dock toward her.

"I'm fine," Karla insisted. "I just need a minute."

She cradled her uninjured foot and made unnecessary wincing faces as she carefully rotated the unharmed ankle joint.

"Should I call your doctor friend?" Ben asked, his brows squeezed together with worry.

"No," Karla said. "Rob is busy with patients today."

What should I do? Think, Karla, think! I know. I'll call Lynn to pick me up. That way, I can avoid getting on the tender without accusing him of anything.

"Ankles are tricky. I know football players who lost their careers because of ankle injuries."

"Good thing I'm not a running back," Karla quipped, hoping her joke referenced the right sport.

"I'll help you up and drive you to the hospital." Ben crouched and steadied himself, preparing to lift Karla off the ground.

Getting back in the car with Ben didn't seem like a much better idea than getting on the yacht tender with him. She was about to protest—as politely as possible—and whip out her phone to call Lynn.

"Oh good! You're still here!" Caitlin Lopez strode toward them with wide, fast strides.

Karla had never been so happy to see her.

"I thought I'd missed you and would have to call for someone to pick me up." Caitlin looked down at Karla's contorted body on the ground. "What happened?"

"She twisted her ankle," Ben replied. "Since you can't drive the tender yourself, you'll have to call someone to pick you up, anyway. I'm going to drive Karla to the hospital."

Caitlin can't drive a speedboat? This would make her a less likely suspect, right? It wouldn't have made sense for her to hide Leila's luggage on the tender if she wasn't able to drive the tender somewhere to dispose of it.

"Oh no!" Either Caitlin's concern was genuine, or she was a better actor than Karla gave her credit for. "Let me help." She pressed her hands against her hips and assessed the situation. "I'll hold her ankle steady while you lift her."

Ben nodded.

"Wait!" Karla said, "I think I'm OK." She lifted her foot off the ground and rotated her ankle. "It's a bit stiff," she fibbed, staring at her shoe to avoid looking either of them in the eye, "but I don't think it's serious enough to warrant a trip to the hospital."

"Are you sure?" Ben asked. "Walking on an injured ankle can make it worse."

"I'm sure," Karla replied.

Ben extended his hand to help her off the ground.

She rose to her feet, keeping her weight on her "good" foot and straightening her dress and bag.

Ben offered his arm and suggested she try a couple of tentative steps.

Karla obliged, adding a subtle limp for effect.

"It already feels better," she insisted.

"Take it slow," Ben cautioned. "Rest and elevate as much as possible for the next few days."

"I will," Karla assured him.

"It doesn't appear to be swollen," Caitlin commented, bending to inspect the unscathed joint.

Caitlin looked different today. She had changed her look. Her short caramel bob was slicked back, she wore large hoop earrings, and her usually neutral makeup was more dramatic. She had a smokey eye and dark red lipstick. Instead of her usual power suit, she wore a teal one-piece, wide-legged jumpsuit with a suspender neckline, and a pair of brown Tory Burch sandals. Her toenails were painted a dark red that matched her lipstick.

"I was lucky. It could have been worse," Karla said. "It's possible I panicked and overreacted." She rolled her eyes and chuckled. "It's been ages since I've worn these shoes. These wedge heels are like walking on stilts."

"Why are you here?" Caitlin asked. "Are you visiting The Aquaholic because your dad is there?"

"My dad is on the yacht?"

Caitlin nodded.

This helped Karla relax. Caitlin's presence combined with the knowledge that Dean was nearby, and the realization that dozens of people milling around the marina have witnessed her with Ben—especially after making such a spectacle of herself with the fake fall—made her more comfortable with getting on the tender.

With Karla using Ben's arm for support, the trio walked slowly onto the deck and toward the speedboat.

By the time they reached the boat, Karla had abandoned her pretend limp, declared herself miraculously healed, thanked Ben and Caitlin for their concern and help, and apologized for making such a big deal out of a minor injury.

"Why is my dad on the yacht?" Karla asked as Ben steered the boat away from the dock.

"Chief Sheridan and a couple of his officers are confiscating Damien's favourite exercise bike," Caitlin explained. "Apparently, it's evidence. He and Damien were vague, but Damien gave Chief Sheridan permission to take the bike and seemed to understand why the police wanted it. I assumed you knew Chief Sheridan was there, and you were joining him."

"Actually, I asked Karla to accompany me back to the yacht," Ben said. "I need to show her something."

"Oh?" Caitlin's interest was piqued.

"She found out about our little secret." Ben smirked at Caitlin. "She's on to us."

"How did that happen?" Caitlin asked, miffed.

Karla tried to hide her panic as it occurred to her that Ben and Caitlin's secret could be that they killed Leila together.

"She found me at the dog park," Ben replied. "She was there with Gucci and her doctor friend."

Karla turned her head back and forth between Ben and Caitlin like she was watching a tennis match, following along as they talked about her like she wasn't there. *What secret? Someone tell me!*

"I hope you'll keep it to yourself," Caitlin said to Karla. "Ben's doing great, but if for some reason he doesn't progress enough to surprise Saskia with a puppy on their wedding day, she would be shattered."

"Of course," Karla said, relieved their shared secret was Ben's exposure therapy and not Leila's murder. "I wouldn't want to ruin the surprise. If Ben can prove that he couldn't have killed Leila, we can ask the police to keep his alibi under wraps."

"Caitlin helped find my therapist," Ben announced.

"Ben's making such good progress, and speaks so highly of his therapist, that I'm considering booking an appointment with her to discuss my own issues." Caitlin smiled.

Karla couldn't tell if Caitlin was joking and wondered what issues she might want to discuss with a professional therapist. Her relationship with her sister? Her limerence with Damien? *It's none of my business,* Karla reminded herself. *Anyway, she was probably kidding.*

"I love your jumpsuit," Karla said, shifting the foot she had elevated for appearance's sake so Caitlin could sit across from her.

"Thank you," Caitlin said, smiling and smoothing her wide pant leg. "I'm trying something different. Something a little more me." She nodded. "It's a nice change."

If she wasn't herself before, who was she?

They left the tender and boarded the yacht. Caitlin offered to accompany Ben for moral support. He thanked her and accepted her offer. Karla and Caitlin followed Ben to the same deck where Karla had found Saskia the previous evening after the social media maven had run from the dinner table in tears.

Ben led them to the same white deck box where Karla and Saskia had sat and talked less than twenty-four hours prior. Ben opened the large white box. Caitlin held the lid for him, even though the hinge locked in place when the box was open all the way. Ben rifled through the contents and came out with a black cinch bag. He closed the box, pulled open the cinch bag, and dumped its contents on the closed lid.

Karla watched as two stuffed dogs—a stuffed miniature schnauzer and a stuffed chocolate lab—a couple of picture books, a journal, and a pen tumbled onto the white box.

"What's this?" Karla asked, assuming it had something to do with Ben's exposure therapy, but not sure.

"This is where I was when that Leila woman was killed," Ben explained. "I told Saskia I was going to the gym, but I came here. I've been coming here three times per week to meet with my therapist."

"Online," Caitlin clarified. "Ben and his therapist have video appointments."

"I see," Karla said. She reached toward the objects on the deck box, then stopped herself. "May I?"

"Help yourself." Ben gestured toward the assortment of dog-themed items.

Karla picked up a book. "*Big Dogs, Little Dogs, A Visual Guide To Popular Breeds*," she read aloud, then leafed through the picture book. She put it down and picked up the other book, Pop-Up Puppies. She opened it to a random page and a cardboard Irish Setter rose from the thick pages. She turned the page and a Jack Russell Terrier popped up in the middle of the two-page spread.

"My therapist can confirm I was here," Ben said. "We spent two hours together." He unlocked his phone. "I can show you the video we watched. It was a video of a dog park." He turned his phone toward

Karla. "It helped prepare me for my trip to The Barking Lot today."

"I believe you," Karla said. "But you need to explain this to the police."

"They won't tell Saskia and spoil the surprise, will they?" he asked.

"I hope not," Karla replied. "They'll only mention it to her if they have no choice. The police aren't here to ruin your wedding gift to your future wife. They're here to solve a murder."

"Chief Sheridan is here," Caitlin reminded him. "You can use my office if you want to have a discreet word with him."

"Thanks, Caitlin." Ben smiled.

Karla texted Dean and asked him to meet them at Caitlin's office. She told him that Ben would like to clarify his alibi. Dean replied that he was on his way.

Rounding the corner to Caitlin's office, Karla's phone dinged.

"My car's ready," she announced. Ben and Caitlin looked at her, confused. "It's been in the shop for days," Karla explained. "It's finally ready, and I can stop relying on everyone I know to drive me around." She checked the time on her phone. "Ben, would you mind if I left to pick up my car? It'll take about an hour. The dealership is in Beaver Creek, the next town over."

"How will you get there without a car?" Caitlin asked.

"Lynn offered to take me," Karla replied.

"Why don't I take you?" Ben suggested. "The

rental car is still at the marina. It'll give me an excuse to drive the Maserati again. It's a nice ride."

"I think you should talk to Chief Sheridan while Saskia is occupied," Caitlin advised. "She's giving a podcast interview right now, but when she's finished, she'll want to know where you are."

"Good point," Ben agreed.

"Why don't I drive Karla to pick up her car," Caitlin suggested, narrowing her eyes on Karla with one corner of her mouth curling into a crooked grin. "It'll give us a chance to talk." She looked at Ben. "As long as you're comfortable meeting with Chief Sheridan on your own, of course."

"I'll be fine," Ben assured her, then fished the Maserati keys from his pocket and tossed them to Caitlin who caught them with ease.

"Road trip." Caitlin smirked at Karla, dangling the fob between her thumb and forefinger.

LEAD-FOOT LOPEZ

Caitlin drove carefully through town, but as soon as they hit the open road, she put the pedal to the metal, leaving Bellbrook, posted speed limits, and her instinct for self-preservation behind them in the rear-view mirror. *Lead-foot Lopez,* Karla mentally nicknamed her.

The windows were down, and the wind roared in Karla's ears. She could practically feel the tangles and knots forming as her wavy blonde hair swirled and billowed in all directions around her head. She was a stark contrast to Caitlin's serene smile, relaxed face, and perfectly smooth hair; the wind hardly touched Caitlin's slicked back bob.

Caitlin pressed a button, and the windows closed.

Karla's hair settled, and she did her best to detangle and smooth her windblown tresses with her fingers.

"I'm glad we have this chance to talk," Caitlin

began. "I have some questions about your ability to detect lies."

"What do you want to know?"

"How long have you been able to tell when I'm"—there was an awkward pause while Caitlin chose her words—"not completely truthful?"

"The past few days," Karla replied. "After Leila's murder." She looked at Caitlin. "I don't *want* to know your Tell, it's just something that happens sometimes. In fact, most of the time I try to ignore people's Tells. I'm sorry if it makes you uncomfortable." She sighed. "This is why I don't disclose it to many people."

"I was in shock at first," Caitlin admitted. "But I'm fine with it now. I'm trying *very* hard to kick the habit." Caitlin chuckled.

This was the first time Karla had heard Caitlin crack a joke. Her hair and makeup weren't the only things that were different about Damien's executive assistant today. *This is going better than I expected*, Karla thought to herself. *I won't bother telling Caitlin she'll probably develop new Tells to replace the one she's become aware of.*

They laughed together. Caitlin laughing at her own joke, and Karla laughing with relief that Caitlin wasn't angry at her for revealing her Tell in front of Damien, which in hindsight she regretted, even though Caitlin had challenged her to disclose it.

"Have you figured out everyone else's Tell?" Caitlin asked. "Can you detect when Saskia or Ben are lying? What are their Tells?"

Karla was neither shocked nor offended that Caitlin was curious about other people's Tells. She had often wondered what she would do if she couldn't detect lies and met someone who could. She figured she would ask them to tell her other people's Tells, and maybe even ask them to teach her how to do it.

"I can't detect everyone's lies," Karla explained, without answering the question. "But the more time I spend with someone, the more likely I'll figure out their Tells. Some people use multiple Tells, which makes their lies harder to detect, and some people don't have Tells. Either I can't figure them out, they're brutally honest, or because they don't experience any stress when they lie."

"Can you teach me how to do it?" Caitlin asked, closing in on the red pickup truck ahead of them.

"I don't think so," Karla replied, watching the pickup truck in front of them grow larger as they sped close enough for her to read the bumper sticker that said, *If you can read this, you're too close.* "Rob suspects it's a combination of neurological and central nervous responses that result from my ADHD and probable SPS." Karla gripped the grab handle and swallowed hard, hoping Caitlin realized how fast they were approaching the pickup truck in front of them.

"So, it's like a symptom?" Finally, Caitlin turned on the indicator, pressed her foot onto the gas pedal and swerved left at the last possible moment, narrowly avoiding the pickup truck before easing back in front of it.

"More or less," Karla agreed, watching the pickup truck get smaller and smaller in the passenger-side mirror. She let out a silent sigh of relief. "It's not a skill I've cultivated or taught myself."

"Well, you've fascinated Damien with your unique skill," Caitlin said, her jaw tensing as she spoke. "He's obsessed with you."

"He's obsessed with the skill," Karla corrected, "and how it could benefit him."

"Are you planning to accept his job offer?" Caitlin tightened her grip on the steering wheel until her knuckles were white, and Karla could discern the shape of the bones underneath her skin.

"No."

Caitlin loosened her death grip on the steering wheel, and her jaw relaxed.

"You're relieved," Karla said, easing the conversation toward a topic she knew was taboo.

"Yes." Caitlin gave Karla a sideways glance from behind her sunglasses. "I guess there's no point in lying to you since you'll probably know, anyway."

"Lying is the best way to help me figure out your Tells," Karla cautioned.

"So, you've probably figured out that, in the past, I've lied to you about a few things."

"Yes," Karla nodded. "Why did you lie to Max and me about your relationship with your sister and her kids?"

Caitlin sighed, and her shoulders slumped. "It's embarrassing," she admitted. "I allowed my career and my feelings for Damien to eclipse every other relationship in my life. I hardly ever saw my sister unless she came to visit me. Even then, I spent most of our time together working, talking about work, or distracted by work." Caitlin's voice grew thick with emotion as she spoke, then her voice hitched on the last two words. "I lost track of everything that was happening with the people I love. The last time I saw my niece and nephew, I couldn't remember what grades they were in or what activities they did outside of school. My sister's marriage fell apart, and I didn't even notice that she was heartbroken and struggling to cope."

She swiped her index finger under her eye behind her sunglasses and sniffled. "Our last conversation was a huge argument over the phone. My sister was fed up with our one-sided relationship. When she called me self-centred and told me I start every sentence with Damien's name, I hung up on her." Her voice was thick with regret and frustration. "I still can't believe I hung up on her. We haven't spoken or texted since."

"That's awful, Caitlin," Karla sympathized. "I hope you can mend your relationships with your family if that's what you want."

"I have lots of reasons for not wanting you to accept Damien's job offer, but the biggest one is that I would hate to watch someone else become so absorbed by Damien's world that they end up abandoning their life and their identity, like me."

"You feel you gave up your identity?" Karla asked.

"I gave up everything for him." Caitlin smacked the steering wheel, and the atmosphere in the car became tense. "I changed my hair, I changed the way I dress, I even changed the way I talk." She shook her head. "I did everything I could to become Damien's ideal woman. I paid attention to the women he dated and figured out what qualities attracted him. I studied them and transformed myself into his exact type." She shook her head and tears streamed down her cheeks from behind her sunglasses. "He should have noticed me. But he didn't, and I'm beginning to think he never will." She inhaled a sharp breath and pulled herself to her full seated height. "I'm tired of being invisible. I'm done. From now on I'm going back to me. The me *I'm* happy with. The *real* me."

"It must be exhausting pretending to be someone else," Karla commiserated. "You deserve someone who loves the real you. If this new look and new attitude are the real Caitlin Lopez, you're awesome. If Damien can't see that, it's his loss. There's someone out there who would love to be with the real you."

Karla believed every word she said to Caitlin, even if she didn't have enough personal experience with true love to back it up.

"Can I ask you a huge favour?" Caitlin asked. "Would you ask Damien how he feels about me? Now that he knows you can tell when he's lying, he'll be more likely to tell the truth. And if he lies, you'll know. I just need to know if I have any chance with him, or if I've spent the past twenty years wasting my time."

"I can't do that, Caitlin," Karla replied. "Damien is my client. It would be unprofessional."

"I understand." Caitlin nodded, but her disappointment was palpable.

"Maybe you should ask Damien yourself," Karla suggested. "Trust your instincts. You'll know if he's being honest."

"I've tried to have that conversation with him so many times but always chicken out," Caitlin revealed.

"I feel like it would open a door that could never close, you know?"

"I think so," Karla replied.

"Once I admit my feelings to him, I can't unsay it. Our working relationship would probably become awkward and unbearable. I'd probably want to leave, but leaving would mean giving up my job and my home." She sighed. "It's not like I have a life waiting for me outside of Damien and my job."

"I can give you a job," Karla blurted, without thinking through the potential ramifications of her statement. "You have all the qualities and experience to be a great concierge. Just Task Me! has concierges all over the world. You could choose your location. I can't provide housing or a multi-million-dollar mega yacht, but I'd hire you in a heartbeat." She paused. "Unless you turn out to be Leila's killer. In which case, I'd have to rescind the offer."

"I didn't kill Leila," Caitlin said. "Do you really think I'm capable of murder?"

"My dad says that, under the right circumstances, anyone could be capable of murder," Karla replied. "Everyone who was onboard The Aquaholic at the same time as Leila is a suspect. The police know you lied about your alibi. You claimed to be in your office all morning, but the surveillance camera aimed at your office door proved otherwise."

"I told the police I was working until you arrived," Caitlin clarified. "They assumed I was in my office. I never claimed to be there. I just didn't correct them because I didn't think it mattered where I was working."

"Where were you?"

"In my cabin," Caitlin replied. "I often work in my cabin."

"What were you working on?"

"I was rescheduling meetings," Caitlin replied. "A few days before we arrived in Bellbrook, Damien had asked me to clear his schedule so he could go with you, Saskia, and Ben to tour Bellcroft."

"We postponed the Bellcroft tour until the next day because we found Leila's body," Karla reminded her.

"The meeting Damien had that afternoon was originally scheduled for next week. I contacted the other party and moved the meeting forward so it would conflict with the Bellcroft tour. When we had to cancel the tour because of Leila's murder, I rescheduled again so it would conflict with the rescheduled tour the next day."

"Why would you do that?" Karla asked, confused.

"Because the people Damien was scheduled to meet with are horrible at time management. They cancel meetings at the last minute at least fifty percent of the time because they have a 'scheduling conflict'." When Caitlin took her hands off the wheel to put air quotes around 'scheduling conflict,' Karla's life flashed before her eyes. "I knew they would probably contact me to cancel just minutes before we were scheduled to video chat with them. I also knew that Damien wouldn't be suspicious because they regularly cancel at the last minute, even when we let them choose the date and time. I was right on both counts."

"You wanted them to cancel so you could be alone with Damien while Saskia, Ben, and I were away from the yacht," Karla surmised. *Saskia was right again! She's good!*

"I was going to have *The Talk* with him and tell him how I feel," Caitlin admitted. "But I lost my nerve at the last minute. I always lose my nerve at the last minute." She shifted in her seat and adjusted her grip on the steering wheel. "But not anymore. I'm going to get Damien alone and tell him how I feel."

"When?" asked Karla.

"As soon as the police arrest Leila's killer," Caitlin replied. "We're both too distracted right now." She glanced at Karla. "Text your father and your sister. Tell them to check my laptop. I'll give them my password. They can contact the people I spoke with the day Leila died and confirm my alibi. They can also get their tech people to confirm that I spent hours replying to emails and doing research for Damien."

Karla did as Caitlin instructed.

They drove in comfortable silence with Caitlin slowing down to about twenty over the speed limit; Karla was relieved when she spotted their exit.

Since last night, Karla had uncovered Damien's alibi—he was at the gym—Ben's alibi—he was on the smaller deck with his virtual therapist, getting desensitized to dogs—and Caitlin's alibi—she was in her cabin yearning for Damien and manipulating his schedule. Assuming these alibis were confirmable by the police, none of them could have killed Leila.

Most of the crew had been accounted for, apart from the deckhand who dropped off Leila's luggage, delivered a Cobb salad to her cabin, and served drinks on the upper deck just before they discovered Leila's body. Apparently, he was on a break, reading alone in his cabin.

The only non-crew member still unaccounted for was Saskia. She claimed to be alone in her cabin. Could Saskia be a killer? She had knowledge of the crime scene that she couldn't have seen firsthand, but she provided a reasonable explanation for how she learned that information. Over the past few days, Karla and Saskia had become friends, or so Karla had thought. Maybe the tears Saskia cried on the deck, and the bonding they did over their complicated relationships with their absent mothers was an act. Maybe Saskia was pretending to be Karla's friend so she could use Karla to find out what was happening with the police investigation. *If only I could tell when Saskia was lying,* Karla lamented to herself. Was she unable to figure out Saskia's Tell because there wasn't one? Was Saskia a sociopath, unburdened by a conscience and felt no remorse about lying… or even murder?

CHAPTER 22

WATER CROWFOOT

"How's your car running?" Rob asked.

Karla, Rob, and Rosalie were sitting on the outdoor patio at Déjà Brew, sipping drinks, nibbling on treats, and watching the world go by.

"Purring like a kitten," Karla replied, sipping her iced tea and watching from the corner of her eye as Rosalie slipped a piece of lemon biscotti to Gucci under the table.

She gave Rosalie an accusatory stare.

"What?" the octogenarian asked, as though she had no clue what she had done. "It fell. I'm old. Sometimes my hands shake and stuff falls."

"Rosalie Howard, your hands are steadier than most surgeons," Rob chided.

Rosalie blushed. "Fine. I gave Gucci a tiny piece of biscotti. He's a good boy. He deserves a treat." Karla's phone chimed. "You should check that," Rosalie said, changing the subject. "It could be Lynn with an update about Harry."

Karla had stopped at home after she picked up her car to take Gucci for his afternoon walk. While she was there, Lynn called from her car. Apparently, Harry had sliced his hand with a rusty tool, or piece of gardening equipment, or something—it was difficult to hear with Lynn and Harry bickering and bantering while Lynn was also talking to Karla on the phone—and they were on their way to the hospital. Harry had been working outside Lynn's cottage when the accident happened. Thank goodness, Lynn was home. Alerted by Harry's loud string of curse words, she tended to his wound right away.

Harry insisted he was fine, but Lynn disagreed and convinced him to go to the hospital, certain he would need stitches and a tetanus shot. She asked Karla to pick up Rosalie and drive her to her weekly garden club meeting; something that Lynn did every week. So, Karla and Gucci picked up Rosalie and drove into town. They came early because Rosalie was craving a flat white and lemon biscotti from Déjà Brew. They ran into Rob at the cafe. She was taking a late lunch.

"It's Lynn," Karla confirmed. "Harry needed ten stitches and a tetanus shot. They're on their way back. Lynn says she's taking him home, feeding him, and getting him settled."

"I bet Harry's not happy," Rosalie said. "He likes to keep his hands busy. This injury will slow him down."

Karla nodded. "In Lynn's text, she said he was in a grumpy mood, complaining that he needed both hands to keep the grounds at Bellcroft in good shape."

"The Petal Pushers will help him out," Rosalie chimed in, offering the services of her gardening club.

"Whether or not he likes it, I've already put our members on notice. The Petal Pushers love a gardening emergency." She sipped her coffee then said, "Remind me to take him a rhubarb-strawberry pie later."

"Did the physician prescribe him an antibiotic?" Rob asked.

"Lynn didn't say," Karla replied.

"Why did they go to the hospital?" Rob asked. "Lynn should have brought Harry to me for treatment."

"You're still getting caught up on your patient backlog from Leila's murder," Karla reminded her. "They didn't want to jump ahead of your appointments."

"I could've made time to give Harry a few stitches," Rob argued, somewhat insulted that Harry took his injured hand elsewhere.

"You can remove them," Rosalie suggested, appeasing the offended doctor.

"Fine," Rob agreed with a small huff, picking up her phone. "I'll text Lynn and tell her to bring him to my office in a week for a follow-up appointment." She tapped her phone screen. "I'd text Harry, but knowing him, he'd ignore it and try to remove the stitches himself."

"Yes, he would," Rosalie agreed with a deep nod.

"Hey! It's three of my favourite people." Max beamed as she approached their table. "My invitation must have gotten lost in the mail," she teased.

Gucci was so excited and in such a rush to greet his Aunt Max that he caught his back paw on his water bowl and flipped it over, spilling the contents all over the sidewalk. But he didn't let that stop him! He scurried out from under the table, wagging his quill-like tail, yelping with glee, and pawing her shins.

Max crouched down to pet her favourite terrier and scratched his neck under his collar as he bounced on his hind legs, trying to cover her face with kisses.

"It's an impromptu gathering," Rosalie explained. "But now that you're here, we insist you join us!"

"I'd love to," Max said with a sigh. "But I'm here on police business." She stood up, gesturing to her police uniform.

"What kind of police business?" Rosalie asked.

"The coffee and donut kind," Rob joked.

"Haha," Max replied. "The murder kind, actually. But I might grab a coffee and cruller to go. May as well, since I'm here."

"You're here about Leila's murder?" Karla asked.

Max nodded. "I'm showing Leila's photo around town." She pulled out her phone and flashed them a post-mortem photo of Leila's head and shoulders.

Aside from being too pale, Leila looked like she was sleeping. The photo included her distinctive tattoos, which should help jog some memories if anyone saw her before she died. "We could really use a lead." Max's voice was heavy with defeat. "Her loved ones must be worried sick by now. We need to identify her, so we can contact them."

"There still haven't been any missing persons reports matching her description?" Rob asked.

Max shook her head. "But the clerk who checked her in at The Seascape Hotel contacted us. He remembered a couple of things that he forgot when we interviewed him."

"Like what?" Karla rested her chin on her hand, giving Max her full attention.

Rosalie not-so-discreetly dropped another piece of lemon biscotti under the table. Gucci forgot all about his Aunt Max and scampered toward the forbidden treat.

"He gave us a good lead," Max started. "Dad is following up on it now."

"What lead?" Karla urged.

"According to the clerk, when Leila checked in, she told him that her boyfriend wasn't expecting her until the next day, but she wanted to surprise him, so she came to Bellbrook a day early," Max explained. "Also, Leila requested a second key for her room. She asked the clerk to keep the second key at the front desk in case her boyfriend showed up at the hotel before she got back from Shearlock Combs. She told him she was going to text her boyfriend from the salon and tell him to meet her at the hotel. The clerk said she was excited to see her boyfriend's reaction to her early arrival."

"Isn't it odd that the hotel clerk forgot all this when you questioned him?" Rob wondered.

"Not really," Max replied. "Most people don't have regular interactions with the police. Especially not because of something as serious as a murder investigation. He's young, he's new at his job, he was probably overwhelmed when we interviewed him the first time. This is one of the reasons we do multiple interviews."

"Did her boyfriend pick up the key?" Karla asked.

"No," Max replied. "The clerk was tidying up the

registration desk this morning and came across the second key. It triggered his memory about her early arrival and the second key."

"Either Leila didn't call her boyfriend from the salon like she told the clerk, or she did phone him but he never showed up at the hotel because he knew Leila was dead, and he wouldn't need the key," Karla suggested.

"If he didn't know Leila was dead, wouldn't he have reported her missing when she didn't show up in Bellbrook, and he didn't hear from her?" Rosalie asked.

"Good point, Rosalie," Max said.

"Did Leila tell the hotel clerk her boyfriend's name?" Karla asked.

They all leaned in toward Max, eager to hear the answer.

"Yes," Max replied. "She said his name was Walter Crowfoot.

"Water Crowfoot?" Rosalie asked, scrunching up her face and cupping her ear as though she had misheard.

"No, Rosalie," Max said. "Walter Crowfoot. Walter." She stressed the L in Walter.

"Oh, that makes more sense." Rosalie nodded. "I thought you said Water Crowfoot, you know like the plant?"

"What plant?" Karla asked.

"Water Crowfoot is a type of buttercup that grows near water. It's a member of the Ranunculaceae family."

"Ranunculaceae?" Karla rolled the word around

her tongue like a hard candy. She squeezed her eyes shut, wracking her brain to remember where she had heard that word recently.

"I don't know of any Crowfoots in Bellbrook," Rosalie said.

"Us either," Max replied, referring to the Bellbrook Police Department. "There are a few Walters, but none with the surname Crowfoot. We don't even have a Walter whose last name starts with C."

"How about The Aquaholic?" Rob asked, looking back and forth from Karla to Max.

Karla and Max shook their heads.

"I haven't met any Walters," Karla replied. "But I haven't met the entire crew. It's shocking how many people it takes to keep a mega yacht afloat."

"There's no one on the yacht called Walter. Nobody with the surname Crowfoot, and nobody with the initials WC," Max added. "Dad and I believe finding Walter Crowfoot is the key to uncovering Leila's identity and solving her murder." She sighed and glanced in the cafe window. "I'd love to stay and chat, ladies, but I should go inside and show this photo to The Posers. If anyone saw Leila in Bellbrook before she died, it would be them," Max said.

"Yes, it would," Rosalie agreed.

"Do we know anything else about Leila's boyfriend?" Rob asked, after Max disappeared inside Déjà Brew.

"She talked about him at length with Lynn at the salon," Rosalie said.

"But she didn't tell Lynn any identifying information," Karla clarified. "According to Lynn, Leila said her boyfriend's job requires him to travel a lot, and he has a sensitive job in a secure environment."

"And Leila also told Lynn that she only sees her boyfriend every few weeks when he flies her to whichever town he's in," Rosalie added. "She said they have to keep a low profile when they're together because of his job, so they don't go out much."

Rob crossed her arms in front of her chest and tilted her head, dubious. "From what you describe, I'd say that Leila's boyfriend is either super famous and avoiding being seen in public with her, or he's married." She shrugged with her palms facing the sky. "And there aren't a lot of famous guys in Bellbrook, but there are a lot of married ones."

Karla and Rosalie looked at each other, mouths agape. Neither could believe they hadn't come to the same conclusion.

As far as Karla was aware, none of the suspects were married, but there was one who was certainly famous and travelled a lot with his social-media-celebrity fiancée.

Gucci panted at Karla's feet, distracting her from her thoughts about Leila's murder. She reached under the table and picked up the overturned water bowl. "I'll be right back," she said, standing up. "Gooch needs water." She shot Rosalie a sideways glance and grinned. "I think the biscotti is making him thirsty."

Rosalie said nothing, pretending not to hear Karla, and sipped her coffee.

CHAPTER 23

MARIGOLDGATE

STANDING IN LINE, Karla's brain replayed Rob's revelation that Leila's boyfriend-slash-potential murderer might have been in a committed relationship with someone other than Leila. In hindsight, Rob was right. His actions, as Leila described them, seemed like the behaviour of someone who had something to hide. Something like a committed partner who had no clue what he was up to.

Was Ben Underwood Leila's boyfriend? Was Leila tired of meeting Ben for short, infrequent secret rendezvous? Maybe she threatened to expose their relationship, causing Ben to panic and kill her. Or maybe Leila confronted Saskia, and she killed Leila to stop the affair from becoming public knowledge, which would destroy her reputation and ruin her upcoming wedding. Maybe Ben and Saskia killed Leila together, and now they're keeping a deadly secret. But if that was the case, surely Saskia would have given Ben an alibi, right? Ben initially told the police that he was with Saskia the entire time Leila was aboard The Aquaholic, but Saskia told the police that she was alone in her cabin. Why would Saskia admit she had no alibi if she was guilty?

Karla stepped out of line and joined Max, who was showing Leila's photo to The Posers at a table near the window. She positioned herself where Max could see her. They exchanged small smiles. Karla stayed far enough away not to interfere in their conversation but close enough to eavesdrop.

"Yeah, I remember her." The brunette ponytail nodded at the image on Max's phone.

"Me too," said the reverse bob, looking over Max's shoulder.

"She was at Shearlock Combs the other morning," added the pixie cut, pointing to the salon across the street. "She was in there a while but came out looking exactly the same, so I don't think she had her hair done."

"You're very observant," Max praised the woman's observation skills. "She had her nails done."

The pixie cut smiled proudly.

"I figured she was a tourist," volunteered the brunette ponytail. "I didn't recognize her as a local, and she looked really happy." She smiled. "She was smiling and had a bounce in her step."

The reverse bob and pixie cut nodded in agreement.

Max put away her phone and pulled out her trusty notepad and pen. "Did you notice anything else about her?"

"Something caught her attention," said the reverse

bob. "Remember?" She nudged the brunette ponytail. "She was smiling and happy, then all of a sudden, she froze."

"Oh, yeah," agreed the brunette ponytail. "She stopped dead in her tracks, and the cheerful expression disappeared from her face."

"It was like she suddenly remembered that she'd left the stove on, or she saw something she couldn't believe," added the pixie cut.

"We assumed she saw The Aquaholic for the first time. It's shockingly huge when you first see it," said the brunette ponytail.

"It had only arrived the day before," added the reverse bob. "Lots of people came to the waterfront that day to gawk at it."

"Did she speak to anyone?" Max asked.

"Not that we noticed," replied the pixie cut while all three of them shook their heads.

"Did you notice which way she went when she left the salon?" Max asked.

"I can't remember," the brunette ponytail giggled. Then the other two started giggling with her.

"We got distracted," explained the pixie cut. "That handsome captain from The Aquaholic showed up."

"He was outside," said the reverse bob. "Right there." She pointed out the window at the sidewalk. "In full uniform." She waggled her eyebrows. "He stopped near the trash can and made eye contact with us through the window. He smiled right at us."

They giggled again, poking and nudging each other like giddy school girls.

"So, you lost track of Leila because you were swooning over Captain Peterson?" Max asked.

"He winked at us," gushed the pixie cut. "And his smile! It was hard to notice anything else."

Max closed her notebook with a sigh.

"Then he came inside and ordered a doppio and a cup of ice water to go," added the reverse bob. "On his way out, he tipped his cap, smiled, and said, 'G'day, ladies,' in the hottest accent we've ever heard."

"If it weren't for the giant wedding ring on his finger, I would've followed him all the way back to his yacht," cooed the brunette ponytail, then she let out a low purr, which encouraged her friends to break into a new fit of giggles.

Karla looked back at the line. It was longer now. She found a table, dropped herself into the chair, and set the Déjà Brew branded water bowl on the small bistro table. She watched as Max thanked The Posers and asked them to contact her should they remember anything else about Leila.

Max slipped behind the counter and showed the photo to the baristas, who stopped taking orders and making drinks just long enough to look at the photo and shake their heads. Max thanked them and quietly left Déjà Brew through the back door.

Ranunculaceae. Karla heard the word inside her head in Rosalie's voice. *Ranunculus,* this time it was Lynn's voice echoing through her mind. Lynn had mentioned ranunculuses yesterday morning when Karla had accused her of flirting with Captain Peterson. Ranunculaceae and ranunculuses. The words were too similar to be a coincidence. They must have had similar meanings, right? Karla unlocked her phone to search for the two similar sounding words on the internet.

"There you are!" Rob's voice brought Karla back to the here and now. "What's taking you so long?"

"Sorry," Karla said, locking her phone and picking up the empty water bowl. "I gave up my place in line to eavesdrop on Max's conversation with The Posers. When they finished, the line was so long, I sat down to wait a minute. Gucci must be thirsty." She motioned to stand up. "I'll get back in line."

"There's no point now," Rob said. "Rosalie left to walk to her gardening club meeting. She took Gucci with her and said she would get him a bowl of water when they get there." Rob sat in the chair across from Karla. "She said you would be OK with her taking Gucci to the Petal Pushers meeting. She said he goes all the time?"

"He does," Karla confirmed, still distracted by Ranunculaceae and the new information Max had learned from the hotel clerk.

"Did you know Gucci is the Petal Pushers mascot?" Rob asked.

Karla nodded. "He's been their mascot for a few months now."

"I didn't know gardening clubs had mascots."

"Me neither," Karla admitted. "Not until Rosalie told me the Petal Pushers had voted unanimously to make Gucci their new mascot."

"Why Gucci?" Rob asked.

"He fits into the old mascot's shirt," Karla replied.

"Old mascot?" Rob's face made it clear she had not heard about Marigoldgate.

"Mrs. Baumgartner's cat, Tabbytha," Karla explained. "Tabbytha lost her job as mascot because she ate Mr. Marshall's prize-winning marigolds. Mrs. Baumgartner's insisted that it couldn't have been Tabbytha because, according to her, Tabbytha hates marigolds."

"They fired Tabbytha without proof?"

"It was a big scandal," Karla told her. "I can't believe you haven't heard about Marigoldgate. It was all Rosalie talked about for weeks. Half the Petal Pushers believed Mrs. Baumgartner and supported Tabbytha. The other half supported Mr. Marshall, believing that Tabbytha ate his prize-winning marigolds as revenge because Mrs. Baumgartner's marigolds won second place behind Mr. Marshall's. It turned out Mr. Marshall caught the crime on his door-bell camera, but a few of the Petal Pushers think someone manipulated the footage."

"Wild," Rob said, shaking her head. "Only in Bellbrook."

"Well, since Gucci's gone to his garden club meeting, I'll return this dog bowl to the barista behind the counter."

They got up, and Karla walked over to the counter to hand in the bowl. Then she remembered she was about to search the internet before Rob distracted her and pulled out her phone again.

"Do you know how to spell ranunculus?" Karla asked as they left the cafe.

Rob sounded out the word, and between them, they figured out how to spell the uncommon word.

Gasp! Karla froze. The words on the screen left her motionless and speechless.

"What's wrong?" Rob asked.

Karla tilted her phone so Rob could see it. "I know who killed Leila."

ROB ENDED the call and put her phone on her lap. "Max said to wait for the police and instructed us not to confront the suspect without them."

"And she'll dig out Leila's ID and bring it with her?" Karla steered the car toward the marina.

"If it's there," Rob replied. "She sounded skeptical that she'd find Leila's ID where you suspect the killer hid it. She said if you're right, the killer is more arrogant than she and Dean gave them credit for.

"The killer is arrogant, all right!" Karla nodded. "If I'm wrong, and Max doesn't find it, she'll get the satisfaction of saying, 'I told you so,'" Karla said. "She loves to do that, so she wins either way."

"Are you sure about this, Karla?" Rob's tone was serious. "Accusing someone of murder is a big deal. If it turns out you're wrong, you can't just take it back and expect them to forget all about it."

"Did you listen to the evidence?" For the second time, Karla explained to Rob how each piece of evidence pointed to one specific person.

"I agree with you," Rob said, "but most of the evidence is circumstantial. If you accuse them of murder, and it turns out they didn't kill Leila, or there isn't enough concrete evidence to convict them, it could cost you a client and your reputation. Not to mention, it would kibosh the celebrity wedding of the year that's supposed to reinvigorate Bellcroft as a world-class event venue and benefit almost every business in town."

"What choice do I have?" Karla asked. "I can't stand by and do nothing while a killer gets away with murder!"

"You could let the police handle it," Rob suggested. "Max said the police would only need a day or two to confirm your theory. Then, they can arrest the suspect, confront them with the evidence, and charge them with Leila's murder."

"In the meantime, there's nothing stopping the killer from realizing the police are onto them and making a run for it. Do you know how far someone with their resources and knowledge can get in one or two days?" It was a rhetorical question. "Far. The opposite side of the world. Somewhere with no extradition laws."

CHAPTER 24

BZZZ... TRY AGAIN

THEY ARRIVED AT THE MARINA, and Karla reversed the car into a parking spot. She turned off the engine, unbuckled her seatbelt, and motioned to get out of the vehicle.

"Hold on," Rob raised her hand in a stop motion. "Let's wait for the police." Karla opened her mouth to protest, but Rob continued. "We have an unobstructed view of The Aquaholic from here. If anyone leaves the yacht, we'll see them," she argued.

"Fine," Karla agreed. "But if the police aren't here in ten minutes, I'm calling Damien and asking him to send a yacht tender to pick me up. You can wait here for the police."

"I'm not letting you board that ship and confront a killer by yourself," Rob protested.

The familiar royal-blue Maserati cruised into the parking lot and parked a few spots away.

"There's my dream car," Rob whispered, forgetting about their difference of opinion.

"It's sleek," Karla commented. "And very fast when Caitlin is behind the wheel."

The passenger door opened, and Saskia got out of the car. Using the front-facing camera on her phone, she checked her makeup and touched up her hair.

Ben got out of the driver's side.

They laughed and flirted as Saskia directed Ben to lean against the sports car with his arms spread out on either side. He crossed his ankles and smiled while she snapped a few photos with her phone, then they switched. Saskia handed Ben her phone, sat on the hood of the car, crossed her long, slender legs, turned her head toward the ocean, closed her eyes, and tilted her face toward the sky while Ben snapped photos of her.

A black electric SUV pulled up. The bald, stone-faced security guard who had accompanied Ben and Saskia to Bellcroft the day before got out of the front passenger side and opened the back door. He stood at attention while Damien and Caitlin exited the vehicle.

"We might not have to go to them," Karla commented. "It looks like they're coming to us."

"What if they catch us staring at them?" Rob whispered.

"They won't," Karla replied. "They don't know what my car looks like. It's been in the shop since before they arrived in Bellbrook."

Damien, Caitlin, Saskia, and Ben gathered in the parking lot, chatting and smiling.

Damien struck a match on the bottom of his loafer and proceeded to toast a fresh cigar.

Caitlin checked the time on her watch and said

something to the others while jerking her head toward the nearby dock. The group started moving in that direction.

"This must be their lift back to the yacht," Rob said, pointing her chin at the speedboat that had appeared in front of the yacht and was speeding toward shore.

"Then it's our lift too." Karla opened the door and jumped out of the car before Rob could convince her otherwise. "Damien," she called, knowing the entire group would stop if he did. "Wait up!" She jogged toward them with Rob running to catch up.

"Karla! What a lovely surprise," Damien said as she approached the group. "What brings you here? Do we have a meeting I've forgotten about?"

Karla opened her mouth to reply.

"O. M. G.!" Saskia declared, interrupting before Karla could utter a syllable. "We just saw Gucci! He was sooo cute! He was wearing a little T-shirt that said, Petal Pushers, with a cartoon sunflower on it." She reached over and touched Karla's forearm. "He was so adorable. I just had to take a picture! I'll send it to you." Saskia turned her attention to her phone.

"We just enjoyed a late lunch at your local pub." Damien squeezed his brows together and looked at Caitlin. "What was the name of that pub again?"

"The Pavlovian," Caitlin replied, then smiled at Karla. "Such a cozy, friendly little establishment."

"We ate outside," Damien continued. "The proprietor called it the beer garden." He puffed his cigar.

"Wonderful food," Caitlin commented. "Fabulous service and such a nice ambience."

When did you all become so talkative?

"I would've stayed longer and had another beer or two," Damien added. "But a bunch of people in Petal Pushers shirts showed up. They were having a loud and heated discussion about a gardening emergency, of all things." Damien chuckled. "Apparently, someone named Harry injured his hand, and the rest of them are fixing to keep his garden in tip-top shape until he gets better." He puffed his cigar and smoke billowed above them. "Sounded like a big garden."

"It was very dramatic," Saskia commented. "Someone named Mr. Marshall refused to sit near someone named Mrs. Baumgartner. Apparently, he was mad at her cat? Anyway, they had to rearrange the whole table. Twice. It was like musical chairs."

"Small town drama," Karla said with a smile.

"When Gucci showed up, it was game over for Ben," Damien said with an eye roll.

"The lady who brought Gucci was super sweet and understanding when she saw how panicked Ben was. She kept Gucci on his leash and everything, but Ben couldn't handle being so close to a dog."

"Who expects to run into a dog at a restaurant?" Ben asked in his own defence. "He took me by surprise."

Karla nodded, hoping Gucci's sudden appearance in the Pavlovian's beer garden didn't set back his exposure therapy, and trying to get a word in edgewise.

"We decided it would be best to leave," Caitlin explained, giving Karla a knowing eyebrow raise. "By the way, how's your car? All fixed?"

"It's good," Karla replied. "It's over there." She gestured vaguely behind her. "The reaso—"

"I hope you and Dr. Mayhew will join us on the yacht," Damien interrupted, and Karla wondered if she would ever speak a complete sentence again without one of them cutting her off.

"Actually, I don't think it's a good idea for any of us to return to the yacht right now," Karla began.

"Poppycock!" Damien declared before she could finish her thought. "We won't take no for an answer. We insist that you and Dr. Mayhew join us for drinks on the upper deck." Damien waved the cigar as he gesticulated with his hands. "It will give us a chance to discuss your new position." He winked and returned the stogie to his mouth.

"New position?" Rob asked.

"Didn't Karla tell you?" Damien asked, clenching the cigar in his teeth. "I've offered her the opportunity of a lifetime."

"You never mentioned it," Rob muttered to Karla, confused.

The yacht tender had arrived at the dock. Captain Peterson used ropes to moor the boat, then hopped off, hoisting a backpack over his shoulder and pulling a dark, wheeled suitcase behind him. He was wearing civilian clothes and a baseball cap instead of his uniform.

"Peterson, what's going on?" Damien demanded upon seeing his ship's captain hurrying toward them with packed bags and civilian attire.

"Family emergency, sir," Captain Peterson explained. "I've already sent for a freelance captain to replace me. He'll arrive tomorrow. In the meantime, the first mate is in charge, and you or Ben can drive yourselves back to the yacht." He tossed a keychain with a triangular key at Ben, who caught it with ease.

"Is there anything we can do, Henry?" Caitlin asked, her face full of concern.

"No, thank you." Captain Peterson nodded. "I need to get to the airport. I have a plane to catch."

"Get in the SUV," Damien instructed. "My driver will take you."

"Thank you, sir." Captain Peterson nodded and continued walking. "I'll be in touch as soon as I can."

The group parted down the middle, creating a direct path between Captain Peterson and the waiting SUV.

As soon as Captain Peterson breezed past Karla, she said, "Walter!"

He stopped. There was a pause before he turned and glared at her with narrowed eyes. "What did you call me?"

"How did you know I meant you?"

He glanced around at the confused faces, then relaxed his shoulders, allowing his backpack to slide to the ground. He pushed the rolling suitcase toward the security guard and bolted.

"Stop him!" Rob shouted.

The security guard sprang into action and scaled the suitcase Captain Peterson had shoved in his way.

Ben gave chase too, leaping in front of the accomplished yachtsman and blocking his getaway, allowing the security guard to catch up and lunge at him. The large bodyguard nabbed the attempted escapee and dragged him back toward the SUV. He twisted Captain Peterson's arm behind his back to stop him from trying to squirm out of his grasp.

"Peterson, why did Karla call you Walter?" Damien asked his soon-to-be-former captain.

"I don't know, sir," Captain Peterson replied. "You'd have to ask her."

Karla felt the weight of everyone's stares on her.

"Walter is Captain Peterson's alias," she explained, without breaking eye contact with the suspected killer. "Walter Crowfoot. At least, that's what you told Leila your name was, right?"

"I don't know what you're talking about," Captain Peterson claimed. "I've never heard that name before."

Karla turned to the group of confused onlookers. "Captain Peterson was Leila's boyfriend," she revealed. "Every few weeks, he would fly her into a town near where The Aquaholic was anchored and sneak away to meet her for secret trysts."

"She has no clue what she's talking about," Captain Peterson said with an awkward chuckle. "I'm a happily married man. I think your concierge might be a few sandwiches short of a picnic, sir."

Damien's face was expressionless. He was giving nothing away. "Keep talking Karla."

"Leila didn't know you were married, did she?"

Captain Peterson said nothing, scowling at her.

"I bet she didn't even know you worked on The Aquaholic, did she?"

Still no reaction from the alleged murderer.

"Two days ago, Leila arrived in Bellbrook earlier than you had expected. She had missed you since your last rendezvous, and she wanted to surprise you, so she came to town a day early. She checked in at the hotel, then visited Shearlock Combs for a manicure and pedicure because she wanted to look her absolute best for you. She was going to text you on your secret burner phone and ask you to meet her at the hotel, but before she did, she saw you. You were outside Déjà Brew just as Leila left Shearlock Combs. She recognized you despite your uniform, and she saw your wedding ring. The jig was up. Leila realized you were married, and she'd figured out you were a liar."

"You have an active imagination, I'll give you that," Captain Peterson said with a chuckle. "Surely you don't believe this woman's inane ramblings, Mr. Casey?"

Two police cruisers squealed into opposite sides of the parking lot, blocking the entrance and exit. Max hopped out of one police car, and Dean got out of the other. There were more sirens in the distance. Backup.

"You're just in time," Captain Peterson shouted, struggling against the large security officer who was restraining him. "Thank goodness you're here. This man is holding me against my will, and this crazy woman is making up unbelievable stories about me and accusing me of murder!"

"No one has accused you of murder," Caitlin pointed out. "At least, not yet." She looked at Karla and nodded for her to continue.

"After Leila realized you were an adulterous liar, she set out to confront you. She returned to the hotel, gathered her belongings, and used fake credentials to sneak aboard The Aquaholic. She bided her time, even ordering lunch from the yacht kitchen. Terrified that someone would realize Leila was there for you, and that she would expose your dirty secret, you killed her. We discovered her body before you finished removing her luggage and other belongings from the yacht and disposing of them."

Max approached the bodyguard and relieved him of his detainee, slapping handcuffs on Captain Peterson, and thanking the security officer for restraining him until the police arrived.

"Where did you get the name Walter Crowfoot?" asked Captain Peterson.

"Leila asked the hotel clerk to keep a second room key at the front desk for her boyfriend to pick up. She told the clerk her boyfriend's name was Walter Crowfoot. You told Lynn that your wife's favourite flowers were ranunculuses and mentioned that you have a garden full of them at home. You gave her the impression that you had expert knowledge of them. Later, my friend Rosalie mentioned a plant called Water Crowfoot that was part of the Ranunculaceae family."

"Oooh, you should have chosen a more random name," Saskia criticized, holding her phone in such a way that Karla wondered if she was recording the interaction.

"The last clue was your wedding ring," Karla revealed. "It's a gorgeous ring, and I found it mesmerizing, but I couldn't figure out why. At first, I thought it was because it was shiny and interesting to look at, but then I realized it wasn't your ring that mesmerized me, it was your finger." She held up her left hand and wiggled her ring finger. "There's no tan line under your wedding ring. You claim to remove your ring hardly ever, yet you have no tan line at all. Despite being one of the most tanned people I've met. Either you remove your ring more often than you claim, or you cover the tan line with self-tanner or something. Either way, you went out of your way to appear unmarried."

"This is all circumstantial." Captain Peterson spat when he spoke. "You can't prove anything!" He scoffed. "The police don't even know the dead woman's name. If she and I were contacting each other with burner phones, as you claim, where's my burner phone? Hmmm?" he challenged.

"Right here," Dean replied, holding up a sealed evidence bag. "Along with Leila Grant's passport and the contents of her wallet. Thank you by the way"—he tipped his head to the captain—"for not bothering to delete the selfies of you and Leila from your burner phone. You should have erased the phone before you tossed it. Rookie mistake. Those photos, combined with the intimate texts between you and Leila, will make it hard for you to deny your relationship with the deceased." He placed the bag on the roof of his patrol car. "I bet when we process these, we'll find your fingerprints all over them, won't we?"

The colour drained from Captain Peterson's face, and he swallowed hard, shaking his head and glowering at the evidence bag in Dean's hand.

"Karla and I watched you toss an old crumpled up paper bag into the garbage can outside Déjà Brew when you were talking to Lynn yesterday," Rob explained.

"You hadn't visited the cafe yet for your usual order, so we figured you weren't tossing the garbage from your morning coffee," Karla continued. "We suspect you hid Leila's ID and your burner phone in her suitcase, the one you hid in the yacht tender, then retrieved it the next morning and disposed of it in a public garbage can, where the police wouldn't be likely to search."

"What do you have to say for yourself, Peterson?" Damien asked.

"Nothing, sir. It's all lies."

"Fair enough," Damien agreed, nodding. "Caitlin, get Peterson's wife on the phone. Maybe she can clear up a few details for us."

Caitlin nodded and unlocked her phone. "Yes, Damien."

"No!" Captain Peterson shouted. "Please don't call my wife."

"Then tell us what happened, Peterson."

"Fine, I had an affair with Leila Grant," Captain Peterson admitted, "but I didn't kill her."

"Was her death an accident?" Max asked.

"I don't know how she died," Captain Peterson replied. "She used the phone in the cabin to contact the quarterdeck. I answered the call. I couldn't believe my ears. How did she get on the yacht, I wondered? Who else knew she was here? She gave me fifteen minutes to get to her cabin, or she would call my wife and tell her everything, then she would announce it through the yacht's intercom system."

"What happened when you got there?" Caitlin asked.

"Nothing," Captain Peterson replied, shaking his head. "When I arrived, Leila was already dead. She was floating in the bathtub. There was a half-eaten salad in the cabin. She could've choked," he suggested, stammering and grasping for each word. "Or maybe she took her own life to get back at me."

"*Bzzz,*" Rob made a game show buzzer sound. "Wrong answer. Try again."

"I don't know what more you want me to say?!" Captain Peterson protested, sputtering his words and blinking from the beads of sweat that were dripping into his eyes. "I didn't kill her. I might be an adulterer, but I'm not a murderer." He fumbled a few incoherent words and shook his head, searching for what to say next. "Do you really think I'm so heartless that I would smother someone to death with a pillow, then cover up my crime by leaving her in a tub of water?"

"*Ding, ding, ding,*" Rob did her best imitation of a bell. "Right answer."

There it was. The holdback. Aside from Rob, the police, and Karla, only Leila's killer knew how she died.

"Henry Peterson, you're under arrest for the murder of…."

"Suffocate?"

"I thought she drowned?"

"She didn't die in the bathtub?"

"He smothered her?"

Damien, Caitlin, Saskia, and Ben's shocked disbelief drowned out Max's voice as she arrested Captain Peterson, reading him his rights and marching him to her patrol car.

CHAPTER 25

FLOTSAM AND JETSAM

THREE DAYS after the arrest

Karla inhaled a lungful of salty sea air and fixed her eyes on the hazy grey-blue horizon line in the distance, watching the tiny white dot as it shrank into non-existence.

"It's hard to believe that tiny speck is a cruise ship-sized yacht," she commented.

"One phone call to Damien Casey, and that cruise ship-sized yacht could be your and Gucci's new home," Rob said, watching Gucci sniff a caterpillar that was inching along the wooden dock. "How did Damien react when you declined his offer?"

"He was disappointed but understanding," Karla replied. "He countered by offering me the flexibility to work for him on a project-by-project basis. I told him I would think about it and let him know when he comes back to Bellbrook for Saskia and Ben's wedding. But I already know the answer will be no."

Saskia had been right when she warned Karla that saying no to Damien would only make him more persistent.

Karla explained to Damien that she had no desire to work in politics. Heck, she had trouble paying attention to Bellbrook's low-stakes, small-town politics, or even the drama within The Petal Pushers, never mind the high stakes political games Damien Casey played. Also, she was averse to using her lie detection ability for financial gain.

"Have you heard from Caitlin?" Rob asked. "How was her flight?"

"She landed early this morning," Karla said. "She's nervous and excited to spend time with her sister, niece, and nephew again."

After Captain Peterson's arrest, they returned to the yacht, and Caitlin sat down with Damien and confessed her feelings for him. She told Karla he was taken aback but did not dismiss the possibility that someday they could be more than friends and colleagues. He told Caitlin he needed time to sort out his feelings.

Then she called her sister and started the process of reconciling their relationship. Caitlin said her sister was so happy to hear from her that they cried together on the phone. Caitlin hadn't taken time off work in years. Damien owed her months of paid vacation time, and she was using a good chunk of it before Saskia and Damien's wedding. She planned to spend her time away from her career getting to know her family again and getting to know herself again. To rediscover the person she was before she reinvented herself in the image of Damien's ideal partner.

Karla could tell Damien was already missing Caitlin and suspected her absence might make his heart grow fonder. Though part of her wondered if Caitlin would still feel the same about Damien after her time away.

"Can you text Caitlin for me?" Rob asked. "Tell her I said thank you for letting me drive the Maserati when we dropped her off at the airport yesterday. She made one of my dreams come true."

"Sure," Karla agreed as they meandered along the waterfront. "When Caitlin texted earlier, she said to tell you the car rental place is picking up the Maserati at six o'clock tonight, so you can drive it until then, but it has to be back in the marina parking lot by six p.m."

"Really?!" Rob's brown eyes lit up, and her smile was wide. "I'll be able to drive it to pick up Josie from her dad's place. She already thinks I'm the coolest mom in the world because of my viral social media sound bites. I didn't even know viral sound bites were a thing."

During Captain Peterson's confession, Karla had noticed Saskia's cell phone and wondered if Saskia was recording the confrontation. She wasn't. Saskia didn't record the confession, she livestreamed it. Millions of Saskians all over the world watched the murderer's confession in real time. Needless to say, it went viral; everything Saskia does goes viral.

It turned out Captain Peterson's wife was a Saskian. Her phone notified her when Saskia's livestream started. According to Max, Mrs. Peterson was at work, sitting in her office when she tuned into the livestream just in time to watch her handcuffed husband say, "Fine, I had an affair with Leila Grant, but I didn't kill her." She watched the rest of the confession and later confirmed to Max that there was no emergency at home. It was Mrs. Peterson's opinion that Captain Peterson wasn't coming home at all but was attempting to evade the long arm of the law. The day after his arrest, she found a charge on their joint credit card for a one-way ticket to Venezuela.

In his formal statement, Captain Peterson claimed he had suspected the police were closing in on him, and his days as a free man were about to come to an end, so he tried to make a run for it while the family was having lunch at The Pavlovian. But they came back early and foiled his escape, thanks to The Petal Pushers, Gucci, and Ben's cynophobia.

Besides Captain Peterson's confession being featured by television and internet news outlets across the globe, Saskians isolated Rob's game show buzzer and game show bell imitations, turning them into a viral social media trend. Rob's voice was trending in thirty-second videos on every social media platform.

"If Josie thinks you're cool now, wait until you roll up in the Maserati and tell her you've met Saskia Casey," Karla teased.

"I plan to enjoy every second," Rob admitted. "It's temporary. By this time next week, the world will have moved on to the next viral trend, and I'll go back to being a boring mom who wears scrubs and makes her eat vegetables."

"You could never be a boring mom," Karla reassured her best friend.

"I have a telephone appointment later today with Leila's family," Rob revealed. "Dean arranged it. They have questions about how she died."

"That doesn't sound like a fun call," Karla sympathized. "Would you like me to be there?"

"I was thinking of asking Lynn to be there. She had more interaction with Leila while she was in Bellbrook than anyone. Other than Captain Peterson, I mean. The family might want to talk to her. She could tell them about their last conversation at Shearlock Combs."

"I'm sure Lynn would do that for them."

Rob's phone chimed, and she checked the screen. "Harry," she said with a sigh.

"Again?" Karla asked. "What does he want now?"

"He wants me to remove his stitches," Rob replied. "He says his hand is itchy, and the stitches limit his ability to do anything."

"He's been asking you to remove his stitches since the day after he got them."

"I know," Rob said, shaking her head. "I keep telling him they aren't ready yet, but he doesn't care. He hates sitting around watching the Petal Pushers putter in his gardens."

"Harry might complain about the Petal Pushers tending to Bellcroft's gardens, but he doesn't complain when they show up with Rosalie's homemade meals and treats," Karla pointed out.

"I don't think Harry's issue is with every member of the Petal Pushers," Rob revealed. "Apparently, Mr. Marshall took it upon himself to plant some of his prize-winning marigolds, prominently, in one of Harry's flower beds. Harry is not happy. He says they don't match the theme of that particular garden. Lynn told him to be nice, so he complimented the flowers, and now he's afraid Mr. Marshall will plant more marigolds. Yesterday, he mumbled something about how it would be a shame if Clancy developed a taste for them."

"I'd better talk to him. We don't need another Marigoldgate," Karla said, shaking her head. "There are still hurt feelings about the last one."

"Maybe Lynn knew what she was doing when she took Harry to the hospital for stitches instead of taking him to my office," Rob pondered aloud. "Maybe she knew he'd pester me every day to remove his stitches."

"You could be right," Karla agreed. "Lynn seems to know Harry better than most of us."

Rob looked at Karla. "Do you think Lynn and Harry will get together now that she's back in Bellbrook?"

Karla shrugged. "I don't know. They have a weird vibe. Sometimes they bicker like siblings, and other times I could swear they're flirting. If something is brewing there, I hope she doesn't break his heart by leaving."

"Where is Lynn?" Rob asked.

"She's researching puppies," Karla replied. "Ben has made such great progress with his exposure therapy that he wants to go ahead and surprise Saskia with a puppy on their wedding day. He gave Lynn a list of requirements, and she's searching shelters all over the country for their perfect dog."

"What breeds did he choose?" Rob asked.

"Small ones," Karla replied. "He can't handle anything bigger than Gucci." The little dog pricked up his ears and tilted his scruffy head at the sound of his name. "Ben came over to visit Gucci last night," Karla continued. "He told Saskia he was taking the Maserati out for one last drive, which wasn't a lie since he drove the Maserati to my place. His therapist was on the phone with him while I held Gucci on my lap. It took quite a while, but Ben got close enough to pet him and even let Gucci lick his hand."

Karla's phone chimed. "It's a notification from the bank," she said, scrunching up her face in confusion. "A money transfer from Damien." She opened the notification, and her eyes almost bugged out of her head when she saw the amount. "A lot of money." She looked at Rob. "But I didn't send him an invoice."

"Maybe it's a deposit toward Saskia and Ben's wedding." Rob shrugged one shoulder.

"Saskia's sponsors are paying for everything related to the wedding, including my consultation fee," Karla explained. "Damien must have sent this by mistake. I'll text him and let him know I'll transfer it back to him straight away." She opened the text messaging app, and her thumbs flew across the screen so fast they were a blur.

Soon after Karla hit send on her message to Damien, he replied.

"What did he say?" Rob asked when she heard Karla's phone chime.

"He insists it wasn't a mistake," Karla replied. "He says the money is a bonus. It's his way of thanking me for helping to solve Leila's murder, saving their reputations, and finding the perfect wedding venue for Saskia. He also says the money is a taste of the compensation I can expect should I decide to work for him."

Karla's phone chimed again.

"It's Damien again," she said. "He says it will offend him if I return the money." She sighed.

"I guess you'll have to keep it." Rob's voice was thick with mock sympathy.

"But it's too much," Karla objected, tilting her phone screen to show Rob the amount of Damien's bonus.

"Holy moly!" Rob blinked twice, and her eyes were wide. "That'll help cover the costs of renovating Bellbrook."

"You're right," Karla agreed. "I can use it to payback some of the money Lynn and Harry invested." She gave Rob an impish grin. "Maybe we could solve a few more murders that earn a bonus and cover the cost of the entire renovation," she teased.

"Bite your tongue," Rob scolded. "The last thing Bellbrook needs is another murder. At this rate, Bellbrook will need a full-time coroner."

"Are you afraid another murder will interfere with your summer plans?" Karla asked with a laugh.

"Aren't you?" Rob rebutted.

Kind of, Karla thought to herself.

Turn the page for a sneak peek of Last Bud Not Least: A Bellbrook Murder Mystery Book 4

LAST BUD NOT LEAST

Bellbrook is full of doom and bloom when the local florist turns up dead.

Karla is tasked with figuring out which suspect has a violet streak strong enough to leaf the local floral artist for dead.

With suspects all clover town talking dirt about each other, can Karla figure out the motive and unearth the killer once and floral?

Find out in Last Bud Not Least: A Bellbrook Murder Mystery Book 4.

ABOUT THE AUTHOR

Reagan Davis is a pen name for the real author who lives in the suburbs of Toronto with her husband, two kids, and a menagerie of pets.

When she's not planning the perfect murder, she enjoys knitting, reading, eating too much chocolate, and drinking too much Diet Coke.

The author is an established knitwear designer who has contributed to many knitting books and magazines. I'd tell you her real name, but then I'd have to kill you. (Just kidding! _{Sort of.})

http://www.ReaganDavis.com/

Follow Reagan Davis on Amazon

Follow Reagan Davis on Facebook, Bookbub, Goodreads, and Instagram